ANGELS IN THE FOG

A WORLD WAR II NOVEL OF THE PACIFIC

A NOVEL BY

SUSAN N SWANN

New Voices Books

Published by New Voices Books

Cover design by Shelbi Graham
Interior build by Will Robertson

ISBN: 978-0-9848645-9-1 paperback.
ISBN: 978-0-9848645-7-7 digital edition

This book is dedicated to my dad, Norman H. Nielson,
and the other men and women who bravely served
in the Pacific theatre. I used his war letters,
as well as other first-hand accounts,
to help tell the story.

In war, you win or lose, live or die – and the difference is an eyelash."

General Douglas MacArthur

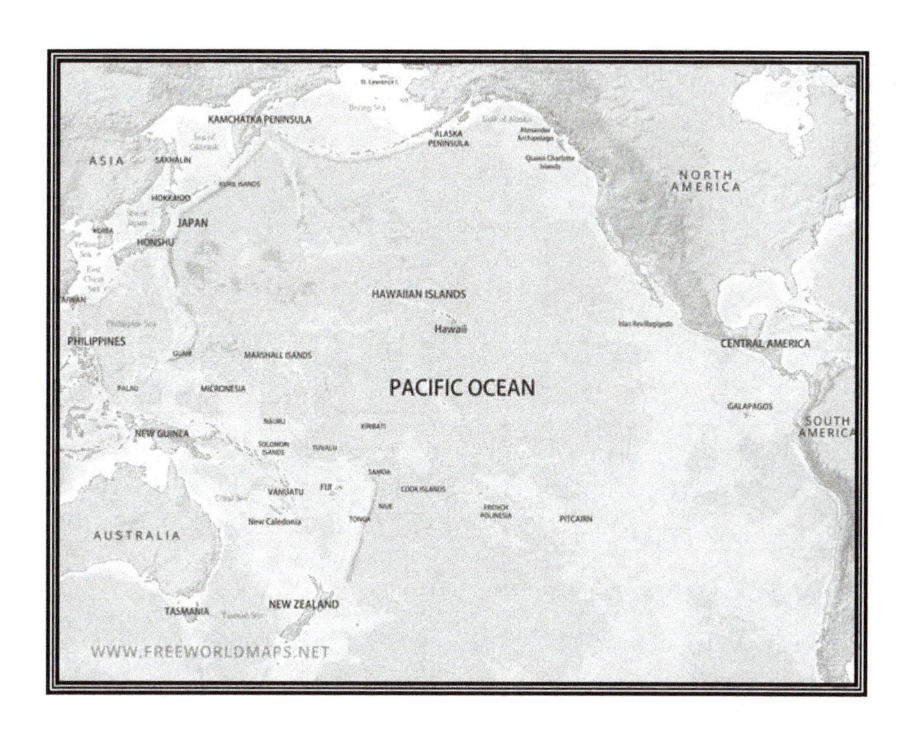

ANGELS IN THE FOG

A WORLD WAR II NOVEL OF THE PACIFIC

PROLOGUE

November 1941

The sun hid behind clouds on a chilly winter morning, the air quiet over freshly fallen snow. I stood at the window, gazing at dark trees stripped of their leaves, and took a deep breath. My life was about to change forever.

Mom walked into the room and leaned against the doorway, staring at my packed bags. I could almost touch her concern. "Lucy," she said, "you could have stayed home and worked at the hospital. Why join the army? Your brother Chris is already serving in the Philippines. Isn't that enough for one family?"

I put my arms around her. "It'll be okay. I'm a nurse, not a soldier, and I'll be in Hawaii. The hospital's a safe place."

She had the strangest look on her face but said nothing. I knew my mother, and her raised eyebrows meant she wasn't convinced. "Let's get something to eat, please," I said. "I'm starving."

Hallie and Alex had come home to say goodbye, and I was happy to enjoy dinner together as a family. Lily was setting the table, and Mom had cooked my favorite, prime rib au jus with garlic butter mashed potatoes and asparagus. For dessert, fresh apple pie, her homemade crusts always warm and flaky. I'd miss her home-cooked meals.

We sat down, joined hands, and Mom blessed the food. Chris's absence was never felt more strongly than during the dinner prayer when she spent an extra few minutes pleading for his safety.

Dad opened the conversation. He was an attorney who loved to talk politics. "Japan is racing through China and on into Indochina," he said. "They're unstoppable. President Roosevelt imposed embargoes first on scrap metal, then aviation fuel, and finally oil. He even froze the Japanese assets in America, but nothing has worked. I'm afraid war may be imminent."

Hallie passed the gravy around the table, then asked, "Did any of you read what the Japanese politician Nakajima Chikuhei said last year? We discussed it in my history class. He claimed there were 'superior and inferior' races in the world, and said it was Japan's sacred duty, as the leading race, to enlighten the inferior ones."

"What happens if the Japanese attack somewhere in the Pacific?" Mom's eyes widened as she looked at me.

I didn't want to say, 'They'd hit the Philippines, not Hawaii,' because that would put Chris in danger.

Alex chimed in, "The newspapers claim America's not worried about war with Japan. We don't want to get directly involved in the war with Germany either."

"I hope they're right," Dad said, spearing another forkful of prime rib.

"I'll be fine serving at Tripler Army Hospital," I said, growing tired of the back and forth.

Lily looked at me, eyes blinking, and I put my arm around her. "I love you, Lucy," she said.

"I love you too, sweetheart." Lily was a sensitive and smart twelve-year-old, going on seventeen. The constant news of war was forcing her to grow up too quickly.

We finished eating, and after tearful goodbyes, Dad drove me to the train station. I'd leave from Salt Lake City, travel west across the country to San Francisco, and then board a ship for Hawaii.

After we arrived at the Union Pacific station, Dad helped me load my luggage onboard, then lingered with me. He waited until the last minute to jump off as the train started pulling away. I looked out the window and waved at him. He waved back, bottom lip quivering, eyes sad.

"I'll miss you all," I mouthed, tapping on the window as the train steamed down the track. We passed the bright blue green waters of the Great Salt Lake, with its swimming patches of salt. I'd grown up floating around in that briny water during summer days with my family, laughing, splashing, and teasing. I cherished those memories but was looking forward to the new waters of the Pacific.

I spent the night in a Pullman car with a few other nurses, and we had the most wonderful conductor who came in and sang to us. His voice was deep and rich, and he knew so many songs. Before long, we all joined in, laughing, and playing games.

We reached San Francisco and spent the night in a hotel near the waterfront. The following day, we boarded a Hawaii-bound transport ship and crossed under the large span of the Golden Gate Bridge in the morning fog. The ship's horn blasted every few minutes, warning of rocky coastlines or the presence of other ships. California's expansive coast became a tiny dot on the horizon, then disappeared in the Pacific Ocean. In a few weeks we'd dock at Hawaii's largest harbor: Pearl Harbor. Excited about my new world, I left the secure and familiar and sailed into the unknown.

CHAPTER ONE

Oahu was just beginning to wake up. I sat in the hospital cafeteria eating our usual Sunday breakfast of powdered eggs and pancakes, leaving little on my plate. Then I took a walk alone through gardens filled with plumeria trees and hibiscus bushes, inhaling their fragrances. I sat on a bench and stretched my toes, grateful for the warm sunshine. At home, it was ice cold and snowing.

I'd been stationed in Hawaii about three weeks, happy on my leisurely tour of duty in one of the most beautiful spots in the world. Why, just last night my nurse friends and I'd been at the Hickam officers' club enjoying jazz at one of the Saturday night dances.

I was finishing a letter from Mom telling me she was happy I wasn't in any danger, when I looked over at the lush green hills and saw plumes of thick black smoke blowing up over the deep blue water of Pearl Harbor. Huge flames shot up into the air. What in the world? My mind floundered. Were we under attack? Then I heard the roar of planes and saw tracer smoke puffs from the anti-aircraft guns. Fear gripped my heart as I ran to quarters to get the other nurses.

They quickly dressed, and we raced for the hospital. Looking up, we could see planes painted with the red rising sun of the Japanese Empire flying low overhead. The planes dropped their bombs, and the ground rolled with enormous shock waves. "I'm betting most of the enlisted men at Hickam Field are still asleep in their barracks," I said to Courtney, waves of nausea surging through my stomach.

"They'll burn to death in their bunks," she answered, face ashen. We looked at each other in utter disbelief and hurried on. Sirens screamed, and people yelled and ran down the street.

We made it to the hospital where the vibrations of aircraft overhead shook the walls. It was terrifying to sit and hear all the noises outside, while inside it was eerily calm and quiet. The attack lasted just over an hour. Then a huge rush of patients came through the door, and chaos erupted.

When they carted the men in, many were already beyond hope. My first two died from severe burns that covered most of their bodies. I could smell their flesh burning. Wounded men lay everywhere, even on the ground, and I wanted to scream.

We began marking the men's foreheads with lipstick to help with triage. Those who couldn't be saved were moved off to the side, so we could focus on those who might be. I'd never pictured myself making on-the-spot life and death decisions like these. We administered shots of morphine to the living and the dying to deaden their pain, struggling to make the men comfortable.

I tried to swab a man's forearm with alcohol for an IV, and his skin came right off in my hands. Courtney looked at me wide-eyed but kept going. I watched a doctor head into the operating ward wearing a cleaning rag that doubled as a face mask.

I saved my next two patients, but I was feeling light-headed. Then a wounded man lying on a cot grabbed my arm. "They destroyed the fleet," he said. "Torpedoes crashed against the hull of my ship, and we started taking on water. The noise was ear shattering with explosion after explosion, and I could smell the fuel burning."

"That must have been terrifying," I muttered with more steadiness than I felt. I could read the fear in his eyes and hoped he couldn't read the fear in mine.

"Am I going to make it?" he asked, clutching my hand.

"Yes, but it'll take time to heal," I said, trusting my new nursing degree.

News began coming over the radio: "We have witnessed this morning the distant view of a brief, full battle and the severe bombing of Pearl Harbor by enemy planes, undoubtedly Japanese. The city of Honolulu has also been attacked and considerable damage done."

Not Honolulu too! I was semi-hysterical. I loved that city.

"It's no joke," the announcer continued. "It's a real war. The public of Honolulu has been advised to keep in their homes and away from the army and navy."

I took a deep breath. "We're at war." My hands shook, and I was terrified by a world that had gone upside down in the last several hours. I walked into the bathroom to wash my hands and found a nurse in tears. "What's wrong, Alicia?" I asked.

"My fiancé Robert is dead. I just saw him out there on the floor, so badly burned I barely recognized him." Tears streamed down her shocked face.

What words of comfort could I offer at a time like this? I put my arms around her.

"It's too much," she said, angrily, pulling away. "It's not just Robert. I hate seeing the fear of death in the men's eyes and then watching them die. Where's God in all this?" Alicia sobbed.

"You just lost your fiancée, and I can't imagine how devastating that is. You have questions about his death and the deaths of all these men. And I do too," I stammered. "The one thing I know is that God loves us, and He feels our pain."

She grabbed a tissue and wiped her eyes, taking a deep breath.

"There are living men out there who need us," I said. "We've got to tend to them."

She nodded, and we went back to the death pit.

An hour later, I stepped to the side to pick up a syringe and thought about Chris. My blood ran cold. If the Japanese had just strafed the heck out of Hawaii, why not hit the Philippines on the way back to Japan? A man, who I thought was dead, moaned. "This one's still alive," I shouted. "Bring morphine."

Night fell, and we worked in almost total darkness. Fearing another attack, we kept the lights low. Some of the corpsmen held flashlights while we tended to the patients. I worked through most of the night and then tried to get a few hours' sleep on a lone hospital cot in an adjoining room.

I pulled on a nightshirt, a sheen of sweat covering my forehead. I wished I could get out of here and go home to my family. Maybe catch one of Alex's basketball games or make cookies with Lily, simple things I'd taken for granted.

Before trying to sleep, I fell to my knees and prayed for Alicia, for Chris, and my family at home. I prayed for those who had lost loved ones. *Dear God, in these darkest hours, please bless the families of the fallen to find peace.* Sobs I'd suffocated all day escaped my throat. *Help me too, God, please help me*, I begged, rolling into bed, staring at the ceiling. Tears streamed down my cheeks until I was bone dry inside.

* * *

Earlier that same day, Hallie and her new roommate, Sally, left church holding onto each other as they walked down the short set of steps, careful their heels didn't slide on patches of ice. They climbed into Hallie's 1940 four-door black sedan and fired up the engine, waiting for the heater core to warm up.

"Christmas is just around the corner, and it's going to be a joyous season. I want a new tabletop radio for my dorm room," Hallie said. "I love listening to Guy Lombardo and his orchestra. How about you?"

"One of those white woolen jackets with a black lapel and collar would suit me."

"Very nice."

Their families had struggled through the Great Depression for the last ten years, but finally a sense of hope and promise filled the air. Newspapers advertised all kinds of Christmas gifts: Diamond rings for twenty-nine dollars and pastries at fifteen cents for a two-pound bag.

As they rode down frosty streets to the University of Utah, Sally turned and said, "I'm relieved America's not at war like most of the rest of the world."

"Me too. My sister Lucy's a nurse in Hawaii, and my brother Chris is a pilot in the Philippines."

"Hawaii is a wonderful place. I wish I were there right now," she said, looking at her watch, shivering. "I'm hungry. It's noon and time for lunch."

"The dining hall at the dormitory won't start serving until 1:00 p.m."

"You'd think they could serve earlier on Sunday."

"No such luck. Want a stick of gum?"

"Sure, why not."

As they neared Carlson Hall at the University, their conversation turned to the movie they'd seen a few weeks earlier, *How Green Was My Valley*.

"That picture was dynamite," Hallie said. "The best part was when the narrator talked about the importance of family living in our hearts long after they're gone."

"Families are forever."

"I think that movie might even win best picture in February."

"I agree. It was that good."

They reached the dorms, and Hallie said, "Let's head straight for the dining room. We can listen to some jazz on the radio until they serve lunch."

They walked into the three-story brick building, furnished in Early American style. The smell of meatloaf, mashed potatoes, and corn filled the air.

"Hi-de-ho," their friend June said, waving from across the room. "Come join me." She counted herself one of the most fashionable among the residents of Carlson Hall, and since silk was often in short supply, she'd taken to painting her legs with a layer of blonde makeup, then lining the back of her legs with black seams. A fashion bridge too far for Hallie.

They sat and ate lunch to the sounds of Count Basie and his orchestra, then lingered over chocolate cream pie. Hallie leaned back in her chair, happy and relaxed.

About 3:00 p.m., the music stopped, and a radio announcer said, "We interrupt this musical program with a live broadcast coming from our NBC affiliate: There has been a severe bombing of Pearl Harbor, undoubtedly Japanese planes. The city of Honolulu has also been attacked. Considerable damage has been done. This bombing has been going on for almost three hours." Then the radio crackled, and the live report ended.

"Holy mackerel! Can it be true?" Hallie asked, jumping from her chair, and running to the telephone, her heart pounding. She thought first about calling her parents, then realized they wouldn't know any more than she did. Hallie picked up the phone and said, "Operator, this is Hallie Forrest. Get me someone at the *Salt Lake Tribune* offices, please."

"Hello, what can I do for you?" A man's voice asked.

"I'm calling to hear more about the bombing."

"We don't have many details yet, but we'll have an extra edition of the paper out soon."

Hallie was sweating and her chin trembled. *Is Lucy all right? Is she safe?*

When the extra edition came out, the headline read: "Japan Declares War on US; Attacks Naval Base at Hawaii. Reported 350 dead and one battleship on fire." Later that day the Associated Press reported that Japan had sunk two warships. Details were inaccurate and dribbling in slowly. Hallie hated that. She needed certainty.

As they heard the AP report, she thought, the Japanese attacked before declaring war. I can't believe it. There was no news yet on the Philippines.

* * *

"Japan is bombing Hawaii!" A man in Chris's squadron shouted. For a minute he thought the guy must be mistaken. Then they heard airhorns blaring.

"My sister's a nurse at Tripler," Chris said, heart racing.

"Betting she has her hands full," the guy stuttered.

The men cursed the Japanese Emperor and his minions, wondering how America had let this happen.

"How could a huge armada of ships make it all the way from Japan to Hawaii without being detected?" Chris asked.

"Yeah," his copilot Sam said. "Where was our intelligence in all this?"

Another man balled his hands into fists, "And why were the US ships left like sitting ducks in the harbor?"

Chris's unit had a few anti-aircraft guns, and the men had dug trenches around the hangars and the mess shacks. The pilots had trained for an attack, but life on the island of Luzon had been relaxed up to now.

The Commanding officer called the squadron together and directed all fighter planes to take off. The P-40 crews were told to stay in the air most of the time, both to stop an attack and to guard against being strafed on the ground. "Ground crews, stay alert," he barked.

At about eleven, the airplanes returned and refueled, ready to take off if necessary. The pilots hadn't seen any enemy airplanes or ships, so Chris and his crew walked over to the mess shack to have lunch. Then they spotted aircraft stippling the sky. Japanese bombers! Chris shouted at his crew and ran for the B17 as bombs started dropping. The bombs made a loud whistling noise and then hit the ground with a roaring explosion, the sound deafening.

The rest of the pilots dashed for their airplanes and tried to get them rolling onto the runway. Crews were desperate to help, but bombs were falling at a frantic pace. The ground quivered, and airplanes exploded. Four P-40s reached the air, but the rest blew apart either on the ground or before they reached the skies. Chris's friend Gene and crew were dead. The two of them had dinner just last night. "No, please God, not Gene," Chris said, as they headed for the skies.

When they reached the air, Jack, the ball turret gunner, began firing from his small seat in the belly of the bomber, as twelve Japanese Zeros attacked their plane. Bullets hit the plane dozens of times, but they didn't take her down. Jack fired back, and they destroyed a few Zeroes, cheering as the enemy planes crashed. Chris stared straight ahead and kept his hands steady on the wheel.

His buddies were dying all around him, both in the air and on the ground. The Zeros were swarming the field, strafing with machine guns, and firing huge cannons. They flew in low and fired into already burning hangers, igniting fuel tanks. They buzzed over the barracks and shot into the men's living quarters. Chris clenched his hands into angry fists.

Then, less than ninety minutes later, the Japanese fighters banked away and vanished into the smoke, leaving Clark Field unrecognizable, and protecting Japan against retaliation for Pearl Harbor. The hangers were destroyed, and most of the planes reduced to charred carcasses. A black plume of oily smoke hung in the sky, and the men were left defenseless against another attack.

Chris returned to base, and his B-17 looked like a sieve, the sides riddled with holes. He laid his hand on Jack's shoulder and said, "Good job, buddy."

"Just glad to be alive."

Chris didn't know how many men in the squadron were dead, but he'd seen two P-40s explode. It was surreal, as if it happened to someone else, on another planet. Chris hadn't had time for fear yet, only anger.

He remembered how he'd cheered as his crew shot men out of the sky and killed them. It had given him a disturbing sense of satisfaction. Then, he thought about something his dad told him before he left for the Philippines.

"When America was fighting World War I," Dad said, "our church leaders advised the men to keep 'all cruelty, hate, and murder' out of their hearts, even during battle. Remember that son, as you do battle."

Chris paled at the memory. He'd killed men out of necessity, but he didn't want to be happy about it. And yet, he had been. He flinched, as if someone had touched him. He felt isolated and frustrated at the world around him.

CHAPTER TWO

Hallie sat in the fourth-floor sunroom at Carlson Hall, waiting for President Franklin Roosevelt to deliver a speech to Congress. She slumped in her chair, eyes closed, and her head spun like a top.

A few weeks after Hallie had moved into the dorms, the house mother said, "I still remember your sister, Lucy. She's the outgoing type, and you're the serious one." Then she quickly added. "I like you both."

"Thank you," Hallie said, smiling but not believing a word of it. Lucy had lots of friends but rarely shared anything personal. Hallie had a few close friends and told them everything.

The President's address began crackling over the radio: "Yesterday, December 7, 1941—a day which will live in infamy—the United States of America was suddenly and deliberately attacked by naval and air forces of the Empire of Japan. The United States was at peace with that nation and, at the solicitation of Japan, was still in conversation with the government and its emperor looking toward the maintenance of peace in the Pacific…

"It will be recorded that the distance of Hawaii from Japan makes it obvious that the attack was deliberately planned many days or even weeks ago. During the intervening time, the Japanese government has deliberately sought to deceive the United States by false statements and expressions of hope for continued peace.

"The attack yesterday on the Hawaiian Islands has caused severe damage to American naval and military forces. Very many American lives have been lost. In addition, American ships have been torpedoed on the high seas between San Francisco and Honolulu.

"Yesterday, the Japanese government also launched an attack against Malaya.

Last night, Japanese forces attacked Hong Kong.

Last night, Japanese forces attacked Guam.

Last night, Japanese forces attacked the Philippine Islands.

Last night, the Japanese forces attacked Wake Island.

This morning, the Japanese attacked Midway Island.

"Japan has, therefore, undertaken a surprise offensive extending throughout the Pacific area. The facts of yesterday speak for themselves...As commander in chief of the army and navy, I have directed that all measures be taken for our defense. Always we will remember the character of the onslaught against us.

"No matter how long it may take us to overcome this premeditated invasion, the American people in their righteous might will win through to absolute victory."

Then Congress declared war on Japan.

Hallie and a group of students took to the streets, the men vowing to enlist in the military. It seemed the guys were all crazy to go overseas. The crowd walked past a fraternity with a large sign outside their chapter house that read: "Our relations with our Upsilon Pupsilon chapter in Tokyo are hereby severed!" Several of the men who hung the sign vowed they'd sign up to serve in the armed forces.

The First Lady, Mrs. Eleanor Roosevelt, in her address that evening, urged women to rise above their fears. "Many of you all over this country have boys in the services who will now be called upon to go into action. You cannot escape a clutch of fear at your heart, and yet I hope that the certainty of what we have to meet will make you rise above these fears. I have a boy at sea on a destroyer. For all I know he is on his way to the Pacific.

"To the young people of this nation, I must speak tonight. You will have a great opportunity—there will be high moments in which your strength and your ability will be tested. I have faith in you! Just as though I were standing upon a rock, and that rock is my faith in my fellow citizens."

Hallie turned to her roommate. "There's got to be a way I can serve my country." The First Lady's words had hit home. "Maybe I could do something with ciphers."

"You'd be perfect. I don't know anyone who can solve a puzzle faster than you."

"Now I have to convince my parents," Hallie said, frowning.

Across the country, all Japanese people became suspect. Were they in on it? Were they saboteurs? The students began hearing words like "yellow rats" and "rice eaters," to describe the Japanese as hatred and suspicion grew. While Hallie understood the fear, she hated the propaganda.

One of her uncles had served a mission in Tokyo, and the Forrest children had grown up hearing about what a beautiful country Japan was and how gentle and generous its people were. But the militants had taken over Japan, and they'd convinced the people it was 'Japan's divine destiny' to expand its powers. A recipe for disaster, Hallie thought.

Hallie and her friends congregated around congested parked cars listening to radios for the latest news. The university finally dismissed classes so the students could tune in to more of FDR's speeches. Hallie couldn't keep Lucy or Chris out of her mind. Remember, rule number one is 'Keep your Cool,' Hallie thought, biting her lip.

* * *

Two days after the bombing at Pearl Harbor, the family received a cable from Lucy. She was exhausted, but uninjured. Hallie was so relieved. But what about Chris? Who knew what had happened to him? She closed her eyes, head pounding.

By Saturday night, distractions from the war were essential. Hallie and Lily went with their parents to the matinee at the Centre Theatre on State Street, a lovely art deco building with a ninety-foot tower above the theatre that could seat over sixteen hundred people. They watched a solid dose of color cartoons, serials, and newsreels, and adored the delightful new main feature, Dumbo. Hallie felt refreshed, a welcome relief.

After the movie ended, they drove to Provo to watch Alex play a home basketball game for his college team. The family never missed one of his games, and Dad was his biggest fan, which wasn't good when he yelled comments to the coach, embarrassing Alex. Hallie looked at her younger brother across the floor, muscular in his blue basketball uniform. Tall, with brown hair and eyes to match, he played center for the team, and no one could tip the ball into the hoop as effortlessly as he could. The girls were attracted to him like honeybees to flowers.

On the way home, the radio announcer said that the White House was going ahead with the annual Christmas tree lighting on the South Lawn, but with a change: The tree-lighting ceremony would follow a patriotic theme. "Looks like the war won't stop the Christmas tree program," Hallie said.

"War is bad business," Alex said. "Has anyone heard from Chris?"

"Not yet," Mom said, tears in her eyes.

The Forrest family lived in Holladay, a suburb of Salt Lake City. Their neighbors down the street had received notice a few days prior that their son had been killed at Pearl Harbor. His mother fainted at the news, and his father was devastated. They'd started planning a memorial service, and then two days later, the army notified them they'd made a mistake. Their son was still alive. Nobody was sure of anything, and Hallie was on edge.

The next day was Sunday, one week after Pearl Harbor had been bombed. The family was in the car, glad to be going to church. They reached the chapel and sat in their usual pew. Hallie whispered to Mom, "I need something to calm me down." Everything seemed magnified, out of proportion.

She patted her hand. "I love you, Hallie," she said, offering a gentle hug.

The chorister stood and opened the meeting with, 'My Country Tis of Thee.' There wasn't a dry eye in the family as the congregation sang, "Long may our land be bright, With Freedom's holy light. Protect us by thy might, Great God our King."

Dad said the opening prayer. When he sat down, Mom held his hand and whispered. "Just the encouragement we needed, Joshua."

He smiled. "Thank you, my dear."

Hallie smiled too, watching them together. Her parents had a good marriage. Not perfect, of course, but whose was? They rarely argued, and when they did, it wasn't in front of the children. Her parents were committed to each other and to honoring their marriage covenants. That's what Hallie wanted someday—but not yet.

A speaker stood and read from Psalm 61:1-4:

"Hear my cry, O God; attend unto my prayer.

From the end of the earth will I cry unto thee when my heart is overwhelmed: lead me to the rock that is higher than I.

For thou hast been a shelter for me, and a strong tower from the enemy.

I will abide in thy tabernacle forever: I will trust in the covert of thy wings."

He set his scriptures down and said, "We must not lose faith. What's right will prevail, and the world will be made safe again someday." Then it was announced that services would end early, so everyone could go home and be with family.

Being at war had taken all the air out of the room and brought what was most important into sharp focus. Hallie was relieved to find a little peace in the chaos.

* * *

When the family returned to their red brick, one-story home, Alex went downstairs to his room in the basement to change out of his Sunday clothes and into something more comfortable.

"Please grab a jar of peaches from the fruit room, Alex," Mom called down the stairs.

"You bet," he said, walking to the windowless room they called the fruit room to retrieve the peaches. His mom had bottled and canned a year's supply of fruit, meat, and vegetables, and Alex's favorite, raspberry jam. He had a sweet tooth, that was for sure. Sugar had been rationed not long after America began supporting Britain in the conflict with Germany. Alex was still trying to get used to molasses cookies.

He walked upstairs, through the dining room and into the kitchen, stomach grumbling. Lily sat on a stool wearing a white apron over her blue-flowered dress, helping their mother cut holes into the dough with an upside-down drinking glass. Then, she folded the circles and placed them on a baking sheet. Alex knew the rolls would take an hour to rise and another twenty minutes to bake, but his mom's rolls were worth the wait. She'd also made fudge with white sugar she still had on hand. No one was better prepared.

"What's for dinner, Mom?" he asked.

"Roast turkey with candied yams and grape salad in sweet cream with brown sugar."

"Topped with pecans?"

"Of course."

"Can't wait."

The family gathered around the table, held hands, and Dad asked Lily to offer a blessing. She prayed for Chris, Lucy, and peace in the world, then blessed the food. The family opened their eyes, and with heavy hearts, said their amens. Then Lily smiled. "Let's dig in." Everyone laughed, relieving the tension.

"Please pass the yams," Hallie said. "Mom, you remember the Brown family who moved to Pennsylvania a few years ago? Kay was my best friend."

Mom nodded, her mouth full of food.

"I got a letter from her yesterday."

"She goes to Bryn Mawr, right?" Dad asked

"Getting ready to graduate. Kay says she got a letter from a department head at her school asking her to meet with him. He asked two questions: 'Are you engaged to be married?' My answer to that would have been no. And the other was, 'Do you like crossword puzzles?' My answer would be yes, just like Kay's. It's all very hush, hush, but Kay says the government is looking for female math graduates."

"Why math graduates in particular?" Dad asked.

"And why the puzzle question?" Alex asked. "If it was some secretarial job, I'd think the question would be, 'Can you type?'"

"It's a mystery," Hallie said. "Whatever the work is, it's in Washington DC."

"What about completing school?" Mom wondered.

"With all the men enlisting, the university is letting students graduate a few months early, so I'll finish in March instead of May. Did you know that the *New York Times* is calling the women joining the war effort, The Lipstick Brigade? A little stupid, but I bet the name sticks." Hallie rolled her eyes.

Dad set his fork down. "Wouldn't you rather stay here and teach?"

"I like solving problems, and I think this job might be working with codes. That's what I want to do," Hallie said, determined.

"You'd be very good at it," Mom commented.

Alex agreed, knowing Hallie had the most book smarts in the family.

"Thanks, Mom," Hallie said. "Besides, Kay says the pay is a lot better than teaching."

Mom seemed relieved that Hallie would at least stay in the United States.

"Good for you, Hallie," Alex said. "I want to get in on this military service shindig too."

"War's not fun and games," Dad said, scowling.

"Don't blow a fuse, Dad, I know that."

"Your dad's worried about Chris," Mom said. "We all are."

"You're right, Mom. Sorry, Dad," Alex said.

"It's okay. I understand you want to do your duty, and I admire that."

"Swell, thanks. Turns out I had enough college credits to enlist as a Private First Class."

"You've already enlisted?" Mom asked, voice rising in surprise.

"In the army. I'll make a good Pfc. First step up the ladder."

"What does a Pfc. do?" Hallie asked, helping herself to more turkey.

"Good question," Alex said, taking a paper from his pocket. "This is what the army says about a Pfc.: 'They are recognized as masters of individual responsibility, and they carry out all tasks and orders assigned to them to the best of their ability.' This will be mostly a desk job, but the battalion they've assigned me to in Maryland has been training a month already, and I won't enlist until after Christmas. There isn't time enough to train on the guns before we ship out."

"You won't be an anti-aircraft gunner, then?" Mom asked, the worry lines in her face dissipating.

"No, Mom." He'd done it for her. Settled for a desk job where he'd be less in the line of fire. He'd wanted to be a gunner, but he'd heard the pain in her voice for weeks whenever she mentioned Chris. "I'll be in the battalion offices, where I'll take on leadership responsibilities. I know I've always been an average student, and it was basketball that got me into college, but Grandma Katie told me I have what she calls a convincing personality, and a style of working others appreciate." The more he heard himself talk, the more he believed his innate political skills would better serve him in an office than on the battlefield.

"People like and trust you, Alex," Mom said. "Those are wonderful qualities for a leader."

"Thanks, Mom."

"I agree," Dad said, "and I'm proud of both of you for wanting to serve."

"I was just getting used to having you two away at college but still close enough to visit often," Mom said, looking down at her hands.

"I promise to write twice a month," Alex said as a loud knock came at the door. "I'll get it," he said. When he came back a minute later, he was waving something in his hand. "It's a telegram."

"Oh, I hope it's not bad news," Mom said, gripping the edge of the table.

Alex opened it. "Cable from the Postal Telegraph, and it's from Chris! This is what he says, 'Knew you'd be worried. Survived the attack. Thoughts are with you. Love, Chris.'"

Mom started crying, and Dad reached over and placed his arm around her as tears of relief ran down her face.

Mom wiped her eyes with her apron. Her children may not all be under the same roof with her, but they were safe. That was the best any mother could hope for.

The church's Christmas fireside was broadcasting on the radio, and the family was anxious to hear some words of hope from their church leaders.

Alex lit a fire in the fireplace, and the family sat together on the couches. As they listened, the words that meant the most to him were: "Only through living the gospel of Jesus Christ will enduring peace come to the world." Alex looked at his parents, and they appeared calm and seemed at peace for the moment, despite the horrors of war.

He was faced with an uncertain future, leaving college, basketball, friends, family, and a girlfriend behind. Sadie had promised to write, but would she be here when he got back? It might be a long time. He was anxious and unsure, the specter of war looming all around him.

The next day, the papers reported that not two, but six US Warships had been lost in the Hawaii attack, and over twenty-seven hundred men had died. The refrain, "Remember Pearl Harbor!" rang across town.

CHAPTER THREE

It took days for us to realize just how bad the attack on Pearl Harbor had been. Hawaii still felt like summer, and when it rained, I loved the tropical energy in the air, palm trees waving in the breeze. But then a Japanese submarine torpedoed a commercial ship, the *Lahaina.* The sub hit the huge freighter twelve times before sinking it, and we lived in constant fear of attack.

I knew my parents would be worried, and I tried to get another cable out, but the lines were jam packed. I felt isolated and frightened, knowing we could be bombed into oblivion any minute.

A melancholy Christmas stretched ahead. Local gardens were donating red poinsettias and hibiscus so they could place small bouquets on graves. Strict blackout measures were enacted, and martial law was enforced. Barbed wire was strung around everything, and a curfew banned civilians from going out at night. Residents even had to black out their windows and paint their car headlights black. It was crazy, scary stuff.

The Sunday after the bombing, I dressed in my favorite Hawaiian dress, pink with green flowers, brown sandals strapped around my feet, and sprayed my hair with light perfume. Even though church meetings had been suspended and the members urged to worship in their own homes, I wanted to visit our beautiful chapel and just sit by the reflecting pool.

I caught a bus into Honolulu and chose a window seat to enjoy the view. Then I noticed that the Christmas lights looped along the streets of Nuuanu Avenue had been turned off or taken down. Many of the military men would spend Christmas digging bomb shelters. Hope was hard to come by.

I reached the chapel, got off the bus, and walked past the old banyan tree. I paused at the huge mural of Christ with his welcoming arms outstretched and gazed with tear-filled eyes. Then I sat down near the long blue pool, remembering my first time in the chapel. I'd gone inside just as sunshine flooded the open doors. The meeting had begun with a heart-felt Aloha, which I loved. It had made me feel welcome and cared for…

Now a man I hadn't seen before walked up. He was tall with muscled shoulders, brown, neatly cut hair, and dressed in a white naval uniform. When he caught me staring at him, a wide smile lit up his face. He had the most engaging eyes. I wanted to look away but didn't.

He came over and introduced himself. "Aloha," he said, offering his hand and taking mine.

Something inside me stirred at his touch. "Name's Matt Hatch."

"Lucy Forrest," I said, smiling. "I'm an army nurse at the hospital here."

"I'm in the navy stationed on the *USS Salt Lake City*. She's a cruiser."

"Really? I'm from Salt Lake City."

"You're kidding. So, we have something in common besides our faith." His eyes twinkled. "I take it there are no services here today."

"We don't know when regular meetings will resume. Were you here during last Sunday's bombing?"

"We escorted the carrier the *USS Enterprise* as it delivered aircraft to Wake Island, so no. I've been here the last few days on leave." He straightened his shoulders and in a warm tone asked, "Say, I know we just met, but how'd you like to take a walk on the beach with me?"

"I planned on eating by the water, and I packed a lunch. Should be enough in here for two."

"Swell," he said offering his arm.

We took a bus to Waikiki, got off, and found a bench along the white sand. "I love it here," I said, opening the paper bag with lunch inside, gazing at Diamond Head in the distance.

"Weather's perfect," Matt said, biting into the ham and cheese sandwich.

"Would you mind slicing this pineapple?" I asked, offering a small pocketknife I carried in my purse.

"Be happy to." He reached for the fruit. "Nice picnic."

"It's pretty simple."

"Being with you beats a fancy lunch in town." He handed me the slices, licking his fingers. "Say, how long have you been a nurse?"

"About six weeks, but it seems like a lifetime." I sighed.

"Bet you've seen some bad stuff." His voice was kind, and he looked interested.

"Our hospital is always full, and we're busy around the clock with wounded soldiers coming from across the Pacific. Yesterday, we helped load the first casualties from Pearl Harbor—at least those who could be moved—onto a ship sailing to San Francisco. A guy on the dock told me the ship would have to follow a zigzag course to avoid torpedoes from enemy submarines. Some of those men were my patients, and I pray they'll make it safely home."

His hand found mine, and he held it. He gazed into my eyes with sincere concern but said nothing. He didn't have to.

"Enough about me," I said, "tell me about your family." I gently removed my hand from his with a rush of conflicting emotions.

"I'm the baby of the family, two sisters and one brother. My dad's a doctor."

"Do you want to be a doctor?"

"No." He smiled. "My dad would want me to go into practice with him, and I don't want to be the boss's son. I'm my own man. How many kids in your family?"

"I'm the second child of five, two boys and three girls."

"Are your brothers in the military too?"

"Chris is a pilot, and I got a cable from Alex yesterday saying he'd quit playing basketball and enlisted in the army."

"Doing his duty. I'd like him."

"Do you play sports?"

"On the rowing team at the University of Southern California. I like to row, but sailing's my favorite. My dad has a boat docked at Dana Point Harbor. What do you do for fun?"

"I paint, mostly landscapes. When I paint, I lose all track of time, which is why I love it."

"Same for me when I sail." He stretched his arm along the back of the bench, and we talked until late afternoon. He listened to me, really listened. He was a man of faith, and there was a lot I liked about him—but I reminded myself I might never see him again.

The sun eased to twilight, the waves transformed to a deep blue, and I sensed a bit of magic in the air. "Just look at that sky."

"It's heavenly, and so are you, Lucy," Matt said, standing, offering his hand.

I rose and leaned into his shoulder. We stood, staring into the heavens.

"It's almost curfew," he said, "and we both have to eat. Please come with me."

"I'd like that." I smiled, my skin tingling.

"How about the Royal Hawaiian? That's where I'm staying."

"I love that hotel's restaurant."

"Me too. Front desk gave me a pamphlet as I checked in. Says the place has been around since 1927. Spanish-Moorish style was popular back then, inspired by none other than Mr. Rudy Valentino himself. It's swank if you ask me."

"A beautiful pink building, and their luau is great," I said, then stopped. "I wonder if they're still having it."

"It's been shortened. Can't have torches lit after dark. You game?"

"Sure am."

He picked up the lunch trash, dumped it in a bin, and we walked along the beach arm in arm.

After we arrived at the hotel, Matt said, "I'll get out of this uniform and put on my best Hawaiian shirt. Wait right there." He smiled.

I stood in the lobby near the window, watching a small white boat with two sails cross the aqua-blue water. There wasn't a more beautiful place on earth.

When Matt came down, he looked more relaxed out of uniform, and we were still in time for the luau. The hostess showed us to a long table and placed two leis around our necks. I felt better than I had in weeks.

Assorted breads and fruits filled the table, and a pig roasted on the spit. We laughed and talked with a few other couples. Everyone liked Matt and his fun sense of humor. He was good with people. And he was just so handsome. We enjoyed the hula dancing until the hostess called us inside to the Monarch Room where staff drew blackout curtains against the view outside.

A band with guitars, ukuleles, and wind instruments took the stage. "Aloha," the leader called over the crowd. "Let's dance!"

"Are you in the mood to dance?" Matt asked.

"Always," I smiled.

He took me in his arms, and we turned around the floor to the song, "Pennies from Heaven." It was my mom's favorite. She'd sung it to me after I broke up with my boyfriend last year, when I learned he wasn't who he claimed to be.

I listened as the band sang the words, 'So when you hear it thunder, don't run under a tree. There'll be pennies from heaven for you and me.' I smiled, looked at Matt, and nestled against his shoulder. This was all happening fast, but I allowed my heart to wonder if he might be one of those pennies from heaven.

The music ended, and we went outside. I called for a military vehicle, and Matt waited with me. He held my face in his hands and kissed me lightly on the lips. I kissed him back, and it was oh, so nice.

As we stood there, I peered into the blackness. "Where is that jeep?"

"You in a hurry? Late night shift?"

"I need to finish writing a letter home to my mom so it can go out tomorrow."

Matt went quiet.

"Is something wrong?" I asked.

"I had a mom once. She died when I was fourteen."

I reached for his hand. "I'm so sorry, Matt. That must have been a terrible loss."

He nodded. "Worst day of my life."

"Do you mind if I ask what happened?"

"Car accident. A drunk driver hit us head on."

"Us?" I asked. "You were in the car?"

"Yes. My mom died instantly, and an ambulance picked me up."

"I'm glad you made it." My eyes watered. "She must have been a very special lady."

"She was the best mom ever. She died, and I lived."

"You can't blame yourself, Matt. She wouldn't want that."

"No, she wouldn't." He looked so vulnerable. "I don't know why I told you all this," he said.

"Because I care, Matt."

He kissed me on the cheek. "Thank you, Lucy. There's something special about you and me together."

I blushed. Could he be the one? Or was I simply on the rebound? Was he any different than my ex-boyfriend? I felt euphoric and disoriented at the same time, my body temperature rising. I moved closer, smiled, and we held hands until the car pulled up.

"Aloha, Lucy, but not goodbye. Until we meet again." Then he kissed me long and deep, and the sparks flew.

I offered a breathless goodbye and climbed into the jeep.

"I'll write," he promised.

"Be careful out there." I was sad that his leave was over. I'd spent one magical day with him and wanted more.

He waved as the driver pulled away.

I leaned back in my seat and gazed into the starry heavens. I knew, just knew. Something inside me whispered that Matt was sensitive, faithful, and I could trust him to be who he said he was. When I finally went to bed that night, his face filled my dreams.

The next morning, I walked back to the hospital, bracing against the blood and missing limbs. Christmas was only four days away.

This year would be nothing like last year when I was safely tucked inside my family home. Instead, I'd be huddled in barracks, taking care of the wounded. I missed my clan. I sighed.

I'd kept it together the past few weeks, and we were saving lives, at least most of them. I walked past the cafeteria and caught a whiff of eggs and bacon cooking. I thought about going in for breakfast, but I'd lost my appetite.

***

Back at Clark airfield in the Philippines, the situation had gotten worse since the attack earlier in December. Besides fighting Japan in the air, the men were battling aggressive Japanese ground troops. Each day, enemy bombers flew over, shelling the airstrip and hitting ruined hangars. They flew at unexpected times, often during the night, leaving the men terrified. One night, Chris turned to his copilot Sam and said, "The US has to get us some help out here or the airfield will be overrun soon."

"I don't know how much longer I can take this, Chris," Sam said, climbing out of the foxhole," shaking.

"Hold tight, buddy. We'll get through it. Say, the CO wants me to take a truck into Manila tomorrow to pick up supplies. Want to ride along?"

"Sure, okay. Anything to get out of here for a couple of hours."

The next day, Chris and Sam made the eighty-mile drive to Manila. As they drove through the nearly deserted streets, they saw buildings that had been damaged or destroyed. "Worse than I thought," Chris said as Sam sat speechless.

Then the sirens started screaming. "Oh, crap" Sam said, holding on to the door as Chris drove under a large tree. They watched as five Zeros howled over the city unchallenged by allied planes. They dropped their bombs, and huge fires enveloped the sky in smoke. Several minutes later, the worst seemed to be over, and Chris said, "Let's get those supplies and beat it back to Clark."

After they arrived, the chief officer called a meeting. "Men," he began, "I don't have to tell you we're trapped like rats. We're outnumbered, and word has just come in that Clark Field will soon be abandoned. We'll be moving to Bataan field."

"Colonel," one of the men said, his hand raised, "the jungle covering Bataan has every tropical, disease possible."

"Bataan won't be a picnic, that's for sure."

Another man spoke up. "The jungle won't be the worst of it, Sir. The Japanese are a savage enemy and see themselves as the master race. We're in for it now."

"Lieutenant, President Roosevelt would never allow General MacArthur to suffer defeat at the hands of the Japanese. I can assure you of that!" The CO looked around to see if there were more questions. Seeing none, he said, "Look for another briefing this afternoon."

On December 24, orders were received at Clark Field to evacuate to the Bataan Peninsula of Luzon. With most of the B-17s destroyed, Chris was now flying a P-40. He and Sam were the first to clear out. They took off, duty bound for Bataan Field, another little dirt airstrip. The rest of the aircraft would also be concentrated there.

As Chris finally neared the airfield, he could see the Juanting River below. The field hadn't been there long, and the sarge said construction hadn't even started until last September. Even at that, there was only one runway that army engineers had hacked out of the jungle. "At least the field is well camouflaged," Sam said, as Chris positioned the plane for a landing.

After they landed and grabbed their gear, one of the men at the field showed them to quarters, which looked more like a shelter than a barracks. It was small, made of wood, and had a makeshift porch built on stilts with a couple of chairs outside. "Looks like this is where we'll be spending Christmas," Sam said, looking around. "Ho, ho, ho."

A group of Filipino soldiers, a few civilians, and Chris and his buddies gathered around a shortwave radio to listen to President

Roosevelt's Christmas message from Washington. When the president said, "We light our Christmas candles now across this continent…from one coast to another this Christmas evening," a Filipino soldier became upset.

He said, "The Japanese soldiers are entering Manila, and your president speaks of Christmas? Why doesn't he help us?"

Chris had no answer, and neither did anyone else. Why wasn't President Roosevelt sending reinforcements?

Worse news came the next day as General MacArthur declared Manila an open city, apparently hoping to spare it from destruction. But the Japanese didn't care and kept the bombs falling as they moved toward the capital. More lives were lost, and Chris was still having a tough time not hating his enemy.

CHAPTER FOUR

It was Christmas Eve in Salt Lake, and the family sat around the dining room table. Grandma Katie was there too. Alex looked at her weathered face, praying that at age eighty-seven she'd still be around when he returned from serving his country. He'd sneaked a piece of her amazing pumpkin pie before dinner. No one asked who'd already had a slice. They knew.

His mouth watered at the roast turkey with dressing, mashed potatoes with giblet gravy, and sweet potato casserole. He looked around at those who meant the most to him in the world and knew next Christmas would be nothing like this one. After the blessing on the food, he relished every bite.

"Please pass the string beans and venison sausage, Alex," Hallie said.

"Here ya go, sis," he said, mouth full of food.

"Thanks. I miss Chris and Lucy," she whispered to him, careful that Mom wouldn't hear. She was sad enough without knowing how deeply Chris and Lucy's absence upset Hallie.

"Me too," Alex said, his voice cracking. "Christmas isn't Christmas without them."

A Douglas fir Christmas tree glowing with lights stood in the corner. It was seven feet tall, but Alex had easily reached the top and added a star. When he was a little boy and had attended a school carnival, he'd stepped up to the free throw line with the rest of the first graders to sink a basket. A male teacher had stopped him and said, "You can't be a first grader. You're too tall. Now, you go on over there."

Mom stepped in about that time and assured him Alex was in the first grade. "Now, let him shoot the basket," she'd said, ever the mama bear.

After they finished dinner, Dad read from the book of Luke. "And there were in the same country, shepherds abiding in the field, keeping watch over their flock by night. And lo, the angel of the Lord came upon them, and the glory of the Lord shone round about them."

Alex's favorite part of the scripture came when Dad read, "And suddenly there was with the angel a multitude of the heavenly host, praising God, and saying, glory to God on the highest, and on earth, peace, good will toward men." Alex startled at the words 'and on earth, peace,' hearing them differently than before.

Dad stopped reading, took off his round glasses and said, "This year, we have a war going on. Two of our family members are serving, and we pray for their safety. Instead of singing, 'Joy to the World,' like we usually do, come round the piano, and Mom will play the hymn, 'I heard the Bells on Christmas Day.'"

They sang the first verse, and again the idea of peace resonated with Alex. "And in despair I bowed my head, there is no peace on earth I said, for hate is strong and mocks the song Of Peace on earth, good will to men." Mom stopped playing, tears streaming down her face. Dad handed her a handkerchief, placing his hand on her shoulder.

"Let's take a deep breath," she said, collecting herself, "and go to the last verse, singing this one with hope." Mom was trying to bury her worry and fear in faith and optimism.

The family sang, "Then rang the bells more loud and deep, God is not dead, nor doth he sleep. The wrong shall fail, the right prevail, With peace on earth good will to men." They held hands and said nothing, hoping it was true.

"Peace will come one day," Dad said, "and we'll all be together again. But we're going to have a very rough go of it until then."

Hallie nodded as if she understood.

"Let me remind you that love and charity for others is still strong," Mom said. "The Relief Society made blankets and gift boxes for the elderly in nursing homes. We delivered them yesterday. Remember, the best way we can help ourselves is to help others."

Dad agreed and said, "Let's pick one gift to open from under the tree before bed." This happened every year, and it was Alex's favorite tradition. If only Chris and Lucy were there to take their turns.

1942

On New Year's Day, Alex rode a train traveling to Washington DC, last stop, Fort Eustis, Virginia. He'd been so busy packing that he hadn't had time to read an article the *New York Times* published about the injured men from Pearl who'd arrived in San Francisco Bay on a ship. Lucy had called from Hawaii Christmas day and told them all about her patients. Alex was proud of his sister for her dedication and compassion.

He read from the *Times*, "Ambulances moved away through the barricades while mothers stood in a steady rain, watching with hopeful eyes as the passengers emerged. The Army Nursing Service put out an all-points bulletin that asked for volunteer women to step forward and help with the wounded. All the men had stories of bravery and death. They were, the *New York Times* noted, filled with cold anger at the Japanese."

Alex put the paper aside and sipped on a ginger ale, thinking, within a month or so, I'll do battle with the Empire of Japan. A sobering thought.

He reached his destination two days later. Alex had been assigned to the 102nd battalion of the army, an anti-aircraft unit, as a clerk in the battalion office.

On his first day of training, he noticed that the food wasn't bad, and the sleeping quarters were warm, but they were filled with men sleeping shoulder to shoulder. And getting up at 5:30 a.m. every morning to the sound of reveille took some getting used to. He'd made a friend, a guy named Norman Nielson, who'd played football in high school, so they were both athletes. Norm had grown up in a rural country town, Burley, Idaho. He'd gone to college at Albion Normal College and taught school before being drafted. He said he wanted to go to law school when the war was over, just like his other five brothers.

"What do you want to do when the war is over?" Norm asked Alex one afternoon.

"Finish my degree in business. Maybe get an MBA."

"Sounds like a good plan."

That night in the barracks, Norm turned up the volume on a football game he was listening to on the radio. Some of the boys started yelling at him to turn it off. "They're not yelling that loud," he grinned at Alex.

Alex laughed. "I like your style."

The thing that bothered Alex and Norm the most was the constant standing in line. They got in formation to eat, to walk, for reveille, for taps, and, as Norm pointed out, "every other thing they have in this man's army."

One morning as they marched along, he told Alex he'd never even held a gun before he trained as an anti-aircraft gunner.

"Me neither," Alex said. "The sarge told me the rifle is my friend, learn to use it. So, I did."

The sergeant called out, "Count, 1, 2, 3, 4, get in step." And then, "To the rear, march—right flank, now left flank. Private first-class Alex Forrest, you missed a step. Gimme five laps!"

Five laps was a piece of cake for Alex. And the good news? It gave him a break from the drilling. Not so bad, he thought, smiling to himself as he sprinted around the track.

In February, Alex, Norm, and the rest of the battalion took a long train trip across the country to San Francisco, and then a few days later, shipped out for parts unknown. When the ship sailed under the iconic bridge, Norm and some of the men called out,

"Golden Gate in '48," and pumped fists into the air.

Alex mumbled under his breath, "So, six years before we come back? Better not be. Sadie will never wait that long."

The ship sailed the Pacific for a few days with no land in sight, the heat almost unbearable. Good thing there was a soda fountain aboard. "Make mine chocolate," Alex always said when he ordered ice cream. The guy who made the meals was a great cook, so the food was good.

At last, the weather turned cooler, and Alex spotted schools of porpoises and flying fish. *Might mean Hawaii.* He looked over the rail.

When the ship readied to dock in Oahu, Alex grabbed a ship-to-shore phone and reached Lucy at the hospital. "I'm in Hawaii," he shouted.

Excitement filled her voice. "I'll find a way to get away. Meet me in the courtyard of the Moana Hotel in front of the old Banyan tree at 3:00 p.m."

"Will do. Bringing a buddy along from Idaho. Want you to meet him."

Alex kept tears out of the corner of his eyes when he walked up to the white H-shaped building an hour later, knowing his big sister was waiting inside. He was surprised at his reaction; he never imagined he'd miss Lucy this way. When Alex and Norm reached the courtyard, Lucy stood there waiting in a blue and white aloha dress, her blonde hair cut shorter than usual. She waved and jumped up and down when she saw Alex.

He ran over, picked her up, and they both laughed. Norm went in search of a table on the lanai. When they all sat down, Alex said, "Lucy, this is my friend Norm Nielson."

"Hello," he said. "Good to meet you."

"You, too," Lucy said, shaking his hand.

"Alex tells me you're a nurse. Not an easy thing in this war. You must be one tough cookie."

"My Grandma Katie is the one who taught me I can do hard things. She was one of the first female medical doctors in Utah."

"Where did she grow up?"

"The small town of Farmington."

"My grandma used to live in Farmington," Norm said.

"They probably knew each other," Lucy smiled. "You're one of the family now, Norm."

"Thanks, Lucy," Norm grinned.

"Be careful, Norm," Alex warned. "Lucy can take anybody on."

"Thanks, hotshot." Lucy laughed and punched him in the arm.

They sat in the warm sunshine, and Alex and Lucy caught up for an hour, while Norm mostly listened. Then he looked from one to the other and said, "If your voices weren't different pitches, I might not know who was talking. The language you use is so similar."

Lucy smiled. "Our parents stressed the importance of an education, and they wanted us to practice what we learned, so we had nightly dinner discussions from the time we were small. We all love to talk, but Alex is the most fun."

Alex laughed and said, "I've missed you, sis."

"Me too," she squeezed his hand, "more than you know."

The three sat until dusk, palm trees swaying around them in a gentle breeze that blew in from the ocean.

The next day, Alex and Norm boarded the ship, and Alex hugged Lucy goodbye.

***

"Hallie," Mom called up the stairs. "Are you ready to go?"

"I'll be right there." The two of them were driving to Tooele to give Grandma Ann a birthday cake. In mild weather, it would take about thirty-five minutes from Salt Lake. But it was the end of February, and it was snowing, so Hallie figured an hour. Mom grew up in the little farming community of Tooele, and Grandma Ann still lived there.

When Hallie went to Grandma's farmhouse as a kid for the weekend, it was like taking a step back in time. She and Lucy slept upstairs in a thinly furnished bedroom with bare wooden floors. Grandma had no indoor plumbing or running water until Hallie was twelve, so she kept a big jug in the corner, called the thunder jug. The girls had to use it during the night if they needed to go to the bathroom. *Yuck. Still gives me the willies thinking about it.*

"Mom, slow down. There's a black and white in front of us," Hallie said. "You don't want the police chewing you out for speeding."

"I didn't realize I was going so fast."

As they neared Tooele, Mom said, "Did you know the army is building a facility here at the Dugway Proving Grounds? The word around town is that they'll be testing biological and chemical weapons."

"Geez. I had no idea," Hallie said. "That sounds pretty scary. I'd hate to be involved in building weapons."

They drove past the old brick county courthouse on their way to Grandma's house. She'd sold the farm after Hallie's grandpa died and used some of the money to build a small, white, wooden ranch-style home that was less than 1,000 square feet. Mom had tried to talk her into moving to Salt Lake to be closer, but Grandma refused. "Tooele is my home, and I'm staying put," she'd insisted. "This is where my memories live."

They parked the car out front and went inside without knocking. Grandma was sitting in a rocking chair, knitting.

"Don't get up, Mother," Mom said. "Look what we brought you."

Grandma set aside her knitting, and her eyes lit up. "My favorite chocolate cake with the white frosting inside. Today's February 24th, and it's my birthday." She grinned, as if they didn't know. "Come in, come in. Can you believe I'm eighty-four?"

Hallie walked over and put arms around her grandma's shoulders, hugging her close.

"It's so good to see you, Hallie," she whispered.

The name Hallie had been her idea. It meant praise the Lord and was the short form of Hallelujah.

"Sit next to me," Grandma said, patting a chair.

"I've got your candles right here in my purse." Hallie pulled them out, along with a book of matches. "Ready?"

"Ready, and I'm not getting any younger, so let's go." She laughed as Hallie lit several candles. A smile filled Grandma Ann's care-worn face as Mom and Hallie sang Happy Birthday. They stayed a few hours, enjoying cake and hot chocolate, until they could see she was tiring, then said goodbye and promised to visit again soon.

On the way home, Hallie drove while Mom leafed through the *Relief Society Magazine*. As soon as Hallie saw it, she knew Mom must have brought it along to teach her something. She was like that, never missed an opportunity. "Listen to what Professor Carlton Culmsee says about the war."

Mom started reading:

"The women replacing men at hard jobs, the old men and the lads extending themselves at war tasks, the soldiers, and sailors in the monotony of drill and watching and waiting—they all need something sound and sustaining. The mother saying goodbye to her son or receiving the news that he is missing in action must be fortified but with a far-seeing faith drawn from eternal sources."

Mom put the magazine down and put her hands in her lap. Hallie knew she was thinking of her own two sons, and Lucy too. As usual, hope and faith sustained her.

"Just think, Mom," Hallie said trying to distract her. "Before long, I'll be replacing some man using my math skills, happy as a coder."

"I'm so proud of you, Hallie."

Hallie wasn't as confident as she tried to sound. She liked a sense of order. Even the dresses in her closet were arranged by color, shoes neatly ordered. Lucy's stuff was everywhere, fall, winter, spring clothes all jammed together. War had disrupted all their lives, and Hallie hoped to restore a sense of predictability in her work with codes and ciphers.

CHAPTER FIVE

I was utterly exhausted and relieved the long shift at the hospital was over. Then one of my patients called out from his narrow bed in a voice so faint it was hard to hear. "Nurse, nurse, I need a nurse."

I walked over to his bed. "What can I do for you, Harry?" He'd been brought in last month from the Pacific and was in rough shape, having lost a leg. While his physical wounds were healing, he was battle scarred and struggled to get through the day.

"I need another shot of morphine," he said.

"Are you in pain? Is it your leg?"

"My head hurts."

I sat next to him on the bed to talk. We'd done this before, and it seemed to help. When Harry was drafted, he'd been a stage actor off Broadway in New York City and was very bright. But he believed his acting career was over, and his eyes had that faraway look I'd seen in patients before.

"Can't get those lines from Macbeth out of my head," he said.

"Which ones?"

"'Tomorrow, and tomorrow, and tomorrow, creeps in this petty pace from day to day.' That's what my days are like. They're all the same. I've been here thirty days, and it's been a lifetime."

"I remember those lines from a high school English class," I said. "Pretty depressing stuff."

"It's Macbeth's soliloquy. His final speech. The way he sees life at the end of it:"

'Life's but a walking shadow,
A poor player that struts and frets his hour upon the stage,
And then is heard no more.
It is a tale told by an idiot, full of sound and fury,
Signifying nothing.'

"Is that how you see your life?" I asked, concerned.

"Yep. I'm that walking shadow, Lucy. Me. Not some other poor sap. Me. Wish I'd died with my buddies. What good am I to anyone now?"

I'd seen soldiers die, not from their wounds, but from lack of hope. And when they lost hope, they usually felt helpless. I wondered if there was something that might encourage Harry to see a better future. "Let's talk about what you have to live for," I said.

"Like what? What's the point?"

"When you leave this hospital, you're going home, soldier. Who and what's waiting for you?"

"I can tell you what my life used to be. My days were full of possibilities. New York City was the place to be before the war."

"I've never been there, but I hear it's wonderful."

There was a small light in his eyes when he talked about his old life. "You have to go, Lucy, when this stupid war is over. The city's alive, vibrant. There's no place in the world like it. My family lives in Pennsylvania, but my friends are all in New York. At least they were, until the war scattered us all over Europe and the Pacific. I want my life before the war back, and that's never going to happen."

"I'd love to see the city someday. It's true you won't get your old life back, but maybe you'll find something new and unexpected."

"Like what? My acting art is dead," he said, folding his arms.

"You love plays. Have you ever written one?"

He looked surprised. "Did once. Sitting on a shelf at my parents' home, collecting dust."

"So, it's never seen the light of day?"

"Never."

"Is it any good?"

"Could be better, but yeah, it has potential." He smiled. "It's something to think about."

Then he asked, "What helps you get through this ugly war, nurse Lucy?"

Matt's face danced through my head. "The anticipation of a future with someone I love."

"Does that someone have a name?" Harry smiled.

"Maybe," I laughed. "We'll see. So, how's your head feeling?"

"Better, thank you."

"I'll come by later and check on you," I said, standing, reluctant to leave a conversation that had been so real. I stopped to pick up my things and heard the rain beating down on the roof as it had been for days.

I wondered how Alex was doing. According to his APO box, he was in Darwin, Australia. He had no idea what he was getting himself into and that worried me. A picture came to my head of little three-year-old Alex dragging around a smiling yellow bunny, almost as big as he was. I loved that little boy. I stopped and said a silent prayer for Alex and Chris: *Please, God, look after them both.*

I was almost out the door when I remembered the lieutenant nurse had asked me to stop by. I wondered what she wanted. Maybe it had to do with the rumors flying around that some of the nurses were being sent somewhere far away.

"Come in, come in, Lucy," she said when I reached her office. "Sit down, please. I have news."

After I took a seat, she said, "You've done an excellent job for us here at the hospital. You care about the men, and the girls look up to you. You're just the one to take over my job here. The army is promoting you to lieutenant."

I was stunned, pleased, and terrified. I hadn't seen that one coming. "Thank you. It's an honor I wasn't expecting. Where will you be? Are you going home?"

"No, I'm being sent somewhere in the Pacific, along with about half our nurses here. We ship out in about a week, which gives me very little time to show you the ropes of head nurse."

I left her office and walked back to the barracks, weighed down with extra responsibilities.

When I came in, Alicia was talking to the others. "Girls! Have you heard the news? We're being sent away." News traveled fast.

"I wonder where they're sending us." She looked at me.

I stepped up and answered her question. "Not all of you will go. The top brass is still figuring out who to send where, but several of you will be leaving. Alicia, you'll stay here with me."

"Good. I want to be where Robert's buried as long as I can," she said, looking out the window. Then she asked, "What's that in your hand?"

"My lieutenant bars. I've been promoted."

"Congratulations," she said. "You deserve it."

"Thanks." I looked at her with gratitude and a sense of expectation. "I'm going to need you to be my right-hand nurse." She flashed a thumbs up sign and smiled.

Early the next morning, the Japanese struck Hawaii again. The attack was so small, I didn't even hear about it until the next day. The pilots must have been counting on the moonlight to guide them in, since all the civilian lights were shut off. Lucky for us, a cover of heavy rain and thick clouds had shrouded the southern half of the island, and the Japanese couldn't find most of their targets.

The March 5th issue of the *Honolulu Bulletin* reported that the bombs from one plane landed in the mountain foothills overlooking the city, shattering a few windows on Theodore Roosevelt High School. None of the students were there, but the sound woke everyone up. I couldn't even imagine what would have happened if the kids had been in school. The paper also reported that the second plane likely dropped its bombs in the harbor water. No one had been injured or killed, thank the Lord. I couldn't make my fear leave, but I refused to let it control me.

The days I got a letter from Matt were happy ones. We'd written every week since he left Hawaii in December, and he'd become my best friend as well as the love of my life. I shared personal details with him. What I thought, how I felt. His words back were supportive, never critical. He'd been so proud of my promotion.

Matt couldn't disclose much about where he was or what he was doing. If he had, the army censors would have cut his letters with blackout ribbons. So, he wrote little anecdotes about the fellas he served with. His stories made me laugh. He always ended with the words, "Don't forget me. Love, Matt." As if I ever could. I tucked his letter back into the envelope and kissed it, my red lipstick leaving a mark.

***

In the Philippines on Bataan, bursts of artillery fire tore across the sky. The exploding shells sounded like thunder. Chris and his crew were infantry now, not pilots. Their uniforms were soaked with sweat from days fighting in the heat and humidity.

Chris looked up from the foxhole and shouted, "I see tanks coming."

"Four of 'em," Sam said, "and dozens of soldiers behind." The tanks fired their cannons, blasting big holes not far from where the men had dug in.

"Get those bottles of gasoline ready," Lieutenant Johnson called down the line. When the tanks rumbled closer, the soldiers stood up and threw the makeshift bombs at the tanks. Two of the tanks erupted in flames, and one fired on the soldiers, killing everyone in the foxholes next to Chris.

"Here comes the infantry," Jack the ball turret gunner shouted.

The lieutenant screamed, "Make every shot count, men." The Japanese soldiers ran toward them, with the Filipino soldiers alongside the Americans using simple bolo swords as weapons. The situation degenerated into hand-to-hand combat.

When it was clear to the lieutenant the Japanese had the advantage, he ordered the men to fall back. As they retreated, they kept firing at the enemy, until they found a new position to hold about half a mile away. Then, they furiously dug more foxholes.

Chris and his crew rolled into the new holes, and he asked Sam, "How ya holding up?"

"Hungry. Haven't eaten since yesterday." Sam and several others were sick with malaria, uniforms spotted with dust and dried blood.

"Me neither," Jack said, "and I'm running out of water." That night, they held their new position and waited for the next attack. The fighting had been going on for days, and the situation was deteriorating. "The enemy is kicking our behinds," Jack complained, "and we're on half rations. What the heck's going on?"

Sam pleaded with Chris, "I don't wanna die." And then he moaned, "I'm so hungry."

"I'm gonna go find us some food," Jack said climbing out of the hole and heading into the jungle. "We gotta eat something."

An hour later, Jack returned with a dead monkey slung over his back that he skinned and cut into pieces. Chris cut wide strips of bamboo that would hold water and lit a small fire. Jack boiled water and cooked the meat. "It's pretty chewy," Chris said, as they ate. "A little greasy and tough, but it's good having something in my belly."

"Guess when you don't have any food to eat, doesn't matter what it is," Jack said.

That night, Sam's fever spiked, and he talked in his sleep.

The next morning, the fighting started again, and the men unloaded their guns on the Japanese until the Americans were forced to retreat. This pattern went on day and after day. "We're slowing the enemy down, right?" Sam asked, delirious.

"No, they're beating us bad," Jack said, making a fist. "I'd swear up a storm if it weren't for Chris. Know how you feel about foul language."

"Thanks, buddy." Chris reached out to Sam. "Do you need another sulfa pill for infections? Here, take some of mine."

"Thanks, Chris," he said. By midnight, Sam was taking his last breaths. Chris called on God to bless him with comfort, and within minutes, Sam was gone. Chris wiped away tears with the back of his hand. Sam was a good friend. It just wasn't right.

Chris and Jack pulled Sam's body out of the foxhole and dug a shallow grave. They said a few words about his bravery, and then Chris put Sam's dog tags in his own pocket. He'd give them to the lieutenant so the army could use them to notify Sam's family that he'd gone to meet his maker on the battlefield.

Just before dawn, Lieutenant Johnson called the men together. "At ease, men. Good morning. I'll make it quick. The sarge here wrote down a message in shorthand that he heard yesterday over the shortwave radio. Came from President Quezon to the people of the Philippines. Read it, Sarge."

"Here goes. 'Thousands of the flower of our youth are being killed and wounded. We have sacrificed everything we can. Japanese Imperial forces continue to ravage our cities and villages...and still there is no help from our friends in the United States.'"

"Gosh dang," one of the men said. "Sounds bad."

"It is," the lieutenant said. "Most of our troops are trapped here on Bataan with no place to go. And help is not on the way."

"I don't get it," Jack said. "General MacArthur knows President Roosevelt. Why isn't he sending us troops and food?"

"I don't know, soldier. But we've been fighting here on Bataan for two months, and we haven't stopped the Japanese. A courier brought a message last night from the colonel. MacArthur has retreated to the island of Corregidor, just off the tip of Bataan."

"What?" Chris asked. "I can't believe it."

"Yep, hear tell the General left those plush headquarters of his behind at the Hotel Manila and left for Corregidor. We'll be getting no troops or supplies from Washington, boys. The fate of our fighting force here on Bataan is sealed."

Chris was so angry, he couldn't speak. His eyes were cold and hard. Jack picked up his canteen and threw it on the ground.

"That's enough, Jack," the lieutenant said. "You and Chris take Tim here and go out on jungle patrol. See what you can find and report back in an hour. Looks like the Japanese are late risers this morning. Must think they already have us licked."

When Chris, Jack, and Tim pushed through the jungle, they ran across the remains of an American soldier. "Take a look at this guy," Tim said, flinching. "His hands and feet are missing."

"So's his head," Jack said. "Look there on the trail. That's his head on a bamboo stake."

Chris flinched. He'd never seen anything like it. "What kind of low life would do something like this to another human being," he wondered, gnashing his teeth.

"Japanese soldiers are animals, pure and simple," Tim said shaking his head. "We should bury what's left of him."

Jack took out his pack shovel and they started digging. It was the second grave Chris had dug in the past several hours, and his anger turned to numbness. He wasn't paying attention when he cut his hand on the edge of the shovel. Chris just stood and watched the blood trickle down his hand.

Jack tore off a piece of his shirt and tossed it to Chris. "Gotta stop the bleeding, buddy."

Chris pressed the dirty shirt against his hand, sad and numb.

Jack and Tim finished digging the hole and put the soldier's remains inside. There were no dog tags around that they could find. "Japanese must have took 'em," Tim said, face red.

"We don't even know who the man is," Chris said. "And his family will never know what happened to him. The army will list him as missing in action."

The three men walked back to deliver their report and spotted fire burning over the trees. They heard men screaming as a lone Japanese soldier broke through the brush pointing his gun.

Chris rolled on the ground, pulled out his gun, and shot the guy right through the heart. But not before that devil had shot Tim in the shoulder.

Tim grabbed his shoulder and said, "Lucky for me, he's a poor shot."

Chris stared at his smoking gun and the dead man on the ground. He'd become the killer he'd trained to be, this time face to face.

CHAPTER SIX

Alex's battalion was headed for the small town of Darwin, an important military base on the northern tip of Australia. They were among the additional American troops deployed after the Japanese bombing in mid-February.

A lieutenant told Alex as they stood on deck, "More than one hundred fighter planes sank three warships, damaged another ten, hit the army barracks, and blasted the town."

"That's terrible," Alex said, the veins in his neck beating a pulse.

"A second air raid left Darwin in chaos, and at the end of the day, there were almost two hundred men dead and four hundred wounded."

"Sounds like the Japanese want to become the masters of Australia."

The lieutenant agreed. "They see Australia as a serious threat because they're allies of the United States."

Alex felt rooted to the spot as they approached Darwin with its bombed-out military base, angry at the damage done to this Aussie town.

A week later, Alex and Norm rode in a jeep down one of Darwin's main streets on their way to the Old Vic Hotel. "Hey, look, on the left," Alex said, pointing to a small, white wooden building with a large red cross painted on its roof. "Must be the hospital. Guessing they were loaded with casualties after the bombing. A sad day."

"We're in for it now, Alex," Norm said.

"This war's gonna be a long haul," Alex said. Then he went silent. He hadn't heard from Sadie since January, and he missed her. "Guess my girl must have found someone else to chase around with," he said.

"Haven't heard from Mildred either. But at least we have a furlough coming up in two days. It'll be one heck of a trip to the Gold Coast."

"Surf, sand, and dancing with girls. Good stuff," Alex grinned. "Say, I brought along that guidebook the army issued to help us adjust to living in Australia, the one titled *Instructions for American Servicemen in Australia, 1942*. It's to help us navigate our way through a country we know nothing about."

"Oh, yeah. Haven't read it yet. What's it say?"

"It starts with: 'YOU and your outfit have been ordered to Australia as part of a worldwide offensive against Hitler and the Japanese. You're going to meet a people who like Americans and whom you will like. The Australians have much in common with us: they're a pioneer people; they believe in personal freedom; they love their sports; and they're out to lick the Axis all the way.' But there are differences too."

Alex and Norm were surprised to find the Australian foods, songs, and customs were vastly different from America's.

"Get this," Alex said. "Australia has a poll tax. It costs six dollars NOT to vote."

"They make sure people are doing their duty. I like that."

"Me too. Says the worst thing an Australian can say about anyone is 'He let his cobbers (pals) down.' A man can be a 'dag' (cutup) or 'rough as bags' (a tough guy), but if he sticks with the mob, he's all right."

"Don't want to get on the wrong side of that." Norm smiled.

"Hey, up ahead, there's the Old Vic. Need me some ginger ale." Alex checked his pockets. "Dang. Left my wallet in my other pants. Can I bum five bucks until we get back?"

"Sure," Norm said, parking the jeep. "Keep the change. I've got extra dough from selling my cigarettes."

"Smart. Hadn't thought about selling them. I usually just give away my four-pack we get with every ration." Alex shook his head. "Didn't know cigarettes were that essential for soldiers."

"Supposed to calm their nerves and relieve boredom, but I don't see it. I'm guessing some of them didn't even start smoking until after they enlisted."

As they walked down the street, Alex said, "Take a look at the Vic's roof. Still damaged from the bombing. What a sad sight. I hear the navy's taking over the place now."

"Get a load of the bank over there, Cashmans, it's even worse. The front is just a big, dark, black hole."

"Bad stuff, this war."

"It's hard not to let it get under your skin."

A few days later, Alex and Norm got a three-day furlough. They boarded a military transport to Brisbane and then picked up a car. It was about a two-hour drive to the Gold Coast, and Norm took the wheel. "Next stop, the Coolangatta Hotel," he said.

"It's billed as having one of the most beautiful beaches in the world. A laid-back surfer's paradise. Boy, do we need this break."

Norm agreed. "I talked to a guy at the barracks who's been to the hotel. He says it's a live music joint with a beachfront deck."

"Is this as fast as you can go?" Alex asked, leaning forward. "Can't wait to get there."

When they found the hotel, they went into the pub, sat down, and joined some Aussie soldiers. One guy at the bar said, "I'm half Scotch and half Soda, but give me a beer." Everyone laughed. Then he looked at Alex and asked, "What'll you have?"

"Ginger ale's good for me."

"We Aussies eat and drink too much," he laughed. "So, good on ya, mate. You're fair dinkum." He raised his glass and walked away.

"That means a right guy," an American soldier sitting on a stool next to Alex said.

"I wondered."

A lady at the bar started singing the American song, "Bless Them All," and the whole bar sang along with her, including Alex and Norm. It was loud and crazy fun.

"Bless 'em all, bless 'em all, the long and the short and the tall

Bless all the sergeants and w. o. ones,

Bless all the corp'rals and their blinkin sons,

'Cause we're saying goodbye to them all, as back to their billets they crawl.

You'll get no promotion this side of the ocean, so cheer up my lads, bless 'em all!!"

Then the gang switched to "Waltzing Matilda." Alex and Norm had a fun time singing along with their new friends until the bar closed at 6:00 p.m. Lights out.

The next evening, Alex and Norm sat on the beach, watching the waves roll in and roasting little sausages over a small fire with the locals. "G'Day, mates," one of the Aussie soldiers said. "How ya goin?" he asked as he walked past in the sand.

"Fine," Norm said. "You?"

"Not bad, but for the mozzies flying about. We grow 'em big over here, so keep an eye out. Now grab yourselves a feed. Got plenty of what you blokes call hot dogs." He laughed.

One of the pretty girls winked at Alex, and he winked back. He hadn't heard from Sadie in so long, he'd decided to move on and have some fun on his time off.

She introduced herself simply as Diane from Darwin, and the two of them sat on the sand together and ate the little franks. Then, Alex stuck marshmallows on sticks and put those in the fire too. Until the jitterbugging started, and he invited Diane to dance.

"We look like a lot of silly old fools dancing around this fire," she laughed.

"Who cares? This party's a real gas," Alex said. When the music stopped, he pulled out a couple of Baby Ruth candy bars from his pocket and gave one to Diane.

"Your Yank chocolate is my favorite," she said.

"Tonight's been the best time I've had since I joined this man's army," Alex smiled.

Two days later, Alex and Norm took the transport back to Darwin and watched the Gold Coast fade away.

***

Hallie was packing for a trip East to meet with an army recruiter when Mom, Dad, and Lily came in with a cable dated April 15. "At least he's alive," Mom said, sobbing as she handed Hallie the telegram.

War Department Telegram: Chris is a POW.
Your son, Second Lieutenant Christopher Forrest
reported a prisoner of war.
of the Japanese government in the Philippine Islands.

'Oh, Mom," Hallie cried, sitting down on the bed.

Mom reached for a tissue. "Chris will get through this. Just you wait and see," she said, optimistically, likely for Hallie's sake.

"I pray you're right," Hallie said, looking at the floor.

Even Dad wiped his eyes, and Lily sobbed as they stood in silence thinking about what being a prisoner might mean for Chris. Mom exhaled the breath she'd been holding and said, "You better finish packing." Then they left her room.

Hallie tucked her diploma in mathematics into the smaller of the two bags. She'd graduated summa cum laude in the top 5 percent of her class and was proud of it. Before leaving campus, she'd picked up two items from the university offices: a copy of her transcript and a letter from the dean praising her logic, persistence, and collaboration skills.

Hallie lugged her bags into the living room where Grandma Katie was waiting. She'd offered to take Hallie to the train station. Hallie had grown up listening to her wonderful stories. *I've never traveled by train alone and never overnight, and Grandma did when she was about my age. I'm a little nervous.*

Lily came up first and put her arms around Hallie.

"I'm going to miss you," Lily said, and then whispered, "I'm the only kid left at home now. Scary."

"You'll be fine," Hallie smiled. "Wait, I have something for you." She went to her bedroom and grabbed a long pearl necklace. It was Lily's favorite, and she'd borrowed it lots of times. "This is for you," Hallie said, coming back into the living room.

Lily took it in her hands. "Really?"

"Absolutely."

"Thank you." She hugged Hallie. "Grandma, get a load of my new necklace. Hallie gave it to me."

"Why, it's just beautiful, Lily. How kind of your sister," she said, smiling. "Are you ready to go, Hallie?"

"I am." But really, she wasn't. Hallie walked over to her parents and hugged them.

"You can come home on leave, you know," Mom said, holding her longer than usual.

"I'll do my best."

"I'll take your bags to the car," Dad offered. "We're going to miss you, Hallie."

Hallie heard a catch in his voice when he hugged her. He didn't tell Grandma about Chris. Not yet.

On the way to the station, Grandma asked, "Are you ready for your new adventure?"

"I hope so."

"I remember when I took my first train trip East to attend medical school."

"You've always been so brave, Grandma."

"Sometimes I was scared too."

"You were?"

"Absolutely. You know, Hallie, out of my six granddaughters, I believe you're the one most like me."

"Really? Why?"

"Because you feel the fear, and then go right out there and do what you know you must do. I'm proud of you."

Hallie looked over at her grandma and smiled. Even at eighty-seven, she was the picture of health. Grandpa Thomas had passed five years ago, and Grandma missed him every day.

When they reached the old red sandstone building with the large Union Pacific Depot sign out front, Hallie hugged her grandma and walked inside.

She loved the terrazzo floor, the stained-glass windows, but especially the ceiling mural that depicted the driving of the Golden Spike, completing the first transcontinental railroad in Utah in 1869.

It was a long ride across country, but Hallie slept well in the Pullman sleeper car, the rhythm of the train rocking her to sleep. After almost seventy-seven hours of travel, she was ready to reach Washington.

The last morning of the trip, she climbed the steps to the observation deck and ate bacon, eggs, and toast for breakfast. Just as she finished, the conductor called, "Washington Union Station, next stop. Please gather your belongings." She hurried down the steps, collected her bags, and held on as the train lurched to a stop. Hallie opened her purse and rechecked her wallet. It was stuffed with enough greenbacks to last awhile.

Inside the station, she could hardly believe her eyes. Compared to the Salt Lake train station, the place was massive. She took the escalator down, gazing up at the large, rounded arches. Her best friend, Kay, would meet her outside and drive them to her apartment in Arlington. She'd already completed training in what she referred to in hushed tones as cryptoanalysis.

When Hallie got to the main floor, Kay called, "Over here." Hallie waved and walked toward her.

They hugged, went outside, and climbed into Kay's new Hudson Nash. "Nice car," Hallie said.

"My parents gave it to me after I graduated."

"You're a lucky lady."

"Don't I know it. What'd you do with your car?"

"It's sitting in the garage at home, waiting until I come back."

The next morning, they drove to the Mayflower Hotel, an iconic building dating back to 1925 and two miles from the National Mall. They were scheduled to meet with an army recruiter. It was the middle of April, and the army was on site meeting with representatives from several women's colleges in the East. Kay's dad, who was an Undersecretary of State, had arranged an interview for the two of them. "This hotel is magnificent," Hallie said when they stepped inside. "Look at this plush carpet and those chandeliers."

She was more than a little nervous sitting across from the army recruiter. He read over her transcript. "Impressive," he said. Then he read the letter from the dean. "Sounds as if you have a good sense of logic and can work well with others."

"Thank you," Hallie said, relaxing a little.

"And you studied a foreign language."

"Yes, French."

"Well, Miss Forrest, you seem to be an inquisitive, well-educated woman. And pretty, too, I might add." He winked.

Hallie bristled. What did her looks have to do with it?

"This job requires gumption. How do I know you have what it takes to do the work?"

"Let me tell you a little about gumption and the women in my family," Hallie said sitting up straighter. "My great-grandmother dragged a handcart across the plains, alone with six children. My grandmother was a suffragist and fought for the right to vote. My mother raised five children—and has now sent four off to serve our country. And me, I graduated top of my class in math. I can assure you the women in my family do not lack gumption."

He smiled. "I can see you're plucky as well. We'll sign you up for a class with a test at the end. Let me warn you that only 50 percent of the women who take the test pass. Still interested?"

"Absolutely."

When they left the hotel, Hallie was glad to have the interview behind her. Kay had already completed the coursework and was scheduled to take the test the following week. If she passed, she was in. "Let's go to the Mall," Kay said. "Then we'll think about dinner."

The afternoon was warm for this time of year, and the sky was blue with puffy white clouds. When they reached the park, Hallie pulled her jacket around her and enjoyed walking along the pond, pausing on the steps of the Lincoln Memorial, gazing at the Washington Monument that rose majestically in the sky.

They climbed the rest of the steps to the Memorial, walked inside, and stood a while in front of the huge statue of Lincoln, discussing his contributions to the country. Then they continued their walk, visiting the other memorials. Hallie thought about her country's war heroes who'd paid the ultimate sacrifice through service. The past and the present came together in ways she hadn't imagined.

When they got hungry, Kay suggested eating at the Old Ebbitt Grill, a landmark in the area, she chose for its delicious American food. After they were seated and had menus in hand, Kay recommended starting with the New England Clam Chowder with its celery, potatoes, bacon, and cream. She didn't have to ask twice.

Hallie decided on the Atlantic salmon with a side salad, and Kay ordered the fried oyster platter. After it got dark, the restaurant closed its blackout curtains against a possible Japanese attack, and the lights on the street were dimmed. They'd both brought flashlights.

"Before I left Bryn Mawr," Kay said, "we sewed blackout curtains and rolled bandages for the soldiers. Such a strange time we live in."

"I know, and I still can't get used to it."

A week later, Hallie began taking the 'cryptoanalysis' class she needed to qualify. That word was not to be used outside class, and the students were all sworn to secrecy about the course content, since they were learning to break codes. After an introduction to ciphers and codes, the women completed problem sets each week and turned them in, often working together in small groups. Hallie studied polyalphabetic substitution ciphers as well as cipher alphabets and loved it all. When it came time to take the test, she passed with flying colors.

In late May, instead of joining the army and becoming WACs, Kay and Hallie went to work for the navy. They hadn't cared much for the army recruiter who'd interviewed them, and besides, with two brothers serving in the Pacific, Hallie said, "I'm betting the navy will be doing more of the code work there than the army."

"I bet you're right," Kay said. "Daddy says the army is a little behind the navy in creating a division for women. But it's coming."

Hallie sent a cable home to the family writing:

My work here in Washington is on the q.t. But it will be challenging, and I think I'll like it.

With love, Hallie.

CHAPTER SEVEN

Back on Bataan, the Japanese continued their relentless bombing until the Americans were forced to surrender in April. Chris's hands shook when he thought about what it might be like to in the custody of the Empire of Japan. He closed his eyes, exhausted, and just laid on the ground, worried about Tim, whose wounded shoulder wasn't healing. But Tim didn't complain because there were so many men worse off than he was.

"Men, you need to get rid of anything you have that the Japanese might think belonged to their troops. Ditch the souvenirs," the lieutenant said, walking up to them.

"Why?" Tim asked.

"Just do it, soldier. It could save your life. Then throw away the rifle firing pins and destroy the rest of the trucks. I've been ordered not to leave anything behind for the enemy."

There was nothing to do but wait for the surrender.

"We've fought for months," Jack said.

"And help never came," Tim said, bitterness in his voice.

"Get some sleep, men," the lieutenant said. "You're going to need it."

Come morning, in the sweltering heat, 12,000 Americans and 68,000 Filipino troops sat on the filthy runways of the abandoned airfield at Bataan. The rumbles of something that sounded like a train caught everyone's attention. "This can't be good," Chris said, getting to his feet with the rest of the troops. "They're coming for us."

"It's Japanese tanks," Jack said, "and lots of them."

"Check out the guys on top with machine guns," Chris said, heart racing.

"Bet they don't go by the rules of the Geneva Convention when it comes to prisoners of war," Tim said, sarcasm in his voice. There were thousands of Japanese troops following the large column of approaching tanks, armed and ready.

"Can't believe this is my life," Chris muttered, as the silence grew. He prayed to God that he'd survive what came next.

The Japanese troops surrounded the men, and using their machine guns to communicate, motioned for the troops to get into groups. One of the Japanese officers stood up in a tank and screamed something in Japanese. Chris had learned just enough of the language from his uncle to understand the words, 'prisoners,' 'three hundred,' and 'Now!' A translator shouted the same words in English.

"Which group of 300 are we supposed to join?" Tim asked. "It's chaos." A Japanese guard hit Tim in the back when he hesitated. He gasped, grabbing the back of his head, and Chris caught him before he fell. Their captors were setting up machine guns every fifty yards or so to make sure no one got out of line.

The officer screamed again, and the translator followed with "Stand at attention. No talking."

When Jack didn't stand straight enough, a Japanese soldier slapped him in the face.

The men stood for hours at attention in the hot sun with no food or water. No one was permitted to speak, and when the sun went down, they stood in the moonlight. Sick men were dropping like flies all around.

Come morning, they were still standing on the field at Bataan, and Chris's legs wobbled with exhaustion. The commander screamed another order. "Strip the prisoners of helmets and valuables!" The guards took pens, watches, anything they could get their hands on.

"This is bull," Jack whispered to Chris.

"Now we know why we were ordered to ditch stuff," Chis whispered back as he heard a man scream. Chris's muscles jumped under his skin, and he winced in horror as a Japanese soldier found a small knife. He took it up to his commander, who shouted something. Then the Japanese soldier dragged the American soldier over to the side and shot him.

"That knife's a souvenir," Tim said. "He didn't get it off some dead man. Just another excuse to kill." A guard punched Tim in the face for talking and laughed. Then all the guards went out of control and started slugging the prisoners for no reason. One hit a Filipino prisoner with a rifle butt, splitting his head open. Then he kicked the dead man. Chris was horrified.

The prisoners were pushed into lines four abreast and told, "If you don't go under your own power, we'll eliminate those who are helping and those who are being helped."

Chris stepped in line with Jack, Tim, and a man they didn't know. "Name's Ralph," the man said under his breath.

Chris acknowledged him without speaking.

They walked about ten miles before one of the guards pulled Ralph out of line and hit him, just for fun. Chris lurched forward and then stepped back. He wanted to help Ralph, but he knew better, having seen a man shot a few miles back for assisting a soldier who'd fallen. When the guard tired of abusing Ralph, he shoved him back in line. The guards looked away, and Ralph whispered, "I need water." He was choking on the dust and blood all over his uniform "When do we stop for water?"

"No clue. Don't know where they're taking us," Jack said, stepping over the body of a prisoner whose throat had been sliced open. The longer they walked, the more dead bodies they found.

By sundown, the men were still walking and had been given no food and no water. "They gotta let us stop soon," Tim whispered. "We gotta rest." When nighttime came, the prisoners were told to drop to the ground and sleep right where they landed. Jack went to relieve himself again, and Chris watched him hurry away, knowing that if Jack got too dehydrated, he'd lose all his strength.

He was still sick when the guards ordered the prisoners to get up and start marching the next morning. Jack told Chris, "I only had to relieve myself once last night, so it must not be dysentery. Maybe it was that snail I ate."

They walked all day the next day, again without food and water, stopping now and then to rest in the heat. Their helmets had been taken away, so Jack always stood with his hands on his head to protect himself from the sun. By early afternoon, they were moved off the road, pushed into close groups where they were nearly on top of each other. It was almost impossible to sleep that night.

The men started marching early in the morning before the sun was out and continued until they couldn't take the heat. One day was the same as the next, as men died all around them. Chris wondered if he'd live to see tomorrow. And why should he live when other men died?

"How long have we been on the move?" Tim asked. "Time's all running together."

"Three days," Jack answered.

They started marching again the next day before dawn, passing a stream around noon. "Finally, water," Tim said, as the guards filled their canteens. One of the prisoners made a break for the stream, went face down, and was shot instantly. The prisoners were then told to drink from animal holes filled with water, the only water they'd had in days, and it was filthy.

"Some of the guys look like skeletons," Chris said, filling his hands with muddy water and drinking it.

"So do you, buddy," Jack said. "Your uniform's hanging off you like it's two sizes too big."

The next day they passed through a small town, and a young Filipino boy flashed the victory sign at the prisoners. Chris smiled at him and then watched as a guard hit him in the head with a rifle butt. "He's only a child," Chris breathed, stomach nauseous.

"The enemy doesn't care who they hurt," Jack grimaced, as a woman offered him food. He reached to take it, and one of the guards shot her in the leg. She fell to the ground, bleeding, and no one dared move a muscle to help.

The seventh day, they reached the town of San Fernando. "This is an old Filipino town named after King Ferdinand of Spain," Ralph wheezed. "I've been here before. They used to have a lantern festival every Christmas until the Japanese took the town in 1941. Good news is there's a train station on the other side of town. Maybe we're done walking."

"Maybe so," Jack said. "The line's stopping up ahead."

Chris climbed onto a mound and looked at the size of the line, front to back, estimating they'd lost more than a quarter of the men since they'd started at the airfield.

A Japanese officer shouted, "All prisoners get on train! All prisoners get on train!"

"This might not be so bad," Chris said, his chest tight. He changed his mind when they were pushed into a hot metal box car with no windows and no ventilation. There were so many prisoners jammed inside, no one could move.

"I have to pee," a man said, as the car lurched forward. There was no bathroom, and no choice but to let it run down his leg. Before long, the floors were covered in blood, mucus, and excrement.

Two hours later, the train stopped, and a few dead men fell out. The others tumbled outside into the heat. "It's hot as blazes out here," Tim muttered, "but it beats being inside. I can't breathe in there." When it was time to move on, the Japanese ordered the living prisoners to put the dead ones back into the boxcars.

By the time they reached Capas, more men had died. Four miles to march to reach Camp O'Donnell.

When the men trudged inside, they found a partially finished camp with a string of barbed wire around it. They were ordered to stand on a platform by the gates for two more hours in the hot May sun. Tim passed out from the heat, his arm and shoulder swollen.

The Japanese commandant stood on a platform above everyone else and started shouting, "You are not recognized as prisoners of war. You are nothing. We will fight this war for a thousand years if we have to, and you will lose."

Jack balled his hands into fists and put one foot forward before Chris grabbed his arm. "Not worth it, buddy. They're trying to make you lose your cool, so don't let them get to you. It'll cost you your life."

Jack stepped back in line, gritting his teeth as the Japanese commandant read a lengthy list of instructions: You will take turns acting as guards, and if anyone escapes, every guard on duty will be shot. You will be fed, but you will work for your food, serving on water and wood details. The Filipinos will live on one side of the camp, and the Americans will be segregated—army, air corps, navy, and marines—on the other and be governed by your own officers. If anyone escapes, the officers will die. Last thing, very important. Prisoners will be obliged to salute all Japanese guards, no matter their rank.

By afternoon, Chris, Jack, Tim, and Ralph were resting inside a little bamboo hut that had six small beds made of bamboo. Jack fell into a bunk next to Tim, who started weeping. Then the rain started pelting the roof.

"You okay, Tim?" Chris asked, unable to raise his head.

"We're not dead." Tim sobbed and repeated, "we're not dead." He took a deep breath.

Chris whispered verses from the Bible. "Though I walk through the valley of the shadow of death, I will fear no evil."

The rain finally stopped a few hours later, and Chris and the other men started setting up mess halls. They were told they'd be allowed to cook rice once a day about noontime. Lots of men had dysentery, and while there were a few American doctors in the camp, they had no bandages and no antibiotics.

It was evening before the food was ready. The men got a larger portion of rice than they'd had since the march began, and Jack had enough to fill his plate. Some of the men couldn't get it down, while others threw the rice up after eating it. There was no doubt in Chris's mind that many more men would die before long. He'd never witnessed so much death.

When morning came, Chris and Jack stood in line with thousands of other American prisoners waiting to fill their canteens. They'd brought Tim's canteen with them, so he could rest. There was only one spigot of drinkable water for the entire camp, and before Jack could get his own canteen filled, one of the Japanese guards shut off the spigot and laughed. Chris and Jack stood without talking, waiting for two hours, before the guard decided to turn it back on. The Filipinos had it worse than the Americans because the Japanese forced them to drink polluted water.

The day before, Chris had seen a man who refused to bow to a guard, get hit with a club. Chris reminded Jack, "Don't forget to bow and thank him."

A guy from Alabama they'd nicknamed Snake because he was so skinny, got desperate and tried to escape, but the Japanese had offered a hundred-pound bag of rice to any Filipino who turned in an escaped prisoner. Someone turned Snake in.

"Can't believe Snake lost his life over a sack of rice," Tim said the next day when they were out digging another slit trench for toilet facilities. They had to straddle them to go to the bathroom.

Day after day, there was nothing to do besides wait in line to fill canteens and eat watery rice around noon, so some men slept all day. The Japanese didn't care what the Americans did, if they stayed inside the compound. Chris, Tim, Jack, and Ralph mostly hung around together and talked, but there wasn't much to talk about. Their anger had deserted them weeks ago and left them numb.

CHAPTER EIGHT

It was late, and most of the nurses had gone back to barracks. I sat in my office at Tripler and picked up a letter that had come earlier that day. I ran my finger over my mother's beautiful cursive script, then tore open the envelope, hoping she'd sent news about my brother. We hadn't heard from Chris since the Americans surrendered at Bataan, leaving him and his buddies stranded—who knew where—as prisoners of war. Having seen firsthand what the Empire of Japan was capable of, I could only imagine how our prisoners were being treated. I looked down at my hands. I'd started biting my nails again.

My dearest Lucy,

I hope my missive finds you well. I know you have a lot on your plate at the hospital, and I hope you're getting enough rest, but I doubt it. I'm proud of the work you're doing in the Pacific, honey, but I worry. I think about you all the time, and we pray for your health and safety night and day. I love you my Lucy goosey.

I rolled my eyes at that line. Would Mom ever stop calling me Lucy goosey? Probably not.

Please keep Chris in your prayers. We've heard nothing from him since the April telegram. What's wrong with this world, Lucy? Your brother's a Japanese prisoner of war, and my friend Chieko Tanasaki has been in an American internment camp in California since the middle of March. She's one-quarter Japanese, and her parents were born here. Can you believe it? I've heard she's working in the camp as a secretary for $14 a month, instead of being a teacher.

You might remember her husband's a doctor? They're paying him $19 a month to be a janitor. What are we doing to these lovely people? I don't mean to go on and on, dear, but it upsets me.

It upset me too. We had Japanese members in our church congregation here who were born in Hawaii. The police picked them up for questioning, along with their children. The Japanese people were not our enemies. The Emperor of Japan and his military were. I prayed we would remember the difference.

Dad's doing fine, and so is Lily. She's worked so hard to excel in school that she's been skipped a grade. I can't believe it.

We got a letter from Alex, and he told us about his battalion shooting down their first planes. Being a Pfc. in the office doesn't keep him out of harm's way. Hallie's begun doing whatever it is she does now in Washington DC. No details.

How's Matt doing? He sounds like a great guy. Just give it time and see how things go when you're with him next. You'll know if, and when, it's right.

I smiled. My relationship with Matt was moving fast through letters alone. I sometimes wondered how I could fall in love with a pen pal so quickly. But I had.

Please take good care of yourself and write when you can. Remember there are angels among us both seen and unseen. You, my love, are one of those angels in this fog of war. Please stay safe.

Mom

Thank you, Mom, I whispered. Then I put her letter in my bag and turned out the lights.

The next day, we had a group of civilian volunteer nurses come in. I called Alicia into my office and asked her to take charge. "You're one of our best and brightest nurses," I said. "Please take on this assignment. I'm assisting in surgery today."

"No problem, Lucy…I mean Lieutenant Forrest. Be happy to."

I laughed. "We're still friends, Alicia. When we're alone, no military formality needed."

She smiled. "You can count on me, Lucy."

"I appreciate it."

"I'll start by teaching them how to make dressings. We could use more bandages."

"Great idea," I said.

When she left, I headed for the surgery area. Doctor Petersen was both skilled and kind. Today, he was doing surgery to put a metal plate in a wounded man's head. Two bullets had blown through our patient's brain, and it was a miracle he hadn't died. Doctor Petersen was talking with John when I walked in, explaining the process and showing him the plate that would be going in his head.

"Remember when we created the plaster of Paris model of your face?" the doctor asked him.

"Memory's foggy, but yes," John answered.

"Good. We used that impression to create this metal plate that we'll be putting in your head."

"Is it going to work, Doc?"

"I'm confident it will. Meet Lieutenant Nurse Forrest," he said, introducing me. "She'll be helping with the anesthesia, and you're in good hands. She doesn't miss anything. She's kind, and efficient." He shook John's hand and left the room.

I could read the fear in his eyes. "How are you holding up?" I asked.

"I'm scared. What if this doesn't work? What if I die, or worse yet, what if I end up a vegetable?"

"Doctor Petersen is the best neurosurgeon we have at Tripler," I said, draping John with a gown. "And I'm going to be there with him. Have you ever had anesthesia?"

"No, never, but I know it'll put me under," he said.

I nodded. "When this needle goes into your arm, you'll go to sleep and won't feel or remember anything. You'll lose awareness and the ability to feel pain."

"What will it be like when I wake up?"

"You may feel groggy, confused, or even nauseous. I'll be right there with medications to help you. Those guys waiting over there are going to wheel you into the operating room as soon as you get the shot. Ready?"

"Ready or not, here comes the shot." He smiled weakly. He was out like a light in about thirty seconds.

During the surgery, the doc placed the metal plate in position. The fit was exact, and its precision amazed me. I checked vitals, and our patient was doing fine, so I continued to watch the surgery, learning a lot about this complicated procedure.

"Okay," the doc finally said. "So far, so good. I'm going to secure the plate now. Please get the silk sutures ready."

"Right here," I said.

He layered the scalp with interrupted sutures of fine silk and placed fifty thousand units of penicillin in the wound. Penicillin was scarce, and we were lucky to have it. I called for the orderlies, and as they wheeled our patient into recovery, said, "Call me when he wakes up."

I sat down and took a break, relieved the surgery was successful. If we'd lost John, I would have been overcome with guilt. I reminded myself over and over that we couldn't save them all. But that never seemed to help when one of them died.

***

Hallie and Kay had been living in a crowded boarding house with six beds to a room for almost a month, and while the gals were nice enough, there was no privacy. Hallie craved her alone time. The girls left together each morning in high heels and dresses and rode the bus downtown to the places where they worked, their clothes clinging in the June heat. After reaching poorly ventilated offices, they were soaked in sweat.

In the Pacific Unit where Hallie and Kay served, the navy had dispensers filled with salt tablets that were supposed to prevent perspiration, but they just made Hallie sick, so she stopped using them. And the women's bathroom? There were cockroaches crawling around on the floor. It was disgusting. But being a coder? That she loved.

It was the women who acted as human computers, built libraries, and translated documents. They'd been trained on secret message systems as well, which Hallie found fascinating. She had learned that there were two kinds of systems. One was a code group, where an entire word or phrase was replaced by another word, a series of letters, or a string of numbers. Since secrecy was the aim, code groups were randomly assigned and put in codebooks, so coders could look up the word or phrase and the corresponding group that stood for it when they needed to. It was the repetitious use of the same code groups that helped them figure out what the messages meant. Hallie found this work captivating and right up her alley.

But deciphering the Japanese fleet's operational code used for the most important messages was much more difficult. They called it the JN-25, and most of the code breakers, both male and female, were having trouble untangling the code. Hallie had overheard the commander of the unit say that America just might lose this war because he didn't have confidence in his coders.

"I don't care much for the guy," Kay told Hallie. "He's a numbskull who thinks of women as merely 'cute secretaries.'"

"That makes me angry. We're so much more than that," Hallie whispered to Kay as he stood lecturing them on what their jobs were.

Kay smiled. "We know more than he does about our jobs. He's clueless."

When he left the room, one of their new friends, said, "Did you know it was a woman who pioneered our work on JN-25?"

"Golly, I hadn't heard that before," Hallie said. "Who is she?"

"Agnes Driscoll. She served in World War I as a code breaker for the navy."

"Why haven't I ever heard her name?" Kay asked.

"Because she's a woman, I imagine. Driscoll started as a code breaker for the navy in World War I, and in early 1935, led the attack on the Japanese M-1 cipher machine. In 1939, she even trained Joe Rochefort." Joe was a top-level supervisor in the Pacific unit, and they all knew who he was.

"Where's Driscoll now?" Hallie asked.

"I hear she was transferred to a team working to break the German naval Enigma cipher."

In May, they'd learned that the navy had found out about a big upcoming Japanese operation. Thousands of messages had flashed back and forth in JN-25, indicating that Japan was sending a massive flotilla somewhere. "Vague indications of an operation to be launched," said one early message.

They got lots of information about the planned Japanese operation, but there was a key puzzle piece that baffled all of them: they'd intercepted a message saying that the Japanese, who often used two-letter geographic designators, were headed to "AF." They couldn't be certain where AF was.

Joe Rochefort and his team had believed that AF stood for Midway, a tiny atoll where the United States had a base used to defend Hawaii and other places in the Pacific.

"What do you think of Joe's idea?" Hallie had asked Kay. "Do you think AF stands for Midway?"

"I don't know. Isn't Joe the guy who supervised the Pearl Harbor code-breaking team? That didn't go so well."

"True. But he's a smart man, and we can trust him."

"I've heard some of the men say the target might be Hawaii again, or the Aleutians."

"Joe told me himself," one of the women chimed in, "that he and Edwin Layton, Admiral Nimitz's chief intelligence officer, are producing a plan."

It turned out she was right. Joe and Layton instructed the men at the Midway base to radio a message—not in code, but in plain English—saying their distillation plant had broken down and they were short on water. The plan was that the Japanese would intercept the bulletin and pass it on to General Yamamoto.

The Japanese unit picked up the message and sent a message back to their fleet saying that AF was short of water. So, AF did mean Midway, and they had the confirmation they needed. "General Yamamoto will have no idea what hit him," Kay grinned, "and we win."

Yamamoto had put his warships in the Aleutian Islands off the mainland of Alaska, thinking Admiral Nimitz would rush to the

Aleutians to counter the decoy attack. But thanks to the analysts deciphering JN-25, Nimitz was aware of the planned attack at Midway. He knew the targets, the dates of the attack, and he had a good idea which forces the Japanese planned to use.

The Japanese had showed up on June 4, expecting to have the upper hand as their carrier task force launched an air strike on the island. American fighters rushed to meet the incoming planes in midair, taking heavy fire but pushing the enemy back, while four waves of US bombers took off toward the Japanese carriers. The Japanese expected to be attacked by planes from Midway, so that wasn't a surprise, but they didn't know the Americans had aircraft carriers nearby. In four days, it was all over.

Those in the Pacific code room stood and clapped when Joe walked into the room after they got the good news about Midway.

"The four-day Battle of Midway was an unequaled American victory," he said. "We're now playing offense, instead of defense. Think of it. An outnumbered American fleet scored a decisive win over an armada of enemy attackers."

The team cheered at his words, and their morale improved. Nimitz also said that code breaking had provided a "priceless advantage" at Midway. Hallie's heart swelled with pride, and she understood that while no one else knew the work she was doing, she did, and that was enough.

Joe concluded his speech with, "This is a clear victory for the code breakers in the Pacific unit. Now the navy will have more confidence in our cryptanalytic units."

Hallie sat back in her chair and took a deep breath. The work that had sparked her personal passion had also benefitted both community and country. *It doesn't get better than that.*

CHAPTER NINE

In my office, I found a copy of the day's *Honolulu Star Bulletin* on my desk. The headline mentioned a Battle at Midway. My eyes blurred. I was sure Matt was with the *USS Salt Lake City* at Midway. In his last cable he'd written, "While I can't tell you where I am, I can say that while I'm not here, nor there, I'm midway in between." His words were cryptic enough to pass the navy censors, but I knew what he meant.

I took a deep breath and read: *Japanese smashed at Midway. Enemy Damage Heavy in Big Ship US Injuries Relatively Light.* The word 'relatively' troubled me. Who knew what that meant? Was Matt one of the men injured or even killed. I read further into the article. *Nimitz Gives First Details; Fight Continues.* A carrier that was already damaged had been hit by three torpedoes, but the article only mentioned Japanese cruisers being hit.

Alicia came into my office. "You found the newspaper I left on your desk."

I'd shared my guess with her that Matt was at Midway. "I did. Thanks."

"The news looks pretty darned good."

"It does, yes."

"I know that look. You're worried."

"I'll feel better when I get a cable from Matt."

A week later, Matt managed to get leave. My dreamboat's coming to town, I thought walking onto the docks. When I saw him, my happy heart beat with relief and joy. He sprinted down the docks, held me in his arms, and caressed my hair. I clutched him and couldn't stop crying. My emotions had been through the wringer the past few months, and I'd kept them safely tucked inside. Until now.

He took out a handkerchief and gently dabbed my eyes, whispering in my ear, "I love you, baby. I love you," He kissed me, and I melted.

I whispered, "I love you too, Matt." My knees were weak.

A soldier passed by and laughed. "Hey, no smooching in public."

"Ah, go take a powder," Matt said. Then he kissed me again. "More of that later."

"How about a walk on Waikiki?" I asked, taking his hand.

"Beach walks are my favorite, and see, I came dressed for it."

"Nice aloha shirt. Is that new?"

"Why, yes, it is," he laughed.

"I read about Midway in the newspaper, Matt," I said, thinking that it was wonderful to be with him and not rushing around taking care of people. "Thanks for the cable saying you were okay. I worried sick until I got it."

"It was a harrowing four days, Lucy. Our cruiser protected the rear of the battle, and we didn't get hit. The good news is the battle stopped the Japanese Empire's string of victories, and it was a savage blow to their navy. They've now lost the ability to invade Australia."

"I'm glad for that."

"It means it's now safe for Australia to move their military power into New Guinea to help us lick the Japanese. I've never liked bullies, Lucy, and we're going to take Japan down. You'll see." He clenched his fist.

I touched his hand, and he relaxed. "What was it like for you, Matt? Being in the middle of the battle?"

"Are you sure you want to know?"

"Yes, I do." Really, I wasn't sure, but I knew it would help Matt to talk through it.

"I watched one of our carrier pilots fly in and dive bomb the aircraft carrier Kaga. His bombs must have hit the forward bridge because flames shot up from there. A few minutes later, there was a huge explosion, and pieces of the ship flew into the air a couple thousand feet high."

I sucked in a quick breath. "Were you frightened?"

"We were all too busy cheering," he grinned. Then the expression on his face changed to fear and sadness. "The terrifying event happened the last day of the battle when a salvo of torpedoes from a Japanese sub hit a destroyer that sank in about five minutes." His voice cracked. "The remains of our American sailors went down with that ship to a watery grave," he whispered.

I put my arms around his waist, and he pulled me to him. "All that loss of life breaks my heart," I said.

"It's devastating. Those men leave parents, wives, even babies behind."

We walked on in silence. When we arrived at the beach, we found a bench, and sat down. Matt held my hand, and we bowed our heads, offering a prayer for the brave men who'd lost their lives at Midway.

We watched the waves roll in and out, and Matt asked, "What are you thinking, Lucy?"

"About how uncertain life is during wartime. It could be years before this conflict is over."

"We're both a little scared. I could be killed in battle. Or you could find someone else at one of those Saturday dances at the officers' club, you out there bebopping until midnight," he laughed.

"Most of those men are drunk and looking for a little skirt. That's not who I am, and you know it." I socked him in the arm, smiling.

"If anybody tried anything with you—" He stopped, suddenly, eyes angry.

"Don't worry, I can take care of myself. You could always find someone else too, you know."

"Besides being in love with you, you're my friend. You see the best in me." He drew me closer. "We can count on each other, the same way we can count on the sun coming up every morning. I love you, Lucy," he said, kissing me. "We belong together."

I knew he was right.

***

The Filipino prisoners were being released from Camp O'Donnell. Thousands of American soldiers prepared to move to Cabanatuan prison, named after a nearby city of about fifty thousand people. Chris had heard of the place from some of the Filipino men he'd gotten to know at Camp O'Donnell. One of them told him, "Think Cabanatuan might be the place you soldiers go. American Department of Agriculture used it before making a Filipino training camp."

"What's it like?" Chris asked.

"About one hundred acres filled with tall cogon grass, divided by road in center. Lots and lots of barracks. Hope you stay safe. Paalam, Chris," he waved.

When Chris and the other Americans reached Cabanatuan, they saw barracks for Japanese guards and barracks for prisoners that were small bamboo shacks. "It looks like there will be more than a hundred prisoners jammed into each of the sixty-foot-long barracks," Chris said, staring. He and Tim, Jack, and Ralph managed to stay together in one of them. There was also a hospital and a water tower enclosed by barbed wire with guard towers. The prisoners were allowed two meals a day of steamed rice, sometimes with fruit or soup, rarely meat. Jack and some of the men took to eating frogs and snails.

Ralph got so thin, he looked like a skeleton, and he had chronic diarrhea. The guards sent him to the hospital that the men had nicknamed 'Zero Ward,' because the chances were 'zero' you'd come out alive. Ralph had become a good friend, and Chris prayed he'd pull through. "He's a fine man, Lord, please save him," Chis pleaded.

But Ralph died days later of malaria, and a burial detail put him in the ground, but not before Chris snatched his tags and put a small twig marker on the communal grave.

Chris covered his face with his hands, and his voice broke as he said goodbye to Ralph. He had no clue what the future might hold for any of them.

The next day, Chris and Jack were forced to watch men tortured, shot, and decapitated for the smallest breach of the rules. Jack said, "Our days here are filled with death. Not to mention the flies and lice." They bathed in the rain, shaved with a knife, and made toothpaste out of charcoal and powdered salt. Their uniforms had turned to rags, and their shoes had no soles.

Chris still read the Bible, refused to use foul language, and tried to plan for a life when he returned home. He kept a journal that he wrote on the backs of can labels and discarded paper, and he attended services every week in the church area. Chris saw men walk by on their way to the urinals, relieving themselves, then stopping to listen to the sermons.

The Japanese didn't allow prisoners to send or receive mail, and Chris doubted that the Japanese authorities had even given the United States War Department the names of the prisoners they held captive, or if they had the list wouldn't be complete. "The Japanese simply don't care," he told Jack. "Our families will believe we're missing in action. I can't imagine what my mom must be going through."

The following day, using his limited understanding of Japanese, Chris overhead the guards talking and concluded that the Japanese were getting ready to ship out as many able-bodied men as possible. Seemed that there was some sort of labor shortage in Japan, and they needed the prisoners to work there in the industries. Chris, Jack, and Tim talked about what that might look like.

"Hope we can stay together in Japan," Tim said.

"Me too," Jack said. "Friends for life."

The next day Chris came down with chills, fever, and the sweats. His heart beat faster, and he grew confused. "Has to be malaria,"

Jack said, touching his forehead. "Must have been bitten a few weeks ago."

When Chris started vomiting, the guards came to take him to Zero Ward. As they carried him out, Jack and Tim walked on either side of him. "They're shipping us out today, buddy," Jack said. Stay strong."

"Hold on, Chris," Tim said. "Please don't die."

Chris smiled weakly and said, "I'm too stubborn to die," praying he was right.

***

In mid-July, the Meridian Hill Hotel for Women opened in Washington. Hallie read the brochure claiming that the hotel was the 'newest and largest hotel built exclusively for women to provide housing for the Government Girls.' So now, instead of calling them The Lipstick Brigade, they were also known as the 'Government Girls.' Hallie smiled. *Maybe someday they'll understand what we did here.*

Hallie and Kay discussed their options over lunch. "Taking a double room and sharing the cost would be good for my purse strings," Hallie said. "What do you think?"

"We can do that. Every room has an outside room, so we can be alone when we want to."

"That's good." Time alone with her thoughts was still high on Hallie's priority list. "A Washington Residential Hotel. I like the sound of that, and it's convenient to the downtown shopping and theatre district."

"Let's take the bus over and have a look."

When they got off the bus near the corner of Sixteenth and Euclid streets NW, they glimpsed the hotel in the distance, and it looked a bit stark. But as they got closer, Hallie liked the sleek, horizontal ribbons of windows, which the brochure claimed was a trademark of the International Style. The brown bricks contrasted with the blond brick of the overall building, but the best part about the exterior was the concrete fleurs-de-lis that underlined the corners. Hallie loved all things French.

They went inside and found the lobby decorated in pinks and greens, filled with comfortable chairs. "This place is heaven on earth compared to where we've been living," Hallie said to Kay.

"Let's go talk to the woman at the front desk and check the prices."

"Hello," she said as Hallie and Kay approached. "My name's Nancy. Are you some of the Government Girls?" she asked.

"Secretaries," Kay responded, crossing her fingers behind her back, giving nothing away.

"Let me show you the dining room," Nancy offered coming from behind the desk. "Dinner in our grand first-floor dining room costs sixty-five cents."

A little pricey, Hallie thought.

"What kind of food do you serve?" Kay asked.

"A typical meal might consist of chicken liver and giblets, potatoes, peas, a hot roll, jam, and dessert, but we do vary the menu. The dining room and cafeteria will be open to the public, and I can assure you the food here will be excellent. We plan to have broiled steak every day."

That surprised Hallie. "Isn't beef in short supply?" she asked.

"Well, yes, but we have ways of working around that." Nancy winked.

Hallie wasn't sure she liked that.

"How much are the rooms a week?" Kay asked.

"Rents range from $8.25 to $9.50 a week, and applicants have to have an annual income of $1,800."

"While my friend and I can afford a double room, I'm betting very few women workers will be able to live here at those prices," Hallie said.

Under pressure from bad publicity, the Meridian Hill's managers lowered the rates, and the hotel soon filled up with Government Girls, including Hallie and Kay. Hallie noticed that none of them were women of color, which shouldn't have surprised her, but it did. She learned that the unwritten rule at the Meridian was that no women of color were allowed. *When will people understand that men and women of all colors are created equal in God's eyes?*

The morning after they moved in, Hallie and Kay were given a list of requirements for living at the hotel. Kay read aloud: "Boyfriends are only allowed in the first-floor lounge, and not in the rooms."

"My parents will be happy about those strict rules."

"Some of the locals are calling this place 'The Purity Palace.' Kay laughed. "Fine by me."

Hallie and Kay enjoyed sunning themselves on the veranda that faced Meridian Hill Park, where they had free wartime concerts. They could even hear the music from their open window.

"When do you think the navy's going to go through with creating a naval reserve for women?" she asked Kay.

"Daddy says it should be coming soon, but it didn't help when the Senate's Committee on Naval Affairs claimed that admitting women into the navy would break up homes and amount to a step backward in civilization."

"I can't believe it, and neither would Grandma Katie. She sent a letter telling me not to give up hope. She wrote that members in congress made similar statements when the women fought for the vote."

"Let's see," Kay said tapping her chin. "Women have been voting for twenty-two years now, and civilization still stands. How about that?"

They both laughed. It was funny, but it wasn't.

On July 30, President Roosevelt signed the law that created a women's naval reserve, intended "to expedite the war effort by releasing officers and men for duty at sea." The women advocating the reserve were victorious.

"We're an official division of the US Navy," Kay said proudly when she read the news in the paper. "The women aren't just an auxiliary, but a naval reserve like the men."

"One day we'll be in uniform the way the WACs are in the army. That might help us be taken more seriously," Hallie said.

CHAPTER TEN

Alex was in the Darwin offices processing service pay. Realizing how much families at home relied on payments from the combat troops, he took his job seriously. When Captain Matson walked into the office, Alex saluted. "Morning sir."

"Morning. How are you this fine day, soldier?"

Alex thought the captain seemed to be in an unusually fine mood. "Good, thank you."

"Come into my office when you're finished."

Matson was sitting behind his oversized desk poring over documents when Alex came in and stood at attention. "At ease, PFC Forrest," he said. "Take a seat."

Alex had squirreled away a notepad and pen in his pocket just in case. Matson was a leader Alex could get behind, a no-nonsense guy who got the job done, but he still had heart.

"There's plenty of room for advancement in this army for a fellow like you," Matson said. "You've earned my confidence, and I believe you'll be a leader I can trust. You're a strategic thinker, and the men like you."

"Thank you, Captain." Alex's leg bounced under the table, his head up. The captain had used the word, 'leader.' Maybe a promotion? Corporal? Sergeant?

"Under normal circumstances," Matson continued, "your next level of advancement would be corporal or maybe sergeant. But your skills would be wasted in those positions, and wartime is anything but normal. I'm giving you what the army refers to as a battlefield promotion. You're now a Second Lieutenant."

Alex's widening eyes did a double take. "I'm honored, sir, thanks for your confidence. What will my new duties be?"

"I want you as my staff officer."

"What about Lieutenant Dean."

"He's remaining in Darwin."

So, what does that mean for us? We must be moving.

"This is what I expect of my staff officer, Forrest. You'll provide me with information and make recommendations, prepare plans, and monitor the execution of my decisions."

Alex was feverishly taking notes, trying to capture every word. It was a lot to take in, and he'd need time to think about the implications of his new responsibilities. When he stopped writing, Mattson went on. "You'll also process information and disseminate it to the men, coordinating with the staff."

"Yes, sir."

"Last, I need you to identify problems and provide me with your analysis. You're good at seeing through what's happening on the surface and figuring out what's going on underneath."

"Thank you, sir. I'll work hard and won't disappoint you."

"I'm counting on it. And now, I need you to coordinate our new assignment. We're leaving Australia in five days."

"Where are we headed?" Alex asked, raising his eyebrows, surprised.

"New Guinea." Alex knew a little about New Guinea, and it was nothing like Australia.

"We won the Battle of Milne Bay yesterday, and it was the first defeat the Japanese land forces experienced in the Pacific."

"Excellent news," Alex said, sitting on the edge of his chair. "It'll improve the men's morale."

"Our victory prevented the Japanese from establishing a base at the eastern tip of New Guinea. The 'Old Man' knew the strategic value of the Bay's location and had a secret base constructed with airfields to protect Port Moresby from an approach by sea."

"General MacArthur's impressive, sir."

"I hope to meet him one day. His staff officer solicited the help of the Papuan New Guinea laborers to build a facility that supports ten thousand men, all while managing to hide the size of the troops from the Japanese," Matson smiled.

"When did they do battle?"

"It started the night of August 25, and the Japanese even landed at the wrong beach." Matson laughed, and Alex echoed. "They were more than twenty kilometers from their objective. Gave us an edge right up front."

"Did they reach the base at Milne?" Alex asked.

"The Japanese launched an all-out attack, and for them, it was a complete disaster. We had massive firepower along the perimeter of the base, and not a single soldier breached our defensive line."

"So, they pulled out?"

"Yesterday, August 31. Milne Bay is secure."

"Gives me more confidence we can beat those devils."

"That's the spirit." Mattson handed Alex his new lieutenant bars. "Put these on and call the men together. I want them here in two hours."

Alex liked the sound of that. "Yes, sir. Thank you, sir," he said, leaving the office, and attaching the new bars to his uniform. *This is huge. A real opportunity for me.*

Alex bumped into Norm when he was out rounding up the men.

"Say, Alex," Norm said. "Are those lieutenant bars I see on your chest?"

"Been promoted to Matson's staff officer."

"Good for you. Wish I had an office position," he smiled.

"You never know what might come your way."

After the men assembled inside, Matson pulled down a wall-sized map of the Pacific and grabbed a pointer. "Men, we're moving here," he said. "To New Guinea. Although it's a primitive island, it's the second largest in the world. On the windward side, which is where we're going, the rainfall runs as high as three hundred inches a year. I'm told that it rains for nine months and then the monsoons hit."

"Won't be no day at the beach, sir," one of the men said.

"You're right, soldier. And with that jungle climate comes malaria, scrub typhus, and dengue fever. So, do your best to stay away from bugs. We leave in five days for Oro Bay on Papua, New Guinea. Lieutenant Forrest here will organize the operation. Any questions?"

No one spoke.

"That's all. Dismissed."

Over the next few days, the men collected their gear and stored it in big wooden crates cut with narrow slats in the sides. The crates were placed on large pulleys, hoisted in the air, maneuvered on board ship, and laid in stacks. Some of the men climbed on top of the stacks and sat, waiting to leave, while others leaned on the rails. Alex had enjoyed his time in Australia and hoped to get back here someday, just for fun.

The radio onboard crackled with the words, "All aboard," and the ship got underway for Oro Bay. Alex watched Darwin fade into the distance, waving goodbye when no one was watching.

When the ship reached Oro Bay, the men disembarked and made their way to quarters. The weather was hot and muggy, but it wasn't raining. They watched the locals finish the last of the bamboo huts built for the American troops. The natives were dressed in loin cloths and took orders from their chief, who stood on the roof sporting a large headdress. It was more primitive than Alex expected. "All right, men," he shouted, "stow your gear inside, then grab your shovels and dig your own foxholes. You'll need them for protection against the Zeros."

For the next several days and nights, it rained continually. Because of the density of the trees, the men couldn't see their hands in front of their faces, and the mosquitoes were so bad that sleeping without netting was impossible. Every day, the Japanese flew over the jungle area where the men camped and dropped their bombs around noon. Alex and his men rolled into their fox holes as far as possible, hoping not to get blasted.

One wet night when rain pelted the trees and tents, a new lieutenant raced into a tent and told the men they were under attack. "Get out there and face the enemy," he ordered. Most of the men grumbled but did as they were told. Alex learned the next morning that Norm had refused to leave the tent, telling the officer, "You're new here. It's only rain." Then he rolled over in his bunk. Even though it was rain, the officer was incensed at Norm's disobedience and reported him to his superiors. Norm was demoted from corporal to private.

Alex came to talk with Norm. "Heard about what happened, buddy."

"Yeah. How stupid is that? I was right about the rain. Such bull."

"I get that Norm, and you were right about the rain. But you disobeyed a direct order."

"It was a dumb order," he grumbled.

"I'm learning that being right isn't the most important thing in this man's army," Alex sighed.

"I'll work hard and get bumped back up to Pfc. and then corporal. You'll see."

"I know you will, Norm. You're a good man."

When Alex sat down to meet with Captain Matson, Alex was in for a surprise. Matson said, "I have a new assignment for you. We need every able-bodied man on the front lines, and that includes you. We have a big battle coming up, and I want you out with the troops on this one."

Alex straightened his shoulders, surprised. "Where are we headed?"

"Buna. About fifteen miles from here. General MacArthur moved his advance base to New Guinea over on Port Moresby, and he's ordered an attack on Buna that begins in a few days. You and your men will have to walk."

"Guessing that will take about six hours."

"Sounds about right. You'll be in Buna around two weeks, and then I'll get another unit to relieve you. Let the men know they're leaving in the morning."

"Yes, sir."

When Alex and the men started the walk, the rain came in torrents along the dirt trails, old native tracks about a yard wide that ran through the jungle undergrowth. The downpour soon dissolved the footpath into calf-deep mud, and the troops stumbled over the sticky ground, slowing them down by hours. They were exhausted by the time they hit ten miles.

They reached the area where they'd be fighting and found another battalion that had already been at battle for two days. "Each of you grab a carton of twenty-four hand grenades," Alex ordered. "Then head for those foxholes over there and wait."

During the night they could hear the Japanese trying to get to the foxholes. "Throw your grenades men," Alex called, and they hurled grenades all night long.

As morning came, he moved the men to a clearing beneath some trees that he didn't realize were infested with Japanese snipers. Alex heard bullets from a machine gun whizz by and ordered the men to drop to the ground. They moved backward as fast as they could on their bellies, bullets hitting the ground in front of them just as the men fell into a trough.

"Two soldiers sneaking up on us, to your front!" Norm shouted from the back. He had a better viewpoint from where he was, and when he yelled, "Duck," they all did. Norm aimed his rifle at the two Japanese soldiers approaching and shot and killed them both. The noise in Alex's helmet was deafening.

"Good job, Norm," Alex said, taking a deep breath. It was the first time he'd been this close to death.

"I hated killing those guys," Norm said, hands trembling. "But it was either them or us."

"You did the right thing," Alex said, swallowing hard.

The night of November 17, Japanese reinforcements arrived aboard six destroyers, bringing a thousand fresh troops. "We're in for it now, men," Alex said. "Get ready."

One of the divisions suffered hundreds of casualties, and the American units lost contact with each other. As the battle wore on, Alex and his men endured hundred-degree daytime heat and nightly rainstorms. He had to put several soldiers out of the line of combat due to sheer exhaustion and disease, some of them covered in tropical sores.

Food became an issue, and the men were existing on a half-pint of rice a day. A week later, some men took to eating tree bark and grass.

Alex and his unit fought fevers, suffering from Malaria and dysentery, the soles of their shoes gone, ripped off in the thick mud. "How much longer before Matson sends the next group to replace us?" Norm asked.

"He's late, and I hope soon, but we keep fighting as long as our weapons will fire." There was no talk of surrender from the Allied Forces.

When reinforcements arrived, Alex marched his bedraggled men fifteen miles back to Oro Bay. He was missing five, three had been shot, and two had died of dysentery. They were his men, and he hadn't been able to protect them. His skin bunched around his eyes, and he walked with a pained stare.

They were a sight when they finally reached base, faces gaunt, black circles under their eyes, uniforms tattered and too large for their thinning bodies. Alex thought he saw tears in the corners of Matson's eyes when they walked past him. "Get some food and rest, men," Matson said, voice resonating concern.

Alex offered Captain Matson a weak salute. "Most of us are back, sir."

Matson's voice cracked when he said, "Did your best, Forrest. Come see me in a few days."

When Alex and Matson met, Matson told him MacArthur had sent Major General Sutherland to the front to assess the situation. "Sutherland's assessment was that the soldiers lacked the will to fight and suffered from aggressive leadership. You were there. What's your view, lieutenant?"

"While most men fought bravely, sir, some Americans did throw down their weapons and run from the Japanese."

“Not good. I’m betting Harding will be replaced.”

It turned out that Matson was right.

MacArthur ordered General Eichelberger to the front to take command, and a new attack on the Japanese began in early December. Matson told Alex, “Rumor has it among the commanders that MacArthur told Eichelberger, “Bob, I want you to take Buna, or not come back alive; and that goes for your chief of staff too.”

“What did Eichelberger say?” Alex asked, his legs trembling.

He said, “Yes, sir,” Matson told him. “What else was he going to say? But the next morning Mac told Eichelberger he was no use to him dead, so I guess that gave him some hope.”

Alex blinked a few times, remembering how casually he’d taken his duties when he’d first enlisted, even smiling back in Virginia when the Sarge told him to take five laps around the track. *From privates to generals, the only way to get through this war is to obey orders.*

Alex heard from men who returned later that Eichelberger did something his predecessor never did: He spent time at the front, exposing himself to risk so his troops would know their commander was with them. The next month, Allied troops occupied Buna Village, and the Japanese pulled out.

Alex thought long and hard about what made a good leader. Despite the rain, hunger, disease, and death he’d faced on Buna, his men knew he was with them. They’d looked at him with more respect since, and Alex was a better staff officer than he would have been without going into battle. It was a strange thing to be happy about, but he was.

CHAPTER ELEVEN

After less than six months at the posh Meridian Hotel, Hallie and Kay were moving again, this time to barracks the navy had built to house female coders. "I'm going to miss this place," Hallie said, looking around the large, empty room.

"Me too. The view most of all." Kay sighed.

"I wonder what our training at Smith College will be like?"

"It won't be anything like going to school there, that's for sure," Kay laughed. "The best part might be having it over."

"Just think. Then we'll be commissioned officers in the US Naval Reserve. Me, an officer in the navy. Never saw that one coming." Hallie's skin tingled and she felt almost giddy.

"It's a good thing we both have college degrees, or we wouldn't have been given the chance to become officers in the 'Women Accepted for Volunteer Emergency Services,' aka the WAVES. Are you ready to go?"

"Let's do it," Hallie said. Kay walked out in front of her, and Hallie closed the door.

By November, they were packing their bags for officer training camp. "Hallie," Kay asked, "have you ever been to the town of Northampton?"

"I've never been anywhere in Massachusetts."

"Not even Boston?"

"Not even Boston."

"That's just not right. It's less than a two-hour train ride from Northampton, so it's an easy trip. We'll go there on our own dime one weekend in early December. Boston is magical around the holidays."

"I'd love to go."

They'd been told they'd be gone four weeks. "At least we have our uniforms," Hallie said.

"I know. The poor girls who left in September had to pack civilian skirts and sweaters, along with those ugly black Oxford shoes with the thick, tough heels. I heard they were hopelessly inadequate for marching."

"One of them told me she'd slipped and fallen on her backside during drills."

"How embarrassing."

Hallie admired her image in the mirror. She looked smart in her fitted navy-blue wool jacket, sleek six-gored skirt, and a short-sleeved white shirt with a tie. Her hat had a detachable top that could be blue or white. She placed it on her head, then picked up the square black pocketbook and strapped it diagonally over her shoulders. "I look so official," she said.

"And soon we'll have Ensign stripes to boot." Kay grinned.

Hallie and Kay locked their bags and left for the train station. It would take about seven hours to get to Boston from Washington DC, so they'd booked an early ticket. When they reached the train, the sun wasn't even up.

They climbed out of the taxi and maneuvered their luggage along the sidewalk. Inside the station, the Presidential suite had been converted to a USO canteen. "I hope they're open," Hallie said. "I'd like to have something to eat while we wait."

"Remember when we were here a few weeks ago? I loved the live music and singing, but it's way too early for that."

Hallie stretched her arms and stifled a yawn.

They boarded at 6:30 a.m., with a few warm muffins in hand. Hallie slept the first two hours while Kay studied the Bluejackets Manual.

When Hallie woke up, Kay handed her the manual, saying, "You might want to have a look at this. I've been memorizing the notes about personnel and ranks, along with navy protocol. There are some silly acronyms in here for the bureaus. She choked a giggle.

"Like what?" Hallie asked.

"BUPERS."

"What in the world is that?"

"A Navy organization that provides administrative leadership and general oversight of the Command. We don't want to forget that one." Kay put her finger to her mouth in a shushing motion and said, "Remember, this is all top secret."

After reaching Boston, they had an hour layover before boarding the train for Northampton. "Now I've been to Boston." Hallie smiled.

"No, you haven't. This city is the home of the American Revolution, and there's lots of history here. I'll start you off in Faneuil Hall when we come back."

They soon arrived at Smith College, which had been transformed into what the navy called the USS Northampton, the official training and staging grounds for the WAVES. The newly built Alumnae House was headquarters, and the women would be drilling on the athletic fields. Hallie shook her head and could hardly believe what she'd be doing for the next month.

While Kay waited in line to check into student housing, Hallie picked up a newsletter. "Listen to this." She nudged Kay. "A WAVE does not slouch over desks and counters when she talks to others; she maintains a neat, clean, well-pressed appearance at all times; she wears her hat straight… and does not wear flowers at any time on any part of her uniform."

"This will take some getting used to," Kay said, snapping her mouth shut.

"We're also required to line our shoes up in the closet with the toes facing out. I mean, I want a neat closet, but really?"

"For the life of me, I'm not sure why that matters, but all right."

"This is the military, and discipline is paramount. Hope I'm ready for this," Hallie said.

"Ready or not, here we come," Kay laughed. When they got to their room, she said, "If you're okay with the top bunk, I'll take the bottom. Never did like heights."

"That's fine by me."

"Don't forget we have to sleep with our heads in opposite directions," she smiled.

"Right. I'll face the door if you don't mind."

They bunked four to a room, and after they settled in, one of their new roommates told Kay her hair was too long and didn't meet navy standards. So, Hallie cut Kay's hair for her at once. She did the best she could, but the back looked a bit shaggy. Then it was lights out at 10:00 p.m. They had to be up at 5:30 a.m.

"I'm not used to waking up to the sound of a bugle," Hallie said the next morning, stalling for time before getting out of bed. She and Kay dressed, then made beds with shipshape square corners. Their blankets had to be folded in half, then in thirds, then in half again, and put at the bottom of their beds. After the beds were made, Kay bounced a quarter on the cover to make sure it was tight enough. Then they put on winter coats.

They mustered on the field with the other women, drilling in a light dust of snow, practicing calisthenics, doing the same exercises the men did. Kay had trouble shinnying up the rope, so Hallie helped her. They were both tired by the time class started.

They studied terminology from the navy's point of view, learning that a work shift was a "watch" and personal possessions were called "gear." If someone got sick, she was put "on the binnacle list." The bathroom was called "the head."

Every day, Hallie and Kay ate breakfast, lunch, and dinner in town at the Wiggins Tavern at the North Hampton Hotel. The food was good, and the muffins they served in the morning were to die for, crispy tops and blueberries that melted in your mouth.

While some of the women roomed at the hotel instead of the dorms, Hallie and Kay had to march into town three times a day to take meals. That meant they often had to put up with the army men stationed in the vicinity. The men would laugh and whistle as the women marched by.

The women returned the men's disrespect by loudly singing, "Nothing can stop the Army Air Corps… except the US Navy!" Then they laughed and marched on, singing as they went.

"Who cares what they think?" Kay asked on one occasion.

They even had to march to chapel on Sundays. While the marching was tedious, Hallie loved having a purpose in this man's war. She and Kay never did make that weekend trip to Boston. They were far too busy. But Hallie planned to come back some day.

When they returned to the Main Navy in Washington DC, they were called the thirty-day wonders. It had been the longest thirty days of Hallie's life, what with all the studying at night, calisthenics every morning, lectures, and even tests that covered navy terms she'd never use. But the reward was receiving her stripes.

Back in the Japanese unit, even as ensigns, Kay and Hallie were the top officers, with no men who outranked them. Kay's hair was again a little longer than it should have been, but who was going to order her to cut it? The men were being shipped out fast, and the new women code breakers were coming in even faster.

CHAPTER TWELVE

For the first time in what seemed like forever, I was traveling beyond the city limits of Honolulu. Dr. Petersen had insisted I take a day off, saying, "Lucy, you need some time for yourself. Go somewhere. You've worked twelve-hour shifts for a month."

"Thank you." I smiled, then invited Alicia to come along. She'd put in as many hours as I had, maybe more.

When we picked up a car from the motor pool, the sun wasn't even up yet, but we were excited to hit the road. Since gas was in such short supply, we wouldn't drive farther than the Nu'uanu Pali Lookout, about five miles northeast of Downtown Honolulu.

I took a deep breath when we left the city limits, as Alicia drove the Pali Highway. The city disappeared, replaced by the shadows of tall trees and thick forests. I leaned against the back of the seat and closed my eyes, a slow smile spreading across my face, shoulders relaxed.

"Heavens to Betsy," Alicia said, as the first hint of color hit the skies. "It's going to be a beautiful day."

I glanced outside my window. "You're right. It's so good to get away from the war for a little while."

"This morning when I prayed, this is what I said: Aloha, God. You must be sad to watch your children fight. Please stop the war."

I sat up and looked at her. "I love that you started your prayer with an Aloha to God, Alicia. Someday, peace will come to Hawaii."

She blinked a small teardrop from her eye and said, "Look up ahead, Lucy. "We're almost there."

I suspected she was thinking about Robert again. Alicia was compassionate when it came to listening to the feelings of others but stayed away from her own. She'd told me more than once she liked to work things out in her head. I never pushed her. "Did you know the word Pali means cliff in Hawaiian?" I asked.

"No, I didn't. I can't wait to see the view."

"It's stunning. Last time I saw it was more than a year ago, come to think of it, just before Pearl was bombed."

We reached the lookout, parked the car, then walked down the road to a large open area enclosed by a steel railing. The wind howled, whistling through the mountains as the sun came up. "It's breathtaking," I said, watching the sun fill the sky.

Alicia leaned against the rail. "Look at those white clouds, puffing over leafy green mountains and blue ocean water. I can see Honolulu in the distance."

"Oahu's lush windward coast is the best ever, and it's even better at sunrise."

"There's a rainbow," Alicia pointed.

Its glow filled the mountains with light. "A symbol of hope. Did I tell you the USS Salt Lake City is coming to Hawaii again?" I asked.

"No," she turned to me, "when?"

"December 15."

"That's next week. Are you excited to see Matt again?"

"I can't wait."

"You met him a year ago, right?"

"Yes, and I wish we'd had more time in person. I spent one day with him when we met, then he came last June for a few days on leave, and we've written every week."

"These days, that's more time than lots of people spend together before getting hitched. What was the name of that nurse who married a solider she met at a dance?"

"Cindy. Remember her wedding? She wore an Aloha dress, and her husband-to-be scrounged around trying to find metal for a ring to put on her finger. They had two days of wedded bliss, then he shipped out to fight, and she went home to the states. Who knows if it will last?"

"Hard to tell."

"These are not normal times. You know we've had dozens of soldiers marry Hawaiian girls, even though the military discourages it."

"Remember the article that ran in *Yank* magazine in June? Headline: *Don't Promise Her Anything—Marriage Outside the US Is Out.* Doesn't seem to be stopping anybody."

"Soldiers are marrying women all over the world, and in a big hurry. Since the war started, there's been a huge increase in weddings. I think it's because people are scared about the future and want to find a little hope and joy."

"Can't blame them for that."

"No, but that doesn't necessarily mean they're right for each other. I'm sure Matt and I are though. In his letter last week, he hinted at getting engaged."

"You were engaged once before, right?"

"Yes," I said, looking off in the distance.

"You mentioned he wasn't who he seemed to be. What did you mean by that?"

"He told me half-truths that a friend of mine discovered, from a friend of his."

"Like what?"

"He claimed he had a solid, B-plus grade point average and was a good student. That turned out to be true for one semester at a junior college. He left out the fact that he flunked out of the university."

"Wow."

"I was too trusting, and I won't make that mistake again. God has given me the capacity to recognize a truly good man when I see one. Matt's a good man." I gazed out over the water as a large group of people joined us at the rail. "Say, I'm starving. Let's drive back to Honolulu and get something to eat."

"How about Waikiki? I know a place that serves the best Portuguese sausage, eggs, and rice. After we eat, we could take a walk on the beach."

"Fun and games. Let's go."

We had a delicious breakfast, a soothing walk at the beach, and even did a little shopping. "The vegetable markets have less and less each time we come," I said.

"The locals seem to grab the veggies before they even get to market." We picked up a few more groceries, returned the car, and went back to base. Dr. Petersen was right. I felt like a new woman.

A week later, I stood waiting on the docks for Matt, watching as hundreds of sailors disembarked from the *USS Salt Lake City*. Where was he? He was usually one of the first ones off the ship. Then I saw him at the back of the line, that signature grin on his face. He was carrying a beautiful bouquet of orange hibiscus flowers that he pointed to, and then pointed back at me. I ran to him and threw myself into his arms.

He handed me the flowers, picked me up and twirled me around, laughing, his eyes bright. "I've missed you," he said, all attention focused on me. It was as if there was no one else in the world.

"Where did you get these lovely flowers?"

"Called the Bretania Florist in Honolulu yesterday, ship to shore, and they made a special delivery earlier this morning," he grinned.

"So thoughtful, and so like you."

"Nothing's too good for my girl."

My heartbeat quickened, and my throat grew thick.

"I love you," he breathed into my hair.

"I love you back." I smiled, kissing him. "I've been waiting and waiting, so excited to see you. It surprised me that you were at the back of the line of sailors."

"I delayed until last because I have an idea. Now that most everyone is off the ship, how would you like to come aboard and take a tour? It's not something we usually do, but I'd like to show you where I spend all my time."

"That's too good to pass up," I said taking his arm. We walked on board, my heels sounding on the metal, and stood in the large bay. "This is huge. How many men can it hold?"

"The Old Swayback carries 87 officers and 576 enlisted men. The guns over there are the big ones, and there are ten of them. These smaller guns are anti-aircraft guns. I've used this one when we're in the middle of battle.

"Have you shot down lots of planes?"

"A few. Worst thing is when one of them gets close enough to see the pilot's frightened eyes as his plane hits the water."

"I can't even imagine," I said, trembling. I put my hand on his arm, and he placed his hand over mine.

We started walking, and he changed the subject. "These are the torpedo tubes. We also have four floatplanes and two amidship catapults."

I'd never been anywhere near this kind of firepower. Being up close and personal with that kind of hardware brought the war closer. Picturing him shooting an anti-aircraft gun reminded me again that Matt lived in harm's way. I prayed in my heart that he'd stay safe.

"Let's go inside, and I'll show you around."

We passed a sizeable room with several chairs, and Matt said, "This is the Combat Information Center. I spend most of my time here unless we're in the middle of a battle."

His eyes were bright, and he seemed happy sharing his life with me.

"Over there is the ship's galley, the compartment where the food is prepared. Would you like to see the kitchen? It's worth it."

"Yes, I would." When we reached the kitchen, I saw massive ovens, griddles, and large steam pots. I'd cooked before and wondered what it would be like to steer through all this equipment. "Are those mixers?" I asked. "They're almost as big as you."

He laughed. "The baker uses these man-sized stand mixers, and the butcher has those band saws that can cut up whole sides of beef. They have lots of mouths to feed."

"I've never seen a kitchen this size."

"Over here's the mess hall, where we stand in very long lines to be served and take all our meals."

"What do they feed you?'

"Lots of salted meats, breads, potatoes, oats, and citrus. Sometimes those little Vienna sausages with sweet potatoes. Check out the fountain, that's the real deal. That's where we get ice cream and lots of it. Navy food is some of the best compared to other branches of the service, and they keep us well fed. Let's keep going, and I'll show you where I sleep. Then we'll get off this tub."

We walked into a room filled with metal bunks jammed together, one stacked on top of another, strung up with chains. There was a thin cushion for a sailor to sleep on, a pillow, and a blanket. "How do you ever get any rest?" I asked. I don't know what I'd pictured, but this wasn't it.

Matt laughed. "Ain't easy. Especially when the fellas start snoring."

"I bet."

"Now let's get out of here and have some fun. What have we got planned?"

"How about a walk on the beach and dinner at my place tonight? My roommate will be out for a few hours."

"Sounds like heaven. You know, I like being stationed in the Pacific, close to Hawaii. Makes it easy to see you sometimes."

"I've just been told something, Matt."

"What is it?"

"A few of the nurses are being transferred to a field hospital in the jungles of New Guinea. I'm going to help with the set up."

He flinched. "Dangerous assignment, Lucy. Allies are still fighting the Japanese in New Guinea."

"Don't worry, I'll be careful," I promised, knowing full well 'careful' was not in my control.

"When do you leave?"

"The end of January."

"So not before Christmas?"

"No." I smiled, grateful we still had two weeks.

"This will be our first Christmas together, Lucy, but not the last. Look, I don't know where I'm going to be next week or even next month and neither do you. What I do know, is that I care about you, really care. You're the girl of my dreams."

"I love you," I said, holding his hand.

"Let's go sit on that bench. I'd like to give you one of your presents early."

When I sat down, Matt dropped to one knee and pulled a small box from his pocket.

This is it, I thought, my face flushed. Inside the box was a shiny diamond ring.

"You're the one for me," he said, gazing into my eyes. "Will you be mine?"

"I want to be together forever, my darling. The ring is lovely, thank you," I said, kissing him on the cheek.

"It was my mom's." He wiped away tears. "I keep it with me to remember her."

"I'll cherish this ring forever," I whispered, knowing what it meant to him. I linked my arm through his.

"My mom would have loved you." He swallowed hard, paused, then said, "One day this conflict will end. We'll bury our weapons of war and have peace again. Then we can be joined for eternity, surrounded by family and friends, in the Salt Lake Temple. How does that sound?"

"Just right," I smiled.

"In the meantime, we'll write. A lot."

"You can count on me," I said, "although when I transfer to the jungle, expect gaps."

We kissed again, he held me, and we said nothing. We'd already said it all, and I didn't want to disturb the moment. Who knew what lay ahead?

CHAPTER THIRTEEN

Hallie was excited to go home on leave for Christmas. It was hard to believe it had only been a year since Pearl Harbor was bombed. It seemed so much longer. Her train was traveling west to Salt Lake City, and Dad had generously upgraded her ticket to a Pullman sleeper car. She planned to be in heaven for five days: no uniform, no work, no responsibility, and no saluting. Hallie smiled at herself when she boarded the train, and the porter placed her luggage in the cabin. Instead of thanking him, she unintentionally saluted. He looked at her so oddly. When he left, Hallie flopped onto the couch and laughed until tears ran down her face. She'd learned to laugh at herself.

Hallie slept in each morning and ate every meal upstairs in the dining car, watching as the world rolled by. After dinner, she read *The Long Winter* by Laura Ingalls Wilder, such a nice escape.

The last morning of the trip, she decided to wear her dress blues. Hallie had brought her uniform along to show her family and decided to put it on for effect so Mom and Dad would see her in it as she walked into the train station.

When the train stopped, Hallie left the car, thanked the porter, and intentionally saluted him this time. He saluted back. "Didn't know you were in the navy, Miss," he smiled. "Thank you for serving our country."

His kind words touched her heart, and she thought about what they meant.

Entering the crowded station, she saw her parents craning their necks this way and that, trying to find her. When they spotted her, it was as if, for a split second, they didn't recognize her.

"You're in uniform," Mom breathed, taking a step back.

"And doesn't she look smart," Dad said, giving her a hug. "Welcome home, Hallie."

Mom held her close, whispering in her ear, "It's so good to see you."

Passersby in the train station stared at her, not used to seeing a woman in uniform. Even in Washington DC, cars often came to a dead stop, blocking traffic, when WAVES walked down the street. One little boy on the train had asked Hallie if she was a nun.

"I guess it's Ensign Forrest now." Dad smiled and took her bag. "How was officer training?"

"It was an experience," Hallie laughed. "I'll tell you all about it on the ride home."

When they got home, Lily saw her in uniform and said, "Jeepers, Hallie, it's you."

Hallie laughed and gave her a hug. "I've missed you."

Dad carried the suitcase into her childhood bedroom, and Hallie changed into civilian clothes. She sat on the bed, gazing around the room, which was untouched and unchanged since she'd left.

In the living room, her attention fixed on the traditional seven red Christmas stockings lining the mantle. A Douglas fir stood in the corner of the room as usual, but it was shorter this year than last. They didn't have Alex to reach to the top and hang the star. Hallie missed having them all together and was sad that it would be a long time before that happened again.

On Christmas Eve, Dad, Lily, and Hallie stood around the piano, held hands, and sang, 'Joy to the World' while Mom accompanied them. They were doing their best to be joyful without the rest of the family, but it wasn't easy. While they'd had no word from Chris, a doctor in the hospital in Cabanatuan had somehow managed to smuggle a scribbled list of patients to the military. It included Chris's name.

Grateful that he was alive, the family prayed every day that he'd survive. Hallie couldn't imagine life without her big brother.

After Dad read about Christ's birth from the book of Luke in the Bible, Mom went to the credenza and picked up the letters Lucy and Alex had sent home for Christmas.

She began with Lucy's letter, saying, "They're here with us in spirit."

Dearest family,

I wish so much that I could be home tonight and enjoy those happy times we had together at past Christmases. I would give almost anything to sit with you on the couch and watch Lily and Hallie open their presents. What a kick that would be. Merry Christmas to all of you.

It's hard to believe this is the second year I've spent Christmas away from home. The weather here in Hawaii has been nice the past few days, with no rain. War or no war, I'm going to miss it here. It looks like I'll be shipping out next month with some of the other nurses, but I can't say where.

I have some really big news to share. I'm engaged to be married to Matt Hatch. I told you all about him in earlier letters, and I know you'll just love him! We're going to wait to be married until after the war ends.

I've enclosed some pictures of places I've been in Hawaii. Please take good care of them, I'll want them back someday. As soon as these pictures reach home, I'll send you the negatives. May God bless you all.

I'll write to you again after the new year.

I love you,

Lucy

"Wow, she's engaged," Lily said, breaking the silence as Mom and Dad looked at each other, surprised.

"I hope she's going somewhere safe," Hallie said, changing the subject.

"When she gets there, we might get some idea based on the APO box she uses to send her letters," Dad said. "So, we'll see." He cleared his throat.

"I'll read Alex's letter next," Mom said, "and then we can look at Lucy's pictures."

Dear family,

Wishing you all a Merry Christmas. We are not in such a bad place where we are right now. We are all tired of the war, but that's to be expected after a full year of it. Who knows how much longer it will take to win this thing?

I got a letter from Sadie telling me she'd found someone else. Good for her. I can hardly remember what she looks like anymore. Ha, ha. Hope she's happy.

I wish I could be home with you, rather than being here.

Your loving son and brother,

Alex

The family sat in silence, thinking about those who weren't home. Mom's eyes filled with tears, and Hallie guessed she was thinking about Chris. Lily broke the quiet asking, "Is it time for presents now?"

Mom forced a smile. "Right after we eat dessert."

"What are we having?" Hallie asked, moving into the kitchen to help.

"Carrot cake."

Not her favorite, but with sugar rationed to eight ounces a week, Mom used carrots to naturally sweeten the cake, replacing some of the sugar.

Yum," Lily said, eating her cake as quickly as possible. "I'm ready to open my present now."

They all smiled. Even though Lily was thirteen now, she was still a kid at Christmas. After Hallie opened her gift, Mom suggested they save Lucy's fun pictures for tomorrow. "Time for bed," she said, rising from the couch. It was still early, but Mom had kept her brave face on as long as she could.

1943

Chris turned over in his bunk, nauseous, feet still swollen. He closed his eyes and prayed, thanking God for the Filipino underground who'd smuggled in quinine tablets, allowing him to recover from malaria. With Japan pretty much running the Philippine government, aiding Americans was a significant risk.

Chris took a deep breath. Time to get up, he thought, standing on wobbly feet, listening as one of his bunkmates babbled out loud again. Chris had gotten used to that, but lately the guy had started seeing things. Didn't do any good to try and talk him out of it. Chris walked over and touched his arm. "It's okay, buddy. Don't give up," he said.

"Are you my dad?" The man asked. "Are you here to take me home? I wanna go home so bad," he sobbed.

Chris felt the man's forehead. He was burning up. "You hold tight," Chris said. "I'll go to the hospital and get you some quinine." Chris reached the hospital as quick as he could on his wobbly feet and spoke with one of the Japanese doctors, explaining the situation. The doc gave him what he needed.

When Chris returned with the quinine, it was too late. The guy was dead. "You're home now, buddy," Chris said, tears in his eyes. Tearing off the dog tags, he rechecked the man's last name before stuffing them into his pockets, then checked under the mattress to see if maybe he'd left a letter. The Japanese captors wouldn't allow men to send mail or receive it, but they still wrote anyway, saving the letters. Chris found one and added the unopened letter to the dog tags.

The guy's family was in the dark about his whereabouts, as Chris's own family was. None of them knew whether their sons had been killed, were lying sick or wounded in a hospital, or were still stuck in some Japanese prison camp.

Chris sat for a minute, head in his hands, and then walked outside to find the burial detail. He no longer had shoes to wear because the Japanese had taken them away from all the men, except the wood chopping detail. A Japanese general who had recently inspected the camp, ordered that Americans assigned to the farm and other work details would now have to go barefoot. It was raining hard when Chris left, and he had no protection against the wind and rain.

The roofs on the buildings were damaged, and the bamboo strips broken. Even the sides of some of them had caved in. The place was a wreck, and the ditches were clogged again. His bare feet sucked through heavy mud. Chris touched the small New Testament Bible he still had in his pocket. It hadn't been easy keeping that little book safe. Before scheduled inspections, Chris either buried it or hid it in a latrine. It was this little book that brought him hope.

Chris went back to the hospital area. The burial party, accompanied by a Japanese guard, met there each morning. "Got a man dead in my building," he told one of the men.

"On our way to the burial ground now. We'll pick up his body and add it to the others."

Death had become all too routine in the camp, and while Chris was still sick, the guard let him come along anyway. When they reached his building, the four men assigned to recover the body placed it gently on bamboo frames. It was a mile and a half walk from the campground to the burial ground. Chris was wheezing by the time they arrived.

He took a few deep breaths and watched as the four men lowered the body into a shallow grave that looked about four feet deep and was half-full of water. Other bodies they'd carried along were then added to the shared grave. Chris counted fourteen bodies in all.

Chaplain Mike said, "The gospel of John tells us, 'I am the resurrection and the life. He that believeth in me, though he were dead, yet shall he live.' Your bodies are no longer subject to disease and death, and one day, you will live again. Until then may your spirits find peace."

Mike touched Chris's shoulder and said, "I'll pray for you."

"Thank you. I appreciate your prayers for all of us."

Chris made his way slowly back to quarters, sat on his bunk, and picked up his Christmas package from the American Red Cross. He still had it. Each man in the camp had received three individual packages, and Chris figured those supplies just might last through early February, if he was careful. The Red Cross had also sent food in bulk for the mess halls, which Chris found a welcome relief from the rice, greens, and carabao meat he'd been eating for months. There were cases of fruit, corned beef, cocoa, canned vegetables, medical supplies, and even games and new books.

Chris planned on spending the rest of the day reading. A few of the internees at Cabanatuan had brought along books—mostly fiction—a few technical books, and some magazines. The Japanese authorities had set aside a small exchange center in the prisoners' area to house the books and periodicals. Chris was looking for something new to read. One of the worst things about prison life was the never-ending boredom, which had literally driven some men crazy.

Chris picked up a dog-eared copy of Steinbeck's, *Of Mice and Men*, its pages soiled and worn. He had read the novella before, but he viewed the mutual dependence of the characters George and Lennie, friends since childhood, differently this time. The ending, where George shoots Lennie in the back of the head to prevent him from being lynched, was especially powerful. Chris sat back and thought about the characters who were doomed to destruction because of events outside their control.

It wasn't hard to find parallels between the theme of the book and being a prisoner of war. Chris had no power over his life either. A few weeks earlier, he'd watched a prisoner attempt to climb the barbed wire fence trying to escape. The guy surely knew what would happen, so either he'd lost his mind, or he hadn't been able to take it anymore. Before the man reached the top of the fence, two guards shot him in the back. There had been several other attempted escapes the previous year. Even though the men knew the likely outcome, it didn't stop some of them from trying.

Still in the building, paging through the book, Chris thought about the new policy the Japanese had recently put in place where the men had to guard each other. The American officer in Chris's building had informed the men how the new policy would be implemented, saying, "You'll now be put on work details with ten men total and placed in a shooting squad. If one man escapes, the other nine of you will be shot."

The men gasped. If one of them lost it and tried to escape, the others would have to rush him, even beating him, if necessary, to preserve their own lives. It might turn into a mercy killing just like in the book.

Chris put the novella back on the shelf and left for the barracks, more depressed than he'd been in months. It had been another rough day that seemed like a week. As he prayed that night, Chris begged that the devastation, hate, and cruelty around him wouldn't ruin his own soul. How can I make that happen? he asked. His mother's words came to him, as clear as if she were in the room. He could picture her kind face as she said, "The best way to help yourself is to help others, son. Just like Jesus showed us."

Chris got up from his knees and blew Mom a kiss. He slept a little better that night.

The next morning as he shaved, Chris thought about what he could do to benefit the other prisoners, and it came to him. He'd get seeds from the canteen the Philippine women ran, plant a vegetable garden, and share the food. He smiled, remembering years as a kid helping his Grandma Ann with her vegetable garden.

Chris found a small shovel and headed outside. Then he laid out rows next to the bunkhouse. Even in January, the weather was suitable for planting, so he started filling his garden with seeds for string beans, corn, and tomatoes. He checked the position of the sun, and it looked to be about noon. Time to get some rice.

He set his small shovel aside when the captain approached. "What are you doing there, lieutenant?" he asked.

"I'm digging a community vegetable garden, sir."

"That's an excellent idea, Forrest. We could use a man like you on the camp administration committee."

"Glad to help any way I can."

"We've proposed new measures to the Japanese, and they've agreed to them. The procedures will create a better sense of order."

"That would be a big help."

"We've convinced the Japanese that there's a need for greater cooperation if we're going to improve the conditions in the camp. And if we don't, the remaining prisoners won't survive. The first thing we're going to do is start a farm. The prisoners will do all the work, and we expect the farm to be producing by about the middle of the year."

"With all due respect sir, it wouldn't surprise me if most of that food goes to the Japanese guards and not to the prisoners."

"That occurred to us too, but we have to give it a try. Even if the guards take a lot of the food, we hope for at least some fresh squash, sweet potatoes, and onion tops."

"Beats what we have now."

"There's another benefit to the men who work the farm. We've convinced the Japanese that with the increased labor on the farm, the men will need increased rations, so they'll each get an extra ear of corn per day, or a tomato, or a few grams of greens. The members of the work details will also be permitted to pick pig weed."

"That's stuff's tough but it will add bulk to their diet."

"You're right, lieutenant. You know, it occurs to me that you're just the man to take charge of the farm. It'll give you a chance to help the other men, while increasing your own odds of survival."

"Yes, sir. Thank you, sir." Chris blinked, amazed.

"In the meantime, keep that vegetable garden going. Some of the men have been catching mice, snakes, and ducks that wander into camp, killing them for food. Every bit we can do to supplement and improve their diets helps," he said, saluting and walking away.

Chris's mother's words came back in a rush. 'The way to help yourself is to help others.' *I'm out planting a vegetable garden to help someone else, and I'm put in charge of the farm, giving me more food? God moves in mysterious ways. Thank you, Mom.* He fell to his knees. *Please know I'm still alive.*

CHAPTER FOURTEEN

I sat on board an early-morning air transport from Oahu to Dobordura on the North Coast of New Guinea with three of my nurses. "I'll miss Hawaii," Alicia said, gazing out the window at the rising sun as the plane lifted off. "I'll be back, Robert," she whispered, blowing a kiss in the air.

It broke my heart to see her sad about leaving Robert's grave behind, and I prayed this would be the beginning of a new chapter in her life. Stomach churning, I knew working at a field hospital in the jungle would be a new challenge for all of us.

"Our flight will take a shade under nine hours," I said.

One of the nurses groaned. "Oh, boy. That's a long one."

"I brought muffins if anyone's hungry," I offered.

After a small chorus of "No thanks," and "Maybe later," I closed my eyes. Sleep eluded me, as I thought about what lay ahead.

We approached Dobordura around 11:00 a.m. the day after we'd left, with the time change. The plane flew over several runways still under construction, and after a bumpy landing, we grabbed our gear and took an old gray army jeep to the field hospital. The leafy rainforest, dense with green trees, was complemented by orchids, tree ferns, and a few lavender rhododendrons. When we arrived, we found thatched huts in a grove of coconut trees.

I estimated the day's temperature at over one hundred degrees Fahrenheit, and the oppressive humidity left a salty film over all of us. I soaked in sweat and mopped my face with my sleeve. My dad was fond of telling me, 'Animals sweat, men perspire, and women glow.' I'm not glowing today, Dad, I thought smiling.

We moved our stuff into our new quarters, and I advised the girls as they unpacked, "Before you do anything, try to take a nap and spend time rehydrating. It's three p.m. yesterday in Hawaii. I'll have a look at our new working conditions and be back soon."

Across the compound, I found a hastily built twenty-five bed hospital. Looking around, I could see there wasn't enough medical equipment to do the work required. The male captain in charge told me the equipment had to be transportable and weigh less than thirty pounds. "We brought all we could carry," he said. "By the way, you need to know the chain of command here. You'll meet the colonel at some point, I'm next in line as captain, and we have two lieutenants." I found his tone civil yet condescending.

"So, with me, there are now three lieutenants," I smiled, hoping to warm him up.

He smirked. "Oh, that's right. I'm still getting used to women being officers."

I stepped forward and continued my questions. "How many medical personnel?"

"Three general surgeons, eleven medical technicians, and another nine enlisted men, with no medical training. They help as assigned. Our aim in the field hospital is to get the wounded out alive so they can be moved to a more permanent hospital."

"It sounds like we have to work fast."

"And non-stop for hours, so take the remainder of the day off and settle in. I'll see you and the rest of the nurses early in the morning. I just hope you and your nurses will be able to stomach what you'll see here. It can be ugly."

"Don't you worry about us. Our last service duty was working at Pearl Harbor. We'll be fine."

That night, I tossed and turned, eventually waking to the sounds of Alicia getting dressed. She pulled on the drab olive long-sleeved shirt and cuffed pants that we were now wearing to protect against relentless, infectious bugs. Pushing the mosquito netting aside, I got up and stretched, doing a few arm twirls and toe touches.

"Good morning, sleepyhead," Alicia whispered, primping in the small mirror we had hanging in the hut.

"Good morning. You're up extra early."

"I couldn't sleep, and I needed to wash my undies."

We'd been told the water wasn't safe, so we had a large canvas sack filled with chlorinated water hanging from a tripod. We were allowed two helmets full per day.

"Would you get some for me too please, while you're in there?" I asked when she opened the bag.

"Happy to," she said, handing me a helmet filled with water and a few Atabrine tablets. It was so hot and humid in the jungle that malaria was widespread, and, for every patient who came in with a battle wound, four more had malaria. We were ordered to take Atabrine to protect us from a similar fate.

"These tablets turn your skin yellow," Alicia said. "Hate the stuff."

"But they make such great dye. I've never seen so much yellow clothing in my life."

Her hearty laugh woke the other two girls. I shuffled to the small white tub in the corner, dumped in the water, grabbed a bar of soap, and washed my face and hands.

After we were all dressed, we stepped outside and found an armed guard waiting to escort us to the field hospital. "I'll be here every morning," he said. "For protection."

When one of the nurses blanched, Alicia quoted Emerson. 'Always do what you are afraid to do.' I don't know about you girls," she continued, "but that about sums it up for me. I'm kinda scared."

"It's okay, we're all a little anxious," I said, shoulders tight. "It helps me to see that red cross painted on the huts, a clear message to the Japanese not to drop their bombs here." I wasn't as positive as I sounded for the benefit of my team.

A voice called over the loudspeaker, "Attention all personnel. Proceed immediately to the admitting ward and operating room."

We broke into a run, and when we arrived, we found three men who had been shot. They were bleeding profusely.

"Get them in here," the captain called, as men rushed the injured to the operating room.

We pulled on white gowns and surgical masks. "Clean this head wound up," one of the doctors said, "and hand me that clamp, please."

The two of us worked feverishly side-by-side trying to save our patient.

"I think we're losing him," the doc said. "I need a sponge."

I handed him what he needed and prayed this soldier would live.

Minutes later, the doc took a deep breath. "He's coming around." I gave him sutures, he closed the wound, and I put our patient's arm in a cast.

I took a deep breath, relieved. And then bombs began dropping a few miles away, shaking everything around us. I steadied myself as the captain shouted, "That means more incoming. Get ready." I prevented my hands from trembling by focusing on our mission as we labored another ten hours in surgery. Then a guard came and escorted us back to the hut.

"A girl can only take so much," one of my nurses said, shaking from exhaustion and dehydration.

I put my arm around her shoulder. "I know you're tired. Me too. Let's get through this together."

After we walked inside, there was a knock at the door. "May I help you?" I asked.

"Got mail for you, ma'am," said a young corporal with red hair and round glasses.

"Thanks," I said, turning the envelope over. I'd cabled my parents our new APO box number in Dobordura a few weeks ago, and true to form, Mom had sent a letter right away. I was tired, but not too tired to read a message from home. I sat down on the floor and began to read.

February 1943

Dearest Lucy,

I imagine you've reached the new field hospital, and I pray you're safe. The only comfort I find with your new assignment is that you're only about an hour away from Alex. (I checked on the map and calculated the distance by car.)

I smiled. Of course, you did, Mom.

I know full well you'll put everyone else's needs ahead of yours. But please, listen to your mother. Get enough sleep and do your best to stay out of harm's way.

Good thing she didn't know about the bombs today.

Dad and I are doing fine. It's snowing a lot, and the roads are slick. Lily is lonely without her brothers and sisters. You and Hallie write each other sometimes, so you know

she's fine. Chris has now been listed as missing in action. But in my mother's heart, I believe he's alive and pray God will spare his life.

Know that your dad and I love you, Lucy, and we pray for you night and day. Keep the faith.

With much love,

Mom

Exhausted, I set the letter aside and fell into bed. I touched my engagement ring, thinking of Matt, and then slept several hours.

Over the next week, we lived through similar emergencies, day after day after day, and then one afternoon as I left the hospital, I thought I saw Alex driving by. Couldn't be. I ran after the jeep yelling, "Alex!" He waved, stopped, and jumped out. "What are you doing here?" I asked, eyes wide.

"Aren't you glad to see me?" he asked, a big grin on his face.

"I've never been gladder in my life." I hugged him, feeling a sudden lightness.

"Took an afternoon off and thought I'd come see how you're doing."

"Come on, let's go to the food hut, and I'll treat you to a ginger ale."

After we sat, I said, "Let's start with you. What's new?"

"Well, I've been promoted to first lieutenant and assigned as a staffer to Colonel Tory. He's on MacArthur's administrative staff."

"Oh, my goodness, Alex. I'm so proud of you—but not

surprised. You always did know how to make yourself indispensable. Did you ever picture yourself doing something like this?"

"Not in a million years, but you know, I like it. More than I thought. The politics are actually kinda fun."

I laughed. "Someday, I bet you'll run for office."

"You know, I just might do that." He smiled.

"Have you met General MacArthur?"

"Just once."

"What's he like?

"Smart, optimistic, but a little cold sometimes. I can tell you, it's not possible for him to talk sitting down. He paces the floor to get his ideas out. Nothing matters more to him than liberating the Philippines."

"How long do you think we have before the war ends?" I sighed. "I've been serving almost fourteen months now, and the abnormal has become normal. I'm getting numb to it all."

"Living with constant intensity wears you out. But we're just beginning to clear the Japanese out of New Guinea, and we've got a long way to go before taking back the Philippines. Are you doing okay here?"

"I'm having a little trouble with the captain," I said, leaning in. It was the middle of the afternoon, so there weren't many people around, but I wanted to make sure no one heard me.

"What kind of trouble?"

"I put together a request that would improve procedures, allowing the field hospital to run more efficiently," I said, folding my arms across my chest.

"That's great. What did he say?"

"That it *might* be a promising idea, and he'd run it past the colonel. Fair enough. When I asked the captain yesterday if he'd heard anything, he smiled and told me the colonel said he'd take it up with headquarters and see what they thought. That could take weeks. I think I'm being stonewalled."

"Hmm. It's possible. Here's an idea. Go tell him you understand how busy he and the colonel are, so you've written up your proposal to send to HQ for approval. But you just need to check the address. Be relaxed, smile, act innocent."

I beamed. "So, I haven't threatened to go around him, but I've implied I might."

"Exactly."

"And when the captain tells me not to worry my pretty little head about it…"

"Smile and tell him you'll hold onto the letter until he hears from the colonel, just in case. I'm betting the captain will get things moving ASAP."

"That's brilliant, Alex. You know, I think you inherited the smooth operator gene in our family. You always knew how to get what you wanted at home, while keeping the peace. Sometimes you did it by asking for forgiveness rather than permission, but it still worked. You were never confrontational, and everybody liked you."

Alex laughed. "You're on to me, sis. Say, I heard the army is building a big new hospital in the Apoka Valley to the west of Port Moresby. Did you know about that?"

"I hadn't heard," I said, ears perking up.

"Construction started early February."

"It's been less than a month, I wonder how it's coming."

"Well, apart from the roads and water reservoirs, the US Army 135th Medical Regiment is doing all the construction. Might be just the place for you when it's finished. Get in on the ground floor of a new hospital. I'm thinking they could use someone with your experience and expertise, and you could ditch the captain." His eyes twinkled.

I looked across the table at Alex and no longer saw my little brother, but a friend, an advisor on military matters, and a confidant.

"What have you heard from Matt?" he asked.

"His last letter said he was in Dutch Harbor, Alaska, near one of our naval bases. He wrote about a huge mess hall at the base that doubles as a theater. Tickets for the military were only fifteen cents, so he bought one and had himself a good old time watching a show."

Alex grinned. "Sounds like he's doing fine."

"Yes, but he worries a lot about me being here in the jungle. He's glad you're close," I said.

"Me too. If you need anything, let me know. I'm here for you."

"And I appreciate it." I smiled.

"Best get going, Lucy," he said, standing and giving me a hug.

I hugged him back, wondering when I'd see him again.

The next day I went to the captain. When I asked for the address, he glared at me and said, "To be clear, you would never send that request yourself. I told you, the request is in progress."

"Great. Please keep me posted."

He softened. "I expect to hear soon, with the outcome we're both looking for."

So now it's we, and not just me. "Yes, sir," I said saluting. "Thank you, sir." Two days later, after my plan to improve our processes had languished for weeks, it was approved, and life got better for the patients and the medical team. We worked faster and more efficiently.

CHAPTER FIFTEEN

Alex sat in Colonel Tory's office with a few other staff members, waiting for a top-secret briefing. The colonel strode in and began, "Men, it comes as no surprise that the Japanese are furious about the allied forces clearing them out of New Guinea. Another attack on the Pacific is imminent."

"Do we know when, sir?" one of the men asked, tone tense.

"The US Navy cryptanalysts have given MacArthur solid intelligence that the enemy is planning another major transport to Lae several days from now."

Alex understood the code breakers were helping win this war against Japan, and ever since Pearl Harbor, their intel had been right on target. He expected, but didn't know for certain, that Hallie was part of that effort in Washington DC.

The colonel continued. "When we became convinced that the Japanese were preparing a major seaborne reinforcement, we stepped up our air searches, and our B-25 bombers have been modified to allow for new offensive tactics."

"What's changed?" Alex asked, curious.

"Noses were refitted with eight, fifty-caliber machine guns for shelling slow-moving ships. Their bomb bays are also filled with five hundred-pound bombs that will be used in the new practice of skip bombing."

"Never heard of that, sir."

"Well, an aircraft attacks a ship by skipping the bomb across the water like a stone. When the bomb is dropped at low altitudes, it smashes the side of the ship with better accuracy."

"The enemy won't know what hit 'em," a man jeered.

Alex agreed. "Pilots will fly in low, and we'll mop 'em up!"

"That's the plan," the colonel said. "I'm meeting in an hour with some of the other officers, including members of the Royal Australian Air Force (RAAF), to chalk up our strategy on the board. We need to make sure this attack goes off like a well-played football game. Every man will know his play, and every man will do his part. Lieutenant Forrest, I have an assignment for you."

"Yes, sir," Alex answered.

"General wants a cameraman up there to make a film record of the show, and I'd like you to go along."

"I'm your man. When do we fly?"

"Tomorrow morning, March 1."

Sooner than he expected.

"I've assigned you and the camera man to a large bomber captained by Lieutenant Dave Bradford. My air force contact tells me he's one of our best pilots, so you should see plenty of action."

Alex hoped the words 'plenty of action' didn't include being shot out of the sky. At least Dave's reputation as an ace pilot preceded him, and that helped.

The planes took off the next morning, in the middle of heavy clouds. "See any transports?" Alex asked Dave.

"Not yet, but they're down there. Pray for clear skies," he said.

By afternoon, the weather had shifted, and word came over the radio from an allied scout plane: "I see them! Slow-moving Japanese transports and destroyers. Go get the enemy, men!"

"We're going in," Dave called as soon as he heard the news. "Hang on." He plunged the plane's nose downward, and the air filled with allied planes dropping bombs.

"I believe the Imperial Empire of Japan has been caught by surprise," Alex said, as bombs crashed into transports packed with Japanese troops heading for Lae. Their ships were ablaze, and black smoke billowed everywhere. "This is a little down payment on what the Japanese warlords did to us with their sneak attacks on Pearl Harbor and Luzon," Alex said above the racket. "My brother Chris was at Bataan, and he's listed as missing in action."

"I'm sorry to hear that," Dave shouted. "I hope he makes it."

"Yeah, me too, thanks."

"The enemy's going to lose this one today, I promise you that."

Alex turned to the cameraman. "Are you getting all this on film?"

"You bet, but I'll have to edit out the footage where my hands were shaking. I've never been so scared in my life. I don't know how you boys do it."

Alex cupped his hands and stared out the window as several PT boats hurled depth charges at three Japanese transports with around a hundred men on board, sinking all of them. Most of the men survived the bombing, and it would be a horrible thing to kill those survivors.

"These guys are within swimming distance of the shore," Dave said. "If we don't take out those boats now, they'll land, join the garrison, and kill our men."

"You're right," Alex said. "We can't afford to be good sports in war, and the Japanese don't surrender."

The Allied bombers and PT boats finished the job two days later, and Alex and Dave attended a debriefing. Alex saw Dave as a brother in battle and didn't want to lose contact.

The colonel said, "The Japanese lost all eight transports and four out of eight destroyers. The allied forces lost three men, and we estimate the Japanese lost three thousand. The Battle of the Bismark Sea was a lopsided naval defeat, thanks to the coordination of the American and Australian air power."

Dave sat next to Alex, and they low-fived under the table, as the colonel summarized. "General MacArthur is pleased and is referring to the Allied victory as a complete and annihilating combat."

The men threw their fists in the air and cheered.

After the briefing ended, Alex and Dave went back to Alex's office and found Norm Nielson waiting. "Norm," Alex said, "always good to see you. What are you doing over this way?"

"Wanted to tell you I've been promoted to private first class and reassigned. Next stop, corporal. Say, who's the new guy?" he asked pointing at Dave.

"Dave Bradford," he said, stepping up and shaking hands.

"Nice to meet you," Norm said. "Firm handshake. You seem like a strong one."

Dave smiled. "Thank you."

"Norm's a good judge of character," Alex said. "Dave here is an army air force pilot and one of the best."

"Do you plan to fly commercial planes after the war?" Norm asked.

"Nope. I plan to go to law school."

"Me too," Norm said. "Solid profession. So, you're brainy too," he smiled.

"What's the army got you doing now, Norm, as a Pfc.?" Alex asked.

"Clerk-Typist at battalion headquarters. Using my brains more than my brawn, and I like that."

"We need men with your smarts," Alex said.

"Thanks, although this morning, they assigned me to grease and take apart a jeep. When I finished, I thought, why not test it out and drive to Port Moresby. So here I am. In a few weeks, the army plans to put me in a school on the identification of aircraft. Maybe I could pick your brain on that one, Dave."

"You bet, anytime."

"Well, I better be going. Got to get the jeep back," Norm said.

"Glad you stopped by," Alex said.

"See you another time." Dave waved as Norm left the office. "Seems like a really good man," Dave said.

"He is. We served in the 102nd together. Norm joined before I did, and he helped show me the ropes after I enlisted."

"Your first army mentor," Dave smiled. "Have you got time to grab some grub?"

"Let's do it. There's a bowl of rice calling my name."

When they sat down to eat, Alex asked, "What do you think about when you're up there in the clouds alone, flying that plane?"

"My gal Aubrey. She's the one that I love, and it's her face I see. It's what keeps me going."

"Do you think she'll wait for you?"

"There's no question in my mind. What about you?"

"My gal Sadie didn't wait."

Dave laid his hand on Alex's shoulder. "The right one is out there waiting for you."

Alex smiled. "Thanks, buddy. I know you're right."

Several weeks later, Colonel Tory handed Alex a brief about a new battle; this one was a big loss for the US Navy. The Allies eventually got the upper hand, but not until the Japanese chose to withdraw.

"What happened to our air support, sir?" Alex asked as he read through the page.

"This was a daylight surface engagement, and our air support wasn't there. It was just the navy against a superior Japanese force. It was sheer luck that our forces managed to escape complete destruction."

"Says here the battle happened south of the Komandorski Islands. Where's that?"

"North Pacific near Alaska."

Alex paled when he heard the location, thinking about Matt. "Sir, do you know if the *USS Salt Lake City* did battle?"

"Hang on. Let me check the details," Colonel Tory said, pulling another sheet of paper from his desk. "Yes, she did. Why?"

"My sister Lucy's fiancé serves aboard that cruiser. Any damage?"

"The Old Swayback took two hits, one of them amidship leaving her dead in the water. Here comes the luck part. She was hidden from the Japanese in the smoke, so they didn't finish her off."

Alex released his breath and asked, "Any casualties listed?"

"Says here two men were mortally wounded and another shot, who went overboard. Reported lost at sea."

Alex's hair lifted on the nape of his neck, and his stomach went rock hard.

***

Hallie had almost reached the Library of Congress when she took a detour to the Tidal Basin. Kay had said that morning over breakfast, "Hallie, you'll find the best view of the spring cherry blossoms at the basin. They're now at their peak."

Hallie had seen the famed cherry blossoms several times, but this spring was something else. When she reached the basin, she stood under the pink blossoms of the flowering trees and breathed in the aroma, enjoying herself. Then she pulled a camera from a large bag and looked across the blue water at the white columns of the Thomas Jefferson Memorial. Hallie framed her shot to include the pink blossoms at the top left and snapped what promised to be one of her best pictures ever. She'd been sending pictures of Washington DC home to the family for months, and Lily would love this one. She adored flowers of all varieties.

Hallie walked over to the memorial and sat on the steps in the sun, taking a rare, few minutes to herself, thinking about her new role. She'd been assigned oversight of the women's work on collateral intelligence summaries. The very idea that collateral intelligence was now women's work made her smile. Her girls would be making trips to the Library of Congress, where they'd have access to such information as the names of ships, faraway cities, or even public figures of interest. They'd be searching for anything that might illuminate the message content they were getting. I feel a little like a spy, she thought, and it's so exciting.

Hallie had always loved libraries, but the Library of Congress made her feel like she was at the university again. She missed those days when life seemed simpler, and she believed everything she read in the newspapers. Not so much anymore.

Kay's girls were working on the electric cipher machine, ECM, for short. It was used to transmit and receive American messages. Hallie and Kay had talked over breakfast this morning about some of the information she'd come across.

"You know what bothers me most, Hallie?" Kay had asked her.

"No, what?" Hallie had replied, mouth full of scrambled eggs.

"The newspaper headlines are filled with how many Japanese soldiers we've killed and how America is winning the war in the Pacific. It's just so much propaganda."

"It's a strange feeling knowing some stuff we read in the papers isn't accurate."

"We're being told what the president wants us to hear. Our incoming messages clearly tell us we're losing the war in the Pacific. Ships are going down, and casualties are high. And we're losing submarines."

"We did win the Battle of the Bismark Sea last month. My mom told me Alex was up in one of our planes at that time."

"He was?" Kay had asked, surprised.

"Guess I forgot to tell you. Did you see the newsreel of the battle at the movies?"

"Just last night."

"Alex flew with the cameraman, and the military declared it a decisive victory. 'Course, our coders are the ones who gave the military the intelligence to make it happen."

"There's no doubt we're winning some battles, but that doesn't mean we're winning the war with Japan."

"You're right. I understand why the government wants to give the American people hope, and this war isn't anywhere near over yet."

Hallie's mind returned to the steps of the Memorial, and she checked her watch. *Time's a wasting. Better get a move on.* She stood and headed in the direction of the library. Her work wasn't going to do itself.

Hours later, after getting a feel for where and how her girls needed to do their research, and doing some of her own, she went back to the offices on the Mount Vernon campus.

Things had changed a lot around there in the past year. The gym at the seminary had been converted to a cafeteria and an incinerator built for destroying classified papers. They even had a pistol range where Hallie had learned to shoot. *Turns out little Hallie Forrest from Utah is a crack shot.*

She took the path in the rear of the compound, which led to the apartment building where Kay and Hallie lived now, called McLean Gardens. It had been built on the former estate of the wealthy McLean family.

When she reached the apartment they shared, Hallie saw a letter from Lucy sitting on the table in the hall. Hallie thought, While I'm living in the lap of comparative luxury, she's on the front lines in the middle of the jungle. My big sister's my hero. Maybe I'll tell her that someday. She smiled and opened the letter.

Dear Hallie,

I'm writing with horrible news! I received a letter from one of Matt's friends on the USS Salt Lake City. Oh, Hallie, Matt is missing. I'm devastated beyond words. The love of my life is gone.

He was standing on deck when his ship came under fire. Matt shoved another man out of the way of incoming fire. He got shot in the stomach and fell overboard. He put his life on the line to save someone else. He's gone, Hallie, he's gone! He couldn't be seen in the surrounding smoke, and he's been listed as missing in action. The letter went on to say the navy thought Matt was dead. I collapsed like a falling building and wept.

My fiancé is dead. I'd give anything to look into his kind eyes, kiss his lips, and hold him close. There will never be another one like Matt.

Miss you,

Lucy

Hallie sniffed and blew her nose with a tissue. As if life weren't hard enough being a nurse in New Guinea, Lucy had lost Matt, her one and only. How devastating.

Hallie wiped her eyes, thinking she'd never had a 'one and only.' She wasn't even sure what to say to men. Her brothers always claimed she was shy, and maybe they were right back then. She didn't date all that much in college. There was little opportunity for that now with a war on—at least not with the kind of man Hallie wanted to marry.

One idiot did make a pass at her in the hall one day, and a colonel smiled and sat on her desk, asking her to make his coffee.

"That's not part of my job," Hallie had said. "Please get off my desk, sir." He'd left in a huff, and Hallie smiled after him. *The work I'm doing with intelligence and ciphers is the highest and best I can do. The getting coffee days are gone for women officers.*

CHAPTER SIXTEEN

Chris walked from the farm along the prison camp's main street on his way to the commissary. The contrast with last year was striking. Back then, the mud had been deeper than his shoes, and bloody water filled the ditches. The air had been filled with the stench of rotting bodies. But now, since the Americans had dug new drainage ditches, Chris was able to move on mostly solid ground.

He couldn't believe he'd been a prisoner of war for over a year. It seemed so much longer. He paused at the new sign on main street, heart beating. A prisoner had named it Broadway, after the one in New York City. At home. In America. Chris swallowed hard.

The Japanese had allowed the prisoners to name the streets and paths at Cabanatuan, so they'd named them after familiar ones in the United States. That small thing gave morale a big boost.

Chris touched his aching tooth, moving it around in his mouth. He'd cracked it biting down on a piece of gravel in a bowl of rice. The Japanese fed the prisoners rice left over from the sweepings on the floors in the warehouse. Even after washing it several times, the rice still had gravel in it. Chris struck his head with a bony fist, trying not to think about his mother's mouth-watering home cooking. He imagined one of her hot buttery rolls with a slice of ham, and his shriveled stomach groaned at the memory.

Besides the rice, the men ate two or three pieces of carabao meat every few days, each one about the size of a big hazel nut, and a few teaspoons of fried fish about as often. Even at that, the food rations were better than they used to be, and the death rate among the prisoners was dropping.

The men still received their military pay, so when Chris arrived at the commissary the Filipinos ran, he purchased bananas, peanuts, a few limes and one coconut then tucked the food into his bag. When he reached the barracks, a few of the men were having a game of cards.

"We're playing poker here," a guy named Gary said. "Care to join us?"

"Thanks all the same," Chris answered, placing his bag on the bunk.

Gary threw down a pair of aces, laughed, and said, "I believe in luck, not God. You like to spout scriptures, Chris. Why do you believe in God? Look around you? What do you see? Suffering, death, man's inhumanity to man. Maybe it makes you feel better to believe, but it's not rational. I have lots of questions."

"I was a pilot before we surrendered. Faith and reason are like two wings on the same plane, and I can't fly a plane with just one wing. Yes, we're here in the middle of fear, isolation, and grief, but the answer is faith."

"Faith and hope keep me going, too, in this miserable rat hole," one of the men said, and others agreed.

"We're gonna die before we ever make it out of here," a solider lying sick on his bunk moaned.

Chris sat next to him on the floor and took his hand.

"No one knows we're here. I've never been so lonely," the soldier cried out.

"You've got us," Chris said. "I know and trust these men as comrades in arms. They'd give their lives for you if they had to."

The men agreed, and a small glimmer of hope returned to the sick soldier's eyes.

"Say, Chris," the barracks officer asked, "didn't I hear that you play the piano?"

"Yes, mostly the organ. Why?"

"One of the Filipino charity organizations over in Manila, with the permission of the Japanese, of course, sent us a small organ to use for religious services, or for programs the entertainment unit runs."

Chris flexed his fingers and couldn't wait to play again. He believed music was one of the highest levels of prayer and could communicate messages of faith and hope. "Where's the organ?" he asked, eager.

"Over in one of the two chapels. Not sure which."

Two buildings at either end of the compound had been designated for religious services. The Catholic chaplains held mass every morning, the Protestants organized Sunday services, and Jewish services were offered on Saturday. There were no services for Mormons, so Chris attended the Protestant Sunday services, and his favorite chaplain was Alfred Oliver. Chris had met him at Camp O'Donnell, and then they'd both been transferred to Cabanatuan. *Can't wait to tell him I can play the organ at church services.*

The next day was Sunday, and he had his chance. When Chaplain Oliver heard the news, he was delighted, saying, "Have a seat at the organ, Chris. Glad to have you aboard." As Chris slid onto the small bench, Oliver said, "I've been meaning to ask you something."

"What's that?"

"We could use assistance in the hospital sitting with the sick and dying, and I thought you might be willing to help."

"Be glad to," Chris said. "The farm is practically running itself nowadays. I'll go over there in the mornings and come to the hospital late afternoons."

Oliver beamed. "Bless you. Now about that opening hymn." He rubbed his hands together.

"How about, *All Creatures of our God and King*?"

"One of my favorites. I'll sing while you play."

When the men gathered and the service began, organ music was included for the first time. More than a few of the men wiped away tears when Chaplain Oliver sang, "Ye, who long pain and sorrow bear, praise God and on him cast your care." The men raised their voices with him at the chorus. "O praise him, O praise him, Alleluia."

Chris's soul was full right up until lineup later in the afternoon. Twice daily, the men were assembled, rain or shine, as American officers took roll under the watchful eyes of the Japanese. As names were shouted out, Chris heard the officer in his barracks cover for the sick man, lying in his bunk, miserable.

Then the Japanese sergeant stepped forward and said, "Now we have slapping contest." He leered. "You all enemies of Japan."

The men froze as the sergeant strode over to Chris and barked, "You, nothing. Stand over there."

Chris did as he was told, then braced himself, knowing what was coming.

"Rest of men, line up here," he said, striking his long wooden stick on the ground.

Chris stood at the head of the line and planted his feet. *We've been stripped of our humanity.* He knew the men would hate hitting him, but they had no choice. When the first prisoner held back and slapped a little too easy, the guard whipped him on the back with the stick and shouted, "Harder! Must hit harder."

Chris tried to stay on his feet while thirty men pummeled him. Then he lost his balance and fell to the ground, face bleeding, broken tooth lying next to him. Chaplain Oliver bent down to help him, and the guard shouted at him, "You next! Get in line." The flag of the rising sun of Japan fluttered above his head. Chris hated that flag.

After Oliver had taken a thorough beating, the men were dismissed. A few of them gathered on either side of Chris and Oliver, lifting them gently, putting arms under their shoulders, their feet dragging back to the barracks. When Chris finally fell into his bunk, he wiped his bloody face with a wet cloth one of the men handed him. He lay staring at the picture of his family, whispering, "I won't give up hope. I won't give up hope. I promise." He touched his mother's face and fell asleep.

The next day was Memorial Day, and the prisoners had been given permission to participate in memorial services for the first time. Chris and the other men wanted to honor their dead brothers, and he made the effort to crawl out of bed, face still sore and swollen.

When they reached the cemetery, he could hardly believe the changes. A few months earlier, the American officers had requested a plan to make improvements to the dilapidated cemetery, and the Japanese had finally agreed. The boundaries of the older graves had been defined and all the ant hills that had invaded the place, destroyed.

Chris spotted a large cross at the entrance and noted that the graves had been built up, leveled off, and the whole area had ditches that held back the flowing stream of water. One of the officers said to him, "Crosses have been erected everywhere with the names of more than two thousand men who died at Cabanatuan."

"The Japanese have even placed wreaths around the cemetery." Chris couldn't believe his eyes. He knew the Japanese believed in honoring their dead ancestors. It's too bad they have so little regard for the living, he thought.

When the men stepped up to the new fence, Chris took the small journal out of his pocket and made a note of the date, May 30, 1943, writing, 'While every man here wanted to attend this special ceremony, only fifteen hundred have been allowed to come.' Chris continued making notes of the service that began with a chorus singing "Rock of Ages," and then, "Sleep, Comrades, Sleep." Protestant and Catholic Chaplains read prayers, and a Jewish Cantor sang, delivering part of the Jewish burial ritual. The Cantor had a resonant voice, and Chris loved his music.

After a final prayer was offered, and with thankful hearts for the opportunity to attend the service, the men marched back to barracks.

Later that afternoon, Chris was stunned when the Japanese provided baseball equipment and allowed the men to play a game. There was no way Chris could run, so he called catcher. After the two teams assembled, they played seven innings, while the rest of the men stood and cheered, smiling, laughing, offering some good-natured joshing. Even the Japanese guards seemed to be enjoying themselves. After it was over, Chris found himself relaxed, a little happy even.

When the prisoners stood for roll call that evening, the Japanese sergeant grinned again. Chris didn't like the look on his face. More torture coming, he thought, closing his eyes. The sergeant said, "We need endurance test. Pick up stones."

Chris and the men in his detail picked up fifty-pound stones and stood in the hot sun for a half hour holding them over their heads. Chris labored under the weight, wavering back and forth, then finally stood strong, looking the sergeant right in the eye, thinking, you won't break me. You won't break me. The burden of this stone hasn't been removed from my arms, but God has made it lighter.

That night, Chris fell to his knees. "Please, God," he pleaded. "I wanna go home. Will I ever get out of here?" An answer came clear to his mind: 'By and By, my son.' A murmur of hope.

Chris strengthened his resolve the next afternoon and went to the hospital to minister to the sick and dying, noting that the conditions around the hospital had improved. Chaplain Oliver told him the patients were being encouraged to help themselves as much as possible. A physiotherapy program had been launched, and it was saving lives. The patients who were well enough were put on work details to improve the grounds and repair the hospital buildings, and Chris was glad that American officers were the ones who handled inspections of all buildings, clothing, and equipment, making sure everything was up to par.

Even the mess halls had hot water to clean the cooking and eating utensils. Chris could bathe more often, and his clothes were cleaner. His morale and that of the other prisoners improved, despite the ongoing torture.

I came to Cabanatuan with malaria. I was tortured and almost died. But I didn't. I'm still here. Dad taught me the highest good in life is not to try and avoid all suffering, because no one ever does. The Japanese control my body, but they will not control my mind. I will look for meaning in my life, I will love my family, and I will choose faith. One day, I'll make it out of here.

CHAPTER SEVENTEEN

Most nights I dreamed about Matt lying dead in the water. Tonight, he turned and looked at me with a sense of hope in his beautiful brown eyes. I sat up, chills running down my arms, pinching myself.

"What is it, Lucy?" Alicia asked.

"Just a dream."

I'd been newly assigned to the 116th station army hospital in Port Moresby and was leaving the field hospital today, excited about my new assignment. Alicia rolled over in her bed across the tent. She'd been promoted to second lieutenant and would take over for me here.

"I can't believe you're leaving us," she stretched. "I'll miss you."

"I'll miss you too, but this isn't goodbye. We'll see each other again."

"We better," she said, voice dropping to a whisper.

Alicia and I had become close friends, and I was sorry to leave her behind. Hoping to lighten the mood, I said, "I bet you're already thinking of ways things could run better around here." I smiled.

"How'd you guess?" She chuckled.

I threw off the mosquito netting around the bed, doused my face with water, and dressed. Just as I threw the duffel bag over my shoulder, I heard a man's voice outside.

"You ready, ma'am?" he called.

I pushed the flap of the old, gray tent aside. "Yes, soldier. Let's go."

"Here, let me take your things," he said, as I hugged Alicia goodbye. He walked me to the jeep, and we drove a couple of hours through the jungle, until we rounded the small hill that overlooked the hospital complex.

"Want me to drive you around the place?" He asked.

"Yes, thanks," I said, seeing several huge huts. "They tell me the hospital has 750 beds."

"Nothin' like our little field hospital," he said, as we drove down the camp's main road, named Main Street. "See there. The generator area is called, New Guinea Power & Lighting." He grinned.

We passed signs for the surgery, mess halls, emergency medical technicians, contagious diseases, and psychotherapy. "This place is huge," I said, amazed. "They even have a Red Cross post and a commissary. And there's a chapel too." That made me so happy. "It's been a long time between services."

When we found the nurses' quarters, he dropped me off, and I thanked him. It looked like a palace compared to the tent villages I'd left behind. The beds had real mattresses and pillows. There were washing machines and separate showers. There was even a flush toilet. I changed into my white uniform and walked over to the hospital. Inside, I found an office with my name on the door. It reminded me of Hawaii and that felt good.

Dr. Herbert Conway, the surgeon in charge, occupied the office next to mine. I had just put my purse in the desk drawer when I heard a familiar voice. I looked up, stunned. Maxine Tate from Tooele, Utah, was standing at my door. "Are you kidding me?" I jumped up and hugged her. Our moms had grown up together in Tooele and were friends until Maxine's mom died of pernicious anemia. So sad.

"When I walked down the hall yesterday and saw your name on the door," Maxine said, "I was as surprised as you are."

"Please, sit down, and let's catch up. My mom wrote me you were with the Red Cross, but she didn't know where. How do you like your assignment?" I asked.

"Love it."

"What are you doing?"

"Our primary job is to maintain troop morale and help with recreation. I hand out sweets, read to our wounded, write letters for disabled patients, run shopping errands, things like that. There are lots of lonely patients who want to talk."

"You always were a caring listener, Maxine. The men are homesick, far away from their families."

"I have to admit I'm homesick too. How about you?"

"Definitely."

She brightened. "Lucy, there's a big Australian hospital in town, so you'll be glad to know there's a social side to our work here. We're often invited to parties held by Australian and American male personnel officers. I've even been swimming and sailing."

When she said the word 'sailing' I was distracted and saddened with thoughts of Matt. As I returned to the conversation, she was saying something about sunbathing. Maxine went on, "A few of the gals even got leave in Australia when they accompanied casualties on medical ships or evacuation flights."

"I've never been to Australia, but my brother Alex has. Maybe someday."

"Is that a ring I see on your finger?"

"I'm engaged," I said, eyes vacant. I paused, avoiding her gaze. "My fiancé is missing in action, presumed dead."

"Oh, Lucy. I'm sorry. I do understand how you feel."

"I remember you lost your husband after being married a year. Such a heartbreak."

"Devastating and unexpected," she said looking away. "But how are you doing?"

"It's so strange not knowing if Matt is dead or alive. It's like I'm stuck in place and can't move forward. I need to believe he's alive. I worry about him all the time. Waking or sleeping, he's in my head and heart."

Maxine held my hand and nodded. "I'll pray for Matt."

"Thank you. Please pray for Chris too. He's still missing in action."

"Your mom wrote me about him. She has lots of faith he'll make it."

"I try and share her optimism. Isn't it weird how fear, death, and disease have become a normal part of our lives? I'm almost numb to it all."

"The abnormal is our normal. But if we think about the war all the time, we lose hope. That's why we need to have some fun. Several months ago, our entertainment parties included female impersonators, and now we have real women, including singers, dancers, and musicians. We even had a movie star here, Gracie Fields. She's a fantastic dancer, and there'll be more like her coming, don't you worry."

"Wow, I can't believe it. I saw her movie *The Show Goes On*. She's a comedian with a beautiful voice.

"Excuse me," a male voice interrupted. "You must be Lieutenant Forrest," he said, walking up to me dressed in a white surgeon's coat, stethoscope around his neck. "I'm Doctor Conway."

I stood and said, "It's a pleasure to meet you, sir."

"I'll get out of your way," Maxine said. "Catch you later, Lucy."

"Wonderful to see you, Maxine. And thank you."

Doctor Conway spent the next few hours introducing me to the staff and showing me around. "We do almost everything here that can be done in any US hospital."

"Impressive."

That evening, Alex came by quarters to take me to dinner. It was wonderful to be living in the same town with family. I couldn't believe my good luck. "You ready to go, sis?" he asked.

"You bet," I said all dressed up in civilian clothes. "It's been a long time since I've dressed for dinner. Where are we going?"

"The Papua Hotel. They have a new officer's club there. I think you'll like it."

"I'll love it. What a stark contrast to my last assignment."

When we got into the car he said, "Thought I'd show you around Port Moresby before we eat."

"Thanks, I'd like that. I hear it's a pretty big city."

"Largest one in the South Pacific, outside of Australia and New Zealand. Port Moresby, also called Pom City or just Moresby, is the capital of Papua New Guinea." He paused. "Listen to me. I sound like a tour guide."

I laughed. "Yes, you do, and I love it. Tell me more."

"Well, Pom City became a trade center in the second half of the 1800s. Conquest of the city has been a prime objective for Imperial Japanese forces for the last year. They've been trying to take the city and cut off Australia from Southeast Asia and the Americas."

"That would be horrible."

"Yes, it would. So last September, Moresby became an important Allied complex of bases, and thousands of troops were staged here. It's been a jumping off point as we've pushed back the Japanese advances. I'm happy to report that we're gaining the advantage."

"I'm glad of that. Has the city itself been bombed?"

"There was a big daytime air raid two months ago in April that included both bombers and fighters. The bombers were escorted by more than one hundred Zeros, and it was the largest force ever to attack Moresby. They flew in at high altitudes, flying in a V formation. Is this too much for you?" he asked.

"No, I want to hear about it. I'm living here now."

"The Australian Army anti-aircraft guns fired a thousand rounds at the attackers. American fighters were scrambled and took to the air, and there were dozens of dog fights in the sky. We damaged several Betty bombers, and while we didn't hit any Zeros, none of them dove down to strafe our ground targets. All our pilots survived and came back to duty, although a few of them had to bail out of their planes."

"Wow. That must have been scary."

"Our air power and defenses at Moresby won, making us too tough a target for the Japanese. We have momentum."

"Do you think they'll attack here again?"

"Not during the day but expect a few nighttime raids. Don't worry, you should be safe at the hospital. Here we are," Alex said, pulling over at the Four Corners of Douglas and Musgrave Streets. "Let's eat. All this talking has made me hungry." He grinned.

He didn't ask about Matt, and I didn't mention his name. I knew Alex was hoping to distract me.

After a delicious meal and relaxing conversation with my dear brother in a lovely setting, I felt like I'd returned to civilization. I slept well that night, no dreams, or nightmares, and woke up feeling energized.

When I reached the hospital, there was a telegram sitting on my desk. It was from Matt's friend. My hands shook as I opened the envelope. Was this it? Did they find his body? The cable was short and to the point:

Matt's back from the dead. In the hospital in Dutch Harbor in a coma. Still touch and go.

"Thank God he's alive," I said lifting my voice to the heavens, tears gushing down my face. I sagged against the wall and then pulled myself together. Matt was in a coma, and he needed me.

Alex was sitting in his office when I burst through the door, out of breath. "What is it? Everything okay?"

I handed him the telegram. "They found Matt," I squealed with joy.

"That's amazing." Alex beamed.

"But he could still die. I must go to him. It might make a difference in his recovery. Can you help me?"

"Sit down a minute, and let me talk out loud, see what we can do. Hmm," he said. "Our best bet is our C-54 skymaster."

"I don't know what that is."

"It's a four-engine transport aircraft that's also being used to fly high-level muckety-mucks and military staff. Colonel Tory asked my friend Dave to take the wheel when we have dignitaries on board. He's the one I flew with in the battle in March. You haven't met him yet, but you'll like him."

"Do you think you can borrow the plane?"

"I'll check today to see if the navy has cargo they could send to Dutch Harbor, and you and I can ride along with Dave as our pilot. Can you get a few days leave? The flight will take about twelve hours. Let's plan for three days total."

"This is an emergency, so yes, I'll make it happen. What about you? Can you take the time off?"

"I can. How about you go check in with Doc Conway, and I'll find Dave. He's always on call in case we need him to fly the staff plane."

"You're the best, Alex."

He smiled and hugged me. "Pack a bag and be here before six tomorrow morning."

"Will do."

The next morning, Alex, Dave, and I took off for Dutch Harbor, Unalaska Island, at 6:00 a.m. sharp. The two of them did most of the talking on the flight. I was tense, often sitting on the edge of my seat, wrapped up in my own thoughts.

Just before sunset, the plane flew over the sky-blue waters of the harbor, and Alex said he spied the naval base, located on the central portion of the island. "This base has aircraft support facilities, munitions storage facilities, barracks, a hospital, and a bomb-proof power plant," he told me. "The United States Navy and Army use it as an operating base, manning coastal defenses on the high ground at the northern and southern parts of the island."

"The runway has only been here a year now," Dave added, bringing the plane in for a landing. "Ever since the Japanese bombed Dutch Harbor last June."

After we landed, Alex and Dave took me straight to the hospital where I hurried inside and found Matt. The gash on his head seemed to be healing, but I couldn't wake him. I talked to him for hours, worried, my throat thick with emotion. Finally, I went outside and waited for Alex and Dave to come pick me up.

"How is he?" Alex asked gently when I got in the jeep.

"He just lies there, not moving a muscle," I said in a faint voice, my face puffy, eyes red. "I'll try again tomorrow."

While we drove, Dave asked, "Lucy, do you mind telling me who found Matt after he went overboard? That was a little over two months ago, right?"

"The doctor said a couple of fishermen found him floating in the water on a huge bomber shell. He had a shark bite on his neck, and his dog tags were missing. They had no idea who he was, but they lifted him on board their boat and kept him alive until they could bring him here. After he was admitted, the docs stitched up his neck and stomach, but no one here knew who he was."

"Geez," Dave said.

"The doctors kept asking around each time a naval ship docked. A few days ago, the *USS Salt Lake City* was back in the harbor, and Matt's friend identified him."

"That's a miracle," Dave said.

"It is, and now we need another one. He's got to wake up."

The next morning, Dave dropped Alex and me at the hospital, then left to pick up cargo. "Before we go inside," Alex said. "Let's stand over there and pray." Grateful tears fell down my face as Alex prayed that Matt would recover.

When we reached Matt's room, Alex whispered, "What's it like to be in a coma? Can he hear us?"

"While he's unresponsive to light, sound, and verbal communication, it's still possible that he might hear sounds around him, like the voice of a person speaking. That's what I'm hoping for," I said, as Alex sat down.

"It's Lucy again, Matt," I said leaning over him. "I love you. I miss you. I need you," I choked, holding his hand, and stroking his skin. "Remember our fun days at the beach in Hawaii? You looked so handsome in your aloha shirt—even when you dropped pork loin in your lap at the luau." I chuckled at the memory.

"Lucy, Alex breathed. "Is that a small smile on his face?"

"Yes," I said, amazed. "Matt … "Matt, come back to me." I gently squeezed his hand.

His eyes opened slowly, and he looked around, confused. I sobbed.

A moan escaped his lips. He seemed to be trying to make sense of where he was.

Alex and I watched as he slowly woke up, trying to focus his eyes, staring off into space. I sat right by Matt's side, holding his hand, praying. When I spoke, he turned his head to hear me, said nothing, and then went back to sleep.

An hour later, the doctor came in on rounds, and Matt woke up. I put my hand up to my mouth and stifled a shout of joy. "Look at you," I whispered.

The doctor leaned over him and asked, "How are you feeling, Matt?"

"My mouth is dry, and everything hurts." Matt shut his eyes.

"You're fortunate to be alive," the doctor said.

"What day is it?" He asked. "Where am I?"

"You're in the hospital, recovering," the doc said.

Matt pulled at his tubes and paused. Then he said, "The last thing I remember is fishermen pulling me out of the water." His head rolled to the side. "It's like I've been asleep for a long time, but I haven't been dreaming. So odd."

"It's given your body time to heal, and it's a miracle you woke up with your faculties intact." The doctor said as he checked Matt's vitals.

"I love you, Matt." I couldn't stop smiling, palm pressed to my heart.

"You're a very lucky man," the doctor said. "We'll want to keep you here under observation for a while."

"Do you think he'll make a full recovery?" Alex asked.

"I'd say his chances are good," the doc said.

"Maybe the navy will discharge him, and he could go home?" I wanted to keep him safe.

Matt said, "In a few weeks, I'll be good as new, and they'll send me back to fight again."

"Do you really think so? You've been injured. Maybe you should go home," I suggested.

"A sailor is a sailor, stitched up or brand new, my darling."

The doctor agreed and left the room.

"I might be wounded, Lucy, but I won't give up," Matt said. "I still have what it takes to push our fight with Japan on to victory."

I had to admire his strength and determination, but I still worried. "Matt," I said, "meet my brother Alex."

"Hey, Alex, Lucy has told me all about you."

"Good to meet you, Matt. Glad you're doing better."

"Thanks. Lucy, when this war is over," Matt paused and smiled, "we'll finally get married." Then he turned to Alex, and asked, "Will you be my best man?"

"I'd be honored."

I locked my worry inside. "It'll be just like the song," I said to Matt, singing the words, "We'll build a sweet little nest, somewhere in the West, and let the rest of the world go by." I laid my head gently on his chest. He smiled and went back to sleep.

CHAPTER EIGHTEEN

It was a hot, sticky June day as Hallie walked the green park path from McLean Gardens to the office. The oaks, willows, and sunflowers are beautiful this time of year, she thought, inhaling their fragrance, feeling relaxed.

When she arrived at the office, Hallie was told the commanding officer wanted to see her. That was unusual. She closed her eyes and took a calming breath before knocking on his door, her smile pasted on.

"Come in," he said, motioning to her. "And have a seat."

"Thank you." She smoothed her blue naval skirt and sat down.

"Ensign Forrest, I understand that besides your mathematics background, you've been taking classes in physics at night for the past several months."

"Yes, sir."

"And how do you like the study of science?"

"I enjoy it." She felt stuck to her chair, shoulders tight. *What was this all about?*

"Are you familiar with Captain William Sterling Parsons, one of our naval officers? He's been working as the experimental officer at the Naval Proving Grounds in Dahlgren, Virginia."

Was the CO considering reassigning her? Hallie had been to Dahlgren once, and it was a little over an hour's drive from Washington DC. She crossed her fingers under the table, praying she could keep her apartment with Kay and commute. "I met

Captain Parsons one night at a social gathering," she said. "They call him Deke, right?"

"That's the one."

"I'm curious. What does an experimental officer do?"

"In Deke's case, he helped develop the radio proximity fuze for anti-aircraft shells. He's got a top-notch mind, and he's been given a new assignment this month as head of the Laboratory's Ordinance Division. That's where you come in, Ensign Forrest."

"What do you have in mind?"

"With your degree in mathematics and growing background in physics," he said, "we're assigning you to work for Captain Parsons. You've also earned a reputation for being discreet which will be essential in your new assignment."

"What exactly will I do?"

"You'll be a junior scientist in the computation group where you'll use numerical methods to solve physical equations. We'll put you in charge of setting up problems for the staff to run on their desk calculators. What do you think about that?"

"That sounds like a new challenge." Now, if she could just keep her apartment with Kay.

"This might be the most important work you've done yet."

"Thank you, sir, I'm looking forward to it. Is the laboratory at Dahlgren?"

"No, and the location is top secret. I can offer you only a mailing address," he said, pushing a piece of paper across the table.

The mailing address had a post office box, number 1663, Santa Fe, New Mexico. Hallie almost fainted as she read the words 'New Mexico,' thinking, I've been living in the East a year and I love it. Now I'm moving to a town in the southwest? *Of course, Mom will love it because I'll be closer to home.*

She regained her composure and tried to sound positive. "My family and I drove to Santa Fe once when I was a teenager. I enjoyed the history and the Native American markets." She didn't want to leave Washington DC, but what choice did she have?

"To be clear, the laboratory itself is not in the town of Santa Fe.

It's somewhere near there, and I can't tell you where it is. You'll find out soon enough."

"When do I leave?" she asked, spirits dropping. It had started out as such a lovely day.

"Two weeks. I have your train ticket here in my pocket. He handed it to her across the table. "Goodbye and good luck," the CO said standing. "And welcome to Project Y."

Hallie left the CO's office, shaking her head wondering, what in the world was Project Y? She went to find Kay, who was standing next to the electric cipher machine.

"Hallie, what is it?" Kay asked. "You're trembling."

"Let's go to your office."

Kay took her by the hand and led her inside. "Is everything okay?"

"I'm being transferred."

"No!" Kay said. "Is it local?"

Hallie shook her head and handed Kay the PO box address.

"New Mexico?! Are you kidding me? What's there?"

"I don't know, top secret. I love Washington, Kay. It's been so much fun, and you're my best friend."

"And you're mine." Kay hugged her. "That will never change, you know that. We've been together since high school."

Hallie nodded, her face white, beads of sweat forming on her upper lip. She was unable to speak.

"It's almost lunch time. Let's get out of here. Where would you like to go?" Kay asked.

"I've lost my appetite."

"Go get yourself some water. You look like you could use it. I'm going to call Daddy and see if he knows anything about this."

When Hallie came back, Kay was just hanging up. "Anything?" Hallie asked.

"He's never even heard of the project. It must really be top secret if the government is keeping it from an undersecretary of state. He said he might be able to stop your transfer, though. Would you like that?"

Hallie started to say yes, then stopped, looking for the right words. It was a tough decision. Her heart wanted to stay, but her head had other ideas. In a voice devoid of enthusiasm, she said, "Thank you, Kay, but no. I'll accept my new assignment. Because it's the right thing to do."

"You never take the easy way out," Kay said, taking Hallie's hand.

Two weeks later, around the end of June, Hallie's train pulled into Santa Fe. She stepped off and spotted a man in uniform. He glanced at a picture in his hand then waved at her. "Over here, Ensign," he said.

He led her to a Ford Woody station wagon and placed her bags in back. A woman in a smart-looking tailored dress was already inside. "Hello," she said as Hallie slid across the seat. "My name's Soni Sandburg." She smiled warmly and spoke in what sounded like a German accent.

"Hallie Forrest. It's nice to meet you."

"You're in the military."

"Yes, I am. You're not, right?"

"I'm from Austria," she said. "I just completed a degree in physics at the University of California, Berkley, and one of my professors, Robert Serber, asked me to come here as a scientist." Soni's blonde hair was piled on top of her head, her narrow blue eyes piercing. She had a smart, self-assured look.

"I've been assigned as a junior scientist. My degree is in mathematics, and I've completed coursework in physics."

"Very good" she said. "Where did you earn your degree?"

"At the University of Utah."

"Are you Mormon?"

"Yes, I'm a member of the Church of Jesus Christ."

"Ah. I'm Jewish."

"My faith has a deep respect for the Jewish people."

"I left Europe because of growing anti-Semitism, Hallie. I think we will be friends."

"I'd like that." Hallie smiled. Then looking out the window, she asked, "Do you know where we're going?"

"Not exactly," Soni said, as the driver headed into the desert. "We'll find out."

Hallie leaned forward and asked the driver, "How long will it take to get there?"

"About forty minutes," he said.

They crossed the Rio Grande, then drove through a red rock canyon where Hallie spotted deer. After living in the East, it was strange to be back in desert country. *I've left near perfect weather for an oven.* As they neared a flat mesa, a sign on the road read, 'Whose son will die in the last minute of the war?'

"That's heartbreaking," Hallie whispered. "I have a brother who's missing in action in the Philippines."

"I'm sorry," Soni said, her voice filled with empathy. "I have a brother in a German work camp in Dachau. I've written him many times and heard nothing. I don't know if he's dead or alive."

The two of them rode in silence, having found something terrible in common.

The car reached the top of the mesa and stopped behind a long line of vehicles. There were MPs everywhere checking ID's and searching luggage. Hallie rolled down the window and spotted a small white wooden security building up ahead with a large sign. 'Los Alamos Project, Main Gate.'

As they waited, the driver explained, "The army took over the Los Alamos Ranch School, which sits on twenty-two thousand acres. There are fifty-four buildings, and twenty-seven of them are houses. That's where the scientists and their families live. There's a dormitory we call the Big House. That's where I'll be taking you ladies."

When they arrived at the dormitory, he got their luggage and walked Hallie and Soni inside. The building looked like a giant cabin with wooden beams crisscrossing the ceiling. The check-in line was long, so the two of them went to have a look around. "Look," Soni said, as they walked the halls. "A library. I'm a book lover," she said, eyes gleaming.

"I like to read too. And see there. Red Cross headquarters." This place might not be so bad, Hallie thought.

Soni yawned. "Excuse me. I've had a long day."

"Let's go see if they're ready to check us in."

When they finally received their keys, the bellman took their luggage upstairs, stopping at Soni's room first. Hallie was just down the hall. "See you later," Hallie said.

"I look forward to it," Soni said with a small wave before closing the door.

I can't believe I'm living in a dorm again, Hallie thought, tipping the bellman. The room was western looking with a queen-sized bed in the center, covered with a red bedspread. "Listen to yourself," she said aloud. "Describing it as 'western looking.' You'd think you came from the East and not from the state of Utah." She chuckled, shook her head, and unpacked.

A few days later, Hallie picked up a paper dated July 2nd, horrified when she read that there were now forty million war casualties across the world. Who could comprehend that number of lives lost? And they weren't just numbers. They were individuals and cherished family members. She wiped tears away with the back of her hand and left the dorms for the commissary.

She stepped along wooden walkways, noticing that American flags flew everywhere. A few children were playing in the street, family members of the scientists who lived here. A little girl with long dark hair and a huge grin waved at Hallie, and she waved back. It was nice to be around children again. They're the hope of our future, she thought.

At the commissary, she purchased her own small flag and several apples. There wasn't much food. The clerk said they had sold out for the July 4th celebration.

When the big day came, it was windy, and dust blew around the streets, as red, white, and blue ribbons waved everywhere. Hallie held tight to her hat, listening to the music of John Phillip Sousa playing over the loudspeakers. Minutes later, the music was interrupted by an announcement over the radio, calling out the names of local boys missing in action. The celebrants stopped in their tracks for a moment of silence.

Hallie and Soni attended a small party, enjoying appetizers that included tiny hot dogs. What was July 4th without hot dogs? Wives of the scientists had baked apple pies, using boxes of prepared pie crust from the commissary. The evening ended with traditional fireworks. As the bright colors exploded in the sky, Hallie couldn't help wondering what next year would be like. Would peace be possible by then?

Days later, the headlines read, "Carnage continues in the Pacific." Hallie sobbed at the news, thinking about Chris, Lucy, and Alex. She sat silent on the bed and prayed, then dressed and went to the lab. She showed the white tag that allowed her into the building because she was a scientist.

Soni looked up and motioned to her. When Hallie walked across the room, Soni whispered, "One of the scientists has been arrested for keeping classified files in his dorm room." Hallie was shocked. What was going on here? All she knew for sure was that the lab was building some kind of gadget. Maybe a complicated radar system of some sort?

CHAPTER NINETEEN

Back in Port Moresby, Alex checked the heat index: 101 degrees Fahrenheit, about right for early September. Sweat ran down his face as he and several other service men crowded around the radio listening to *Zero Hour*, an English-language music and news program produced in Japan and beamed across the Pacific. Alex was tapping his hands on the table and bouncing his head to 'Boogie Woogie,' by the Tommy Dorsey orchestra. At least the music was good.

One of the female broadcasters broke in at the end of the song and in an insulting tone asked, "Hey, Joe, whatcha doing out here?"

"Time to mock the GI's again." Alex rolled his eyes, sorry to hear the song end.

"You boys should be home on the farm getting your chores done and sitting down to supper," she said, then paused for effect.

One of the men laughed. "Guess she thinks we all grew up milking cows."

"Well, I did," another responded. "And I wish I was back on the farm right now."

Alex put a comforting hand on his shoulder, as the broadcaster said, "Or maybe you should be taking in a show, walking down Broadway, sipping a Coke."

"That would be me," another man raised his hand.

Then with a nasty smile in her voice, the broadcaster threatened, "Where we live, is where you die."

The room went silent and one of the new recruits gulped. Alex said, "Don't pay attention to her." He clenched his fist, angry at the propaganda. "I know we're all homesick, and sometimes this crap is hard to hear. But you just wait. We'll be wiping the enemy out of New Guinea, soon," he said, as Perry Como sang, "Goodbye Sue, all the best of luck to you." The men had a good laugh at his timing.

That evening Alex attended a small briefing with Colonel Tory. "Men," the colonel began, "tomorrow, there will be an airborne assault on Nadzab, our goal being to support the Australian advance on Lae. He placed his pointer on the map. "It's here at the head of the Huron Gulf. Lae will be the first target of Operation Postern."

The men listened with increased attention as Tory continued. "General Kenney told me about an hour ago that General MacArthur has decided to accompany our paratroopers on the assault."

Alex was dumbfounded. "Sir," he asked, "is it smart to have our commander in chief risk his life? And for what?"

"Thinking the same thing," another said. "We don't need some Japanese aviator shooting a hole right through him."

The colonel put his hand up for silence as the room buzzed. "The whole idea started when Kenney told Mac he wanted to go with the paratroopers, saying they were his kids, and he wanted to see them do their stuff. That did it for Mac. He said they'd both go. Kenney tried to talk Mac out of it, and you can guess how that went."

The men nodded.

"Mac shook his head and told Kenney 'It will be the first taste of combat for these parachutists, and I want to give them such comfort as my presence might mean to them.' He's right that it will mean a lot to the men." Then he turned to Alex, "Forrest, I want you to escort him on board the plane and fly along with him."

"I'd be honored, sir," Alex said, face shining through the sweat still running down his face.

The next morning, Alex stood with the General, observing that even though MacArthur was sixty-two, he looked like a man of fifty: broad-shouldered, flat-hipped, and slim. As they walked over to board the plane, Mac's steps were quick and confident. He wore a flier's leather jacket Kenney had given him, name tag pinned to his chest and four white stars painted on each shoulder. Alex had never been this close to MacArthur before, and he admitted to being a little star struck. He worried about the General's safety. If they lost him, they were toast.

Seeming to sense Alex's anxiety, MacArthur whispered, "The only thing that disturbs me is the possibility that when we hit the rough air over the mountains, my stomach might get upset. I'd hate to throw up and disgrace myself in front of the kids." Then he smiled, and Alex did too, muscles relaxing. The men fell in line to greet the general as he walked the line, stopping occasionally to say hello and wish them luck. The men had somehow found out he'd be watching today and were glad to see him.

Alex and MacArthur took off in a lead B17, followed by several hundred C-47s, and flew across the tall Owen Stanley mountains. The planes laid down a thick smoke screen so the enemy below couldn't see the men making their first combat jump. Then one of the B17's engines broke down. Alex gripped the seat as the plane rocked, and the pilot suggested they turn back. In classic MacArthur style, he said, "Carry on. I've been with General Kenney when one engine quit, and I know the B-17 flies almost as well on three engines as on four." And so, on they flew, Alex not as confident as the General.

As they reached the other side of the mountains, more than fifteen hundred paratroopers, clutching weapons, equipment, and machetes to cut through the jungle, jumped from the planes. As they filled the skies, the pilot turned and said, "It'll take the men just over a minute to reach the ground." Alex watched out the window of the plane at the stream of men dropping over target. He caught his breath when two men's chutes failed to open, smashing them into the earth.

When the three B-17s that carried the top brass returned to Port Moresby, MacArthur told the crews, "Gentlemen, that was as fine an example of discipline and training as I have ever witnessed." It was an experience Alex knew he'd never forget.

Four days later, Tory told his staff that the Allies had secured the large Japanese base at Lae. "The whole operation was a big success," he smiled, "and we want to capitalize on it. The Australians are preparing to advance on Finschhafen."

"We're not going along?" Alex asked.

"MacArthur believes that the Japanese defending the area are pretty small in numbers."

But the General was mistaken. The Australians sent a request for reinforcements, indicating there were far more Japanese forces in the area than intelligence had estimated. "Now are we going in, sir?" Alex asked Tory when he briefed the staff.

"Don't know yet. My guess is that the US commands will agree to send in a large infantry battalion to relieve the Australians, with no navy. Very risky for them. I'm betting the infantry will make an amphibious assault with cover from the air."

The colonel's assumptions were correct. Alex heard that his old battalion would participate with the troops going in at the end of the month. He asked the colonel if he could accompany them on the next series of attacks. "I admired the General's decision to be with the paratroopers, the mark of a real leader. I'd like to be with my former comrades in arms for this mission."

"Permission granted," the colonel said. "And Forrest."

"Yes, sir?"

"Come back alive. I need you here. See you in a month or so."

Alex saluted and walked out of the office, shaking in his shoes.

The day he joined the battalion Norm shook his hand and said, "Hey, Alex, good to see you. Heard you volunteered to accompany us. I'm impressed."

The rest of the men agreed.

"Great to be with you guys again," Alex said.

"What do your connections at the top tell you?" Norm wondered.

"The goal is to extend the Australian perimeter towards Jivenaneng and establish a company there. End goal is to take Finschhafen."

The next several days were filled with heavy fighting as the men pushed their way through the thick jungle, crossing several rivers and fighting through the kunai grass. Seeing they were outnumbered, the

Japanese withdrew, and the Allies took control of the Finschhafen airfield.

A week later, Alex and his battalion were on a ship crawling along the coast of New Guinea, Norm froze in place and said, "Up there, Alex. I count eight Japanese dive bombers coming for us."

"Man the guns," someone shouted. Alex's heart raced, and he covered his ears as the antiaircraft guns fired at the planes, taking five of them down. The air corps took out the other three planes. "That was a close one," Norm said, and Alex nodded, staring at the Japanese airships all around them. "I hope I never have such an experience again."

"You and me both, brother," Alex exhaled, watching smoke fill the sky. They landed at Scarlet Beach and prepared for another attack.

A few days later, around 4:00 a.m., four barges filled with Japanese soldiers moved toward the beach, their engines muffled. It was pitch black outside and they were close to shore before the Americans spotted them. One man ran around whispering to the Australians and Americans waiting on the beach, "Wake up, wake up. Man your guns."

The men shot round after round at the enemy using .50 caliber machine guns. Alex saw two American soldiers engage a group of Japanese led by a bugler and a couple of guys with flame-throwers. Alex was horrified when an enemy soldier tossed a hand grenade into the weapon pit, and a man screamed, "My, legs, my legs!" The other guy was hit too, but they kept on firing. Until another grenade took them both. Tears rushed to Alex's eyes as he blasted the Japanese over and over with his machine gun, the rat-a-tat-tat echoing in his ears.

When Alex returned to Port Moresby, Norm and the rest of the battalion stayed behind to help build the new base at Finschhafen, giving General MacArthur a solid basis for an attack on New Britain, which was just across the straits.

After MacArthur's troops took Talasea and Rabaul, Hirohito's one hundred thousand infantrymen, who were still in Rabaul, started digging new trenches, putting on their thousand-stitch belts. Alex was sure they would fight to the last man when the Americans came for them. "When do we send more troops to Rabaul?" he asked Colonel Tory.

"We don't," he chuckled. "The Japanese never surrender, so we're going to just leave them there waiting in the jungle for troops that will never come. All those troops want is the chance to give their lives before they are killed or to eviscerate themselves in honorable seppuku. MacArthur is denying them that honor, and it will frustrate the Japanese beyond words."

"So, rather than dishonoring themselves, they'll starve in the jungle, refusing to surrender?"

"That's right. Mac calls it the bypass strategy. It's brilliant, don't you think?"

"Yes, sir," Alex said smiling from ear to ear.

"The Japanese don't see that we're cutting off essential lines of communication and supplies, rendering their defenses useless. And we save American lives."

"Here's to us," Alex said, raising his bottle of ginger ale.

"I know you don't drink the strong stuff." The colonel laughed. "What we're doing is part of the timetable for Mac's eventual triumphant return to the Philippines. The General told me once that while the Japanese are very efficient, it's their rigid image of themselves that will make them lose in the end."

"What do you mean, sir?"

"They can't imagine they could ever lose, and that's what prevents them from planning for that possibility."

"So, we win because the Japanese can't see themselves as losers?"

"That's the long and short of it. When the Japanese are attacked, and they don't know what's coming, we have the advantage. Mac compares their inflexibility to a fist that can't loosen its grasp once it has grabbed something. I've heard him say more than once: 'A hand that closes, never to open again is useless when the fighting turns to catch-as-catch-can wrestling.' We'll get these guys, Forrest. But it's going to take time."

CHAPTER TWENTY

Thanksgiving had come and gone, and November was a rough month in the Pacific for the soldiers and my nurses. Many of the wounded men survived the attacks, but it broke our hearts when our patients didn't make it.

Matt didn't give any hint in his letters about what he'd been through. "I'm fine, Lucy," he'd written. "Don't worry about me."

I got the real story from Alex, who'd told me, "Reports say the *USS Salt Lake City* fought off repeated torpedo plane attacks in the Gilbert islands. It was a rough go."

My face lost its color. "Did the ship take any direct hits?"

"No, but they were engaged in a bloody and vicious battle for three days before the Allies secured the Tarawa Atoll."

"That's so scary," I'd said, voice wavering with fear…

I spent the morning at the hospital scrubbing open wounds, removing pieces of shrapnel, and applying bandages. Then I sat on the edge of an empty bed for a minute to catch my breath.

If Dad were here, I knew what he'd say. His favorite scripture came from Isaiah. "Those who trust in the Lord will renew their strength. They will soar on wings like eagles; they will run and not be weary. They will walk and not faint." I could react with fear or chose to be brave. I got up and kept going.

I passed the bed of a patient who liked to joke around even though a doctor had amputated his hand earlier in the week. Sometimes the choice came down to either laughing or crying.

"What are we eating today"? he asked.

I winked and said, "I'm guessing Spam."

"You mean ham that didn't pass its physical?" He grinned. "Hate the stuff."

I laughed.

"You always like to beat your gums," another patient said to him. "Never stop talking. Me, I'm so bored, I'm completely cheesed."

Some of the men were not seriously ill, just restless. "You're going to like what Maxine and I have planned this afternoon," I said.

"The lady with the Red Cross?"

"That's the one."

"What are you going to do?"

"If I told you, it wouldn't be a surprise."

They liked to talk and kid around to keep their spirits up. But they were troubled about babies they'd never met, parents who were getting old, and friends they'd lost in battle. And me? I worried about Matt every minute of the day and night and wouldn't stop until this war was over, and we were safely home.

"See you later," I told the men and walked on, checking on the patients in all four of my wards. My nurses were doing a good job, no one needed anything, so I went back to my office.

Christmas was just around the corner, and I had something exceptional for Matt. Would he ever be surprised. I sat at my desk and took out pen and paper to write a letter. Matt loved cowboy movies, and his favorite was *Stagecoach* staring John Wayne. I smiled as I wrote:

December 20, 1943

Dearest Matt,

You won't believe who I met at the hospital. John Wayne! He was sitting by a patient's bedside comforting him, and they were swapping stories. He's here doing a USO show. I managed to snatch a few minutes of his time and get this enclosed autograph for you! As he scratched out your message, he told me, "I'm here to entertain the troops. I have no special act but hope to get by on appearances." He smiled.

As if John Wayne needed a special act.

Then he said, "With brave service members risking their lives in battle, it's the job of those of us on the home front to provide encouragement to our protectors overseas." I thanked him, he shook my hand, and wished you well. Then he went to talk with a few more patients. He's an amazing guy.

I miss you, my darling. I want to see you, not just picture you in my head. This war has got to end soon. But no matter how long it takes, I will wait, knowing you're waiting for me too. I wish we could go out to dinner. Do things that normal couples do. You are with me always. We are united in mind and spirit.

I love you,

Lucy

As I sealed the envelope and pressed it to my heart, Maxine walked in with Alex and Norm. Norm was in Port Moresby on leave for a few days. "Are you ready?" Maxine asked, handing me a green and red elf hat with bells on top that jingled. We all chuckled as we put on our hats, then practiced our four-part harmony one more time. I thought we sounded pretty darn good.

When we strolled through the wards singing Christmas carols, many of the men sang along, making it more festive. As we sang, "Joy to the World," my mind flashed home. I could picture our tall white mantle lined with red and green Christmas stockings, fire glowing in the fireplace. There'd be a brightly lit green fir in the corner decked with red holly boughs and ornaments with cheerily wrapped packages underneath. I was hit with a wave of homesickness but carried on.

Our last number was the new Bing Crosby hit, released a few months ago to honor soldiers serving oversees. As we sang the lyrics, "Christmas Eve will find me, where the love light gleams, I'll be home for Christmas, if only in my dreams," some of the men broke down and cried. My eyes filled too. Alex handed me a tissue, I squeezed his hand, and we shared a bittersweet smile.

On Christmas Eve, we had a dinner that included roast beef, cucumber salad, and fresh lettuce. The mess hall had been transformed with local cogon grass and lots of oriental lanterns.

We nurses were dressed to the hilt in our 'best clothes,' stunning in long-sleeved tan army shirts, necks that tucked under our chins, and pants that danced over wool socks supported by large flat heeled shoes.

After we ate, we listened to recordings of the latest records from home, then got ready to watch the motion picture show, *This is the Army*.

Maxine stood and introduced the movie on behalf of the Red Cross. "Warner Brothers claims this is the most important event in the history of entertainment. The music is by Irving Berlin and features both Lieutenant Ronald Reagan and Sergeant Joe Louis, members of the Armed Forces. Other talented corporals and sergeants will be singing and dancing, all in Technicolor. I hope you enjoy the show." Everyone clapped.

Near the beginning of the picture, the indomitable Kate Smith sang, "God bless America, my home sweet home," at the top of her lungs. Those words pierced my heart. There was nothing like being in a war and hearing patriotic words. I gripped the arms of my chair when the film showed actual footage of the bombing at Pearl Harbor. I froze, remembering the very day it happened, beads of sweat on my forehead as a plane caught fire and crashed into the ocean, killing the pilot.

Then the film grew more lighthearted. When Ronald Reagan danced with his movie sweetheart, it made me nostalgic for Matt and our evening together at the Royal Hawaiian. I was crazy for that guy.

Alex and Norm laughed out loud as the male chorus dressed in army uniforms marched and sang, "This is the Army, Mr. Jones, no private rooms or telephones. You had your breakfast in bed before, but you won't have it there anymore." There were comics telling jokes, lively dance numbers, and even acrobatics.

The words of the last song, "We won't stop winning until the world is free," were true. We all stood and cheered at the end. It was a patriotic motion picture that conveyed a sense of American optimism and dedication to the war effort.

At about mid-morning on Christmas Day, still Christmas Eve in Washington DC and Salt Lake City, President Roosevelt delivered a radio broadcast. This was my third Christmas away from home, and I listened intently to the President's message, these words resonating:

My Friends, on this Christmas Eve there are over ten million men in the armed forces of the United States alone. One year ago, 1.7 million were serving overseas. Today, this figure has been more than doubled to 3.8 million on duty overseas. By next July 1, that number overseas will rise to over five million men and women.

I couldn't believe how many men and women were serving in this war. And so many others supporting the war effort at home. One thing was for sure. We were united as a nation.

But everywhere throughout the world, through this war that covers the world, there is a special spirit that has warmed our hearts since our earliest childhood—a spirit that brings us close to our homes, our families, our friends, and neighbors: the Christmas spirit of "peace on Earth, goodwill toward men." It is an unquenchable spirit.

Our Christmas celebrations have been darkened with apprehension for the future. We have said, "Merry Christmas, a Happy New Year," but we have known in our hearts that the clouds which have hung over our world have prevented us from saying it with full sincerity and conviction.

And even this year, we still have much to face in the way of further suffering and sacrifice. Many bigger and costlier battles are still to be fought.

I knew the word 'costly,' was not only in dollars, but in lives still to be lost. There were men in this very room who wouldn't see another Christmas.

But, on Christmas Eve this year, I can say to you that at last we may look forward into the future with real, substantial confidence that, however great the cost, "peace on Earth, goodwill toward men" can be and will be realized and ensured. This year, I can say that. Last year, I could not do more than express a hope. Today, I express a certainty, though the cost may be high, and the time may be long.

Increasingly powerful forces are now hammering at the Japanese at many points over an enormous arc which curves down through the Pacific from the Aleutians to the jungles of Burma. Our own army and navy, our air forces, the Australians and New Zealanders, the Dutch, and the British land, air and sea forces are all forming a band of steel which is slowly but surely closing in on Japan.

The war is now reaching the stage where we shall all have to look forward to large casualty lists: dead, wounded, and missing. War entails just that. There is no easy road to victory. And the end is not yet in sight. For surely our first and most foremost tasks are all concerned with winning the war and winning a just peace that will last for generations.

I shivered thinking about men who'd died on remote islands of the Pacific whose remains might never be found. I hoped that peace, when it finally came, would last for generations.

On behalf of the American people, your own people, I send this Christmas message to you, to you who are in our armed forces. In our hearts are prayers for you and for all your comrades in arms who fight to rid the world of evil.

We ask God's blessing upon you—upon your fathers, mothers, and wives and children—all your loved ones at home. We ask that the comfort of God's grace shall be granted to those who are sick and wounded, and to those who are prisoners of war in the hands of the enemy, waiting for the day when they will again be free. And we ask that God receive and cherish those who have given their lives, and that he keep them in honor and in the grateful memory of their countrymen forever.

God bless all of you who fight our battles on this Christmas Eve. God bless us all. Keep us strong in our faith that we fight for a better day for humankind, here and everywhere.

After the broadcast ended, I went back to the hospital. Mom had sent me a bag of heart-shaped candy, so I put one piece on each bedside stand in the sick ward, wishing the men a Merry Christmas. It wasn't much, but it was something. Most of them hadn't received their packages from home yet including me. I had a card from Hallie that I hadn't read. I'd been saving it for today.

I walked back to my office and opened it. Inside sat a Christmas card decorated with sparkly green and red tree ornaments. The glittery red one had Merry Christmas written in cursive. The card read, 'The best thing about Christmas is family to share it with, whether we're together or just close in our thoughts.' Hallie had included a picture of herself. Her smile brought back memories, and the memories brought back home.

That night for dinner, we ate a small portion of turkey, some sweet potatoes, corn, dressing, and raisin pie, which was quite good. Once again, I hadn't understood just how much home and family meant until I was so far away, for so long. I'd come to love and appreciate my family in ways I hadn't before. And I missed Matt, oh, so much. "Merry Christmas, my darling," I said aloud as I finally tumbled into bed, blowing him a kiss.

CHAPTER TWENTY-ONE

It was a dreary Christmas day in the prison camp. Chris paused a moment as he dressed and thought, I've been a prisoner almost eighteen months. It was unbelievable. He shook his head, reached for the tattered sheet music under his bunk, and said a prayer. Then he tightened his belt another notch around his skinny waist and touched his eyes. He could almost feel the dark circles.

Chris walked to the hospital, entered Zero Ward, and found a particular bedside. The soldier lying there had been shot in the back while trying to escape. He wasn't going to make it. Chris touched the man's arm. No response. Hoping to offer some Christmas comfort, he began singing, "O Holy Night." When his rich tenor voice reached the words, "For yonder breaks a new and glorious morn," the man rolled over with difficulty and seemed to see right through him. Chris stopped, got down on his knee, and whispered the words, "Oh, hear the angel voices."

The tired soldier grabbed Chris's hand and with eyes shining said, "I can hear them. I really can." Then he took a last gasp of air and shuddered, a prisoner no more.

Chris closed the soldier's eyes and whispered the rest of the words:

"Truly He taught us to love one another.
His law is love and His gospel is peace.
Chains shall He break for the slave is our brother,

And in His name all oppression shall cease.
Oh, night divine."

Chris bowed his head, laid his hand on the dead man's shoulder, and said, "This is your night divine, be with Him." Then he pulled the thin blanket over the man's face and removed his dog tags.

As Chris shuffled back to his barracks, he remembered singing 'O Holy Night' with the church choir. Those Christmases were worlds away. His heart broke as he thought about his family, who had no reason to believe he was alive. "All I want this year," Chris said, speaking with the heavens through a shining star, "is to send a letter home."

When he got back to barracks, he read the telegram from the American Red Cross wishing him a Merry Christmas and Happy New Year. They had also sent more games that the men could play in their almost nonexistent leisure time. The men held contests every month to maintain morale, creating wood carvings and doing metal work.

Chris wasn't good at handiwork, so it was his job to judge the next day's contest. "Some of this stuff is really good," he said, turning over a beautiful carving of a bluebird in flight. Chris stopped and wished he were that bird and could fly out of there. He couldn't even imagine what freedom felt like anymore.

1944

Chris marched his gang of one hundred out the gate and into the fields where they dug the long rows of camote sweet potatoes and planted mongo beans. Chris guessed there were about two thousand men working on the farm, always from 6:00 a.m. to 5:00 p.m. They wore no shoes, and they had little clothing to protect them from the sun. Chris held his nose as his gang carried human excrement in buckets, the only fertilizer they had for the crops.

Most of the farm guards were especially cruel, and the Americans had given them names like Liver Lips, Beetlebrain, and

Simon Legree. "Hey, men," Chris said as they marched, "we got Big Speedo today." He was a guard from Osaka and used to be a cop. He was resolute but fair. Chris had even seen him hit other Japanese guards who abused the prisoners.

"At least we can talk and joke a little with him around," one of the men said.

"Yeah, as long as we get our work done," another answered.

Chris led his men in one of their favorite camp songs as they thinned the crops.

"We'll all be back next Christmas Day
We'll see the lights of Old Broadway,
Until then a song of cheer we'll play.
Happy days will come again
Frisco lies just o'er the hill
The USA will be there still
With what it takes to fill the bill
When sailing day draws near."

"The weather today doesn't feel half bad," a laborer said when they ended the song. "I'm guessing only around eighty-six degrees."

"Too bad December and January are the coldest months at Cabanatuan," another groaned.

"At least we have lime salts now to keep down the lice."

Six hours later, Simon Legree replaced Big Speedo, and the men stopped talking. Except one poor sap a few rows over who kept up the chatter.

"The guy's got rice brains," one of the men next to Chris whispered. "He's in for it."

Legree beat the talker mercilessly with a stick until he could no longer move and lay bloody on the ground. Then Legree shouted at the others "What you looking at? Get back to work."

The rest of the men turned to him and bowed their heads several times before resuming their labors. "I'd like to punch that guard in the gut," one whispered to Chris.

"I know. But remember, we can't oppose, insult, or offend the Japanese."

"Yeah, yeah," he said as Legree stepped farther away. "If we break rules the guards can kill us if they want."

"Yep, doesn't pay to push or test them," Chris said. "As the colonel likes to say, put your shoulder to the wheel and do your best."

That night as the men lay exhausted in their bunks, they talked about food. Again.

One said, "I don't even dream about women anymore. All I dream about is food. Gimme some chocolate syrup on mashed potatoes."

Another said, "I'll take whipped cream over a whole stick of butter."

"How about a bacon, lettuce, and tomato sandwich," someone said after a few minutes of silence. The men turned over in their beds and moaned, holding their stomachs.

Another guy piped up saying, "Let's pool our money, buy a grocery store, and never leave."

It was self-inflicted torture, but somehow it helped. An hour later, they all gave up on food and drifted off into another depressed sleep.

The next evening after farm detail, Chris prepared to go to Zero Ward to see what words of hope he could offer the men still there. Only about five hundred men were left in the hospital. The Japanese had ordered the rest of the men to go to work, whatever their physical condition. Lots of them struggled, and some didn't make it. The Japanese were indifferent.

Chris still spent time at the hospital when not on work detail. On his way to Zero Ward, one of the Japanese translators approached him. Speaking in broken English he said, "You skinny and weak, but still, you go hospital every day to help. Why?"

"The men need faith and hope."

"You Christian?" He asked.

"Yes."

"I Christian too," he whispered, peering over his shoulder. "You must tell no one."

"I promise," Chris said, surprised.

"We all God's children. I hate what we Japanese doing here. You help these men and risk own life. Give hope when life hopeless. What your name?"

"Christopher Forrest. Chris."

"Maybe you like Saint Christopher," he smiled.

"I'm no saint," Chris said, "but I won't let cruelty and hatred destroy who I am."

When Chris went inside the ward, a prisoner was saying, "One day is the same as another. You can't tell them apart. This should be the prime of my life, and it's the worst time ever."

A second man said, "You're right. We're scrawny men, sad men, bruised and broken men."

A third man said, "Faith brings me peace. It's how I connect with God."

Chris agreed. "God watches over us, and Christ promises us life beyond death. Our situation in prison reminds me of Job in the Old Testament of the Bible. Job was a just and rich man. Forces of evil tried to take away Job's faith by destroying his property and killing his children. Job was really depressed, tore his clothes, shaved his head, and called on God. But it just got worse, and Job came down with boils. That's when he started wondering why he had even been born."

"Some days I feel that way too," the first man said. "I've asked God why I was ever born to live in this misery."

Chris put his hand on the man's shoulder. "Job came to understand how short life is and how certain we all are to die. He continued to weep and sit in sack cloth and ashes. Even his friends despised him."

"At least we have buddies here who care about us," the second man said.

"Makes a big difference," Chris noted, returning to his story. "When Job reached the end of his rope, he cried out to the Lord, repented of his anger and despair, and prayed for his friends. I think the key for him was refusing to be consumed with anger and despair and praying for his friends. God blessed the end of Job's days even more than the beginning. Job went on to father more children, regain his prosperity and live until he was an old man. As he reached the end of his life, he believed in the certainty of a resurrection."

Chris paused, then continued. "Hopefully, we'll go home someday, recover, and live until we're old men like Job."

The men were quiet as they looked around wondering which of them would survive another year.

Then the day came when the Japanese finally allowed the men to send a message home! But only twenty-five words. The Japanese guard ordered, "You can write every two months, but be careful what you say. No talk about life here," he threatened. "You can also get letters."

Unexpected tears of gratitude and hope spilled from Chris's eyes. He found some paper to write a draft. He wrote, scratched the words out, counted, and tried again. My card might be censored and not ever even reach home, he thought. It could end up instead on the bottom of the ocean on some bombed Japanese ship. But it comforted him to write and send it. He knew it would mean everything to his family if his message got there.

Mom and Dad,

I'm alive! In a labor camp. I can only write a few words. Please pray for me, write me soon.

Love, Chris

That was it. Twenty-five words. He couldn't wait to get a response. If it took forever, he'd wait for it. Chris buried his face in his hands and wept.

CHAPTER TWENTY-TWO

Alex stretched his feet under the desk and wrote a cable of congratulations to the men of the 102nd Battalion. They were his people, and he was proud of their excellent work for the war effort. He'd planned to ask Dave to get the staff plane and fly him the short hour into Lae so he could see the guys in person, but in a few hours, he had to meet with a reporter from *Life Magazine.*

Alex wrote: *My compliments on being awarded bronze stars for your last three campaigns. Well done, men. Norm, you, and the others who'd already enlisted before Pearl Harbor also received the National Defense Ribbon. You've done your nation proud.*

He tucked the cable into an envelope, just as a corporal walked in and handed him another one. "This just came for you, sir."

"Thanks. Take this one with you and get it off to the 102nd, please."

The corporal saluted and walked out.

The return address on the envelope was home. Alex held it in his hands a minute, then pulled out the cable and read: *Chris is alive! In a camp in the Philippines, but he's alive. Thank the Lord! Please tell Lucy.*

Alex leaped from his chair, heart pumping, grateful that his brother was no longer missing in action. He grabbed his cap, ran outside, and jumped into a jeep for the short ride to the hospital.

Lucy was standing in the sunshine laughing and talking with Maxine when he pulled up. Lucy startled when she saw his face and ran to him. "Is everything okay?"

"It's better than okay," he grinned. "Here's proof," he said, handing her the cable. "Couldn't wait to give you the good news."

"He's alive," Lucy squealed. "I can't believe it." Happy tears glowed on her cheeks.

Alex threw his fist into the air. "Here's to you, Chris Forrest."

"We love you, Chris," Lucy shouted, hands cupped around her mouth. Then she asked Alex, "Can you come inside for a minute?"

"Wish I could. Got a meeting in less than half hour."

"How about some dessert tonight at my place? We could celebrate Grandma Ann's birthday. Today is February 24th, you know."

He smiled. "You're on." Alex pulled away, waving over his shoulder. He didn't tell Lucy that in three days, he'd board the cruiser Phoenix and be part of the attack on the enemy garrison at Los Negros. She was happy about Chris and didn't need something new to worry about.

On Sunday, Alex picked up General MacArthur at Lennon's Hotel, and they flew to Milne Bay. After they landed, Alex escorted the General to the gangplank of the Phoenix where he strutted aboard, corn cob pipe in his mouth. "That'll be all, soldier," Mac said to Alex. "Be here first thing tomorrow for my briefing with General Krueger."

As ordered, Alex was right on time when Krueger came aboard and handed MacArthur a sheaf of new G-2 reports, saying, "The enemy has strengthened their garrison on Los Negros. This won't be easy."

"Nothing worthwhile ever is," MacArthur said, eyes determined. Alex heard from the newly promoted General Tory that Mac spent most of that night alone, standing at the rail of the ship, gazing into the dark water, a bright moon shining overhead. Mac had a lot on his mind. This was an important and risky operation.

At dawn, the Phoenix dropped anchor in Hyane Harbor off Los Negros where they were met with a bombardment from Japanese batteries on shore. Alex stood on deck with the *Life* correspondent, who was furiously taking notes. Alex read over his shoulder: "One salvo went over the ship. The second fell short. Men on the deck, expecting that the third might well be on the target, were preparing to get behind anything handy when it hit." The reporter's eyes were filled with panic. "I've never been in battle before," he told Alex. "It's scary."

"It is, and it's something you never get used to," Alex said, hands clenched.

Six hours later they all went ashore as the rain poured down around them. The fighting was heavy. While the GIs on the ground wore steel helmets, Mac just stood there in his trench coat and cap and awarded the Distinguished Service Cross to the man who had led the first wave. Alex stared at him and thought, it's like he doesn't even know he's in immediate danger. Then to his surprise, Mac began strolling inland. Alex and the rest of the staff begged him not to expose himself to the guns.

MacArthur lit up his corncob pipe, blew out the match, and explained that he wanted to get "a sense of the situation."

Alex walked with him until they reached the airstrip. God only knew why the Japanese didn't kill them. When they reached the strip, the General wandered up and down, digging into the coral surfacing to see how good it was.

After MacArthur was satisfied that they wouldn't need to evacuate the airfield, he reboarded the Phoenix, drenched and covered in mud. That night he sailed back to Finschhafen and flew to Moresby, likely to pace his veranda and put in place what his generals could expect next.

"Look at this," Alex said to Tory the next morning. "One of the men picked up some plans the Japanese accidentally left behind at the airfield."

Tory called in a translator, who said, "We're in for a major counterattack in a few days. The Japanese plan is to tap into the American phone lines and use an English speaker to order an American platoon leader to pull back. Their goal is to create a hole in the American lines."

Tory rubbed his hands together. "We'll be waiting for them with heavy artillery and mortar fire."

The next night, the Japanese attacked. During one of the assaults, Alex and the men listened to the Japanese troops sing, 'Deep in the Heart of Texas' while blasting away at the Americans. He'd come to know the Japanese strategy for breaking morale well enough that it didn't surprise him, but their disrespect angered him every time. His body tensed, nostrils flaring.

In the end, the Japanese counterattack failed, and that gave Alex a supreme sense of satisfaction. He flew back to Moresby on the staff plane with Dave, telling him that the win would speed up MacArthur's advance to the Philippines. Dave said, "That might mean we get home quicker."

"I'd like to think you're right." Alex looked out the window, thinking of Chris. Being alive was good. But how much longer could he hold out under wretched conditions? Alex shook off the thought for now, turned to Dave, and said, "Admiral Nimitz's drive across the Pacific, taking the Gilbert and Marshall Islands last month, gets our B-29 bombers that much closer to Tokyo."

"The closer we get to Tokyo," Dave said, "the more likely the Japanese are to surrender."

"I wouldn't count on it. In Japan, they're talking about the war maybe lasting one hundred years. And that doesn't bother them."

"You're kidding me."

"Nope. For the Japanese, their honor is tied up in fighting to the death. When the situation is hopeless, a Japanese soldier is taught to kill himself with his last grenade, or charge without weapons in a mass suicide. The shame of surrender is buried so deep in their souls that I can't imagine what it will take for their leadership to admit defeat."

Dave's shoulders drooped. "I hope the war in the Pacific won't drag on for another three years, let alone one hundred."

"The first two months of this year have been a turning point in our favor, so there's hope."

The following day, Alex was in Tory's office in Moresby listening to him describe the next offensive at Hollandia, called Operation Reckless. That name gave Alex pause, after hearing how high the risks were in carrying it out.

Tory pointed his stick at the map. "We'll make a large amphibious landing deep behind the front lines here in New Guinea. The Joint Chiefs of Staff have directed the United States Pacific Fleet to provide air support for the landings."

"That should help our troops on the ground," one of the men said.

"Frankly," Tory continued, "MacArthur's officers are advising him against it. Including me. I'm not sure we can get enough air cover to neutralize Hollandia. We've been trying to convince the General to land at Wewak instead."

"What did he say to that?" Alex asked.

"MacArthur thinks the Japanese have moved their troops forward to Wewak, anticipating that's where we'll strike. If he's right, that leaves Hollandia poorly defended."

"You don't need to tell us who won that argument." One of the men grinned.

"No, I don't," Tory answered. "On April 22, we hit Hollandia."

Five days after the attack, the Americans scored another win. Tory summarized the strategy for his staff. "The Americans passed the Japanese at Wewak, leaving them to fight their way through the jungle to find us. They didn't reach Hollandia until weeks later. By then, lots of them had dysentery or malaria, and their soldiers were demoralized and starving. We captured the main airfield, and large numbers of the Japanese escaped through the jungle, while others actually surrendered willingly. There are still over one hundred thousand Japanese soldiers stranded at Rabaul."

"So, the General did it again," Alex said. "He put together a plan against the advice of his staff, and in the end, it was the right move."

"Correct, and it was magnificently executed," Tory smiled. "It was a military masterpiece. Hollandia will now be converted into a major Allied military base and will become MacArthur's new headquarters. We're all going along, men, so get ready. One step closer to the Philippines."

Alex had dinner with Lucy that night and told her the news about the upcoming move. She looked disappointed. "I'll miss having you close," she said.

"Not for long, maybe. By summer, we'll have a hospital in Hollandia. Think about it."

Lucy's eyes brightened at the new possibility.

"What do you hear from Matt?" He ate another generous bite of steak.

"By now, the *USS Salt Lake City* is on its way to Pearl Harbor."

"Pearl? Why there?"

"It's just a stopover on the way to California. Matt says they're going back for what he called shakedown trials and gunnery training. They'll be at the Mare Island Navy Yard northeast of San Francisco for a few months. He'll spend some time with his family."

Alex looked off into the distance and said, "He's a lucky man."

"Without going into detail, it won't be easy for him."

CHAPTER TWENTY-THREE

Hallie removed the pink rollers from her hair and dressed in black pants paired with a frilly white blouse. She fit in better with the rest of the scientists in civilian clothes. Once dressed, she ate a light breakfast of eggs and toast and could hear the radio blaring from the room next door. The noise woke up her cat, Whiskers. He stretched, sat at her feet, and purred to be fed. Hallie had found him lost in the desert and taken him in. She loved her little friend.

After they finished eating, Whiskers curled up in a ball on the round rug in the corner and went back to sleep. Hallie envied him. The scientists were working ten to twelve-hour days six days a week. She was exhausted but exhilarated to be building something that might end this long and very bloody war.

Hallie put on her sunglasses, stepped outside, and enjoyed the May sunshine as she walked across the compound. She strode through the dusty streets, looking off in the distance at the mountains and green pine trees. She thought about how much the place had changed since she'd first arrived a little over a year ago. There were two places to eat now, more than one library, a laundry, a veterinarian's office, and a cantina where they could enjoy a soda and lunch. Even the entertainment was good, with stage plays being presented. *The Wizard of Oz* had been excellent.

Hallie moved from Fuller House into the new dorms, built for anyone who was unmarried. She'd never had a roommate here, and she was fine with that. When she wasn't working, and the weather was good, she liked hiking into the hills. The view in the canyons was stunning.

Hallie walked past T Building, which housed Robert Oppenheimer and his staff and the theoretical physics division. It was connected by a long, covered path to the chemistry and physics building. Near the rim of the mesa, above Los Alamos canyon, sat the building where the cyclotron was located. Hallie worked in the tech area, not far from the two-story, four-unit family apartments, which had been painted a dull green.

As Hallie crossed the compound, a voice thundered over the loudspeakers announcing a mandatory tech staff meeting in ten minutes.

After the large crowd had assembled, the head of tech stood up front and called, "Can I get everyone's attention, please."

Plutonium was on everyone's mind, and it was Hallie's best guess that was the purpose of the meeting. What they called the 'Thin Man' project had been abandoned after one of the scientists determined that the rate of spontaneous fission in plutonium, bred in a nuclear reactor, would cause a nuclear chain reaction before the core was fully assembled. A frightening thought.

"There is a path forward," the director said, "despite the plutonium issue. We will still build a working gadget to drop on Berlin. Hitler is working to develop an atomic bomb, and we must get there first. So next July, we're going to drop a bomb on Berlin. Then we're all going home. Knowing we did the right thing."

Hallie was shocked. She'd always heard that the army would detonate the gadget where it would do no harm but be a threat, a show of force. When the Axis saw it, they'd surrender and there would be no more wars ever.

Soni looked at her and whispered, "A bomb on the city of Berlin?"

A man next to them said, "But we'll have peace. No more loss of American lives."

Are we inventing the end of the world?

A few weeks later, Hallie stood at the chalkboard, puzzling out a design equation for the gadget while the men on her team made suggestions. The door flew open, and a breathless man panted, "BBC broadcast. Turn on the radio."

Hallie turned the radio on, and the words crackled: "Thousands of Allied troops have begun landing on the beaches of Normandy in northern France at the start of a major offensive against the Germans. Thousands of paratroops and glider-borne troops have also been dropped behind enemy lines, and the Allies are already said to have penetrated several miles inland."

Everyone sat up straighter in their chairs and listened with attention.

"The landings were preceded by air attacks along the French coast. We have got all the first wave of men through the defended beach zone and set for the land battle."

"This is it," one of the men shouted. "The beginning of the end of Hitler's War. Maybe we won't need the gadget after all."

"Even if you're right," another said, "what about the Japanese? I lived there for five years, and I know these people. They won't crack, even when faced with certain defeat. They'll fight to the bitter end. That, my friends, is the difference between the Germans and the Japanese. That's what we're up against."

The radio announcer described the landing of airborne troops, saying it "was on a scale far larger than anything there has been so far in the world" and that it had taken place with extremely little loss.

Hallie glanced at the calendar on the wall. *June 6th.* A red-letter day for the Allies.

A little later, President Roosevelt said during a news conference that the invasion did not mean the war was over. "You don't just walk to Berlin, and the sooner our country realizes that the better."

One of the scientists interrupted the news conference. "But we did catch the Axis powers by surprise, forcing the Germans to fight a two front war again just as they did in WWI. I predict the Germans won't be able to handle a war coming at them from both sides."

A week later, the army divided up the old Ranch School truck garden east of Fuller Lodge into victory-garden plots. But they had no water to spare for irrigation.

The morning of July 4, J. Robert Oppenheimer gathered the staff. Hallie was always pleased to interact with the head of the entire project. He was a tall, nervous man, who moved with his limbs swinging, his head usually a little to the side, and one shoulder higher than the other. All the women found him handsome with his wispy black hair and piercing blue eyes. Hallie thought he looked like a younger version of Einstein. And he was almost as smart.

He lit his usual cigarette and coughed before speaking. Oppie, as the staff referred to him, knew what the important problems were and struggled with the issues to find a solution, He discussed his concern with the group. Hallie had no end of admiration for the man.

"As you know," he said, "the planned plutonium gun had to be abandoned, and we've been forced to make implosion research a top priority, using all available resources to attack it. With just twelve months to go before the expected weapon delivery, a new fundamental technology—explosive wave shaping—must be invented and made reliable. The implosion method has now been transformed from an intriguing possibility into a difficult necessity. This will require large scale research efforts, and I'm counting on each and every one of you."

A buzz of questions circled the room as Oppie left the building. Then the staff reorganized.

The head of tech told Hallie, "I want you in the implosion group. You'll run the model and design division." That was a big step, Hallie thought, blanching. But another challenge she was eager to embrace.

While an implosion weapon looked like a long shot, it had to happen. Every day that went by, another 220 US service personnel died in the war. At that rate, a year from now, the country would lose another eighty thousand men.

The meetings wrapped up, and the compound was readied for the July 4th barbecue. Hallie was looking forward to more relaxing conversation. Of course, there would be hot dogs, all kinds of salads, and some delicious desserts. Some of the men's wives were excellent cooks.

The day of the party was a warm one. Hallie arrived early, picked up a plate, and started through the line. As she scooped potato salad onto her plate, she peeked at the man standing behind her, wondering who he was. She thought she recognized him from a church meeting she'd attended last week.

'I don't think we've met," he said. "My name's Trent Monson."

"Hi, Trent. Hallie Forrest. Where are you from?"

"Utah. How about you?"

"The same."

"Are you a steno girl?"

Hallie bristled. "I run the model and design division. And those steno girls that you refer to are human computers and very talented women."

"I've insulted you, and I didn't mean to," Trent apologized. "I was told that some of the best minds in America work here, and you're obviously one of them."

Hallie laughed. "Thank you, but I wouldn't go that far."

Trent smiled and said, "I'm not such a bad guy. Give me a chance. Can I join you for lunch?"

Hallie had to admit he was attractive, and he must be smart, or he wouldn't be assigned here. "Sure," she said. "Let's sit over there."

After they sat down, Trent said, "When I got here, I had to take a lie detector test. Is that normal?"

"Yes. We all did. Security is very tight around here. I've even had my room searched a few times. We live under the Federal Espionage Act."

"Did they find anything?" He laughed.

Hallie grinned. "Of course not."

As they ate and talked, she found Trent a bit irreverent and sarcastic, which she liked. He was also passionate about what was important to him and said, "When I believe in something, I'm all in. Across all countries we're losing millions of people a year in this war. Can you believe that? This must stop. While we value the lives of others, our enemies don't. I don't doubt the importance of what we're doing here."

Hallie listened until a tarantula walked across the ground, distracting her. Trent picked up his empty plate, deftly scooped up the huge spider, and threw him back to the desert.

"Yuck," Hallie said. Trent smiled and touched her hand.

The following Saturday, Hallie accepted when Trent asked her to a local square dance. They dressed in their best western shirts, boots, and jeans. When the dancing began, Hallie and Trent formed the usual square with three other couples and faced the middle. As the traditional country music played over the phonograph, their only goal was to have fun. Trent took her hand in his as they promenaded around the room. They had a great time, and Hallie was breathless by the end of the evening. She loved being with Trent in this mountain resort. It felt so natural.

When the party ended, he walked her back to the dorm where he lived too, giving her a gentle goodnight kiss. "I'll see you tomorrow in church," he said, walking down the long hall to the much larger men's section.

Hallie was anxious to tell Soni all about her evening and hoped she was awake. Hallie figured she would be absorbed in a book. She knocked on Soni's door. "Are you still up?"

"Come in," Soni called out. "The door's unlocked." Classical music was playing on her record player, and she was sitting on the bed, a glass of wine in hand. A packed suitcase was on the floor next to her.

"What's this?" Hallie asked, taking a seat at the desk. "Are you going somewhere?"

"I've resigned my position here. I'm leaving Los Alamos and going back to Berkeley."

"But why?"

"I guess someone has to build this gadget, but I've decided I don't want it to be me. We're building an atomic bomb that will set off an explosion with the power of twenty thousand tons of TNT. That's powerful enough to destroy an entire city."

"I don't think we'd ever do that," Hallie said. "We'll set it off outside a city, and the power of the bomb will end the war, because the Allies have it, and the Axis knows about it."

"That's optimistic. The most frightening thing is that the decisions to proceed, and in what way, are not left up to the scientists. It's the politicians that will decide. Every man and woman here owes his/her authority to the President, and Roosevelt has reserved the nuclear weapons policy for himself. That's one man with the power to destroy everything. We have no voice in the military uses of the weapons we're building here. I can't live with that, Hallie, so I'm leaving."

Hallie didn't know what to say. She was torn. Was Soni right?

Soni dropped her voice to a whisper. "We need to be careful what we say here. I have it on good authority that all conversations are recorded. Be discreet, my young friend. I'll miss you."

"I'll miss you too, and I wish you all the best."

When Hallie got back to her room, she noticed that Whiskers wasn't himself. Pus was coming out of his mouth again. The Hill's army veterinarian had told her last week that the cells in the cat's jawbone were dying, a sign of radiation poisoning from tech area contamination.

She picked Whiskers up and held him close, tears in her eyes. His tongue swelled, and his hair began falling out in patches in her hands as she stroked his back. Whiskers died that night.

CHAPTER TWENTY-FOUR

The rain beat down on the corrugated tin roof of the new hospital, and I heard cockatoos screeching in the trees. I'd moved to Hollandia, New Guinea, a beautiful place with its mountains, harbors, and large lake. But we were behind enemy lines, and anything was possible. The muscles in my neck tightened, and my heart hammered in my rib cage.

The hospital was ready to open its doors to patients tomorrow, and today had been set aside for staff orientation. I waited next to my new friend, Lori, a war correspondent who spent a lot of time covering hospitals. She'd been a fashion model before the war and was now a crack journalist and photographer for *Life Magazine.* It wasn't easy being an accredited female journalist, especially in the Pacific.

Lt. Colonel Watson, Chief of Surgical Services, cleared his throat and held up his hand for silence. He described the way the hospital was organized, pointing to a sketch taped to the wall.

"The surgical wards are all of standard size and design," he said, "and are arranged in pairs, with a utility building containing two offices, a kitchen, and a storeroom, between each pair. There's a latrine and shower for each of the four wards, and each ward is equipped with forty hospital beds. The wards are divided into two groups. The one consisting of sixteen wards is in the main hospital area near the surgery and clinic buildings. All patients received on the surgical service will be admitted there."

Watson certainly had a thorough and precise way of explaining things. He seemed a bit stuffy, but I could be wrong.

"The other group, consisting of eight wards, is in the convalescent area. Patients are transferred to these wards in the main area when they have sufficiently recovered to permit them to undergo graduated physical training preparatory to their return to duty."

Men in combat recovered simply to return to action. Unless they were so severely wounded that they had to be sent home, it was back to the battlefield.

Watson finished by telling us there were a total of 960 beds with additional beds in several tents. Apparently, all the buildings except the wards were screened. That meant bugs as far I was concerned. Why not screen the wards?

I'd been promoted to captain before I left for Hollandia, and in my new position, I'd be supervising therapeutic facilities for both outpatients and ambulatory hospital patients. The physiotherapy department and the brace shop were housed in separate buildings, so when the staff meeting ended, I walked over to the brace shop. Lori came along, and what I found surprised me.

"Lori, see that? What they use for splints and belts?"

"Yes, it's as if they cleaned up after an air battle. Look at the plywood, old canvas, and that Japanese red star on the scrap of aluminum."

"It's from a plane, I bet."

"I wonder if that makes our boys depressed or invigorates their recovery."

"I hope it helps them. The usual medical supplies we get through normal channels will be a long time coming. This is a primitive area without railroads, highways, and shipping facilities." I shook my head. "We'll have to make do with what we have while I investigate ways to improve the supply chain."

"You know what, Lucy," she said. "You're optimistic even when life is darkest. You're a smart leader who is genuine and accepting of others."

"Thank you," I smiled. "Faith and hope are the two crutches I lean on every day. I admire your skill as a journalist."

"Thanks for the compliment."

"I'm glad we're here serving together."

"Me, too, friend."

I waved goodbye and told Lori I'd see her later. Then I went back to the barracks. There were desks and bureaus for our belongings, and our beds were couches with netting to keep the bugs out. We had showers but needed to use our helmets to take a bath. The facilities were bigger and better than the last field hospital where I worked but not nearly as nice as Port Moresby. The good news? We weren't far from the New Guinea Beaches. I sat down to write a letter to my parents.

July 31, 1944

Dear Mom and Dad,

I hope all is well at home. I arrived last week in Hollandia, Dutch East Indies with the 27th General Hospital. It's the furthest forward of all general hospitals in the Southwest Pacific Theater. But don't worry, we're well protected.

I hoped I was right.

The food here is fine, but repetitious. I haven't been very hungry lately. It's just been so hot and humid. I do like the nurses I'm supervising.

You know, it's funny. When I left home all I wanted was something new. And now, after so much change, I wish I could just come home. But we still have a job to do here.

My mind flipped for a minute between my old life and my new one. I grew suddenly still, astonished at the change. I was an officer/supervisor and engaged to my soul mate. Who would ever have guessed? Not me.

Alex will arrive at the end of August. It means a lot to both of us that we'll be stationed in the same area again. He, however, will live in one of the quarters that have been built on the top and sides of the tall hill between the blue waters of Lake Sentani and the sea. General MacArthur will move in soon too, and his family will follow.

Alex told me what a posh place MacArthur's headquarters is. He said that the commander in chief will have a home here 'befitting his rank.' Alex said some of the aides had installed rugs and furniture sent up from Australia.

Sounds nice to me. Some of the men here have been complaining because he'll be the only officer in the Pacific who has the privilege of having his family with him.

I've made a new friend named Lori. She and I are going to the beach for a picnic now, so I'll write again soon. Hugs to Lily.

Love,

Lucy

A few hours later, Lori and I sat next to a large bay. The beach was wide, sandy, and beautiful with its green palms waving overhead. It reminded me of Hawaii, which I still missed. I gazed out over the water and could see a white egret. Matt would love it here. Lori had brought along a simple meal for us of beef in a tin, papaya, pineapple, beans, and cucumbers. She liked to eat healthy.

I said, "Did you know that we've just about beaten the mosquito here? A very big deal."

"What do you mean?" Lori asked.

"Malaria has been almost as tough an enemy as the Japanese, and our medical teams and scientists have now reduced its punch against our troops. Besides saving lives, Alex tells me that the threat of mosquitos and malaria is no longer given serious attention when planning tactical operations. The Japanese haven't been so lucky."

Lori made notes. "This might make a good story," she said. "Do you think Alex would mind?"

"I'll ask him."

"Thanks."

When we finished eating, we waded in the ocean, laughed, and splashed in the water We knew there were warships out there somewhere, but just for today, it didn't seem to matter much.

We came ashore, and Lori suggested we see a few of the landing strips. We climbed into a jeep and took off, stopping at several. Every landing strip we found was littered with wrecked Japanese Zeros. Lori took lots of photographs. I gazed up at the mountains, thinking about the Japanese soldiers still hiding out there. I felt sorry for them, really. They were cut off, had nowhere to go, and refused to surrender.

When we reached headquarters, I found a letter waiting from Matt. The USS Salt Lake City had docked in the San Francisco Bay area for repairs during the month of June, and he'd had time to see his family. The letter sounded like he hadn't eaten much or slept well. Peace eluded him when he returned to the house where he grew up. He still missed his mom.

I reached for a tissue.

Matt was the kind of guy who did everything at full throttle, and he was successful at what he did. But he managed his emotions by toughing them out. I wished I could be there with him. Sit next to him, brush his hair out of his face, kiss his lips and then hold him tight. He told me he loved the way I took care of him. And I loved the way he cared for me.

***

Alex sat in his office in Port Moresby reading over a communique General MacArthur had issued on D-Day in the European theatre. He highlighted the strategic importance of the Hollandia-Aitape operation, writing:

"We have seized the Humboldt Bay area on the northern coast of Dutch New Guinea, and our ground troops have landed at Aitape, Hollandia.

"We are pushing forward to secure the local airfields. Our feints over the past weeks apparently deceived the enemy into concentrating the mass of their forces forward into those areas, thus leaving the vital sector of Hollandia vulnerable and making possible our surprise movement to his rear."

Mission accomplished, Alex thought, reading on, relaxing in his chair.

"The enemy army is now completely isolated, with its communication and supply lines severed. Its present strength is estimated at sixty thousand. The total remaining forces of these two armies, which are now themselves surrounded, are estimated at one hundred and forty thousand. Since the start of the campaign, they have lost 110,000 men, 44 percent of their original strength of a quarter of a million, and the remainder is now neutralized and strategically impotent."

The allies were winning. We didn't start this conflict, Alex thought. The Japanese did. But we'll be the ones to finish it. It was beginning to dawn on them that their sad fates were sealed. MacArthur was a great general. He wasn't a perfect man, and there were some who found him arrogant, but Alex liked him.

Alex cleaned out his office and paused to take a last look. Tomorrow he'd board a plane to Hollandia. Port Moresby was behind him now, and he looked forward to seeing Lucy. Alex hoped she was adjusting to life in Hollandia. He was, after all, the one who'd suggested that she request the new assignment.

Lucy is always open to new challenges, and she's a first-rate supervisor, he thought. With Hollandia being the new front of the war, they'd need her skills at the hospital.

Growing up, Alex hadn't been as close to Lucy as he was to Hallie. But now, after shared wartime experiences, they could talk about anything and usually did. No one could make him laugh like she did.

Alex closed his office door for the last time and walked into the staff briefing room for a meeting of the top-secret project called Musketeer II. The objective was to seize the Central Luzon area in the Philippines and establish bases for further operations against Japan. Seizing Leyte would divide the Japanese forces in the Philippines.

As they waited for MacArthur, General Tory turned to Alex and said, "Did I tell you that less than a week ago now, on July 26 to be exact, General MacArthur went to Pearl Harbor to discuss future plans for the war in the Pacific with Admiral Nimitz?"

"No, you didn't," Alex said.

"MacArthur had no idea that the President of the United States would be there."

Alex's eyes widened as he listened to Tory, thinking that he, Alex, was only about two degrees of separation from the President of the United States. He could never have imagined that when he was back in Utah playing basketball.

Tory went on. "President Roosevelt invited MacArthur and Admirals Halsey and Nimitz to dinner. After eating, the president pulled out a map and, pointing to Leyte, apparently said, "Well, Douglas, where do we go from here?"

"No better man to answer that question," Alex said, knowing it wouldn't be long before MacArthur kept his promise to return to the Philippines.

Just as he finished that thought, MacArthur himself walked into the room, and the men all sat up straighter, anxious to hear what he had to say.

"The Philippines," MacArthur said, "is American Territory where our unsupported forces were destroyed by the enemy. Practically all the seventeen million Filipinos remain loyal to the United States and are undergoing the greatest privation and suffering because we have not been able to support or succor them. We have a great national obligation to discharge."

The next day, Alex and General Tory flew with Generals Kenney and MacArthur to new headquarters in Hollandia. Alex's tension was apparent as they boarded the plane, and like a fly on the wall, he heard General Kenney describe their descent into Hollandia.

"See how the deep green hills of central New Guinea form a backdrop of peaks, ravines, and jungle growth that is almost unreal. Little cone-shaped green islands, with native houses on stilts cling to their shores and dot the lake. And look there, behind the camp and perhaps two miles away, a five-hundred-foot waterfall seems to spring out of the center of Cyclops Mountain, dark and forbidding, with its crest covered with black rain clouds."

Kenney is quite poetic, Alex thought. Who knew?

A few weeks later, he heard some of the troops call MacArthur's headquarters "Dugout Doug's White House" referring to his "fabulous villa overlooking dreamy Sentani." Some of them were so angry, they even canceled their war-bond purchases. They had no idea how much MacArthur had sacrificed to win the advantage in this war. Alex shook his head and remembered one of Abraham Lincoln's favorite statements: "You can please some of the people all of the time, you can please all of the people some of the time, but you can't please all of the people all of the time."

CHAPTER TWENTY-FIVE

Chris couldn't believe he'd been rotting in solitary since July. It seemed longer than six weeks, and he'd marked each passing day off on the wall. The Japanese referred to solitary as the sweat box. Chris was trapped in a tiny bamboo cell that was meant to sweat the truth out of him. His arms were heavy and his chest tight as he moaned in despair.

Chris doubted that he could even stand up now, after sitting in an uncomfortable squat position for so long, and he had horrible sores on his legs from the hard bamboo floor. When he slept, which wasn't well, he had trouble closing his eyes. That had started even before he was thrown into solitary. It was like he always needed to be on high alert, wondering when a guard might bang on his door. That's when the nightmares started.

During the day, Chris read from his Bible, courtesy of small beams of light that came through the tiny boards in his cell. He'd had dysentery for a week now, so the floor was filthy and slick, and the stench sickened his stomach. He tried to take heart, but he didn't know how much longer he could survive this way.

Chris closed the Bible and rocked back and forth. He remembered how hopeful he'd been at the beginning of the year after the Japanese relaxed the rules, and he could contact his family. He'd received a letter every week since then, and that's how he'd kept hope alive. That stopped when he was placed in solitary. Chris suspected that the Japanese guards had torn up the letters when they came in and thrown them away. He stared off into space, seeing nothing.

Food was more plentiful last January too. Then life changed for the worse around June. The Japanese cut the rice rations down by about a third. Eventually even the commissary shut down, and the cases of men with malnutrition went up. Chris knew the American officials had complained to the Japanese. But they turned a deaf ear and did nothing. The more they believed they might be losing the war, the worse they treated the prisoners.

The Filipino Red Cross in Manila tried more than once to get permission from Japanese headquarters to supply the camp with sorely needed food and medical supplies, but permission never came. The Americans and Filipinos responded by setting up an underground to bootleg small amounts of food and medicine into the camp.

Chris and many of the other prisoners built traps to capture and eat birds, and they also stole seeds and added them to the gardens. Desperation was the order of the day.

Then in the summer, the guards caught about sixteen Americans and several Filipinos stealing seeds. Chris was among them. He and his buddies were horribly beaten and thrown into solitary, that dark, lonely sweat box. Chris didn't know what had happened to the Filipinos, but he guessed they'd been executed for trying to help. Chris shuddered at the thought and moaned again.

His mind tried to escape the sadness that he feared might cost him all hope. His vision blurred for a moment, and his body felt cold. His mind went to Hemmingway's *For Whom the Bell Tolls*. He'd read it not long before he joined the service. Chris thought about the loss of innocence in war and understood it in a way he never had before. He realized that loss happened on both sides of the equation, for the prisoners and the guards. Chris had come to place an even higher value on the precious nature of human life since he'd been confined. He wanted to live so that his life mattered. It would never be about money or fame for him.

Chris opened his Bible and read again from the book of Job. Chris believed that God would save him in the end, like he did Job. Chris prayed that his own story wasn't over. Then he lapsed into a coma. The next day, he was released from solitary and sent to the hospital.

It wasn't until early October that Chris began to recover. Physically he was doing better, but the nightmares continued. A few of the other prisoners came to visit. The prisoners up at camp number one had rigged up a secret radio that they tuned in to San Francisco radio station KGEI. They'd been getting news about the war for some time. "The Japanese are being badly beaten here in the Pacific," one of the prisoners whispered to Chris. "We think that's the reason they're starting to empty the camp and send us to Japan. The word around here is that we're going to be exchanged for Japanese soldiers the Americans are holding. Then we'll get to go home!"

"I'm happy for you," Chris said, still weak.

"You just keep getting better, buddy," one of the other men said. "And before you know it, your turn will come to get out of this hell hole."

"I hope you're right," Chris said with a feeble smile. "Best of luck to you, men." He shook each man's hand.

After they left, he looked up at the ceiling, closed his eyes and prayed that he would be sent to Japan too. A voice came to his mind saying, "You won't be going to Japan." Chris opened his eyes wide. What did God have in mind for him? Was he going to die? He had no idea. Chris put himself in God's hands and went back to sleep.

***

Hallie was still living in the middle of nowhere in her own kind of camp at Los Alamos. She pressed her lips together and wrinkled her nose, head shaking lightly. She was growing tired of all the gossip in this small community of scientists and their families, and several cliques. The best thing about living there was Trent Monson. Hallie and Trent had been dating steadily for a couple of months. Being with him felt natural. And since they were both scientists on the implosion project, they had lots to talk about.

Hallie missed her work in Washington DC, though, and her friend Kay. She'd loved the coding she'd done there with its clear-cut benefits to the war effort. Here, she felt more conflicted, weighing over and over the pros and cons of building an atomic bomb.

Hallie had tried to examine the question from all sides and wasn't any closer to producing the right answer, if there even was one. She understood that the work the scientists did here, if it succeeded, would end World War II with Japan. But the whole idea of the bomb's potential gave her stress headaches. She often thought about Soni's decision to leave the lab at Los Alamos because the 'gadget' the scientists were creating might not just end the war. It also had the potential to destroy all humanity.

Hallie was harboring a secret she couldn't share with anyone she knew, besides Trent. She certainly couldn't tell her family, the people she loved and trusted most in the world. A few days earlier, she'd written a private letter home that mentioned nothing about the bomb, and the censors had still given it back to her, placing their comments in the margins. She had to make changes and rewrite it.

Hallie had grown up with the belief that secrets were destructive and that the truth would set her free, but there were no easy answers to this dilemma. Her commanding officer told her, "Hallie, if this works, we can not only end this war but every other war." But at what cost, she wondered.

When Hallie left the dorms that day for the labs, she found a letter waiting for her at the front desk. It was from Kay. Hallie sat down in a chair in the lobby and read it.

Dear Hallie,

I still miss you here in Washington DC. Daddy has told me about what's going on at the labs in New Mexico. Knowing you, I'm guessing you might be having mixed emotions about the work you're doing. Let me tell you about the intelligence we've been getting about what the Japanese are doing to our prisoners of war, now that they can see they're losing. None of this information will be secret for long.

The Japanese are beginning to empty the prisoner of war camps and ship the men to Japan to be used as slave labor. I pray that your brother Chris can stay at Cabanatuan. He's safer there, at least for now.

Hallie trembled. Chris was alive but maybe not for long. Then her nostrils flared. It wasn't just her brother. What about all the other brothers, fathers, and sons who'd died or were still in harm's way because the Japanese had started this stupid war when they bombed Pearl Harbor? They were the aggressors, not the United States.

The prisoners have been conned into believing that they will be exchanged for Japanese prisoners being held by the American forces. The men think they're going home. No such luck. Instead, the men are being packed into ships so tightly that dozens of them are suffocating from the heat and lack of oxygen. Most of them have dysentery, and if they die their bodies will be casually thrown over the side. The mortality rate on these ships is reportedly over 70 percent.

I'm also sorry to tell you that we've gotten intel about the Japanese planning to kill the prisoners in some of the camps. When they get ready to leave, and they don't know what to do with the prisoners of war, they'll just kill them.

If Chris wasn't sent to Japan as slave labor, he may be shot if the Japanese surrendered at Cabanatuan. Hallie bared her teeth and cracked her knuckles. She quaked with rage at the enemy. Japanese soldiers were behaving like inhumane animals who cared for only themselves.

Hallie, the Emperor of Japan will never surrender without an incredible show of force. Please never doubt that you're doing the right thing for our country. Daddy told me that on average, 220 US Service personnel die every day. That's every day, Hallie. It adds up to over 6,600 in a month, and that doesn't include our boys who have been wounded or disabled.

Hallie did the math in her head. If using the gadget could shorten the war by even six months, it would save almost forty thousand American lives. In a year, almost eighty thousand lives would be spared. The empire of Japan had already been at war with China since 1937, when China resisted the expansion of Japanese influence into its territories. That was seven years ago.

The war in the Pacific had been going on for three years. Hallie estimated that in another four years, three hundred and twenty thousand more American lives would be lost. That was unacceptable.

Japan believed their divine destiny was to rule the world. The emperor had to be stopped. Sadly, it might take something literally explosive to force him to surrender. Hallie no longer felt conflicted as she finished Kay's letter.

I admire you, Hallie. I always have. You're smart, you're brave, and you can do this.

Your friend,

Kay

Hallie folded Kay's letter and put in her pocket. Hallie missed her days as a code breaker when life was more certain, and she wasn't faced with the worst kind of moral dilemma. She stood, left the lobby, and walked back to her work on the implosion project.

CHAPTER TWENTY-SIX

It was dawn as Alex gazed out the window at the huge convoy of combat and amphibious vessels anchored below in Hollandia's blue waters. He'd never seen so many ships in one place. He stood tall, a knowing smile on his face. The high command in the Pacific had been orchestrating this promised return to the Philippines for two years. It was go time.

There was lots to be done between now and when the order was called for the ships to leave for Leyte. Minesweeping task groups had been working for the past two days, and Alex trusted they'd found them all. But there were no guarantees.

When he reached General Tory's office, the general was on the phone but waved Alex in. He sat waiting, listening to a one-sided conversation. Even at that, it was obvious that weather might be a concern when the ships landed. "A typhoon?" Tory asked. "Headed toward the Leyte Gulf area in the next few days. I see, yes."

They weren't leaving for two days, and Alex knew it would take another few days to reach their objective. They could only hope the typhoon would be over by then because that kind of weather could be fatal to the operation.

Monday, October 16, MacArthur led his staff aboard the cruiser *USS Nashville*. He was in high spirits. "Only a year earlier," he said, "you were bogged down in the humid, filthy, sweltering swamps of New Guinea, fifteen hundred miles away from the nearest Filipino."

And now, we're on a ship ready to take back the Philippines.

At exactly sixteen hundred hours, the order was given, and the convoy sailed. Alex spent a sleepless night in his bunk, tossing and turning, heart pounding. While this was a red-letter day, and he was excited, the mission was dangerous.

The next day the convoy crossed the equator without any issues and Alex participated with the men in both battle drills and abandon ship drills that took a good part of the day. They had to be prepared for anything. While they drilled, the ship made timely progress toward the objective.

That afternoon, Alex met with the rest of the staff as Tory reviewed the role of the ground forces. "In the next two days," he said, "the first assault begins. The 6th Ranger Infantry Battalion will land under the protection of naval gunfire and take the small islands here," he pointed to the map, "that guard the entrance to Leyte Gulf. The men will place harbor lights on Homonhon Island and the northern tip of Dinagat Island to guide the safe passage of the convoy into the gulf."

A man next to Alex whispered, "If people at home only knew what went into planning a flawless operation like this."

"I know," Alex smiled. "When they watch the landing on the movie newsreels, it will all seem like it just magically came together."

His thoughts drifted to Lucy. Ten days after the scheduled landing at Leyte, Lucy and twenty-six other nurses, part of the first and second field hospitals, would leave New Guinea and come to the Philippines. With any luck, the enemy would mostly be contained by then. But it could be a hazardous mission for the nurses.

The night before the scheduled attack, the tension on board the ships ran high. Alex could almost make out the shoreline in the distance. He listened as evening prayers came over the radio. The prayers helped lessen his fear until he heard a few men across the room wondering out loud if this was the administration of their last rites. During the night, destroyers nearer the shore shelled the Japanese forces on land.

The convoy reached its destination just before midnight. It was black outside, and there was no moon in the sky. All lights on the ships had been shut off, so they wouldn't be visible to the Japanese. Alex passed by MacArthur's quarters and could see him from the open door. The General was reading from the Bible. Alex stopped and heard him mutter, "I pray that a merciful God will preserve each one of those men on the morrow."

In the early hours of October 20, 1944, Alex scribbled in his journal: *We entered the calm, glassy waters of Leyte Gulf. General MacArthur has chosen to call this A-day, to match D-Day, the landing on the beaches of Normandy. The typhoon ended about a week ago, which was welcome news.*

Alex put his pen down at the sounds of reveille, thinking about the men on board the transports dressing in the holds by the red lights. This was it. There was almost no talking as the men sat on the bunks and checked their weapons. Others went to find the chaplains, Alex included.

He asked the chaplain to pray specifically for the men of the 102nd. They were part of the Sixth Army and had been ordered to take and set up beachheads in the Dulag and Tacloban areas to secure airfields for naval and air bases. When the chaplain finished his prayer, Alex offered a silent prayer for his buddies.

Then he went up top as General MacArthur handed ear plugs to now President Sergio Osmeña of the Philippines and a few others. Alex put in his own ear plugs as the battleships and cruisers started a fierce barrage. He watched smoke plumes coming from the shore and heard the thunder of the battleships. MacArthur peered through binoculars as the battle began.

At 0900, the battleships stopped firing, and the cruisers and destroyers moved in closer to the shore. The transports assumed their positions, ready to evacuate their cargoes of men and munitions. Alex watched as men and tanks poured from the bellies of the ships and onto the beaches at Leyte. He was amazed that these relatively new landing ships could facilitate amphibious assaults on almost any beach. The fifth cavalry was one of the first to reach the beaches.

A few hours later, General Tory observed, "We're not encountering much opposition from the Japanese. Looks like resistance is light."

Admiral Kinkaid called Tory over the ship's phone moments later, saying, "The execution of the plan is as nearly perfect as any commander could desire."

After an early lunch in his cabin, General MacArthur came back on deck wearing a newly pressed khaki uniform, sunglasses, and his usual field marshal's cap. Then at 1:00 pm, he called for his landing craft.

Tory, asked, "Are you sure, sir?"

"Yes, I'm ready."

"Get the General's landing craft," Tory ordered and then turned to Alex. "You and I will go too."

The invasion had been going on for four hours when MacArthur climbed down a ladder to a barge, his staff and war correspondents following him aboard. The coxswain stopped at the transport John Land to pick up Osmeña.

Alex had made sure the reporters and cameramen were waiting on shore to capture this historic moment. As they moved closer, Alex could still hear mortar and small-arms fire coming from the highway leading to Tacloban and the hills nearby.

MacArthur turned, saluted Osmeña, and said, "You are home at last."

He smiled. "Yes, General."

As the Nashville's launch neared the beach south of the city of Tacloban, one of the men reported to Alex that the launch wouldn't be able to get close enough to shore to allow for a dry landing.

Alex told one of MacArthur's aides to radio the beachmaster and ask for amphibious craft to take MacArthur's party the rest of the distance to dry land. He did just that, and when the aide came back, he said, "The beachmaster wasn't very helpful. He's consumed with hundreds of landing craft unloading amid incoming sniper fire. He said, "Let 'em walk."

Alex was upset until he realized what a great picture the cameramen could get of the General wading ashore.

A grim looking General MacArthur with President Osmeña and General Kenney following closely behind, waded in water up to their knees. CBS correspondent Bill Dunn and Staff Sergeant Francisco Salveron accompanied them.

Alex waded in behind, knowing it wouldn't be appropriate to be in the picture. He handed MacArthur the radio telephone for his speech then stepped away, listening as General MacArthur spoke:

"People of the Philippines, I have returned. By the grace of Almighty God, our forces stand again on Philippine soil. The hour of your redemption is here. Rally to me. Let the indomitable spirit of Bataan and Corregidor lead on. As the lines of battle roll forward, rise, and strike. For your homes and hearths, strike. For future generations of your sons and daughters, strike! In the name of your sacred dead, strike. Let no heart be faint, let every arm be steel. The divine guidance of God points the way. Follow in His name to the Holy Grail of righteous victory."

Alex's spirits soared.

That first afternoon on Red Beach there were still snipers tied in the trees or piled into 'octopus traps,' Japanese foxholes. Alex could hear the enemy soldiers, again shouting insults in broken English: "Surrender, all is resistless!" and "How are your machine guns feeling today?" The Japanese were going down.

MacArthur climbed into a jeep and went within one hundred yards of the front lines. Alex said, "There are Japanese soldiers right up ahead."

"You can't fight 'em if you can't see 'em. Let's go," MacArthur replied.

It wasn't long before a soldier riding on the back with a gun, jumped out of the jeep and shouted, "Take cover!" They all did, scrambling into the undergrowth. But not the general.

With admiration in his voice, a soldier said, "He's the greatest general since General George Washington. Washington won the war with the British, and MacArthur is winning the war with the Japanese."

Alex watched as an officer walked up to MacArthur and said, "Pursuant to an act of Congress, you have been promoted to the rank of General of the Army. Such promotion to take effect 18 December,1944, by order of the President."

"Thank you," MacArthur said, pleased.

"Sir, we thought you should get these new stars on as soon as you can. You've got your fifth star. Congratulations."

A five-star general, Alex thought. And who deserves it more? MacArthur had returned to the Philippines as promised.

Three days after A-day, the Filipinos gathered for a victory celebration in Tacloban. Alex attended the special ceremony, again organizing members of the press. General MacArthur stood with President Osmeña, who proclaimed that Tacloban would also be the temporary capital of the Philippines until the complete liberation of the country. The crowd cheered.

CHAPTER TWENTY-SEVEN

Not long after the soldiers landed at Leyte, I packed my footlocker and suitcase for our voyage to the Philippines. I instructed the nurses to bring helmets, backpacks, and gas mask cases. "The transport is waiting outside," I said, "so gather your gear. The men will load our stuff onto the trucks." This was it. We were going to the front of the war, assigned as part of the first and second field hospitals in the Philippines. We climbed aboard and settled in our seats. I took a deep breath as we drove over red ground, through leafy green rainforests.

After my twenty-six nurses and I reached Hollandia Harbor, we boarded the *John Alden*. I'd miss this beautiful tropical spot. It was a funny feeling to know I'd lived here and loved things about it, but probably wouldn't ever see it again. I'd hardly had time to say goodbye to my nurses, but they'd be well cared for with Alicia.

While we waited to sail, a call came in on the ship-to-shore radio. It was Matt! I couldn't believe it. My heart drummed in my chest, and I quivered as I said, "It's so good to hear your voice. Where are you?"

"We're still in Leyte Gulf, which is why I was able to get a call through. Not only did the battle rage around us, but we were sailing in what felt like a hurricane."

"Was your ship damaged? Any casualties?" I held my breath.

"No, neither. We were some of the lucky ones."

"Thank heaven. I've been worried about you for days. I love you, Matt, so much."

"I love you more than all the stars in the sky," he said. I could hear him smile. Then his tone shifted. "I still can't believe the army is sending nurses into this battle zone. We haven't won yet, you know."

"We're the first to go, and someone needs to care for our wounded. I have to do my part."

He paused, and then his voice lightened. "Say, where will you be stationed?"

"Tacloban."

"Not far from where I am right now. When do you land?"

"We're scheduled to dock November 1."

"Get this. I can be there to meet you."

"Really? Seeing you would be a dream come true," I sighed.

"Where are they setting up your temporary hospital?"

"At the Palo Cathedral."

"You're going to be busy, so much to do. I hope we get a little time together."

I wanted to be with Matt. Really be with him. I wanted a husband, and he needed a wife. In my heart, I knew what was right for us. "Let's have a chaplain marry us at the cathedral and be promised to each other for eternity after the war ends."

Matt didn't even question my suggestion. He whooped with joy and agreed. "I'll meet you at the cathedral when you get there. I'll be ready and waiting with a chaplain and your brother Alex."

"Perfect." Then I wondered aloud what I should wear.

"Do you still have that pink and green Hawaiian dress you wore the day I met you in church?"

"It's right here in my trunk, but it's bad luck for the groom to see the bride before the wedding day," I chuckled, "so I'll surprise you."

"I'll be the one in the white navy dress uniform. Just in case you don't recognize me," he laughed.

I smacked a kiss into the receiver and hung up the phone. I couldn't believe it. Me, a bride. Happy tears glistened on my cheeks. It was time to marry my soul mate.

The ship began to move, and we were underway. I sat on the deck where the breeze was cool, and there were no bugs. I began to relax until I heard the voice of Tokyo Rose over the ship's radio. I was surprised to hear her say, "Oh, girls, I feel so sorry for you. You'll never get there. I hope you realize how terrible your parents are going to feel."

Her words rattled me, and I feared what else Tokyo Rose and the Japanese knew about our mission.

I felt a little better as we neared Leyte, after being told that the battle to take the beaches was almost over. But as we approached, I saw three battleships. We watched a Japanese kamikaze pilot, plane loaded with explosives, crash directly into a ship, setting it on fire. I pressed my elbows into my sides, making my body as small as I could as we passed by.

A few hours later, an announcement came over the radio about a typhoon. When it hit, we ran below deck to avoid winds that blew at more than ninety miles an hour. I rubbed sweaty hands on my pants, praying.

The *John Alden* landed at the Harbor on Leyte November 1, my wedding day. We docked, watched as our gear was loaded onto trucks, then drove in a convoy to the city of Tacloban. We soon reached the church the American liberation forces were using as a hospital, the stately Palo Cathedral. It was built in 1596. I peeked inside, and it was so beautiful. I quickly found a bathroom and changed into my pink and green Hawaiian dress. It wouldn't be much of a surprise, but I knew Matt would be happy.

I spotted him wandering around the cathedral, stifled a squeal, and called his name. He turned, and I held my arms up in a V for victory. The grin that I love spread across his face, and he sprinted over to me. He wrapped me a in hug, then pulled a ring from his pocket. It was made from airplane parts, and it was nothing like my engagement ring. It didn't even matter. He handed it to Alex, and I gave Matt a paper with our favorite Elizabeth Barrett Browning poem written on the page. He smiled. "Perfect." We both loved poetry.

The three of us stood in front of the chaplain, and looking into Matt's eyes, I said, "How do I love thee, let me count the ways. I love thee to the depth and breadth and height my soul can reach."

Then Matt said, "I love thee with the breath, smiles, tears, of all my life; and, if God choose, I shall but love thee better after death."

My lips parted, and I leaned forward, breathless.

After we said our 'I do's,' the chaplain turned to Matt and said, "You may now kiss the bride." Matt kissed the new Mrs. Lucy Hatch, and I kissed him back.

Alex had brought a small cake a Filipino woman made for the occasion. We sat down to enjoy her creation, and the chaplain joined us. Although this wasn't the way I'd always pictured my wedding day, I'd never forget it, that was for sure.

I sighed, disappointed that I couldn't spend tonight with Matt. I'd imagined my wedding night in many ways. Tending to the wounded never entered my mind. But I was here serving God and country.

As a wedding gift, Alex had arranged for us to stay in a hotel the following night and pre-paid our night's lodging, which was so nice of him.

"What's the name of the place?" I asked Alex while we finished our cake.

"The Hotel Alejandro."

"So, it was named after you," I grinned.

"Very funny," he laughed.

It was good to hear him laugh again. With all the responsibilities on his shoulders, he'd become so serious.

An hour later, I hugged Matt goodbye and changed into my nurse's uniform. I was still on duty, and we were expecting more than three hundred patients.

The next evening, Alex and Matt picked me up in a jeep, and we drove to the hotel where we found a beautiful white mansion, five stories tall. Alex told us it was built in 1932, not as a hotel, but as a home for Dr. and Mrs. Alejandro Montejo. "It has a cafe, guest rooms, and party halls."

"Despite the war, it's beautiful," I said, as we walked inside.

"Are the military officers using it as a place to meet?" Matt asked.

"Yep, ever since we threw the Japanese out. They were utilizing it as a base. The owners, the Montejos, are good people. They're opening their hotel doors to war evacuees from Cebu and Negros. But tonight, they're reserved a room for you. Your keys will be waiting at the front desk."

"Thank you, Alex," I said, kissing him on the cheek before he left.

Matt and I dined on chicken marinated and cooked in adobo sauce, rice, mango, and pineapple. It was delicious.

We went up to our room on the fifth floor. He insisted on carrying me across the threshold before we spent our first night as man and wife. That made me smile. He gently set me down and took me in his arms. Then we bonded in a new way, happy together.

Early the next morning, he shipped out, and I waved a sad goodbye. We knew we might not see each other again until the war ended. But when it did, we still planned to meet in Hawaii for our honeymoon. My shoulders slumped. I'd miss him so much. But it was back to the house where I now lived with the rest of the nurses.

Some generous Filipino families had put all of us up in several of their homes. The houses stood on stilts, made of bamboo, layered with palm leaves on the roofs and sides. The family pig and chickens lived underneath. Outside, stood an open fireplace with a mud and stone hearth for cooking. When we needed a lavatory, they handed us big milk cans.

That night, the Japanese planes flew over the house twenty times. We could hear enemy fire as we tried to sleep.

The next morning, we were back at the cathedral serving our patients their breakfast. We listened as the priest conducted morning mass. He let us use the sacred baptismal to scrub up, which was very generous. We had two nurses for every one hundred patients.

Several days later, thinking of Matt, my eyes glazed over and spanned the room. I did a double take. Could it be? It was Alex's friend, Norm, and I hoped he was okay. I moved to his bedside. He didn't seem injured, but one of the nurses held a bucket and Norm vomited into it. "Do you know what's wrong?" I asked the nurse.

"I'm not sure yet. But he's lethargic, and his heart's pounding."

Norm's eyes were sunken. I gently pinched his arm, and the skin didn't return to its original position for a few minutes. "It's cholera," I said. "We've got to keep him hydrated or we could lose him."

"Is that you, Lucy?" Norm asked glancing up from the bucket before he vomited again. "God has sent me an angel."

"Hi. I'm so sorry you're sick."

"My legs are cramping, and my nose is so dry."

"I'm guessing you took in some bad water. You're in for a rough four or five hours, but don't worry. We'll get you better," I said squeezing his hand. If we didn't keep Norm properly hydrated, he could go into shock and die. "I'll take it from here," I told my nurse, wanting to ensure Norm received the water required for his recovery.

By evening, his symptoms had subsided, and we sat and talked.

"I'm feeling a lot better," Norm said lying flat on his back. "It was cholera, right?"

"Yes."

"I know I could have died. Thanks for helping a guy out."

I patted his hand. "I'm glad I was still here. I'm being transferred to the Hospital Ship, *Hope*, until the end of December. One of the nurses on board injured her spine, and I've been assigned to take charge of the rest of the nurses until they find a replacement."

"Sounds dangerous. Is it?"

"Maybe, although there's a big red cross painted on the side of a white ship, so I'm hoping the enemy will leave us alone. You know, I've learned flexibility being a nurse in this war. I never thought I'd serve on a hospital ship, but then I never thought I'd supervise nurses in a cathedral in the Philippines either." I smiled. "So, when did you get to Leyte, Norm?"

"About five days ago, and I don't have to tell you how awful the battle has been. And it's not just the fighting. I feel bad for the natives, Lucy. Most of them haven't lived in their homes for a long time. The Japanese have caused them a lot of trouble. I've watched the Filipinos coming out of the hills, and they're in bad need of clothing."

"It's so hard for them. I bet it won't be long before our government starts bringing in clothes," I said.

"Hello," a happy, familiar voice smiled.

I turned, surprised. "Maxine, you're here. It's wonderful to see you." I gave her a hug, and she hugged me back.

"How long have you been in Tacloban?" I asked.

"I came on a hospital ship with the Red Cross and landed on Leyte the same day MacArthur did. How are you, Norm?" she asked. "Good to see you."

"Another angel of mercy," Norm smiled. "I'm recovering form cholera."

"I'm glad you're doing better. Here, have some toiletries, courtesy of the Red Cross," Maxine said, handing him a bag.

"Thank you." Norm pawed through the bag looking for little treasures.

"What's your assignment here on Leyte?" I asked Maxine.

"Maybe the most important was organizing a refugee camp."

"That's fantastic. Norm and I were just talking about the Filipinos needing clothes."

"I've noticed the same thing. We're working on it," she assured me. "I've also helped set up sacrament meetings for our church here in Tacloban. I hope you can join us Sunday."

"That would make me very happy. I'll be there." Then I paused. "I've been thankful so many times for you and the Red Cross."

Maxine hugged me. "Thanks for your service too, Lucy. I best be passing out more of these bags. See you in church," she waved.

It wasn't long before I began supervising nurses on the hospital ship *Hope*. Serving on a ship was a whole new experience. At night, we worked in the dark, using only dimmed lights inside the ship. The men were happy to trade filthy foxholes for the clean hospital beds jammed close together and stacked like brick layers.

We cared for badly wounded sailors, two with shrapnel wounds to their brains and one with a broken back. Many were horribly burned, and we heard guns fire from the beach as we cared for our patients. It was frightening.

By mid-morning the second day, two hundred more casualties came in from the hills. A few hours later, I went up top for a short break. The sky darkened, and the temperature dropped. I held onto the rail as the wind whipped the waves so high that I couldn't see more than a hundred yards away. The skipper finally had to move the *Hope* because other ships were floating too close to us. It was hard enough to tend to the patients without the wind.

The next day, we took the men back to Hollandia for more permanent treatment. We weren't there long before the ship turned around and sailed back to the Philippines. Then we loaded more wounded men and transported them back to Hollandia. We crisscrossed the ocean several times.

Thanksgiving Day, we pulled into the harbor before daylight on the tail end of more harsh weather. The water wasn't bumpy, but the sky dumped torrents of water. We'd hardly dropped anchor when small craft and barges loaded with the wounded surrounded us. More than six hundred men came on board during the downpour. The chilly wind whipped sheets of water onto men with anguished expressions, attempting to control their pain. When we finally got them into hospital beds, we discovered that the diseases they'd developed in the tropics made their wounds more difficult to treat.

We were able to feed them a Thanksgiving dinner, of sorts. We had hot soup, beef steak, and potatoes. The guys wolfed down the food as if it might be the last that they'd ever eat.

One week prior to Christmas, we were back in Leyte. By noon that day, the ship was fully loaded with new battle casualties from the landings on Mindoro. The boys we'd just taken in told us that it was "the worst Japanese air attack they had ever witnessed. The suicide bombings were terrible."

Our beds filled quickly, and this time we had to put the wounded on the mess hall tables and extra folding cots throughout the ship. The captain told us that the USS Mercy had been called early that morning and would be able to come in and pick up the men we couldn't cram onto our ship.

We worked all the next day and night. A little before daybreak, an air alert went off. We were parked in the middle of a group of destroyers, and I could hear their call to "General Quarters," "Man Your Battle Stations," and the command to the gunners, "Man Your Guns." We all waited for the whistle of a bomb to drop.

The silence on board the Hope was profound. The wounded in the wards were tense, and they gripped the bed side rails, their noses peering over as if they were ready to crawl under bunks and tables.

We got lucky when our fighter forces drove off the enemy before they could drop a bomb. I heaved a huge sigh of relief, and we all relaxed.

An hour later, the captain said they'd found a replacement for me on board ship, and I could stay behind in Leyte. I was overjoyed.

I watched the *Hope* leave Leyte Island with 708 casualties on board and pleaded with God for the safety of everyone on board.

A few days later, Alex and I met for lunch in Tacloban.

"Let's talk over there, away from everyone," he said, finding a table.

"What's up?" I asked.

He looked off in the distance. "We've learned that on December 14, the Japanese executed almost 150 American prisoners of war."

"That's horrible. Was Chris there? Was he killed?"

"No. It wasn't Cabanatuan."

"You're pretty sure he's there, right?"

"Yes."

"Where were the POW's slaughtered?"

"Palowan Prison Camp near the city of Puerto Princesa."

"How far is that from here?"

"'Bout a two-day jeep and ferry ride. Lucy, it was a mass murder," Alex said, staring off in the distance again.

"Did they line the men up and shoot them?"

"Worse. The Japanese sounded an air raid warning, knowing the prisoners would jump into the covered trenches. Then the guards grabbed barrels of gasoline, doused the men, and set them on fire."

There were no words for that travesty.

"Prisoners who tried to get out of the flames were shot with a machine gun," Alex said.

"Did anyone survive?" I asked, eyes full of tears.

"Ten men escaped by climbing over a cliff that ran along one side of the trenches. We just learned about another one, Private First-Class Eugene Nielsen from Logan, Utah, if you can believe it. He managed to escape the fire and make his way to the beach. The guards shot at him, but he just kept swimming."

"How long did he have to swim?"

"Almost nine hours. Then he reached a neighboring island where Filipino guerrillas rescued him. They contacted the Australians, who picked him up. The Aussies told us."

"A man of courage and strength."

"You better believe Eugene's story will help motivate the generals to liberate the rest of the POW camps in the next few months.

"Before the same thing happens."

"Exactly. I'm hoping we'll get Chris out soon."

Alex and I observed a moment of silent prayer for the 139 POWs who'd died. Then we held hands and prayed for our brother Chris.

1945

CHAPTER TWENTY-EIGHT

Alex waited at 6th Army headquarters south of Lingayen Gulf in the Philippines. MacArthur's forces landed in early January, and he had renewed hope for Chris's rescue. He couldn't imagine the horrors his brother was suffering.

Colonel White, General Krueger's intelligence officer, took charge of the day's briefing. Everyone in the room listened with intense interest to the American guerilla chief, Major Lapham, as he said, "When I heard about MacArthur's landing on Luzon, I grabbed a horse and rode thirty miles behind enemy lines to the Sixth Army spearheads."

The man has guts, Alex thought.

"I have critical information about the POWs from Bataan," Lapham said, leaning forward. "Based on observation and information my Filipino guerillas gave me, there are about five hundred POWs, mainly Americans, still stuck in the Cabanatuan camp. They're at risk of being murdered."

Just like the men at Palawan last month, Alex thought, sweating. *We can't let that happen again.*

A large man stood and walked to a wall map of Luzon. He pointed at the Sixth Army's most forward position. "We're twenty-five miles west of the prison camp," he said.

Lapham said, "There are about nine thousand Japanese soldiers in the general area of the stockade, and they're getting ready to withdraw."

Alex's body stiffened knowing if the Japanese pulled out, they'd massacre the prisoners before they left.

Lapham confirmed Alex's worst fears when he said, "Unless these five hundred POW's can be rescued, the Japanese will murder them when the Sixth Army spearheads approach the camp."

White stood. "I'll go find General Krueger and let him know we recommend a crash operation to rescue the prisoners."

Later Alex heard Krueger had given the operation a thumbs up, so he went to General Tory's office to review the operational plan for the rescue.

"The scheme looks simple, but it's perilous, Tory said. "Two teams of Alamo Scouts will leave twenty-four hours in advance of the mission to get a look the camp. Then a force of more than one hundred rangers will take a winding course through enemy territory to reach their destination. When they get there, they'll have to sneak up on Cabanatuan in the dark, kill about 250 Japanese soldiers, and get the prisoners out."

Alex let out a low whistle. He knew these rangers were skilled but unproven in battle. He hoped they'd be able to pull this off with few casualties. He said, "I'm betting it won't be easy getting five hundred weak, probably puny, and maybe confused men back to us. You know my brother is in that camp, sir. With your permission, I'd like to accompany the rangers." Tory turned to Alex and raised his eyebrows. Before he could object, Alex said, "I do have combat experience, sir."

"You're my staff lieutenant, and I need you here. You won't have any jungle cover. You'll be walking through dry rice paddies out in the open. The Japanese will have tanks, and you'll have only bazookas and hand grenades to combat them. You sure you want to do this?"

"Chris is my brother, sir. He's been living in awful conditions ever since Bataan." Alex's eyes were flinty with resolve. "He'd do the same for me."

Tory nodded. "Permission granted. I'll let Colonel White and Lieutenant Colonel Mucci know. Mucci is the leader of the 6th Ranger Battalion.

"Yes, sir. Thank you, sir."

Alex went to find Mucci, who shook his hand, welcomed him aboard, and said, "The Rangers will hit Cabanatuan at 7:30 p.m. on January 29, 1945, only fifty-four hours from now. Then we'll have about an hour of darkness to crawl across the ground to the stockade where we wait for the signal to bust through the front and rear gates. I want you at the front gate."

"I'll be there."

"This will be a tough but rewarding task, and we'll succeed by luck and the grace of God."

"I'll pray for that."

"I'm going to give every man the chance to choose not to go on this mission without worry that anyone will question his courage or dedication."

The decision was put to the men, and no one backed out.

Long before daylight on January 28, the Ranger camp readied for the sixty-mile ride to the province of Guimba. The men wore green fatigues and cloth hats, with no insignia specifying rank. Right around 5:00 a.m., Alex heard the shout "Load 'em up!" The men climbed into seven GI trucks, and Colonel Mucci followed in a jeep.

We're heading into the enemy's backyard, Alex thought.

One man reminded, "We've got to maintain an element of surprise if we're going to be successful."

"Failure is not an option," Alex said, fists clenched in his lap.

When they reached Guimba, they stopped for a while and waited to walk the rest of the way to Cabanatuan. The plan was that if the raiders ran into trouble either going in or coming back, they would radio the P-61 Black Widow airplanes based near Lingayen Gulf. Alex prayed they wouldn't have to use those radios. His friend Dave stood by one of those planes just in case. Alex told him all about Chris.

Just after 2:00 p.m., the Rangers, with Colonel Mucci in the lead, marched eastward from Guimba. Each man carried a canteen and two day's rations and was armed with automatic rifles, pistols, bazookas and rockets, hand grenades, and trench knives. Even the medics carried guns. That's unusual, Alex thought.

Two Filipino guerillas guided the gaunt men over flat rice paddies to the Licab River, where they crossed the stream. They waded through mud, the mosquitos buzzed, and the sun burned hot overhead. Alex could see beads of sweat on the men's foreheads, upper lips, and damp patches under their arms. They marched in wet boots until they reached the command post of the Filipino guerilla chief. Eighty of his guerillas joined the Rangers for the next leg of the march, bringing the group to a total of two hundred men.

When it got dark, Alex could hear odd sounds in the rice paddies, as his eyes tried to penetrate the black night. A few minutes later, he heard the banging of Japanese tanks. When he lifted his head above the long cogan grass, he saw the outline of ten tanks rumbling down the road. The men held their collective breath as the tanks passed, bodies tense, foreheads creased with fear.

Mucci ordered the men to get down and crawl on all fours so they wouldn't be spotted. Then the moon came out from behind the clouds. Alex wiped clammy hands on his pants. This was not good. As they came up on a small bridge, Alex could see a Japanese tank parked nearby. He watched as Captain Prince took out a map.

"Look here," he said. "There's a deep ravine. It would be safer if we crawled about one hundred yards through the ravine underneath the Japanese tank." Mucci agreed, and the Rangers dropped to their knees again and moved toward the bridge. Alex's heart pounded so hard he was afraid the Japanese might hear it.

It took about an hour to creep through the ravine, but they made it to the woods without being spotted. "Double-time it, men," Mucci ordered. The men ran across the open country for two miles and then slowed to a fast walk.

It was 4:30 a.m. and not quite daylight, the morning still, no hint of wind, and no birds chirping. Alex and the tired Rangers, along with the Filipino guerillas, reached the barrio of Balincarin, five miles north of Cabanatuan camp. As Alex sat down for a brief rest, he heard Lieutenant Tombo, intelligence chief for the guerillas, describe what they were facing up ahead. "There are six to eight hundred Japanese combat troops bivouacked along the Cabu River, a few hundred yards northeast of the POW enclosure. There may be as many as five thousand Japanese troops deployed around Cabanatuan town."

Alex stood with resolve and moved forward with the rest of the men who walked until dusk, until they reached Plateros. His uniform was caked with dust, and he was sweating profusely. As they neared a group of Nipa huts, Mucci ordered the men to keep quiet. "We're only a mile and a half from Cabanatuan."

The men acted as ordered until giggling Filipina teenage young women dressed in white and carrying leis made of fresh flowers, approached. Behind them stood the rest of the barrio's smiling residents who asked Mucci if they could sing songs.

"Yes," he said, "but please sing softly. We're twenty-five miles behind Japanese lines."

The soldiers choked up when about forty Philippine voices joined in a quiet, and slightly off-key rendition of "God Bless America." The song stirred deep into Alex's heart.

That afternoon the men were given a final briefing. "Here's what we're going to do," one of the ranger officers told them. "We'll sneak up to a low knoll seven hundred yards from the front gate and wait until it gets dark. Then we move across the paddies to the Cabanatuan stockade. A P-61 Black Widow will buzz the camp over the treetops to distract the Japanese. The guerillas will then cut the phone lines leading out of camp, so the Japanese commander can't turn on the alarm."

Alex nodded, palms again dripping sweat.

"Murphy's platoon will then move around to the rear gate. At 7:30 p.m., they'll fire into the Japanese barracks and kick off the raid."

By 6:00 p.m. it was dark. Captain Prince signaled the men to move on. They dropped to their bellies and crawled slowly forward. When

Alex looked up, he could see Japanese guards in the watchtowers. He prayed, "Please God, don't let them see us." Then they waited.

Alex knew a few of the guerillas had placed a time bomb on the Japanese side of a wooden bridge, set to go off at about 8:00 p.m., just when the enemy force would be on the bridge trying to cross to Cabanatuan.

Alex heard a Black Widow plane fly in low and fast, buzzing the POW enclosure. Then it pulled up and headed back to base, a maneuver to trick the Japanese into thinking the Americans were coming at them from the air instead of the ground.

At only twenty yards away, Alex could see Japanese soldiers lazing around in their underwear in the still-lit barracks. One of the platoons hit the barracks with an ack-ack-ack of bullets. Then a couple of the men fired at the guard in the tower, taking him out. He never knew what hit him.

A soldier jumped from the ditch and ran to the eight-foot-high front gate. Using the butt of his Tommy gun, he pounded the oversized padlock. It didn't give, so he pulled out his.45-caliber pistol and aimed it at the stubborn lock. A Japanese soldier a few yards inside the gate fired at him, knocking the pistol from his hand. Alex saw another man raise his automatic weapon and fire at the man who had shot his buddy. The first guy picked up his pistol and fired at the lock again, shattering it.

When he pushed the heavy gate open, a horde of men followed him inside, pitching grenades. They were crashing through both gates now. The Rangers were outnumbered two to one, but they had surprise on their side.

As he ran, Alex could hear orders being shouted in Japanese as a hut burst into flames. The Japanese soldiers screamed as their bodies were punctured with flying grenade fragments.

***

At first, Chris and the men in his barracks thought the Japanese had started killing the prisoners when they heard machine gun fire and more explosions. One of them screamed when troops burst through the door.

"It's okay," one of the soldiers said. "We're Americans."

Chris couldn't believe it. Was he going home? Those green angels carefully helped him up on his bare and swollen feet.

"If you can walk, head for the main gate," another soldier said, "If not, we'll carry you." He put a man on his back.

Some of the prisoners broke into tears. Chris couldn't remember the last time he'd been treated with such kindness. He'd been a prisoner almost three years.

A few of the POWs hugged and kissed the rangers, sobbing, "Thank you! Thank you! Thank God, you've come!" Many of them were barefoot and wore only underwear.

An older POW refused to move and just sat there on a bunk staring at the ceiling.

"Come on, pal, we got to get going," one of the rangers said softly.

"No, no," he said in a whisper. "I'm a goner. Help get the other fellows out."

The ranger leaned forward and gently picked up the prisoner, who was mostly skin and bones, and placed him on his back.

Chris wrapped his bony arms under another prisoner's shoulders and urged him out the door. A few of the men fell, and Chris helped them up. "We've got to keep moving," he said.

As they walked outside in the dark, Chris was amazed as a ranger fired a missile from a stovepipe looking weapon, destroying a guard tower. "What's that?" he asked.

"It's a bazooka," one of the soldiers told him as he herded the hospital patients forward as fast as he could.

He'd never heard of it. One man walking next to Chris had gangrene in his foot, and he was limping. "You okay, buddy?" Chris asked.

"I'll make it," he said. "My adrenaline's keeping me going."

More heavy fire erupted as they shuffled on, and Rangers ran from hut to hut, shouting at the top of their voices: "We're Americans! This is a prison break! Get to the front gate!"

About halfway to the gate, the older POW who'd said he was a goner, gasped and went limp. The ranger set him down and Chris checked his pulse. There was none. "I'm afraid it's too late for him," Chris said, bending over his body, hands clasped, lips moving in prayer.

Another prisoner came out of one of the barracks walking only on one leg. He was moving faster than Chris. Seeing Chris's surprise, he turned to him and said, "If you think you're about to be killed, you don't let a little thing like having only one leg slow you down."

Chris smiled, shuffling a little faster.

Alone, or in twos, a steady flow of POWs moved to the main gate.

Chris stopped, stared ahead across the compound, and saw... Alex? When their eyes met, Chris didn't miss the look of shock and sadness. Chris gazed down at his feet, ashamed. Alex ran up, a grin splashed across his face "You're a sight for sore eyes," he said putting his arm around him. "Thank God you're alive." Alex brushed away a tear.

"My little brother came for me," Chris sobbed. He couldn't believe it.

"We've been a long time coming," Alex said as a bullet whizzed past Chris's ear.

Alex pulled out his Tommy gun, turned, and fired in the direction of the shot. An enemy soldier dropped to his knees. Alex put a bullet in his head just to be sure.

Chris looked at him, shaking. "You have a job to do. Don't worry about me. I'll keep walking."

"See you at the river," Alex said, pointing to the Alamo scouts. "They'll escort you to the Pampanga River where veterans of behind-the-lines operations in New Guinea are waiting."

Chris slowly walked away, continuing to help other prisoners who faltered.

CHAPTER TWENTY-NINE

Alex checked his watch. Twenty-eight minutes had passed since the first shots were fired at Cabanatuan, but it seemed like hours. Hundreds of Japanese soldiers had been killed, and about five hundred freed POWs were being led north. Mucci said, "We lost two army rangers and twenty-one guerillas."

"Brave men who gave their lives for others," Alex said, pained, as a bright red flare colored the night sky. Alex thought of all the rangers and Alamo scouts who read the signal in the heavens with relief. They could pull out now. One step closer to going home.

Mucci and Alex moved to the front of the long line of POWs who were more like hobbling robots than men. One prisoner couldn't get up a three-foot bank. When Alex put out his hands to help, the man had no muscles at all—only bones.

They'd gone a couple of hundred yards when bullets whizzed past them. Everyone hit the dirt, trembling. No one was hit. One of the rangers told the POWs, "Remove any outside white clothes. The Japanese probably spotted you in your underwear."

Without a word, the prisoners got up, took off their underwear, and walked on, bare foot and naked.

Mucci turned to Alex, "There are twenty-six, two-wheeled carts each with a carabao waiting on the north shore of the river. We asked the Filipino villagers twenty-four hours ago to round them up to transport the prisoners."

"Not much notice, but they came through."

"Almost every farmer has a cart and carabao, and all of them who were asked parted with possessions they use to make their living."

Alex shook his head, blinking back tears. "The Filipinos have hearts of gold."

Shortly after 10:00 p.m., Alex, Mucci, the first rangers and the freed prisoners pushed into Platero. The others followed in a constant flow. Then excited natives welcomed the Americans with open arms. Many talked and laughed despite the rangers trying to quell the chaos.

The freed prisoners sat down on the dusty road, still stunned. Then some of them laughed and talked noisily. Or broke into tears. Others remained silent. The Filipinos gave them tomatoes to eat, and the relief trucks brought in hamburgers. "If this is a dream," one skinny POW said, "don't wake me up!"

CHAPTER THIRTY

"Pack up and get down to Guimba by this afternoon. Set up and be ready to take patients immediately!" Brigadier General Hagins ordered the 92nd evacuation hospital. I'd been assigned to the evacuation hospital after leaving the *Hope*. It was another temporary assignment until the evacuation hospital left for the island of Cebu. One thing for sure, the range of experience continued to broaden my skills.

Things moved quickly from there as our several-hundred bed hospital raced down the road to a town nearly fifty miles away. Most of the staff didn't know why, although there were rumors. Alex had told me why we'd been assigned to this town, but I never shared what he communicated in confidence. We're all in this together, the women as well as the men.

When we reached Guimba, we drove to the rambling frame buildings of the town's elementary school, where we would set up to care for the wounded.

In practiced rhythm, the men unloaded the trucks. The simple process involved moving the beds first, then the surgical equipment, followed by the linens. The Red Cross attached to the hospital had come along, bringing small bags full of toilet articles, pen and paper, candy, and gum—anything they thought might boost the men's spirits.

By nightfall, we had power, a supply room, operating room, laboratory, and wards with sheeted cots in tidy rows, just waiting.

The hospital sent trucks out to meet the incoming caravan of men, who were still walking. We were ready.

Two days later, around noon, the liberated prisoners from Cabanatuan arrived. Many were naked, skin on skeletons, their eyes vacant. About half of them were in carts pulled by carabao. The other half stumbled along on foot. I wasn't prepared for how gaunt and ragged the men looked. Where was Chris? I couldn't wait to see him again.

My eyes scanned every man with his hair color, my stomach nauseous as I realized how badly these men had been treated. A few minutes later, I saw him with Alex. My two brothers, walking arm in arm. Chris looked like death warmed over, chest caved in, shoulders stooped. My heart broke, and tears ran down my face as I dashed to his side. I held him in my arms and could feel his bones. "I've dreamed of this, Chris," I whispered in his ear. "I love you."

He sobbed. "I love you, Lucy. I can't believe it."

"You're free, Chris." I bottled up my breath, trying to calm down.

"The three of us together again." Alex beamed with joy.

"The war, the rescue," Chris said, head down. His hands shook.

I held his hand. "Come with me and I'll get you registered. Then you and the rest of the men can take a shower, and we'll get you into some new clothes." The seriously ill and injured soldiers went right to the wards, and the others went to the tents. Chris was put in a tent.

To a man, the former prisoners were excited to get the Red Cross kits. I smiled as Chris dumped the bag on the bed. He was like a kid at Christmas. You'd think we'd given the men expensive gifts. Seeming to read my mind, Chris said, "We've gone without basic items for so long, even the little things matter."

We treated the men to our best care and handled them gently. Many of them who had held up resolutely were so touched by our tenderness, they broke down and cried.

Then the reporters came to document the men's stories. Lori was with them, and I was happy to see her again. We shared a quick hug, and she started snapping pictures. We witnessed a young man who had lost his arm on Bataan eat half dozen eggs, a large helping of ham, and lots of biscuits with jam. In ten minutes, he threw it all up.

Hours later, I was able to find a phone and call my parents to give them the news. When Mom heard that Chris was alive, she asked me to repeat what I'd just said.

"Yes, Mom," I said softly. "It's true. Chris is back."

Mom sobbed. "He's safe, he's safe."

"We've prayed non-stop for his rescue," Dad said, voice trembling.

"Chris is coming home," Mom breathed.

Dad said, "We've been hearing patchy radio reports of a heroic raid on a Japanese prison camp in the Philippines. That was Cabanatuan, right?"

"Yes, Dad."

I could hear the pride in Dad's voice as he said, "I can't believe three of my children had a part in this historic raid. You just can't make this stuff up."

Just before noon on February 1, a dusty jeep carrying a five-star general arrived at the 92nd Evacuation Hospital. I watched the people of the village smile, wave, and call out to General MacArthur. The jeep stopped, he climbed out, shook hands, and hugged many more of them.

Next, he came to meet the survivors of Bataan and Corregidor, the emaciated ghosts who had been liberated from Cabanatuan. The more mobile POWs had been moved to another camp earlier that morning, and Chris was one of them. I was sorry he wasn't here to meet the General.

When MacArthur stepped out of the jeep, his face looked grim. I walked behind him into the reception room. Haggard veterans, some of them on crutches with missing legs went up to him, raising their arms in weak salutes. Others reached out to touch him. Some broke out in sobs.

The general shook the hand of one man after another, deep emotions visible on his face. "God bless you, General," one of the men rasped. "Thank God you came back!" another said. In a voice choked with emotion, MacArthur replied, "I'm a little late, but we finally made it."

I ventured outside to find Alex, who stood with Colonel Mucci, swarmed by scores of war correspondents and photographers. Lori smiled from the back of the crowd. Mucci told the story over and over of the raid that freed the men, as the reporters continued to ask questions, his face weary.

Mucci took little credit for what had happened, pointing to Captain Prince and the rangers who breached the stockade. "They were the ones who brought the POWs to safety," he said. Mucci also praised the Alamo Scouts and the Filipino guerillas. "Make no mistake about it," he said, "we couldn't have pulled it off without them."

When the crowd dispersed, I moved over to a rickety table where Lori sat. She introduced me to the man next to her. "Lucy, this is war correspondent and photographer Carl Mydans of *Life Magazine*."

"It's nice to meet you," Mydans said.

"And you," I said with admiration. "I've seen your photos and read some of your articles."

He placed his hands over the tattered portable typewriter in front of him. He seemed to be searching for just the right words. I read over his shoulder as he typed: "Every American child of coming generations will know of the 6th Rangers, for a prouder story has never been written...."

CHAPTER THIRTY-ONE

The Americans freed from Cabanatuan were returned to the United States as soon as possible. Chris was among the largest group of about 280 men who sailed for the San Francisco Bay on the transport ship *General A. E. Anderson.* It would take thirty days to cross the Pacific.

During that time, Chris and the other men ate well and gained weight. He started to fill out his clothes again. His spirits lifted, and he felt better.

Chris was still onboard ship when news came that US troops had recaptured Corregidor and Bataan. Men stood up on the tables where they were eating, slapped their thighs, and raised their arms above their heads. Then they clapped and cheered at the news.

As the hoots and hollers subsided, Chris's face grew dark. Rather than being a hero of the war, he had been a prisoner of war.

One of the men echoed his thoughts, asking, "What will America think of us?"

"Will we be labeled as cowards because we surrendered?" another asked.

No one knew what to expect.

When they neared San Francisco, ships, boats, and even a few yachts circled around their ship as she broke through the harbor. Chris heard bells, whistles, sirens, and a band played a rip-roaring rendition of "California, Here I Come."

California, here I come,
Right back where I started from
So, open up that Golden Gate,
California, here I come.

Chris leaned on the rail and looked out over the water. He remembered when he'd first sailed to the Philippines and passed under this bridge. He was a different man now. Hemingway's words from, *A Farewell to Arms* sank into his brain. 'The world breaks everyone and afterward many are strong at the broken places. But those that will not break it kills. It kills the very good and the very gentle and the very brave impartially.'

Tears filled Chris's eyes. He'd lost very good and very brave buddies in the war, and their faces still haunted him. As well as the faces of enemy soldiers he'd killed. *Who am I now? A broken man, still suffering from night terrors and anxiety?*

It would take time to begin to heal his broken spaces. He worried about the impact his lingering battle fatigue would have on his parents. They were coming to San Francisco to meet him in a few days and planned to accompany him home by train. They'd upgraded his ticket to a Pullman car that the three of them would share. What if he called out in the night or woke up screaming? He did that sometimes.

Chris pulled himself out of his head as the ship sailed under the Golden Gate Bridge. The POWs could see thousands of people frantically waving tiny American flags. There were huge banners that read: "Welcome Heroes of Bataan and Corregidor" and "God Bless You Heroes."

"They think we're heroes," Chris whispered. His mouth quivered and he choked up.

Moments after their boat docked, the former POWs gathered on deck to pray, thanking God for their rescue. Then they left the ship, walked down the gangplank, and pushed through jostling and shouting crowds of people. The noise, the people. It was almost too much.

When Chris climbed on board the buses that would take them to Letterman Hospital where they'd spend the night, his tense body relaxed, muscle by muscle. He would spend the night in a safe place.

Early the next morning, they were up and at it again. The men rode in a caravan of army sedans through a huge parade in downtown San Francisco. Thousands and thousands of cheering people lined the route. And the bands. So many bands, all playing as loud as they could. Some of the men covered their ears.

When the sedans reached the city hall, the POWs stepped out and stood in front of a platform filled with civilian dignitaries and military brass. They listened to prayers, welcoming speeches, and all sang, "God Bless America." It was exhilarating in some ways and hard to cope with in others.

Back at Letterman Hospital, while Chris waited for his parents, he heard some of the men phone home. For many, their voices were filled with happiness as they reconnected to loved ones.

But for others, it was a disaster. One walked over to Chris and told him his wife was dead. Another said his family had moved and couldn't be found. One poor guy told Chris he'd lost two children. The group of men grew as they sat together and commiserated.

Another said, "My wife abandoned our children and put them in an orphanage. Can you believe it?" Tears ran down his face. He stuttered, tried to get out another sentence and failed.

Someone else joined the group, and in a voice filled with disbelief said, "I just found out my wife has been living with a boyfriend since Bataan."

"Get this," still another said, "both my dad and mom died. My brother and sister took my part of the inheritance."

Chris listened and responded with the respect and empathy they deserved, no judgment. Coming home isn't all sunshine and roses, Chris thought. That's for sure. The war wasn't over for these men, not yet. Their wounds went beyond their bodies.

Chris could see the pain in the men and in himself too. He wondered where God was in all this. He knew in his head that God had never left him, but he didn't feel it in his heart. He prayed for himself and for these men, that God's grace would shower them with love.

CHAPTER THIRTY-TWO

Inspired by his success at Cabanatuan, MacArthur ordered American forces into Manila to liberate the nearly thirty-seven hundred civilians incarcerated at the University of Santo Tomas. American families locked up behind the gates had suffered along with the Filipinos. They'd eaten dogs, cats, and even rats to survive. The detainees were deliriously happy when help arrived. Then the fires started.

Alex and the rest of Tory's staff listened as MacArthur's pilot Dusty Rhoades radioed the message, "The entire section of the city is a mass of flames that are rising two hundred feet in the air from the center of the city," he said. "The spectacle is an appalling sight."

Alex was incensed. Instead of withdrawing from the city, the Japanese were destroying it. He prayed for those trapped in their path.

Tory read a communique from Major General Beightler: "We are powerless to stop it. We have no way of knowing in which of the thousands of places the demolitions are being controlled. Big, modern, reinforced concrete and steel office buildings are literally being blown from their foundations to settle crazily in twisted heaps."

"Are we getting any reports about other civilians in the city?" Alex asked.

"Not yet," Tory answered. "We need some preliminary investigations. In a few days, American soldiers will cross the Pasig

River and retake southern Manila, block by block. I'm assigning you and Lieutenant Ben West to go along and get what stories you can from the survivors. We want to build a case against Japanese war crimes.

"Yes, sir," the two men said in unison. Ben nodded at Alex, whose lips were tight, and his fists clenched.

Two days later, Alex and Ben were with a second lieutenant and his team surveying the Dy Pac Lumberyard in Manila. In the tall weeds, they found dead Filipino women, some in flowered dresses and others in nightgowns. Even worse were the dead infants who lay beside them. Alex stared with pain etched on his face, briefly closed his eyes, and bit his lip. They counted 115 dead. "The adult bodies," Ben choked, "their hands are tied."

"Let's order a team in to give them a dignified burial," Alex whispered, as Ben went over to talk to one of the guerillas.

When Ben returned, he said, "There are rumors about a massacre behind the Presidential Palace. We should go there now."

In a field behind the palace, Alex and Ben found hundreds of dead men who had been suspected guerillas. An American Pfc., throat thick with pain said, "It appears that whole families have been executed."

Alex stared, saying, "The men have been beheaded, and their wives and children killed with bayonets. There's so much blood, it's running in streams in the dirt."

There were hundreds more dead civilians in the destroyed dining hall at Saint Pauls' College. One of the survivors told Alex and Ben, "The Japanese marines promised us safety. We didn't know that they'd loaded the chandeliers with explosives, until the chandeliers fell to the floor and blew up in our faces. I barely survived the attack."

Another one said, "Some who didn't die in the blast lurched out through this collapsed wall. The Japanese went after them, then shot and bayoneted them. I walked out of here over dead mothers and their children." He sobbed.

Alex looked away, the vision burned into his brain of mothers, daughters, and sons lying dead together.

The following afternoon, he and Ben went to the Red Cross headquarters, thought by many to be a sanctuary. Instead, it proved to be a slaughterhouse. Even before they opened each door, the stench told Alex and Ben what they'd find. Still, the sight of working men and women sliced open in the chest, pained expressions frozen on their faces, beautiful dresses with bright flowers stained with blood, conjured up visions of evil Japanese marines. They had stormed in, going room by room, shooting and bayoneting more than fifty civilians. There were two infants on the floor—one looked less than a week old. The sight of the brand-new baby made Alex choke. *Hope and love had been snuffed out with the blow of a bayonet.*

A man approached them and introduced himself as being Jewish, saying he'd escaped Germany and then survived the Japanese attack by pretending to be dead. "They murdered my fiancée," he sobbed.

Alex swallowed hard as the man wandered away, distraught, pointing him to a rescue truck waiting outside.

"I can't believe what the Japanese are doing." Ben shook his head. "They're butchers."

"These soldiers are no better than cannibals," Alex grimaced.

That same day, Japanese forces surrounded the German Club, a big social hall where more than five hundred civilians were jammed into the crawlspace for protection against the gunfire. The enemy soldiers poured gasoline on the club's furniture and then lit matches.

Alex and Ben arrived to survey the damage and speak with any survivors. The women who tried to escape got the worst of it. One of the survivors told them, "The Japanese caught us, poured gasoline on our heads, and set our hair on fire."

Alex ground his teeth and clenched his jaw, summoning up enough courage just to get the facts down on paper.

Enemy troops killed former constables, police officers, and even some priests. Ben was Catholic and said, "The Japanese must have believed our priests were loyal to the United States, but that's no excuse. When men of God get brutally assassinated, you know the stakes of war can go no higher."

"This isn't just a fight between two armies to take Manila," Alex said. "It's a human catastrophe." That night, he played the stories he'd heard from survivors over and over in his head as he wrote down the details. Shock turned to anger, and he didn't sleep much.

When he woke up the next morning, it was Valentine's Day. Alex's body sagged as he laid in bed and remembered great parties at home with girls he'd dated. He rolled over with a heavy sigh, thinking that he'd give almost anything to see just one friendly face from home. Then he sat up. Mom had written a few weeks ago that a friend from Mapleton, Utah, was only two hours away at Clark Field.

Alex got up, told Ben he'd be back later, and found a jeep. He made the drive to Clark Airfield to find his friend. While his family called him Norman, Alex preferred using his friend's middle name, Willis. Their mothers knew each other well, and Alex remembered fun times he'd had with his pal growing up. Willis had loved the outdoors, his dog, and teasing his sisters. More than once, Alex had gone to Mapleton for a July 4th breakfast. He appreciated his friend's easy-going smile. The guy never frowned or said a bad word about anybody.

Willis had been serving in the engineer core, building roads and bridges and barracks to meet the needs of the army. He was one of the lucky ones with enough points to rotate out of the service. He'd be home by August.

Alex couldn't wait to see him again and catch up on the mundane and normal: old girl friends, swimming in Utah Lake, fireworks. He wanted to talk about anything but war and death.

When he reached Clark, Alex parked the jeep and went inside. He asked about his friend. The officer standing behind the counter motioned and said, "Come into my office, please." His face was serious.

"Is everything okay?" Alex asked, gripping his hands together.

"You might want to sit down."

Alex took a chair, face pale.

"I'm sorry to have to tell you that Norman Willis Bird was just killed."

No, no, no. Alex was nauseous. "What happened?"

"He was driving a truck and backed up the hillside off the main road when an underground Japanese mine exploded. Unfortunately, it hadn't been found by our detection instruments. He and three other men lost their lives."

Alex left the office in disbelief, dragging his feet, and went back to the jeep. Despite the heat of the day, his fingers were cold, and he had trouble catching his breath. His buddy was dead. He wanted to go somewhere and hide where no one could find him.

But he and Ben still had interviews with survivors back in Manila. Alex sat in silence for a moment and then started up the jeep, leaving his dead pal behind.

Alex and Ben went first to a home at 1195 Singalong Street, a street that sounded so light and happy. But Japanese troops had cut a hole in an upstairs floor and then marched everyone from blindfolded teenagers to grandfathers inside and made them kneel. A Japanese marine then slashed each man's neck with a sword before kicking his body into the hole inside. Two hundred men had died and only nine survived. One of them said, "I watched body after body tumble down the hole into a pyramid of tangled arms, heads, legs, and torsos."

Another survivor said, "I placed my hand and arm on the floor. I could feel several inches of blood."

Predatory Japanese troops had assaulted families in their homes, pulled some out of bomb shelters, and then executed them in the streets. "The Japanese wanted to be sure that everybody was dead," another survivor said. His eyes stared into nothing.

The worst for Alex were the rape stories. The Japanese soldiers gathered up hundreds of women and locked many of them inside the once beautiful Bayview Hotel. As Alex and Ben approached the regal building and walked up the steps, they reminisced about MacArthur's wife. "This is where Jean MacArthur lived, before she married the general," Alex said. "She still talks about the beautiful sunsets."

"The Japanese have turned it into a house of horrors," Ben said.

One of the women told them, "I was raped between 12 and 15 times during the night. I can't remember exactly how many times."

Scores of women had been assaulted. Most of them were hesitant to even talk about it.

When MacArthur got word of the stories, he was outraged. On February 17, he wrote, "Desire full details of all authenticated cases of atrocities committed by the enemy in the Manila area as soon as possible."

Two Filipino Supreme Court justices had been killed. The Japanese didn't discriminate, Alex thought. Old and young, rich, and poor, men and women, healthy or sick. They murdered them all. Because dead men don't speak.

The army managed to capture some Japanese orders left on the battlefield. That's when Alex and Ben learned that the brutalities had all been part of a grand master plan. The Japanese soldiers had been ordered in advance, as part of an organized strategy, to "decimate the city and exterminate its inhabitants," one order stated. "All people on the battlefield with the exception of Japanese military personnel, Japanese civilians, and special construction units will be put to death."

It also said, "Because the disposal of dead bodies is a troublesome task, they should be gathered into houses which are scheduled to be burned or demolished. They should also be thrown into the river."

The architect of the Japanese horror in Manila, Rear Admiral Sanji Iwabuchi, finally realized he was facing imminent defeat and killed himself.

"Good riddance," Ben said.

The day after Iwabuchi took his life, Alex and Ben walked behind MacArthur and his staff into the red-carpeted halls of the Malacañang Palace which had been left untouched. The General officially restored the capital to Osmeña, and other loyal Filipino officials, saying, "The enemy has unnecessarily destroyed this beautiful city. But by these ashes he has wantonly fixed the future pattern of his own doom."

Alex had no doubt that Japan would be defeated. If they'd just surrender and save lives.

MacArthur continued, "On behalf of my government I now solemnly declare, Mr. President, the full powers and responsibilities under the constitution restored to the commonwealth whose seat is here reestablished as provided by law. Your country, thus, is again at liberty to pursue its destiny to an honored position in the family of free nations. Your capital city, cruelly punished though it be, has regained its rightful place—citadel of democracy in the East."

Alex heard MacArthur's voice tremble and watched as the General buried his face in his hands and wept. After wiping his eyes on his sleeve, MacArthur said: "In humble and devout manifestation of gratitude to almighty God for bringing this decisive victory to our arms, I ask that all present rise and join me in reciting *The Lord's Prayer.* After everyone stood, the present company bowed their heads and began. "Our Father who art in Heaven, Hallowed, be Thy name."

Alex wiped his eyes as he repeated the words to the familiar prayer, which was so dear to his heart.

Three days later, American forces secured the city of Manila, but not before 613 city blocks had been leveled. Official Army investigators interviewed still more victims and produced thousands of pages of sworn testimony. Others photographed wounds and walked through slaughter sites with the survivors, making diagrams and taking pictures.

Page after page of testimony showed the struggle victims had in understanding why the Japanese had been so cruel. Many were bitter and hostile. No one could really fathom the widespread bloodbath. American investigators used words like "diabolical," "inhuman," and "savage," and wondered how anyone who called themselves human could do this to another.

"This orgy of looting, raping, and murder defy credence, were it not for the mass of indisputable evidence establishing its commission," one report read.

Life Magazine journalist Carl Mydans wrote: "Those residents who were able, fled—a perilous journey through an apocalyptic wasteland. All morning we had seen the long files of people walking mutely rearward past advancing infantry. Some of them limped with improvised wound dressings. Many of them walked, heaven knows how, with open wounds." Internee Robert Wygle described the parade of wounded who came to Santo Tomas in search of help. "They are so far beyond recognition that, in many cases, one can't tell whether they are men or women, boys or girls, dead or alive."

Tory told Alex that Manila was the nearest thing to a hometown General MacArthur had. "In this city," MacArthur had told him, "my mother died, my wife was courted, and my son was born."

There were others who had appreciated this once beautiful city. "To live in Manila in 1941," CBS news correspondent Bill Dunn said, "was to experience the good life."

Not anymore, Alex thought. The Japanese have ripped out her heart, and mine too. I'll never be the same man. And even if the people back home read all about it, they'll never understand what it was like to listen to the stories firsthand and feel the pain of those who survived. War is so arbitrary. Why does one person die and another live?

When he got his next letter from home, Mom had included a poem her friend Eva Bird had written about her dead son.

"We followed him through many lands,
In jungle dense, on white beach sands,
In inky blackness on the sea,
Where phantom ships and men did flee,
We followed him!
He has returned but to his God.
Of his brave deeds we are so proud.
May we in our groping find the way,
To life eternal and endless day,
Of peace with Thee and him,
At Last."

Alex set the letter aside. It was a poem of hope written by a mother with deep and abiding faith. *No matter what horrors we face in this life, there is a better life to come.* Alex cried like a baby, relieved no one was around to hear his sobs.

CHAPTER THIRTY-THREE

When the 92nd evacuation hospital left for the small island of Cebu, I joined the 126th General Hospital, a huge tent city of more than thirty-five hundred people, carved out of a muddy swamp. With Alex in Manila, and me an eighteen-hour jeep and ferry ride away, we wouldn't see each other much anymore. That made me sad. I guess I'd been spoiled having him close for so long.

I'd miss Maxine too. She'd been sent to Manila as a war relief worker, among one of the first large groups of American Red Cross women to arrive after American troops reached the city. I hoped Alex would run into her. Maxine was quite a gal, loving, always asking after others, never talking much about herself. She had a great love for the Filipino people.

The colonel in charge asked me into his office and said, "Captain Lucy Hatch, congratulations on your promotion to major! You've served admirably under fire in field hospitals, on a hospital ship, and recently in an evacuation hospital. You've worked under difficult conditions and risked your life."

I was speechless, thoughts scattered, too excited to think as he continued. "It's my pleasure to express heartfelt congratulations for your service. Thanks for a job well done." Then he handed me my new oak leaf insignia and said, "I'm confident you will continue to serve your country with vigor and apply yourself faithfully to the task of supervisor of the head nurses."

My mouth fell open slightly when he told me what I'd be doing, and I forgot to blink. I saluted, thanked him, walked away, and waited for the transport bringing in our new nurses from Hollandia. I was happy that Alicia would be one of them.

When they arrived, I loaded them onto a jeep and drove them around the new compound. "This is the 126th General Hospital," I told them. "There's a water system that can handle one hundred thousand gallons of water a day, a big generator system, steam plants, and an incinerator. Over there's the washing room for clothes. It has actual machines."

"Wow," one of the nurses said. "I was expecting something more primitive."

"Nope. We also have young Filipina girls who come to wash and iron our pants and shirts," I said.

"That's very nice," Alicia observed.

"It helps us, and it helps them," I said. "They need the money. Nurse's quarters are up ahead, there at the far end of the compound."

We arrived, got out of the jeep, and I showed them around their new living area. "There are six to a tent," I said. "Check out the iron beds and the T-bars with bug netting. You'll find clean sheets and towels on your bed."

"The pillow looks kind of fluffy," Alicia said. "Where do we keep our stuff?"

"In the five-by-seven storage area over the bed. There's just enough space."

"Great," Alicia said, preparing to unpack.

"It's quiet too," I said, "except for the geckos that like to hang out in the palm trees that cover the tents."

"You know I'm fond of those little green lizards," Alicia laughed.

I smiled and said, "You girls get yourselves settled. I'm off to write an overdue letter home.

When I reached my new office, I sat alone and wrote another letter to Mom and Dad. In my last one, I told them I'd married Matt. While Mom wrote back that she understood, I could read her disappointment between the lines, and I was sorry for that.

March 10, 1945

Hi Mom and Dad,

I hope you're both well. I miss you.

I'm now serving with the 126th General Hospital outside Tacloban. I've been promoted to major, an honor I wasn't expecting. It's surreal that I've attained the highest officer rank in the Women's Army Corp. Do you remember last June when nurses became entitled to pay and allowances equal to male officers? My pay goes up now, a big help when the war ends.

The hospital is so big here that the CO told me it has more beds than there were in the whole state of Nevada in 1943. Can you believe it? There are offices and supply rooms as well as a chapel made from bamboo. We're holding Easter services there tomorrow. Our hospital has put together a quartet. I hope the chaplain's sermon gives me the spiritual uplift I need.

There's still a lot of fighting going on out here. Monday, we could have as many as ten thousand new patients. But I have the day off tomorrow, and Alicia and I are heading for the beach to swim in the Pacific where I hope not to get tossed around too badly by the breakers. We'll bring lunch and air mattresses to sit on.

That's it for now.

Love, Lucy

I sealed my pages in the envelope and went to mail the letter. Next Saturday night, we'd have the formal opening of an officer's club here at the hospital. We'd have dinner and then dance to a Nickelodeon. A nice break from the boxes and tents, and the food should be good.

I wouldn't be dancing without Matt, of course, and I continued to worry about him. Alex had cabled that the *USS Salt Lake City* was still in Iwo Jima, and I'd been scared to death. Matt had been in the middle of a huge battle for three weeks, ever since the US Marines invaded.

When I dropped my letter off, the corporal handed me one. It was from Matt. I tore it open immediately.

Dear Lucy,

I know it's been a while, and I'm sorry, my love. Our ship has spent the last several weeks providing fire power for the Marines here at Iwo Jima. When we first arrived, I listened to Tokyo Rose over the radio telling us to write our last letter home because we were about to die. We tried to ignore her, but she was right. Two of my shipmates were killed.

Lots of lives have been lost on both sides of the struggle, but this loss was deeply personal. These men were my friends, my comrades in arms. We've served together more than three years. They're like family. Better than family in some cases. I'm devastated, Lucy.

You know I believe in a forever after, but it doesn't change my sadness over the loss of my friends. Even Jesus wept.

I'm told we're leaving soon for Okinawa. Happy Easter, my darling wife.

I love you,

Matt

"Oh, Matt, my dear husband," I whispered. "You've been through so much. Happy Easter to you too, my love. I pray we can be together again soon."

The battle of Iwo Jima lasted another two weeks before the soldiers raised the American flag of victory. It was one of the bloodiest battles in history, and Matt survived unscathed. I learned from Alex when he got a call through to me that the allied win was due in large part to the Navajo Code talkers.

"Thank the Lord for the Navajos. Their language is unwritten, right?" I asked.

"Yes, and by assigning a Navajo word to key phrases, the Code Talkers are able to translate three lines of English in twenty seconds, instead of thirty minutes."

"That's incredible. Are they with the army?"

"Marines," Alex said. "Leadership told us that six Navajo Code Talker Marines effectively transmitted more than eight hundred messages without a single error and were critical to our victory at Iwo Jima." He paused. "I'm glad Matt's ok."

"He's safe, thank God. I miss him so much." I tried to swallow the lump in my throat that never seemed to go away.

CHAPTER THIRTY-FOUR

Hallie chewed her lip as she read the sign she traveled past daily, thinking about the ever-increasing security in this complex on the hill.

What you see here
What you do here
What you hear here
What you leave here
Let it stay here.

She rubbed the dust of Los Alamos out of her eyes and kept walking. Hallie didn't like secrets, but she had no choice. Things were moving ahead quickly on the gadget, the name the scientists used for the weapon of destruction. Trent was privy to information that the weapon design for the uranium gun bomb had been frozen a few weeks ago. He'd told her, "Confidence is high enough now that it's fit for combat."

"So that's why our focus has shifted to implosion," Hallie said.

"Exactly. And I hear the design for the implosion device is set to be approved any day now."

"Then we'll need to test it. If it works, and I'm betting it will, that's when the tough decisions are made."

"You mean as in, how will we use the gadget?"

"Yes, and should it be used to end the war in the Pacific. We also need to study the radiological effects of the test. The bees in my hives are dying in droves, and mums that should be white are brown and dying."

"No one's even testing that stuff. You're right, Hallie."

"Thanks. Some of the male scientists around here treat me like a secretary."

"They're idiots," Trent said, leaning over and kissing her on the cheek.

She smiled and kissed him back on the lips.

"That was nice," he said.

"I love kissing you," Hallie said, snuggling up against his chest.

"I'll second that," Trent smiled.

Hallie reached up and touched his hair, her face radiant. Time to change the subject, she thought. "Say, have you heard about Oppenheimer's new Cow Puncher Committee?" Hallie asked.

"You mean the one whose purpose is to 'ride herd' on the implosion weapon?" Trent laughed.

"That's the one."

"Then there's Project A, with the responsibility to prepare and deliver the weapons for combat."

"Last I heard, there's a test scheduled in July, three short months from now." Hallie looked at her watch. "The scientists are meeting right now."

"Let's go join them. I bet physicist Leo Szilard will speak in opposition to using the gadget."

As Hallie and Trent entered the back of the room, one of the female scientists was saying, "There have been more than sixty accidents in the tech area since the beginning of 1945. That's way too many and the chemicals are dangerous to our health. We can't leave things in the hands of politicians and military men."

"I think we need exposure limits and hazard pay," another said.

"The bomb may be inevitable," a physicist spoke up, "but the scientists should have a say in how it's used. We're not going to have that say."

Hallie whispered to Trent, "I heard President Roosevelt is forming a committee to decide how the bomb will be used and who it gets dropped on."

"There are no scientists or engineers on his committee," Trent said.

Szilard started circulating a petition asking for the names of fellow scientists who felt the same way he did.

"We might not need this bomb," someone else spoke up as the petition went around. "Hitler is finished, and the military knows the Germans don't have a bomb."

"But the military still plans to drop an atomic bomb on a Japanese city, killing maybe fifty thousand people, most of them civilians, women and children," a scientist said.

"That would be tragic," Trent spoke up. "And yet I've heard estimates that one hundred thousand civilians lost their lives in the battle over Manila. This war has to stop, but the Japanese refuse to surrender."

Another agreed saying, "This gadget is going to end the war with Japan. It will save American lives."

There is no easy answer, Hallie thought as the discussion raged on. No one really knows what will happen if we drop this bomb.

On April 12, a new dimension was added to the problem, as the scientists at Los Alamos heard an announcement blaring over the outside radio speaker.

President Roosevelt has died. Reports have emerged suggesting he suffered a cerebral hemorrhage. The president was sitting for a portrait when he complained of a terrific headache. He has been one of the greatest leaders of this country and humanity. He was a wise and patient leader in the greatest war ever fought for freedom. The President died at his home in Warm Springs, Georgia at the age of 63.

"That means Truman's in charge," Trent said to Hallie, "and that could change everything."

The Secret Service rushed Vice President Harry S Truman to the White House, and he was sworn in by Chief Justice Harlan Stone.

"Truman's been serving in the senate, and he's been vice president for less than three months," Hallie said, concerned.

"He has very little experience, and we don't know him well enough. Will he listen to the experts, the military, or just go rogue?"

A few days later, snow littered the grounds, and the usually busy streets were quiet. Los Alamos mourned along with the rest of the nation. The scientists, their families, and the military men waited in the large theatre for President Roosevelt's memorial service. As the head of the entire project, Oppenheimer was scheduled to deliver the eulogy.

Hallie remembered the promise Roosevelt had made to the nation after Pearl Harbor was bombed. "No matter how long it may take us to overcome this premeditated invasion," he'd said, "the American people in their righteous might will win through to absolute victory."

Trent reminded them, "It was Roosevelt who authorized the atomic bomb research and development project here, gathering the brightest scientific minds to create a device that he hoped would end the war."

"He's led our country for more than twelve years," Hallie said, still stunned. "Through the Depression and Pearl Harbor. What will we do without him?"

A physicist turned to them. "Without Roosevelt, there's no one we know at the top."

Hallie wondered what Oppie would say today. He knew some of his scientists had doubts about the atomic bomb. She watched him walk slowly to the stage, down the middle of thousands of people who had crowded into the long rows of wooden benches.

When he reached the stage, he stood, a lowered American flag behind him. Then, in a voice that wasn't much louder than a whisper, he began the eulogy.

"When, three days ago, the world had word of the death of President Roosevelt, many wept who are unaccustomed to tears, many men, and women little enough accustomed to prayer, prayed to God. Many of us looked with deep trouble to the future; many of us felt less certain that our works would be a good end; all of us were reminded how precious a thing human greatness is.

We have been living through years of great evil and of great terror. Roosevelt has been our president, our commander in chief and, in an old, unperverted sense, our leader. All over the world, men have looked to him for guidance and have seen symbolized in him, their hope that the evils of this time would not be repeated; that the terrible sacrifices which have been made, and those that are still to be made, would lead to a world more fit for human habitation. It is in such times of evil that men recognize their helplessness and their profound dependence.

One is reminded of medieval days when the death of a good and wise and just king plunged his country into despair and mourning."

Oppie opened a book and continued:

"In the Hindu scripture, in the Bhagavad Gita, it says 'Man is a creature whose substance is faith. What his faith is, he is.' The faith of Roosevelt is one that is shared by millions of men and women in every country of the world. For this reason, it is possible to maintain the hope, for this reason it is right that we should dedicate ourselves to the hope that his good works will not have ended with his death."

After he finished, the scientists and their families stood, bowed their heads, and were silent for a few minutes, sad and concerned about the future.

As the crowd dispersed, Hallie heard Oppie tell one of the physicists, "Roosevelt was a great architect. Perhaps Truman will be a good carpenter."

"We'd better hope so," the physicist answered.

Trent whispered to Hallie, "After years of research and billions in taxpayer dollars, Oppenheimer knows he'd better deliver as promised, and soon."

CHAPTER THIRTY-FIVE

Tory gathered his staff for what he told them would be an important and historic announcement. Alex expected everyone in the room knew what was coming, but still an excited buzz circled the room. About a week ago, as bombs pounded on Hitler's bunker, he and his wife of two days, Eva Braun, killed themselves. Then yesterday, Field Marshal Keitel signed the formal surrender terms. The world would forever remember May 7, 1945. The war in Europe was over.

President Truman was about to share the news with the United States, and Alex and the others listened via radio as Truman read his declaration.

"Germany has surrendered to the UN. This is a solemn but glorious hour. I only wish that Franklin D. Roosevelt had lived to see this day," the president said. *"Thanks to the Providence which has guided and sustained us through the dark days of adversity into light."*

Truman went on to speak about the horrific cost the Allies had paid to "rid the world of Hitler and his evil band."

"Let us not forget the sorrow and the heartache which today abide in the homes for many of our neighbors.... We can repay the debt which we owe to our God, to our dead, and to our children only by work, by ceaseless devotion to the responsibility which lies ahead of us.

If I could give you a single watchword for the coming months, that word is work. Work and more work. We must work to finish the war. Our victory is but half won.

Alex's jaw tightened as he wondered what horror was needed to defeat the Japanese. We still might have to invade Japan, he thought.

Truman went on to say, *The Far East is still in bondage to the treacherous tyranny of the Japanese. When the last Japanese division has surrendered unconditionally, then only will our fighting job be done."*

The word 'unconditional' punched Alex in the gut, and the color drained from his face. He shuddered thinking what that would take, as Truman ended his two-and a half minute address.

Newspapers across America put out special editions with bold headlines. *The Pittsburgh Press* led with "V-E Day Proclaimed. Japan Next." *The Hattiesburg American* called out, "Japs Being Measured for Burial Kimono." *The New York Daily News* headline simply said: "It's Over."

A week later, Alex received a rare letter from Chris. He hadn't heard from him since he'd reached home, and Alex worried how Chris might be adjusting.

Hey Alex,

Bet you're even more excited than I am about the end of the war with Germany. We'll stop the Japanese next!

I'm trying to get on with my life back here in Utah, but the camp horrors won't leave me alone. I get nightmares and flashbacks, dreaming about the men I couldn't help or save. Always on high alert. Then my hands started trembling. I told Dad about the nightmares. He reminded me that I was home now. That I was fine. So, I stopped talking about it.

Last Sunday, Grandma Katie came to dinner. I can't believe she's ninety and still practicing medicine. She told me she's delivering babies for children she delivered. Our grandma is something else. After we ate dinner, she suggested we take a walk to the park, where we sat down on an empty bench.

Grandma Katie mostly asked questions and just listened to me talk. Then she said, "Chris, your wounds are inside. You can't see them, but they're still there." Her words shocked me. Then she told me it was nothing to be ashamed of.

I bawled like a baby, and she held me. Then she suggested I contact an army doctor. I asked her why my faith wasn't enough to heal me. She said that God gives us both light and knowledge, and He wants us to use all the tools at our disposal. She said physicians of the mind are one of those tools.

So, I called the army and they're sending me to Mason General Hospital on Long Island for several weeks. It opened last year to treat men like me. Pray for me.

Your brother,

Chris

Alex blinked away tears and set the letter aside. He prayed. "Please, God, help my brother."

Alex then learned about the proposed invasion of Japan. Tory shared an internal communique on May 25, advising his team that the US Joint Chiefs of Staff had approved Operation Olympic, code name for the invasion of Japan.

Alex asked Tory, "Is there a date set?"

"Yes," Tory answered. "November 1. It's hush, hush."

A few weeks later, Japanese Premier Suzuki announced that Japan would "fight to the very end rather than accept unconditional surrender."

Japan here we come.

The next day, Alex took a depressing walk along the streets of Manila's business district. There were only two buildings that hadn't suffered damage. He thought about lines from a letter he'd received from Norm Nielson, who'd observed, "Sometimes I wonder why things like this couldn't be settled without this great loss of life and material."

True words, Norm, Alex thought. Manila alone had lost 100,000 to 240,000 Filipino civilians. The Japanese either massacred them or they'd died from the artillery and aerial bombardment the Japanese and US forces used in the battle for Manila.

The city had lost its beautiful Spanish colonial architecture. Government buildings, universities and colleges, monasteries, and churches, along with their treasures dating back to the founding of the city, had been decimated. It was hard to believe that Manila was once called the Pearl of the Orient.

Alex wandered into a studio of the former Japanese-controlled Radio Manila, which had been used to broadcast anti-American propaganda. He thought about the messages he'd heard from Tokyo

Rose and clenched his fists. Then he felt a tap on his shoulder that startled him. "Hi, Alex," a woman said.

Alex turned and hugged her. It was Maxine. "Great to see you."

"You, too."

"Say, I heard you were one of the American Red Cross relief workers awarded the Liberation Ribbon last month."

"I was honored."

"I understand that the Chief of Staff of the Philippine Army made the presentation."

"He did," Maxine smiled, "to several of us who assisted the army in the distribution of Red Cross Chapter-made clothes."

"A big help to the people here. What are you doing in this empty studio?"

"Checking out the place. Once the war ends, Tokyo Rose's radio broadcasts will be finished, and I'll be the radio announcer, broadcasting hope and faith, not fear and propaganda."

"That's incredible. Congratulations!"

"I've mentioned our religious heritage to the Red Cross, and they've endorsed securing and using recordings of the Mormon Tabernacle Choir. What do you think about that?"

"I can't think of anything more uplifting than their music. You're quite the woman, Maxine. I'll let Lucy know I ran into you."

Alex hugged Maxine goodbye, wished her the best, and then left for staff headquarters.

He gazed into the distance as he walked, thinking about his friend Norm again. He was one of the lucky ones. Corporal Norman H. Nielson had served enough time to return home and had been honorably discharged from the army in Virginia. "Thanks for your service," Alex said, touching the brim of his hat, lengthening his stride.

By June 18, the Japanese resistance ended on Mindanao in the Philippines. Four days later, the Japanese lost Okinawa as the US Tenth Army completed its capture of the island. Tory told his staff, "The Japanese lost about a hundred thousand of their one hundred and twenty thousand men on Okinawa. They're clearly defeated.

And yet, thousands of Japanese soldiers are still fighting, falling on their own grenades instead of surrendering." Tory shook his head.

"If the enemy fought that fiercely for Okinawa, what will they do to defend their homeland?" Alex asked.

"Good question," Tory said. "The only option I see now is to invade Japan. MacArthur has estimated that invasion would cost one million American casualties, not to mention countless Japanese lives."

CHAPTER THIRTY-SIX

The *USS Salt Lake City* had docked at Leyte for repairs and relaxation. Matt and I were happily spending as much time together as possible. The day after the ship landed, he and I drove around the circle from Tacloban to Dulag to Dagami and back in a jeep. This time I drove, and it was lots of fun. "These jeeps are quite the vehicles," I said, shifting into gear.

"And you're a pretty good driver, Lucy," Matt said, grabbing the armrest as I rounded a corner.

"Just pretty good?" I laughed as we pulled to a stop. I'd brought along a picnic of tenderloin steak, beans, and fruit.

Matt patted his belly as we ate. "The steak is delicious. Thank you."

"I love being with my man."

After we finished, we drove up to the top of a high hill overlooking Tacloban Harbor. "I never tire of this view," I said.

"You can still see white clouds reflected in the calm water." Then as the daylight dimmed, he put his arm around me.

We heard people singing. Behind us, across the hillside, we spotted a line of lights and people holding torches. They carried a lit cross, stars, and lanterns. As they made their way around the treacherous curves on the path, they gyrated to the sounds of a chant we didn't understand. We stood with the lights of the city of Tacloban below us and the lights of the Christian religious ceremony on the hillside. It was moment I'd never forget.

Matt said, "When the war with Japan ends, we can take that long overdue honeymoon in Hawaii. Chances are good we'll pass through there on our way back to San Francisco."

"I can't think of anything better," I said, giving him a long, drawn-out kiss, sighing. "I guess we better get back."

"Do you have an early morning tomorrow at the hospital?"

"Yes, and I've been asked to supervise a men's surgical ward for the day."

The next day, as I walked around the ward, it still surprised me that many of the boys weren't any more than eighteen or nineteen years old. They were still just kids but with horrible wounds. One of them had an awful chest injury, and I watched a nurse carefully dress his wound. He was brave and didn't complain, but I could see the pain carved on his face. War is always the same, I thought. Young men are wounded or die at the peak of their lives.

Around noon, I ran into Alicia. "Hey, come and have a look at this," she said, her step light. We walked over to a large tent, and when we went inside, I was surprised to find a lovely lounge with a rug, several tables, and padded chairs. The couch was covered in pink cloth. "Can you believe it's pink?" Alicia asked. "So fun," she smiled, "and all for the nurses."

"Look, there's even a stove and bread and cheese over there," I said, stomach grumbling.

"Thanks to Major McKay." Alicia always gave credit where it was due.

"You know, our hospital is like a village. We're one big family who works hard, and we even have fun when we can."

"We're all friends, and that means everything," Alicia said.

I picked up bread, cheese, and juice, and we relaxed in two of the lounge chairs. "We've been through a lot in this war, Alicia. I want us to be friends forever."

"Me too," she said. "In the kindness of friendship, there's laughter."

"I've loved your distinctive laugh since I first heard it at Pearl Harbor and knew I wanted to be your friend. You make my heart smile." I looked at my watch and said, "Guess I better get back."

"I'm going to find our new little Filipina girl, Diwa. She's been washing our shirts and pants, and she's probably almost finished."

"Give her a hug from me."

An hour later, Alicia came rushing into my ward. "Diwa's gone missing. Her mother is frantic. I'm going to go help her look."

"My shift here lasts another two hours, and then I'll join you."

"We'll find her by then. See you back at the tent."

When I reached the tent, Diwa and her mother were inside. Diwa was wrapped in a towel, crying. "I'm so glad to see you," I said putting my arm around her shoulder.

"Missy Alicia, she find me. I slip into water and could not get out. Was holding on a branch. She waded into rushing water and get me."

It was like Alicia to put her own life at risk to save someone else. "Where's Miss Alicia now" I asked.

"Don't know," Diwa sobbed. "I was resting on bank of river and told her I was hungry.

She said she find me some fruit, but never come back. So, I walk here."

With a rush of anxiety, I went for Matt, and the two of us took off looking. My heart beat with fear. Where was she? An hour later, we hadn't found her, so the nurses from the 126th general joined the search. No luck.

The next morning, we still didn't know where she was. "What if she never comes back?" I asked Matt horrified. Please let this be a nightmare and not for real. I had to believe she was alive. "Please come back to us, Alicia," I whispered. I felt like an anvil was sitting on my chest, weighing me down with worry.

Later that afternoon, Matt and I went back to the place Diwa had last seen Alicia. This time we found some torn cloth in the bushes and what looked like handprints in the dirt. Matt pulled his gun, and we followed the trail. We heard someone moaning. It was Alicia!

"Thanks be to God, you're here." I rushed to her side.

"I fell and broke my ankle and couldn't get up. I dragged myself as far as this tree to hide from the Japanese soldiers. I prayed you'd come." She reached out for me.

I sat by her side and hugged her. "I'm so grateful we found you."

Then Matt tore off his shirt, and I wrapped it around her ankle.

Alicia gulped water from a canteen Matt offered, then said, "I was close to my grandma who died, and I could feel her presence last night, giving me hope that you'd come," she whispered. "My grandma loved me so much, and so does my mom. I have nieces waiting at home, and someday I'd like a daughter of my own. My family needs me, Lucy, and I need them." She bowed her head. "I have so much to live for."

"Yes, you do, and your good friends back at the hospital love you too and have been worried sick."

Matt and I put one of Alicia's arms around each of our shoulders and carried her back to the 126th General Hospital where a doctor put her ankle in a cast and ordered her to get some rest.

July 5, the military declared the Liberation of the Philippines. We were all so excited, we had a big celebration. "It's only a matter of time until this war ends," Matt said, holding my hand, as we ate supper. "I'm sorry to leave you again, Lucy, but the USS Salt Lake City sails tomorrow."

"I love you so much. Please stay safe."

"I will, my darling."

The next day, Matt waved at me from the deck of the cruiser as she left for Japan. The thought of him being so close to Japan gave me chills.

CHAPTER THIRTY-SEVEN

Hallie and Trent took an early morning hike in the sandy, red hills outside Los Alamos. "Are you up for the fourth of July picnic today?" He asked, climbing higher.

"I don't know. Maybe I'd rather just be with you."

"I like that answer." He kissed her, smiling.

"Whew. I'm getting a little winded," Hallie said. "Do you mind if we take a break?"

"Not at all. There's something I want to tell you anyway," Trent said, as they sat down on a large, flat rock. "Out here in the desert where the military isn't tapping our phones is a good place for it."

"Sounds secretive."

"Very."

"I'm all ears."

"Did you know Utah has played a role in this whole bomb thing?"

"No, I didn't," Hallie said, doing a double take. "What is it?"

"It started at Wendover Airfield, a base along the Utah–Nevada state line."

"That's a pretty remote area."

"And apparently perfect for Operation Silverplate. Guy in charge is named Tibbets, and he's put together a first-rate flight crew. Their job is to drop the gadget."

Hallie sucked in a quick breath and asked, "How do you know all this?"

"Ryan is a pilot out there." Ryan was Trent's little brother, and Trent would regularly get lost in nostalgia sharing memories of their childhood in Utah.

"Was he allowed to share this information?"

"The military told him last September: You don't discuss with anyone where you are, who you are, what you're doing. With your wife, your mother, your sister, your girlfriend."

"Wow. So, why'd he tell you?"

"They didn't say anything about telling your brother," Trent laughed. "No, it's because I told him about what we're doing here in Los Alamos. We've been communicating through secure two-way radio."

"What if you get caught?"

"We won't. Ryan told me the ground crews left at the end of April, took the Western Pacific Railroad to Seattle, and then boarded a ship to Tinian. Ryan and the B-29 crews will fly out later."

"What and where is Tinian?"

"A small island in the Northern Marianas, located fifteen hundred miles south of Tokyo. We have an airbase there."

"So, it's the launch point for dropping the bomb."

"That's what Ryan says."

"I hate thinking that dropping the bomb is inevitable."

"We'll see how the test here goes. Twelve days and counting."

The morning of July 15, Hallie and Trent pulled out binoculars and watched as a truck backed up to a tower and stopped. The driver pulled a canvas cover off the truck. In the sunshine of the day, Hallie could see the bomb gleam. She focused her gaze on that steel globe spiking with wires, switches, screws, and diagnostic devices. Inside the 8,000-pound shell sat thirteen and a half pounds of plutonium wrapped inside explosives. Workers moved the bomb up into position and placed mattresses underneath it.

The door opened in the floor of the steel shed that sat on top of the tower. Steel cables dropped and workers hooked the bomb to the cables, and an electric winch started hoisting it up. Hallie froze when one of the cables came loose, and the gadget rocked back and forth. *Thank the Lord it stabilized.*

Once the bomb was in position, technicians inserted electrical detonators into openings on the steel casing. Hallie could see Oppenheimer talking to a guy named Hornig and suspected he was being asked to tend to the bomb until morning. Good plan, Hallie thought. There were lots of people here at the test site who knew how it worked, and some of them weren't above sabotage.

Then the heavy rain started. Hallie and Trent pulled on raincoats and started walking. Unusual weather for Los Alamos, Hallie thought, picking up the pace. When they got back, the dirt roads were flooding.

By four thirty the next morning, tension was running high in the bunkers filled with scientists and the military. Some of the technicians put together a betting pool, asking, "Who wants to estimate the size of the explosion?"

This is supposed to help, how? Hallie wondered, her anxiety growing by the minute. One man bet the explosion would be like setting off forty-five thousand tons of TNT.

"Too high," Oppie said, "I'll take thirty thousand tons."

Then Enrico Fermi said, "How about some side bets? If the bomb ignites the atmosphere, will it destroy just New Mexico or the entire world?"

Oppie was not amused, and Hallie hoped some of the more vigilant scientists could help Fermi convince Oppie to at least delay the test.

Major General Groves bristled when Fermi told Oppenheimer that with the winds gusting up to thirty miles an hour and the rain still pouring down, it was a tough time to set off a nuclear bomb.

"He might be right," Hallie whispered to Trent. "We could all end up getting soaked with radioactive rain."

Fermi told Oppenheimer, "There could be a catastrophe."

An army meteorologist spoke up next and predicted the storm would clear by sunrise. General Groves folded his arms across his chest.

Trent said, "I bet he's wondering what he'd have to tell Truman about delaying the test."

After a lengthy discussion, Groves and Oppenheimer decided to keep the test scheduled for 5:30 a.m. and hope for the best.

Right around five, Groves left for another bunker to watch the final countdown. Groves and Oppenheimer were set up in different bunkers just in case things went awry. The project couldn't afford to lose two key leaders at the same time.

Hallie and Trent had already hopped into a truck and driven twenty miles northwest of ground zero. "At least the rain and wind have stopped," Hallie said as they drove. They were headed for Compania Hill where the press and VIP observers from Washington were waiting to watch the explosion, along with many of the scientists. Reporter William Laurence and Vannevar Bush, head of the US office of Scientific Research and Development, would be among them. He'd been the lead scientist on Roosevelt's committee and then in May had become a part of the committee that advised Truman on nuclear weapons. Hallie had heard of him, but they'd never met. She did know that he was fully in support of dropping the bomb.

The visitors had come in from Albuquerque in a group of three buses, three automobiles, and a truck full of radio equipment. There seemed to be more than expected.

They were waiting now at the Alamogordo bombing and Gunnery Range for the Trinity nuclear test, the first time an atom bomb would be detonated on earth.

Trent parked the jeep, and he and Hallie stood on the outer part of the circle among those waiting for instructions on what to do when the bomb went off.

A soldier pulled out his flashlight and read the orders. "You'll hear a short siren at zero minus five minutes. When it goes off, find an acceptable place on the ground to lie down." He looked around for questions. When there were none, the soldier continued.

"At zero minus two minutes, you'll hear a long siren sound. You need to lie prone on the ground immediately, face and eyes directed toward the ground. Do not watch for the flash directly but turn over after it has occurred and watch the cloud. Stay on the ground until the blast wave has passed. That will take about two minutes."

Even though it was pitch dark outside, several of the scientists including Hallie and Trent applied sunscreen to their hands and faces. They knew what atomic energy could do.

In thirty-millionths of a second, observers in the pre-dawn darkness saw an intense flash of light, followed by a huge blast wave and a loud roar. With the explosive power of twenty thousand tons of TNT, a light "brighter than the noonday sun" was seen more than two hundred miles away. The sound carried close to one hundred miles.

A yellow and orange fireball spit upward and spread across the sky. Then a breathtaking mushroom cloud rose about forty thousand feet in the air. Heat seared across the desert, vaporizing the steel tower, and blasting a crater six feet deep and more than a thousand feet long in the desert floor. Hallie gasped and took a step back when she noticed that a herd of antelope that had been grazing near the tower had disappeared. She saw no signs of life within a one-mile radius of the blast. Not a rattlesnake, not a blade of grass. No one could see the radiation generated by the explosion, but they all knew it was there.

The business of warfare had changed in an instant.

Concerned by the bright flash and the deafening roar, people living near the air base immediately began calling military authorities. The military told residents and police an ammunition dump had exploded, but that everything was under control.

People in Albuquerque flooded an *Associated Press* reporter with telephone calls, wondering what had really happened on the base. The reporter said if the army didn't respond to comments, he'd put out his own story.

So, the army issued a statement, of sorts. "This isn't even true, of course," Trent said as he read it to Hallie. Listen to this: "Several inquiries have been received concerning a heavy explosion which occurred on the Alamogordo Air Base reservation this morning. A remotely located ammunition magazine containing a considerable number of high explosives and pyrotechnics exploded. There was no loss of life or injury to anyone...Weather conditions affecting the content of gas shells exploded by the blast may make it desirable for the army to evacuate temporarily a few civilians from their homes."

The army's smokescreen dumbfounded the reporter. He wrote: "The Atomic Age began at exactly 5:30 Mountain War Time on the morning of July 16, 1945, on a stretch of semi-desert land about fifty airline miles from Alamogordo, N. M., just a few minutes before the dawn of a new day on this earth."

When General Groves and Oppenheimer got together, Hallie watched a big smile spread across the general's face. "I'm proud of you," he said to Oppie.

Oppenheimer straightened his shoulders and said, "I believe the bomb will shorten the war." Then he whispered, "Now I become death, destroyer of worlds," a passage of Hindu scripture from the Bhagavad Gita.

Some of the men celebrated and slapped one another on the back. Hallie shook with fear.

Others were more restrained. Bainbridge, the test director, called the explosion a "foul and awesome display." It was clear what would happen if the bomb were dropped on a Japanese city.

Yes, it might shorten the war. But at what cost?

The next morning, Trent and Hallie ate breakfast in a diner, the bright sun shining through the café's windows. Trent held a copy of July's *Atlantic Monthly* in his hands, saying,

"Vannevar Bush makes his position crystal clear in his essay 'As We May Think.' He wrote: "This has not been a scientist's war; it has been a war in which all have had a part. The scientists, burying their old professional competition in the demand of a common cause, have shared greatly, and learned much. It has been exhilarating to work in effective partnership."

What do you think of that?" Trent asked.

"In an effective partnership to do what? Destroy humanity?"

"Who knows what the right thing to do was? We were actors in this movie, not directors," Trent said.

"I wanted to make the world a better place. Not destroy it."

"Whatever the result, our work at Los Alamos is finished, Hallie. Let's get out of here and go home."

"I'd like that." Then she paused and asked, "What does that mean for us, Trent?"

"Thought you'd never ask," he smiled, taking something out of his pocket. "Does this engagement ring suit your tastes?" He grinned.

"What took you so long?" Hallie laughed.

"Does that mean, yes?"

Hallie threw her arms around him, nodding. He kissed her.

***

The day after the nuclear test, Alex was attending a two-week conference in Potsdam, Germany, with General Tory, General MacArthur, and staff. The big players were President Truman, Prime Minister Winston Churchill, and Premier Joseph Stalin, who were there to negotiate terms on how to administer Germany, peace treaty issues, etc. The surrender of Japan would also be discussed.

Alex knew he'd never meet the real bigwigs. That was okay. He wanted to hear the discussion about what to do with Japan, which would begin in a few minutes. He was sitting in the back of the room with Tory.

The meeting opened, and Alex listened first to General Dwight Eisenhower state his opposition to the use of the bomb. "The Japanese are already defeated," he said. "It's not necessary to hit them with the awful thing."

General MacArthur agreed and said that the Japanese would have been willing to surrender as early as May if the US had allowed them to keep the emperor. Several of the admirals agreed with MacArthur.

Alex was dumfounded. *Why not let them keep the emperor. What did that matter?*

Even President Truman's chief of staff spoke up saying, "The Japanese are already defeated and ready to surrender. The use of this barbarous weapon at Hiroshima and Nagasaki is of no material assistance in our war against Japan."

The Soviets had already agreed to invade Manchuria, Korea, Karafuto, and Hokkaido. That would deal a death blow to the Japanese resistance. We don't need the bomb, Alex thought.

On July 26, Truman, Churchill, and Chinese President, Chiang Kai-shek, issued the Potsdam Declaration, which outlined the terms of surrender for the Empire of Japan. The ultimatum stated that, "if Japan did not surrender, it would face prompt and utter destruction."

Alex found out later that on that very day, components of the atomic bomb called "Little Boy" were unloaded by the cruiser *Indianapolis* at Tinian Island.

Three days later, a Japanese submarine sank the *Indianapolis*, killing 881 crew members and leaving survivors adrift in the water for two days.

Why didn't the Japanese give up instead of continuing to dig their own graves? Alex wondered. The awful price is more lives lost on both sides.

CHAPTER THIRTY-EIGHT

Sunday, August 5, a courier arrived from Washington with word for MacArthur that an atomic bomb would be dropped on an industrial area south of Tokyo the next day. The decision had been made. General Groves cabled MacArthur that he'd arranged for some photographers and film makers to 'be on hand for the event, saying he wanted a record.'

MacArthur asked Tory to reign in the press. "Got it," Tory had said. "This may be hard on the crew of the *Enola Gay*. The last thing they need is to feel like they're in the middle of a stupid movie."

Tory told Alex and pilot Dave to take the staff plane ASAP and fly to Tinian.

The next morning, they met the flight crews. When one pilot introduced himself as 'Ryan Monson from Utah,' Alex asked, "Any relation to a guy named Trent Monson?"

"He's my brother. How do you know him?"

"Trent is engaged to my sister Hallie."

"Small world in Utah," Ryan smiled.

"Are you on the *Enola Gay*?"

"No. One of the B-29 observer planes." Ryan said softly. "I didn't know anything about this mission until a couple of hours ago. Then they told us our planes could be seriously damaged or destroyed by the shock waves from some kind of bomb." Ryan's eyes were wide. "We might not make it back alive."

He was right, and there wasn't much Alex could say. He placed his hand on Ryan's shoulder. Ryan said, "You're almost family and we're on our way to meet with a chaplain in a few minutes. Could you come with me please?"

Alex nodded. "You bet."

When they met with the chaplain, he read a long prayer he'd written on the back of an envelope. Men from all religious backgrounds came to the chaplain, hoping to find peace and, for some, find God before heading into the eye of an atomic bomb. After the chaplain finished, Ryan's friend Besser said, "As Jews, we're more likely to give thanks after surviving than to ask a special favor beforehand."

"Makes sense," Alex said. "In a way, it's like saying, 'thy will be done.' Reminds me that while God hears our prayers, we don't control the outcome."

They walked into the mess hall for breakfast, and Ryan said, "I might be too nervous to eat."

"I don't know, Ryan," Alex said. "Food looks pretty good and there's lots of it."

"You're right. If this is my last meal, I better enjoy it." Alex ate oatmeal and Ryan stuffed himself full of bacon, eggs, steak, and pineapple fritters.

Ryan was still eating when Alex said, "See you on the tarmac."

He and Dave climbed into a troop truck. "Time to go check on the reporters," Alex said. "I want to get there before the crews do."

When Alex and Dave reached the empty planes, there were reporters and filmmakers everywhere. "Might be more than a hundred," Alex said in disbelief. "Don't know how much good I can do here." Alex walked around and shook hands with several reporters he recognized.

When Colonel Tibbets arrived with the crew of the *Enola Gay*, he seemed stunned and totally unprepared for all the attention. "I should have warned him," Alex whispered to Dave. "Thought he'd been briefed."

"Don't think so," Dave said. "The men aren't dressed for a photo opportunity. Besides their green overalls, one guy is wearing a Dodger's hat, and there's another with a knit ski hat."

Alex shuddered. "The men's pockets are full of rosaries and rabbits' feet. They're scared."

The crew of the *Enola Gay* had been asked to pose for pictures and speak on camera. A guy named Lewis on the crew gathered the rest of them to finish a briefing. A reporter interrupted, handed Lewis a pen and a notebook, and asked him to keep a record of the flight that the *New York Times* would publish later. Lewis smiled, turned to the enlisted men, and said, "You guys, this bomb costs more than an aircraft carrier. We've got it made. We're going to win the war, just don't screw it up. Let's do this really great."

Alex rolled his eyes. Lewis's words weren't for the men. He was grandstanding for the reporters.

One of the photographic officers spoke up and said, "I need to get the official crew shot." The enlisted men kneeled, and the officers stood over them. When the picture was snapped, Tibbets turned to his crew and said, "Okay. Let's go to work."

Tibbets stepped into his plane, grinned, and waved at the waiting crowd as a photographer snapped his picture. Then he prepared to move his plane down the runway.

"I happen to know that this is Tibbets's first mission in three years," Dave said. "He's had his hands full being in charge of this operation."

Alex agreed and said, "We need to head for the control tower. We'll be there with one of the generals and a *New York Times* reporter to watch the take off."

When they reached the tower, the chaplain was there too. Everyone was attentive as Tibbets called the tower. "Dimples Eight Two to North Tinian Tower. Ready for takeoff on runway Able." The tower cleared him for takeoff.

The B-29 worked itself down the runway, carrying its heavy load. Alex wasn't sure if they'd make it before they hit the water at the end of the runway. At the last possible minute, the plane struggled into the air. Everyone in the control tower cheered and watched as the plane climbed to a cruising altitude and headed for Japan.

Alex came down from the tower, and Dave said, "I've got an FM radio here. Ryan gave me the right frequency to listen in to the *Enola Gay*."

"You're kidding. That's great. Let's go sit over there. They sat off to the side of the tarmac and soon heard Tibbets tell his crew, "We are carrying the world's first atomic bomb." The crew members gasped so loudly that Alex could hear them.

Then Tibbets said, "When the bomb is dropped, Lieutenant Beser will record our reactions to what we see. This recording is being made for history. Watch your language and don't clutter up the intercom."

Good advice, Alex thought. History matters.

Less than an hour later, he and Dave heard Tibbets say over the intercom, "It's Hiroshima." A few minutes later Tibbets told the crew. "On glasses."

Dave turned to Alex and asked, "Why the glasses?"

"To protect their eyes from the blast. This is it. No turning back now."

Tibbets called out, "Five, four, three, two, one." Then they heard the bombardier, "Bomb away!"

"There she goes," Tibbets said. As the bomb dropped, the *Enola Gay* flew away from the blast. When the bomb hit, Tibbets said simply, "Oh, my."

When the planes returned, Alex watched for Ryan to get off the plane, then met him on the tarmac. Ryan's face was pale, and it took him a minute to speak. "It was horrible," he said. "There was death in that big mushroom cloud. Innocent people, women, and children. The city was on fire, and the air filled with black smoke."

What have we done? Alex quaked.

Ryan went on. "Minutes before we had seen a city, with boats in little channels, trolley cars, schools, houses, factories, stores. It was all destroyed in an instant."

Tibbets said, "War, the scourge of the human race since time began, now holds terrors beyond belief."

That same day, before news of the first nuclear holocaust had reached MacArthur, he'd called an off-the-record press briefing at

Manila City Hall and said, "The war may end sooner than some think. Russian participation in the struggle against Japan is welcome."

Alex was back in Manila Tuesday. Even after the bomb destroyed Hiroshima, Japan still refused to surrender. The next day, the Soviet Union revoked its treaties with Japan and invaded Manchuria. The pressure's on, Alex thought. This might do it.

That afternoon MacArthur issued another statement: "I am delighted at the Russian declaration of war against Japan. This will make possible a great pincer movement which cannot fail to end in the destruction of the enemy."

The Emperor of Japan knew about the bomb and the destruction it caused when it hit Hiroshima. Still, he did not surrender.

The following day was Thursday, August 9, and a second bomb destroyed Nagasaki. Three days later President Truman suspended B-29 raids on Japan.

It was August 15, before Emperor Hirohito ordered an end to all hostilities at 4:00 p.m. Tokyo time.

Everyone on staff in Manila listened spellbound to every word of Hirohito's surrender message to the Japanese people as he spoke:

"We have ordered our government to communicate to the governments of the United States, Great Britain, China, and the Soviet Union that our empire accepts the provisions of their joint declaration," he said, referring to the allies' demand for unconditional surrender.

"The enemy has begun to employ a new and most cruel bomb, the power of which to do damage is, indeed, incalculable, taking the toll of many innocent lives. Should we continue to fight, not only would it result in an ultimate collapse and obliteration of the Japanese nation, but also it would lead to the total extinction of human civilization."

Hirohito could be right, Alex thought, shaking. Soviet spies may already have given the secrets of the atom bomb to Russia. He listened keenly as Hirohito went on.

"To strive for the common prosperity and happiness of all nations, as well as the security and wellbeing of our subjects, is the solemn obligation which has been handed down by our imperial ancestors and which lies close to our heart."

Alex thought the emperors' words suggested that the military hadn't forced him into his decision. Instead, he had replaced the imperial creed of war with an ideology of peace.

Hirohito then asked his people to shoulder the burdens of peace, humility, and lower status. *"The hardships and sufferings to which our nation is to be subjected hereafter will be certainly great,"* he warned. *"However, it is according to the dictates of time and fate that we have resolved to pave the way for a grand peace for all the generations to come by enduring the unendurable and suffering what is not sufferable."* He ended by asking his citizens to *"Cultivate the ways of rectitude, foster nobility of spirit, and work with resolution" so as to "keep pace with the progress of the world."*

When the address ended, Tory turned to his staff and said, "I'm afraid that 'enduring the unendurable' might mean weathering Japan's almost complete collapse."

Alex didn't understand what he meant by that. Social collapse? Economic collapse? What would it mean for this once great nation of good people?

Then Tory said, "President Truman, with the approval of Clement Attlee, Stalin, and Chiang Kai-shek, has appointed MacArthur Supreme Commander over rebuilding Japan. I'll be going with him. Most of you have more than enough points to leave the army, and if that's your decision, I'll honor it. But we could use you in Japan. It won't be easy trying to rebuild the country."

The room grew quiet. Alex took a deep breath, and the next words out of his mouth surprised him. "Count me in for another year," he said, raising his hand. "What we've destroyed, we should rebuild." It was the right thing to do, but he wanted to go home. *Next year.* He squared his shoulders as several others volunteered.

"Thank you, men," Tory said. "We leave for Japan with General MacArthur at the end of the month where he'll formally oversee the ceremony officially marking Japan's surrender. This will be a proper surrender ceremony on board the *USS Missouri*, which will be docked in Tokyo Bay. President Truman will be there too, and after hundreds of carrier-based planes fly overhead, he'll declare Victory over Japan Day. We have heard that on that same day,

General Yamashita will surrender and be put on trial in Manila for the Japanese atrocities that he sanctioned here.

I have no doubt he'll be found guilty, Alex thought. The evidence against him is overwhelming.

CHAPTER THIRTY-NINE

The war with Japan was over! My hands were wrapped around the wrist of a patient taking his pulse when word came across the radio at the hospital. The war was officially over. The United States and its allies had finally prevailed. The patient pulled his arm away and sat up, whooping, and hollering along with all the men around him. I ran out of the ward to the nursing station, finding it crammed full of doctors, orderlies, and my nurses, who were throwing their white hats into the air. It was crazy. We hugged and cried and kissed each other, dancing with anyone we could find.

The next day reality set in, and we sat around and talked about the news of the atomic bomb dropping, guilt mixed with joy. One of the nurses said, "I'm relieved we won't have to invade Japan."

"Me too," I said. "The casualties for sure would have been even worse."

"You're right, she said. "And the war has ended!"

It was still hard to believe. A few days later, I got a letter from Hallie, now in Salt Lake.

Dear Lucy,

A whole group of us mobbed Main Street in the damp rain when we heard rumors that the war was over. We stood 25-deep in front of the Salt Lake Tribune-Telegram building waiting for verification. Then we saw the headline spread across the Tribune's display windows, 'Japan Surrenders to Allies.' I can tell you things got raucous from there. There must have been 20,000-plus people downtown shouting, crying, singing, and dancing for joy.

Trent and I are getting married next week in the Salt Lake Temple. I wish you could be here. I can't wait for you to meet him, and me to meet Matt. War is so strange, isn't it? You don't know Trent, and I don't know Matt. That would never have happened under normal circumstances. I'm so glad this war is over! Have a safe trip home.

See you soon!

Love,

Hallie.

The talk among the nurses turned to how and when we might get home. No one knew for sure, so our work at the hospital went on. But the load was lighter. Then we got word that those nurses with thirty-five points could go home. I had forty, so I was on the list! But I knew it might take months to find a ride on a ship.

"I wonder what it will be like at home?" One of the nurses asked, worry lines on her face.

"Will people be happy to see us?" Another questioned.

No one knew the answer.

"I think so," someone else said, chin up. "We are heroes, you know."

"Do you think people have moved on without us?"

I said, "Just as we've changed over the past several years, our friends and family at home have too. We may have to get to know each other again."

We found ourselves with more free time, so we formed groups and went out and had fun together. We went swimming, sightseeing, and just sat around and talked. Mostly we waited for word that it was our turn to be released from service. Then I got a call from Matt.

"I've been discharged," he said. "In a few days, I'll be boarding a navy troop transport."

"I'm so happy for you."

"Get this, we'll be stopping at Leyte on our way to San Francisco! I told the captain my wife was waiting there to go home, and he made room for you on the ship!"

"Are you serious?" I grinned into the phone.

"Yes, my darling. He also told me we have a scheduled stop at Pearl Harbor."

"So, Hawaii here we come?" I asked, stunned.

"Exactly. We dock at Leyte the middle of September, so I'll see you then."

"Yay! I'll go find the CO and give him my notice."

"Can't wait to see you. Bye for now."

"See you soon!"

I hung up the phone and sang the old song, "Happy Days Are Here Again."

Then I sat down and wrote a letter to my parents.

Dear Mom and Dad,

I'm coming home! I have enough points to be discharged, so I'm leaving the service. It'll take a while to get there, but I'm leaving on a navy transport with Matt, first to Hawaii and then San Francisco. I can't wait to cross under that Golden Gate again!

Matt and I want children, and I'd like them to know their uncles and aunts and their children to come. I want my babies to live close to you, their grandparents. I also want to continue my medical career.

I'll miss the nurses I served with. I'll never bond with colleagues like this again. We've shared dangers, illness, and fatigue, all mixed in with occasional fun times. We're the best of friends.

Well, that's it for me. Save me some ice cream and loads of fresh vegetables. Matt and I are excited to see you.

Love,

Lucy

When I received a package from Mom several weeks later, it was filled with magazine articles, some from the *Saturday Evening Post* and *Reader's Digest*. The stories had lots of advice for soldiers and their families. The women's magazines—*Ladies' Home Journal*, *Redbook*, and others—featured articles that I guessed meant to prepare wives, girlfriends, and mothers for what everyone thought would be a tough time of readjustment.

I read headlines like, "At First He Might Find it Easier to Live Without You Than With You." Another piece encouraged women to ask themselves the question. "Has Your Husband Come Home to the Right Woman?" Another headline asked, "What if He Comes Home Nervous?" I thought about Chris, and my eyes watered.

***

The sun was barely up when Dad drove Chris to Hill Air Force Base, just south of Ogden, Utah. A pilot would fly him into Long Island for treatment. Grandma Katie had taken Dad aside and suggested he listen to Chris and consider his feelings, rather than giving him the buck-up speech. That made the drive to Hill more pleasant for Chris

After they reached the base, Chris pulled his case from the trunk and Dad hugged him goodbye. Chris hadn't shared many details about the horrors he'd endured, but he knew Dad heard his screams at night, watched him jump around loud noises, and felt him tremble uncontrollably when they sat on the couch.

Chris returned Dad's hug. Then he walked out onto the field and met the pilot who would take him to New York.

"Hi," the man said. "Name's Marc Lee."

Chris shook his hand. "Chris Forrest."

They climbed aboard and Marc said, "I'm with the 75th Air Base Wing here at Hill. We're a replacement training unit."

"I used to fly for the Army Air Force in the Philippines."

"Bet you saw lots of action."

"Yes," Chris said gazing out the small plane's window. His hands trembled so badly, he sat on them.

"So, we're flying into Mitchel Field today, a US air base in Long Island," Marc said. "Why are you going there?"

Chris took a deep breath and thought, might as well tell him. There is no shame. There is no *shame*, he repeated in his head. "I'm going to Mason General Hospital, run by the United States War Department. They treat psychological casualties of the battlefield." Chris forced himself not to look down at his lap.

"Those wounds are just as real. I have a buddy who came back from France, shell-shocked."

"How's he doing now?"

"Still struggling. It might help to tell him about this hospital. Let me know if it helps."

"I will. Thanks, Marc."

After landing, Chris climbed into one of many waiting cars with some of the returning soldiers whose ship had sailed into Long Island Harbor from overseas. The men were still dressed in uniform and hadn't been discharged from the service. They were going to Mason General first for treatment. Good thing he'd worn his uniform. He didn't want to stick out like a sore thumb.

When the convoy of cars reached Mason General, Chris saw a large, dusty-brown brick building with several wings and lots and lots of windows.

The men left the cars and were led into a large room with stacks of wooden folding chairs. After they sat down, the man up front said, "At ease, men. On behalf of the commander and staff at Mason General Hospital, I want to extend a hearty welcome."

After a brief orientation, Chris stood in line and checked in at a long table. The guy asked Chris for his last name. "Forrest," he said. Then he was assigned to a bunk with a little desk in a large sleeping room. Chris stowed his things and put a small picture of his new girlfriend, Whitney, on the nightstand. They'd been friends at church before the war, and they'd been dating some. When his hands shook, she held them in hers, kissing his lips.

A regular medical doctor checked him and said, "You'll meet with a psychiatrist next. You'll find that modern psychiatry makes no division between the mind and the body. They're both connected."

Chris met a man at lunch who was paralyzed. "The doc told me today there's nothing physically wrong with me," he said. "Guess it's all in my mind."

"That's tough," Chris said, "and I can relate. See these hands and how they shake? There's nothing physically wrong with them either."

Another soldier added, "I have crying spells that I can't stop."

"I guess we're all broken in some way, and that's why we're here," Chris said. "A psychiatrist I met with before I came told me battle neurosis is not chronic. The good news is we can hope to be repaired."

After lunch, a nurse attached metal disks to Chris's scalp and gave him an electroencephalogram. "This will help us track your brain activity," she said, turning on the machine. Then a psychiatrist came in and administered a Rorschach test. Chris was given a series of ink blot images and asked what they looked like to him. After providing his responses he asked, "How do my answers help you?"

"We use a series of complex algorithms to help us check your emotional functioning."

So many tests, Chris thought, trying not to feel like a guinea pig. He found the doctors and nurses generally kind and caring, and that helped.

That night as he tried to sleep, he could hear other men tossing and turning. Sometimes moaning. One screamed. The nurses came in to help, and Chris tried to go back to sleep.

The next day, he sat in a small room with a window, his chair facing outside and told his story of the war to a psychiatrist. The doc listened, took notes, and asked interested questions.

"How are you getting along now?" he asked.

"Okay, I guess."

"You were overseas, right?"

"Yes, sir."

"Where?"

"The Philippines."

Do you feel changed from who you are when you first went over?

"Yes."

"How?"

"I used to be upbeat. Not so much anymore." Chris described bombed-out planes, the march from Bataan, and friends he'd seen tortured and killed in the prison camps. "A lot of my buddies died," Chris said. "Good men lost their lives." He slumped in his chair and pulled his arms close to his body.

"What happens to you when you think about them? How do you feel?"

"I feel sad, and I miss them. I wish I could have saved them."

"Tell me about the camps."

"I did all right in the beginning. I tried to find purpose and help others. I read the Bible and wrote in my journal. But the last six months were the worst."

"How so?"

"The Japanese stepped up the torture when they found they were being defeated. I started waking up from nightmares afraid I was going to die."

"Every man has his breaking point," the doctor said. Chris could see a lump in the doctor's throat.

The hospital gave Chris individual hypnosis sessions a few times each week. The psychiatrist led him into a deep state of relaxation and then using guided conversation tried to help him begin to release his fear and survivor guilt. Though relaxed, Chris was always fully aware of what was going on. The psychiatrist took him back to Cabanatuan in his mind, and Chris remembered.

"It's all right," the doc said. "You can tell me. Where are they taking you?"

"Solitary." Chris's hands shook violently as he talked about his months in solitary.

An hour later, the doc said, "You're away from Cabanatuan. You're home now. When I wake you up, you'll feel relaxed, no pain. But you'll remember everything I said."

The hypnosis and talk therapy began to help. After the first few sessions, the trembling stopped for the rest of the day. Then for two days. Over the course of several weeks, the nightmares decreased, and Chris all but forgot that his hands used to shake badly.

He took up drawing and painting with several other men and came to understand why Lucy loved creating her art. Applying a brush to canvas took him out of his head and gave him something else to focus on. He even learned how to play the guitar. But then music had always had the power to calm him. One day he even tried his hand at carpentry, making hobby horses for the neighbor kids.

Chris liked the group therapy sessions best, because he got to know the other men as they shared their war experiences. He wasn't alone. They also did fun things like play baseball, watch movies, and eat ice cream. He could feel himself healing.

There were lots of phone booths around the hospital, so Chris called home regularly. He suspected his parents could hear the change in his voice. He was more relaxed, upbeat, even positive.

On his last call home, he said, "The docs said they could help me here, and they have. I've surfaced the emotional conflict that caused a lot of my distress. I feel like I can breathe again."

"You sound really good, son," Dad said.

He paused. "I've finally been able to forgive the Japanese insurgents." Chris swallowed hard. "That was the hardest thing of all." Chris knew he couldn't move forward with seeds of bitterness still growing in his heart.

"We're excited to have you come home, Chris," Mom said, her voice soft.

"When I get there, I hope my family and friends treat me the way they did before the war. Not like someone who had a problem."

"We will, son," Dad said.

"We love you," Mom said.

"I'm ready to start thinking about the future. I want a wife. Kids. But first I'll start on that advanced degree."

"Do you want to go to law school?" Dad asked, hope in his voice.

"No. I want to be a psychotherapist and help people heal. My life will be filled with faith, family, and science." Chris hung up the phone and sat in silence. Then he prayed for God's grace because he had lived when so many others died.

CHAPTER FORTY

Alex walked the deserted streets of Nagasaki. He'd come from Tokyo, and while he expected the destruction to be bad, it was far worse than he'd imagined. The bomb rendered more than five square miles of Nagasaki a desolate wasteland. There's nothing left, Alex thought as he watched a man wheel his bicycle down an empty street. The fierce might of the bombs had reduced the buildings on either side to rubble.

Alex wanted to speak with a few Marines, the first to land on Nagasaki in September. He spotted a man almost as tall as he was, a friendly looking sort with black hair and glasses. Alex walked up and introduced himself to a guy named Tom Perry. "Have you got time for a few questions?" Alex asked.

"Sure," Tom said with a friendly grin.

"How long have you been in the service?"

"Just about a year. I was serving as a missionary for the Church of Jesus Christ of Latter-day Saints in the northern states when I received my draft notice. I went home and opted to join the Marines. After boot camp, we were sent to Saipan. I stayed there until we came here."

"I was at BYU on a basketball scholarship when I joined up after Pearl."

"It's nice to meet a fellow believer in Christ," Tom said.

"What was your assignment on Saipan?"

"I reviewed casualty reports coming in from the front line and assigned incoming Marines to where they were needed. A group of servicemen and I also spent our free evenings building a small chapel on Saipan so we could have a place to worship."

"Making life better here in Japan is important to you."

Tom nodded. "Yes, it is. Now let me ask a question. You've served in the military a lot longer than I have. I'm guessing you could have gone home by now. Why didn't you?"

"I felt impressed to stay and help rebuild Japan. And Nagasaki is unbelievable," Alex said, staring again at the deserted streets.

With a catch in his voice and tears in his eyes, Tom described the moment the ship he was on came to Nagasaki. "We ran topside as we pulled into the harbor. All I saw was devastation. The city had been built going up little canyons. Everything in those canyons was completely leveled."

Alex's eyes grew wet as he listened to Tom.

"I'll never forget the experience of seeing the devastation that occurred here because of the bomb, for as long as I live. The people we saw were bewildered. They had not even had time to bury their dead."

Alex shook his head. "It's all so hard to take in," he grimaced.

"At night we can still hear children rummaging in garbage cans for food."

"The people here have suffered so much. But the children…" his voice trailed off.

"I found a little boy on the streets the other day just about out of his mind from hunger. We took him back to our quarters, fed him, and cleaned him up. We then found one of the interpreters to see if we could find out where his home was. He used to live in the atomic bomb area, and all of his family were killed as a result of the bomb. Since that time, he has been wandering around by himself eating and sleeping where he could find a place."

"Is there anything I can do for him?"

"We fixed up a place for him to stay out in the buildings behind our barracks and have been saving part of our chow for him."

"God bless you, Tom Perry."

"We've tried to take care of as many of them as we could. When we realized we couldn't help them all, we appealed to a group of nuns who had not been allowed to function during the war. They set up an orphanage to take the little fellows we were bringing in."

"You're doing a lot of good, and I'd like to be part of that. I'll be here a week on leave before I have to back to Tokyo."

"You chose to come to Nagasaki on leave?"

"I had to experience it for myself. Is there anything I can do to help while I'm here?"

"We've got some service projects going on in the evenings, if you'd like to join us."

"I'd like that. What kinds of things are you doing?"

"Along with a group of Japanese people, we're working with two Protestant ministers whose churches were bombed and partially damaged. We're replastering walls, painting, and getting the chapels in condition for church services."

"I'm pretty good with a paint brush," Alex offered.

"You're welcome to join us." Tom smiled. "We could use an extra pair of hands."

"I'll come every night this week. Thank you, Tom, for service that goes beyond the call of duty."

"I've fallen in love with the Japanese people. I want to help them rebuild their city and their faith."

"I have an uncle who served a mission to Japan before the war, and he loves her people too. You're just the kind of man this world needs right now, Tom." He's one in million, Alex thought. The pure love of Christ is written all over his face. I wish there were a million more just like him.

A week later, Alex went back to Tokyo with a changed heart beating in his chest.

After Tom was discharged and reached home, he shared a letter about the day he left Japan.

I'll never forget the experience we had when we left. Several of us who had worked on the church buildings were at the train station, waiting to be taken to a port of embarkation. Another group, in which there were some rough men with their girlfriends, was there. Some of them were teasing us because we were so different, having spent our time rebuilding churches when we could have been having fun.

Then I heard something and looked out in the distance. About two hundred of these great Japanese people, we had helped get back into their churches, were coming over a hill, singing 'Onward Christian Soldiers.'

Alex set the pages down and waited to regain his composure. He could hear the song being sung in his own head, and it was one of his favorites. He wiped his eyes and kept reading.

They showered us with gifts, which they could not afford, in thanks for what we had done. After we boarded the train, they lined up and held out their hands. We leaned out the windows and they touched our fingertips as the train pulled away. Our experience was such a contrast from what those other Marines had on their last day in Japan.

"Thank you, Tom," Alex said aloud, as he thought, this is what happens when your actions show universal love and brotherhood. You deliver faith and hope in a time of crisis.

CHAPTER FORTY-ONE

The day my ride home neared Leyte, I stood waiting, suitcase bulging at the seams. Like most of the nurses, I'd collected lots of souvenirs. I grew impatient for the ship's arrival, longing for the look of love in Matt's eyes. When the ship docked, he ran down the gangplank, I jumped into his arms, and we kissed. Then he whispered in my ear, "Wait 'til you see our room. There's a dresser with a mirror, a private shower, and a real john."

"Talk about living in your lap of luxury. It's so good to see you, my darling. No more separations for us."

He held me close, and I squeezed his hand. As I picked up my suitcase, he gently took it from me. "I'll get that," he smiled.

Together we strolled up the gangplank and onto the ship, ready to begin our new life. We went right to our room and put our things away. A few minutes later, I noticed Matt had a faraway look on his face. "What is it, Matt?" I asked.

He raised his eyebrows saying, "I've been hearing about the shock of peace from some of my buddies who've been home for a few months."

"What does that mean?"

"Happy families put out big 'Welcome Home' signs in neighborhood streets, and then take a picture of 'the homecoming kiss.' That's when the adjustment begins. I haven't even met your parents, Lucy, and we'll be living with them, at least at first. Housing will be hard to find."

"I haven't had a chance to tell you yet," I grinned. "They found us a small apartment over a bakery and already put down a deposit. We won't have to live with them after all."

Matt's mouth dropped open, and he whooped. "That's great news, Lucy. Very nice of them." Then he asked, "How far from the university?"

"Several long blocks. You could walk it, if you had to, but there's a bus."

"Great. Good thing the GI bill will pay for law school."

"And I'll find a job to get us started. For now, let's just enjoy our time together."

He kissed me and we stretched out on the bed together. Then I snuggled against his chest and fell asleep in his arms. It would take about three weeks to reach Hawaii, and Matt and I weren't in any hurry.

As we made the trip across the water, we relaxed in ways we hadn't in a very long time. There was no enemy for Matt to fight and no wounded for me to tend. I did meet several other nurses on board, and it was fun to compare notes. Mostly Matt and I just sat in the sun, watched the waves roll by, and ate our daily dose of ice cream.

When we docked at Pearl Harbor, I sent a cable to my parents, letting them know we'd arrived. Then we checked into the Royal Hawaiian where we'd spend two nights before getting back onboard the ship for San Francisco. We unpacked, slipped into our bathing suits, then ran out the back of the hotel to the beach. We spread out our towels, laid down, and Matt couldn't stop smiling at me.

That evening a group of us nurses put on our class A uniforms with ribbons and battle stars and overseas stripes. The men dressed in uniforms too, and we went into Honolulu to walk the lit streets of a once familiar downtown. We were out for a fun dinner, but the war had altered Oahu. We passed lots of empty restaurants.

"I guess people aren't dining out much yet," I said.

"I heard the war's been hard on Hawaii's tourist business," Matt said.

One of his friends agreed. "The people here are banding together to launch ad campaigns, hoping to attract visitors."

"They couldn't come to a more beautiful place," I said. Then I whispered to Matt, "I think I'd just as soon eat back at the hotel."

"Me too." We wished the others a good night and went on to the Royal Hawaiian.

We changed our clothes, and I put on a new aloha dress I'd bought earlier that day.

"It's beautiful," Matt said. "But don't throw the old one out, please."

"I'll keep it forever," I said kissing him.

We made our way downstairs and saw tables filled with pork, pineapple, coconuts, and rice. The hostess put two leis around each of our necks and showed us to a long luau table. When it was time to begin, the bandleader said, "Welcome to Hawaii where the war is over, and the Spirit of Aloha is strong again."

Everyone clapped as he continued. "The word aloha is more than a friendly way to greet you. Aloha means love and is spoken in all Polynesian languages. Aloha is the light inside that tells me you are my brothers, my sisters. So again, welcome to Hawaii."

I dabbed tears from smiling eyes and said, "Our love blossomed like a flower here. Now the petals are expanding."

Matt kissed me. "Hawaii will always be our special place."

The hostess announced, "We begin our musical program tonight with a song written in Hawaii and made popular by Bing Crosby in the 1937 motion picture, *Waikiki Wedding*. Please enjoy the song, *Sweet Leilani, Heavenly Flower*."

Men with ukuleles played, and hula dancers swayed as lovely voices sang the words:

"Sweet Leilani
Heavenly flower
I dreamed of paradise for two (Leilani, la-li-le)
You are my paradise completed (Leilani, la-li-le)
You are my dream come true."

I leaned against Matt's shoulder. "I wish we could have been married here."

He whispered in my ear, "Be right back."

"Where are you going?"

"Trust me," he smiled.

I drank pineapple juice and soaked in the music until Matt came back, grinning from ear to ear. "What are you up to?" I asked.

"I called the Hawaiian temple over on the North Shore. How would you like to have our marriage sealed for eternity there tomorrow instead of waiting until we get home?"

"Oh, Matt, what a great idea. How did you make it happen so fast?"

"I spoke with a Rawsel William Bradford. He's here serving from Utah, and guess what? He's Dave's uncle. You remember Dave, my pilot friend."

"You're kidding me."

"Nope. He lives here with his wife and children, giving guided tours of the temple grounds to returning servicemen. He'll perform the ceremony for us first thing tomorrow morning before the buses loaded with soldiers show up. That is, if you don't mind getting up early."

I laughed and hugged him. "Sunrises in Hawaii are the best. This was meant to be, Matt. How blessed I am to have you."

"I'm the lucky one. Like the song said, you are my dream come true. The front desk has already arranged for a car to drive us to North Shore." He stood, offered his hand, and I danced with my penny from heaven until after 10:00 pm. This time without blackout curtains.

I woke up early the next morning to a tropical breeze gently blowing in from the open window. I rolled over and felt the bed for Matt. He wasn't there, but I could hear the shower running.

When he finished, I showered, we dressed and went downstairs. Our car waited out front. A golden sun came up through red clouds as we drove the thirty miles to Laie.

An hour later, we watched the soft waves of the Pacific Ocean roll against the shore about half a mile east of the temple. To the west lay tall, rugged green mountains and sugarcane fields. It was breathtakingly beautiful. We drove through the entrance of the four-foot lava rock wall surrounding the grounds, and the car dropped us at the temple bureau of information where we met Rawsel Bradford. "Aloha, and welcome," he said, stepping up to us and smiling.

"Aloha," I said shaking his hand. "Thank you for blessing our lives today."

"Nothing will give me greater joy than joining the two of you forever."

I sneaked a peek at Matt thinking, I love him so much. I'm honored to be his wife in this life and the next. Then I gazed up at the lovely cream white temple. Brother Rawsel said, "There's plenty of time for me to give you a short tour of the grounds before we go inside for the ceremony. Would you like that?"

"Yes, please," Matt and I both said in unison.

He told us temple construction began in the middle of World War I, then added, "The 1918 flu pandemic pushed its dedication to November 1919."

My eyes widened. A difficult beginning, but the people persisted, their faith resilient.

"Come this way," he said, and we strolled the grounds. "The Hawaii temple combines ancient and modern designs, from structures similar to the ancient temple in Jerusalem and pre-Columbian ruins in America."

"It's majestic," I breathed as we strolled down the cement walkway bordered on either side by beautiful lawns lined with green shrubs. Tall palm trees waved like new friends.

"The temple forms the shape of a Greek Christian cross with four sides of equal length," Rawsel continued, "symbolizing the gathering together from the four corners of the earth spoken about in the book of Isaiah in the Bible."

We passed three gently rising, rectangular reflecting pools filled with blue water. Tropical plants stood along the sides, littered with pink hibiscus. "The gardens are lovely," I said.

Rawsel replied, "It really is one of the most beautiful spots on the islands. Tourists used to visit the temple grounds every year, and now they're returning. Servicemen are now coming in daily in droves on island tours the military offers. I'm here to show them around."

"I bet the men like being on the grounds," Matt said. "I know I do. It's so peaceful."

"Our servicemen and women face a worrisome future. Many have told me they've felt the sweet and peaceful influence of the temple grounds. My friends the Bellistons said that at the height of the war, in front of the Lani-huli house over there near the temple, Hawaiian, Samoan, and Japanese kids played volleyball with some of our soldiers here."

"The temple served as a beacon of hope and peace," I said.

"That's exactly right," Rawsel nodded. "Are you ready to go inside? President Clisshold has asked temple workers and local members to come early to accommodate your request to be sealed today."

"That's so generous," I said. "Thank you."

"I promise this will be a highly spiritual occasion for you."

We went inside, dressed in simple white temple clothes, and walked down halls graced with beautiful murals. We entered one of the rooms, kneeled across an altar from each other and joined hands. Gazing into Matt's eyes. I wondered how eternity could be any better than this moment. Then Brother Rawsel uttered sacred words and we promised to be together forever.

We moved into another room to enjoy the quiet. Matt and I sat side by side on one of the soft couches in the middle and stared up at the stained-glass walls encircling the ceiling. The pictures represented the Tree of Life, its web of branches reminding us how a family grows from generation to generation. I whispered to him, "We'll soon add our babies to the family tree." He smiled, and with a full heart, I enveloped his hands in mine.

The next day we boarded a ship for San Francisco. An ocean breeze tussled my hair as I stood on deck, a light rain misting my face. We watched the blue of Hawaii fade into the distance, on our way home to a new peacetime life that I prayed would be filled with happiness, love, and family.

EPILOGUE

December 1945

Lily and I stood outside the home where we'd grown up, staring at the winter sky. A light snow began to fall, and we caught the scattered flakes on our tongues, laughing. Across the valley, the snow-covered mountains of the Wasatch Front towered in the distance.

My mind drifted back to the war-filled Christmas of 1941, following the attack on Pearl Harbor. I'd sobbed as I listened to Bing Crosby's new release on the radio, *White Christmas*.

"I'm dreaming of a white Christmas,
Just like the ones I used to know.
Where the tree tops glisten, and children listen,
To hear sleigh bells in the snow."

I hadn't been sure my siblings and I would come back in one piece, let alone enjoy another white Christmas together.

I took a deep breath of gratitude. Chris, Hallie, I, and our spouses were here for Christmas Eve tonight with Mom, Dad, and Lily. We hadn't expected Alex and couldn't believe it when he walked through the door an hour ago on leave from Japan, surprising us all. This promised to be the best Christmas ever.

Lily and I gazed at the ascending moon peeking out from behind wispy, white clouds and she said, "If there really were a man in that moon, I think he'd be smiling down at us right now."

I hugged her close.

"I'm glad we're all home together this year. I missed you," she said.

"I missed you more," I smiled. Lily was seventeen, and I'd lost four years of watching her grow up. How had the war changed her? What had it been like for her living at home without her siblings? I had no answers to these questions yet.

"I've noticed that none of you talk much about the war," she said.

"The war was so horrible that we don't want to talk about it. The memories are just too painful."

Lily nodded. "May I ask you about something else?" She asked.

"Of course," I smiled.

"This is my first year at the university, and I'm interested in pre-law. Do you think I'd make a good lawyer?"

"You're one smart cookie, Lily, and you'd be good at anything you chose to do. If that's your dream, follow it, but know it won't be easy. Returning male veterans are taking the jobs back, and women who served are being sent home. I couldn't even get hired at the hospital."

"And you were an officer with lots of experience," she said, surprised.

"Our country is happy to emerge from the war-torn years, and I understand that. I am too. We all want a normal family life and economic prosperity, but I need to work while Matt finishes law school."

"I'd like to practice law and be a wife and mother. I know that will be a balancing act." She pressed her lips together, looking determined.

"Just be prepared for criticism, because the concept of a strong 'Rosie the Riveter' is fading into oblivion. But you'll have my support," I promise.

"Thank you, Lucy," Lily said shivering in the snow. "It's getting cold out here, let's go inside."

We walked into the house, hand in hand, and stood in front of our traditional Douglas Fir Christmas tree, lights glowing, full branches wrapping down over cheery red and green packages. Dad was carving the turkey and Grandma Katie was placing silverware on the table.

We sat down to a big meal and returned to our once 'usual' social and political discussions over dinner.

Dad turned to Alex, passed him the sweet potato casserole, and asked, "What's the inside scoop about Japan?"

"Well, while others disagree with MacArthur, I'm glad he allowed the Japanese to disarm themselves and threatened to punish any of our soldiers who dare hit any of theirs."

"His actions show a lot of respect for the Japanese people," Hallie said.

"He's a standout in a world filled with hatred, and people who are asking for a harsh government for a defeated people," Alex said, his body tense.

"We need to remember what Christ taught us in the Book of Luke," Mom said, touching his arm, "Love your enemies."

"That's the only road to lasting peace," Chris agreed, as his wife Whitney took his hand, which still shook sometimes. After all Chris had been through as a prisoner of war, he still believed in loving his enemy.

We finished our meal, and before dessert, Mom sat at the piano. The rest of us put our arms around each other and sang, 'Joy to the World,' at the top of our lungs. We were home.

BEHIND THE BOOK

I read and researched dozens of books before writing this story, working hard to be true to the historical details, down to the movies and music of the time. *Angels in the Fog* is a mixture of fiction and fact, with characters that are both real and imagined. I loved immersing myself in the time period.

Researching this book, even before I knew there would be one, was exciting for me. I spent time in several locales in the Pacific important to this story. I traveled two weeks in the Philippines with family, visiting important wartime sites such as Manila, Corregidor, Clark Field, Leyte, and Tacloban. I marveled at the life-sized statues at Leyte that mark the spot where MacArthur and his men returned to reclaim the Philippines.

During the war, my dad enjoyed spending what leave he had in Australia and always hoped to see the country again. But he contracted pancreatic cancer and died at the age of sixty. Several years ago, I took a month off work and traveled to Australia to see what all the fuss was about. I loved this beautiful country and her people. You were right, Dad.

I paid my respects at Pearl Harbor in Hawaii, honoring the memory of those who lost their lives during the surprise Japanese bombing that started World War II in the Pacific. I lived on Oahu for a year on work assignment, and the islands hold a special place in my heart.

SELECT SOURCES

The Army Nurses of World War II, Betsy Kuhn

Prisoner of the Rising Sun, William A Berry
Grimm, Maxine Tate, BYU library collection

An American Caesar, William Manchester

The Manhattan Project, Editor: Cynthia C. Kelly

Poem by Eva Bird (used with family permission)

Let There Be Light, John Houston film documentary

The Laie Hawaii temple, A Century of Aloha
(includes Rawsel William Bradford)
L. Tom Perry, first-hand account of Nagasaki

ACKNOWLEDGEMENTS

Deepest appreciation goes to my sister-in-law, Marcia Nielson, for assisting with the research, reading countless drafts, editing, and supporting me from beginning to end. To my friend, Dee Foster, who came up with the idea of using a family to tell the story.

I'm grateful to Soni Rice, an editor and friend, who helped both me and my characters when we got stuck. To Brenda Sevcik, my writing critique partner, and other members of the Roswell Writer's group.

To my niece Amelia Nielson-Stowell for her invaluable editorial polish. To amazing beta readers: Lori Wynne, Barbara Thompson, Mimi Douglas, Gail Murray, Karen Paavola, Melissa Newman, Karla Nielson, and Dodie Truman Stallcup. I couldn't have done it without you.

A note of fond appreciation also goes to Ralph Staplin and Chris Waggener for fact checking the history. To my niece Emily Plane for combing through military records to trace the movement of the 102nd Battalion.

Writing a book is not a solitary endeavor.

CPSIA information can be obtained
at www.ICGtesting.com
Printed in the USA
LVHW080746250622
722115LV00033B/1224